SNOW CRASH

NEAL STEPHENSON

PENGUIN BOOKS

PENGUIN BOOKS

Published by the Penguin Group
Penguin Books Ltd, 80 Strand, London WC2R ORL, England
Penguin Group (USA) Inc., 375 Hudson Street, New York, New York 10014, USA
Penguin Group (Canada), 90 Eglinton Avenue East, Suite 700, Toronto, Ontario, Canada M4P 2Y3
(a division of Pearson Penguin Canada Inc.)
Penguin Ireland, 25 St Stephen's Green, Dublin 2, Ireland (a division of Penguin Books Ltd)
Penguin Group (Australia), 250 Camberwell Road,
Camberwell, Victoria 3124, Australia (a division of Pearson Australia Group Pty Ltd)
Penguin Books India Pvt Ltd, 11 Community Centre, Panchsheel Park,
New Delhi – 110 017, India
Penguin Group (NZ), 67 Apollo Drive, Rosedale, Auckland 0632, New Zealand
(a division of Pearson New Zealand Ltd)
Penguin Books (South Africa) (Pty) Ltd, 24 Sturdee Avenue, Rosebank,
Johannesburg 2196, South Africa

Penguin Books Ltd, Registered Offices: 80 Strand, London WC2R ORL, England

www.penguin.com

First published in the United States of America by Bantam Books 1992
First published in Great Britain by Penguin Books 1993
Reissued in this edition 2011

008

Copyright © Neal Stephenson, 1992
All rights reserved

Grateful acknowledgement is made for permission to reprint a
drawing from *The Origin of Consciousness in the Breakdown of the
Bicameral Mind* by Julian Jaynes. Copyright © Julian Jaynes, 1976.
Reprinted by permission of Houghton Mifflin Company.

The moral right of the author has been asserted

Printed in England by Clays Ltd, St Ives plc

ISBN: 978-0-241-95318-1

www.greenpenguin.co.uk

> **snow** *n.* . . . . **2.a.** Anything resembling snow. **b.** The white specks on a television screen resulting from weak reception.
>
> **crash** *v.* . . . . — *intr.* . . . . **5.** To fail suddenly, as a business or an economy.
> —*The American Heritage Dictionary*
>
> **virus.** . . . . [L. *vīrus* slimy liquid, poison, offensive odour or taste.] **1.** Venom, such as is emitted by a poisonous animal. **2.** *Path.* **a.** A morbid principle or poisonous substance produced in the body as the result of some disease, esp. one capable of being introduced into other persons or animals by inoculations or otherwise and of developing the same disease in them. . . . **3.** *fig.* A moral or intellectual poison, or poisonous influence.
> —*The Oxford English Dictionary*

1

The Deliverator belongs to an elite order, a hallowed subcategory. He's got esprit up to here. Right now, he is preparing to carry out his third mission of the night. His uniform is black as activated charcoal, filtering the very light out of the air. A bullet will bounce off its arachnofiber weave like a wren hitting a patio door, but excess perspiration wafts through it like a breeze through a freshly napalmed forest. Where his body has bony extremities, the suit has sintered armorgel: feels like gritty jello, protects like a stack of telephone books.

When they gave him the job, they gave him a gun. The Deliverator never deals in cash, but someone might come after him anyway—might want his car, or his cargo. The gun is tiny, aero-styled, lightweight, the kind of gun a fashion designer would carry; it fires teensy darts that fly at five times the velocity of an SR-71 spy plane, and when you get done using it, you have to plug it into the cigarette lighter, because it runs on electricity.

The Deliverator never pulled that gun in anger, or in fear. He pulled it once in Gila Highlands. Some punks in Gila Highlands, a fancy Burbclave, wanted themselves a delivery, and they didn't want to pay for it. Thought they would impress the Deliverator with a baseball bat. The Deliverator took out his gun, centered its laser doohickey on that poised Louisville Slugger, fired it. The recoil was immense, as though the weapon had blown up in his hand. The middle third of the baseball bat turned into a column of burning sawdust accelerating in all directions like a bursting star. Punk ended up holding this bat handle with milky smoke pouring out the end. Stupid look on his face. Didn't get nothing but trouble from the Deliverator.

Since then the Deliverator has kept the gun in the glove compartment and relied, instead, on a matched set of samurai swords, which have always been his weapon of choice anyhow. The punks in Gila Highlands weren't afraid of the gun, so the Deliverator was forced to use it. But swords need no demonstrations.

The Deliverator's car has enough potential energy packed into its batteries to fire a pound of bacon into the Asteroid Belt. Unlike a bimbo box or a Burb beater, the Deliverator's car unloads that power through gaping, gleaming, polished sphincters. When the Deliverator puts the hammer down, shit happens. You want to talk contact patches? Your car's tires have tiny contact patches, talk to the asphalt in four places the size of your tongue. The Deliverator's car has big sticky tires with contact patches the size of a fat lady's thighs. The Deliverator is in touch with the road, starts like a bad day, stops on a peseta.

Why is the Deliverator so equipped? Because people rely on him. He is a roll model. This is America. People do whatever the fuck they feel like doing, you got a problem with that? Because they have a right to. And because they have guns and no one can fucking stop them. As a result, this country has one of the worst economies in the world. When it gets down to it—talking trade balances here—once we've brain-drained all our technology into other countries, once things have evened out, they're making cars in Bolivia and microwave ovens in Tadzhikistan and selling them here—once our edge in natural resources has been made irrelevant by giant Hong Kong ships and dirigibles that can ship North Dakota all the way to New Zealand for a nickel—once the Invisible Hand has taken all those historical inequities and smeared them out into a broad global layer of what a Pakistani brickmaker would consider to be prosperity—y'know what? There's only four things we do better than anyone else

> music
> movies
> microcode (software)
> high-speed pizza delivery

The Deliverator used to make software. Still does, sometimes. But if life were a mellow elementary school run by well-meaning education Ph.D.s, the Deliverator's report card would say: "Hiro is so bright and creative but needs to work harder on his cooperation skills."

So now he has this other job. No brightness or creativity involved—but no cooperation either. Just a single principle: The Deliverator stands tall, your pie in thirty minutes or you can have it free, shoot the driver, take his car, file a class-action suit. The Deliverator has been working this job for six months, a rich and lengthy tenure by his standards, and has never delivered a pizza in more than twenty-one minutes.

Oh, they used to argue over times, many corporate driver-years lost to it: homeowners, red-faced and sweaty with their own lies, stinking of Old Spice and job-related stress, standing in their glowing yellow doorways brandishing their Seikos and waving at the clock over the kitchen sink, I swear, can't you guys tell time?

Didn't happen anymore. Pizza delivery a major industry. A managed industry. People went to CosaNostra Pizza University four years just to learn it. Came in its doors unable to write an English sentence, from Abkhazia, Rwanda, Guanajuato, South Jersey, and came out knowing more about pizza than a Bedouin knows about sand. And they had studied this problem. Graphed the frequency of doorway delivery-time disputes. Wired the early Deliverators to record, then analyze, the debating tactics, the voice-stress histograms, the distinctive grammatical structures employed by white middle-class Type A Burbclave occupants who against all logic had decided that this was the place to take their personal Custerian stand against all that was stale and deadening in their lives: they were going to lie, or delude themselves, about the time of their phone call and get themselves a free pizza; no, they deserved a free pizza along with their life, liberty, and pursuit of whatever, it was fucking inalienable. Sent psychologists out to these people's houses, gave them a free TV set to submit to an anonymous interview, hooked them to polygraphs, studied their brain waves as they showed them choppy, inexplicable movies of porn queens and late-night car crashes and Sammy Davis, Jr., put them in sweet-smelling, mauve-walled rooms and asked them questions about Ethics so perplexing that even a Jesuit couldn't respond without committing a venial sin.

The analysts at CosaNostra Pizza University concluded that it was just human nature and you couldn't fix it, and so they went for a quick cheap technical fix: smart boxes. The pizza box is a plastic carapace now, corrugated for stiffness, a little LED readout glowing on the side, telling the Deliverator how many trade imbalance–producing minutes have ticked away since the fateful phone call. There are chips and stuff in there. The pizzas rest, a short stack of them, in slots behind the Deliverator's head. Each pizza glides into a slot like a circuit board into a computer, clicks into place as the smart box interfaces with the onboard system of the Deliverator's car. The address of the caller has already been inferred from his phone number and poured into the smart box's built-in RAM. From there it is communicated to the car, which computes and projects the optimal route on a heads-up display, a glowing colored map traced out against the windshield so that the Deliverator does not even have to glance down.

If the thirty-minute deadline expires, news of the disaster is flashed to CosaNostra Pizza Headquarters and relayed from there to Uncle Enzo himself—the Sicilian Colonel Sanders, the Andy Griffith of Bensonhurst, the straight razor–swinging figment of many a Deliverator's nightmares, the Capo and prime figurehead of CosaNostra Pizza, Incorporated—who will be on the phone to the customer within five minutes, apologizing profusely. The next day, Uncle Enzo will land on the customer's yard in a jet helicopter and apologize some more and give him a free trip to Italy—all he has to do is sign a bunch of releases that make him a public figure and spokesperson for CosaNostra Pizza and basically end his private life as he knows it. He will come away from the whole thing feeling that, somehow, he owes the Mafia a favor.

The Deliverator does not know for sure what happens to the driver in such cases, but he has heard some rumors. Most pizza deliveries happen in the evening hours, which Uncle Enzo considers to be his private time. And how would you feel if you had to interrupt dinner with your family in order to call some obstreperous dork in a Burbclave and grovel for a late fucking pizza? Uncle Enzo has not put in fifty years serving his family and his country so that, at the age when most are playing golf and bobbling their granddaughters, he can get out of the bathtub dripping wet and lie down and kiss the feet of some sixteen-year-old skate punk whose pepperoni was thirty-one minutes in coming. Oh, God. It makes the Deliverator breathe a little shallower just to think of the idea.

But he wouldn't drive for CosaNostra Pizza any other way. You know why? Because there's something about having your life on the line. It's like being a kamikaze pilot. Your mind is clear. Other people—store clerks, burger flippers, software engineers, the whole vocabulary of meaningless jobs that make up Life in America—other people just rely on plain old competition. Better flip your burgers or debug your subroutines faster and better than your high school classmate two blocks down the strip is flipping or debugging, because we're in competition with those guys, and people notice these things.

What a fucking rat race that is. CosaNostra Pizza doesn't have any competition. Competition goes against the Mafia ethic. You don't work harder because you're competing against some identical operation down the street. You work harder because everything is on the line. Your name, your honor, your family, your life. Those burger flippers might have a better life expectancy—but what kind of life is it anyway, you have to ask yourself. That's why nobody, not even the Nipponese, can move pizzas faster than CosaNostra. The Deliverator is proud to wear the uniform, proud to drive the car, proud to march up the front walks of innumerable Burbclave homes, a grim vision in ninja black, a pizza on his shoulder, red LED digits blazing proud numbers into the night: 12:32 or 15:15 or the occasional 20:43.

The Deliverator is assigned to CosaNostra Pizza #3569 in the Valley. Southern California doesn't know whether to bustle or just strangle itself on the spot. Not enough roads for the number of people. Fairlanes, Inc. is laying new ones all the time. Have to bulldoze lots of neighborhoods to do it, but those seventies and eighties developments exist to be bulldozed, right? No sidewalks, no schools, no nothing. Don't have their own police force—no immigration control—undesirables can walk right in without being frisked or even harassed. Now a Burbclave, that's the place to live. A city-state with its own constitution, a border, laws, cops, everything.

The Deliverator was a corporal in the Farms of Merryvale State Security Force for a while once. Got himself fired for pulling a sword on an acknowledged perp. Slid it right through the fabric of the perp's shirt, gliding the flat of the blade along the base of his neck, and pinned him to a warped and bubbled expanse of vinyl siding on the wall of the house that the perp was trying to break into. Thought it was a pretty righteous bust. But they fired him anyway because the perp turned out to be the son of the vice-chancellor of the Farms of Merryvale. Oh, the weasels had an excuse: said that a thirty-six-inch samurai sword was not on their Weapons Protocol. Said that he had violated the SPAC, the Suspected Perpetrator Apprehension Code. Said that the perp had suffered psychological trauma. He was afraid of butter knives now; he had to spread his jelly with the back of a teaspoon. They said that he had exposed them to liability.

The Deliverator had to borrow some money to pay for it. Had to borrow it from the Mafia, in fact. So he's in their database now—retinal patterns, DNA, voice graph, fingerprints, footprints, palm prints, wrist prints, every fucking part of the body that had wrinkles on it—almost—those bastards rolled in ink and made a print and digitized it into their computer. But it's their money—sure they're careful about loaning it out. And when he applied for the Deliverator job they were happy to take him, because they knew him. When he got the loan, he had to deal personally with the assistant vice-capo of the Valley, who later recommended him for the Deliverator job. So it was like being in a family. A really scary, twisted, abusive family.

CosaNostra Pizza #3569 is on Vista Road just down from Kings Park Mall. Vista Road used to belong to the State of California and now is called Fairlanes, Inc. Rte. CSV-5. Its main competition used to be a U.S. highway and is now called Cruiseways, Inc. Rte. Cal-12. Farther up the Valley, the two competing highways actually cross. Once there had been bitter disputes, the intersection closed by sporadic sniper fire. Finally, a big developer bought the entire intersection and turned it into a drivethrough mall. Now the roads just feed into a parking system—not a lot, not a ramp, but a system—and lose their identity. Getting through the intersection involves tracing paths through the parking system, many braided filaments of direction like the Ho Chi Minh trail. CSV-5 has better throughput, but Cal-12 has better pavement. That is typical—Fairlanes roads emphasize getting you there, for Type A drivers, and Cruiseways emphasize the enjoyment of the ride, for Type B drivers.

The Deliverator is a Type A driver with rabies. He is zeroing in on his home base, CosaNostra Pizza #3569, cranking up the left lane of CSV-5 at a hundred and twenty kilometers. His car is an invisible black lozenge, just a dark place that reflects the tunnel of franchise signs—the loglo. A row of orange lights burbles and churns across the front, where the grille would be if this were an air-breathing car. The orange light looks like a gasoline fire. It comes in through people's rear windows, bounces off their rearview mirrors, projects a fiery mask across their eyes, reaches into their subconscious, and unearths terrible fears of being pinned, fully conscious, under a detonating gas tank, makes them want to pull over and let the Deliverator overtake them in his black chariot of pepperoni fire.

The loglo, overhead, marking out CSV-5 in twin contrails, is a body of electrical light made of innumerable cells, each cell designed in Manhattan by imageers who make more for designing a single logo than a Deliverator will make in his entire lifetime. Despite their efforts to stand out, they all smear together, especially at a hundred and twenty kilometers per hour. Still, it is easy to see CosaNostra Pizza #3569 because of the billboard, which is wide and tall even by current inflated standards. In fact, the squat franchise itself looks like nothing more than a low-slung base for the great aramid fiber pillars that thrust the billboard up into the trademark firmament. Marca Registrada, baby.

The billboard is a classic, a chestnut, not a figment of some fleeting Mafia promotional campaign. It is a statement, a monument built to endure. Simple and dignified. It shows Uncle Enzo in one of his spiffy Italian suits. The pinstripes glint and flex like sinews. The pocket square is luminous. His hair is perfect, slicked back with something that never comes off, each strand cut off straight and square at the end by Uncle Enzo's cousin, Art the Barber, who runs the second-largest chain of low-end haircutting establishments in the world. Uncle Enzo is standing there, not exactly smiling, an avuncular glint in his eye for sure, not posing like a model but standing there like your uncle would, and it says

The Mafia
you've got a friend in The Family!
paid for by the Our Thing Foundation

The billboard serves as the Deliverator's polestar. He knows that when he gets to the place on CSV-5 where the bottom corner of the billboard is obscured by the pseudo-Gothic stained-glass arches of the local Reverend Wayne's Pearly Gates franchise, it's time for him to get over into the right lanes where the retards and the bimbo boxes poke along, random, indecisive, looking at each passing franchise's driveway like they don't know if it's a promise or a threat.

He cuts off a bimbo box—a family minivan—veers past the Buy 'n' Fly that is next door, and pulls into CosaNostra Pizza #3569. Those big fat contact patches complain, squeal a little bit, but they hold on to the patented Fairlanes, Inc. high-traction pavement and guide him into the chute. No other Deliverators are waiting in the chute. That is good, that means high turnover for him, fast action, keep moving that 'za. As he scrunches to a stop, the electromechanical hatch on the flank of his car is already opening to reveal his empty pizza slots, the door clicking and folding back in on itself like the wing of a beetle. The slots are waiting. Waiting for hot pizza.

And waiting. The Deliverator honks his horn. This is not a nominal outcome.

Window slides open. That should never happen. You can look at the three-ring binder from CosaNostra Pizza University, cross-reference the citation for *window, chute, dispatcher's,* and it will give you all the procedures for that window—and it should never be opened. Unless something has gone wrong.

The window slides open and—you sitting down?—*smoke* comes out of it. The Deliverator hears a discordant beetling over the metal hurricane of his sound system and realizes that it is a smoke alarm, coming from inside the franchise.

Mute button on the stereo. Oppressive silence—his eardrums uncringe—the window is buzzing with the cry of the smoke alarm. The car idles, waiting. The hatch has been open too long, atmospheric pollutants are congealing on the electrical contacts in the back of the pizza slots, he'll have to clean them ahead of schedule, everything is going exactly the way it shouldn't go in the three-ring binder that spells out all the rhythms of the pizza universe.

Inside, a football-shaped Abkhazian man is running to and fro, holding a three-ring binder open, using his spare tire as a ledge to keep it from collapsing shut; he runs with the gait of a man carrying an egg on a spoon. He is shouting in the Abkhazian dialect; all the people who run CosaNostra pizza franchises in this part of the Valley are Abkhazian immigrants.

It does not look like a serious fire. The Deliverator saw a real fire once, at the Farms of Merryvale, and you couldn't see anything for the smoke. That's all it was: smoke, burbling out of nowhere, occasional flashes of orange light down at the bottom, like heat lightning in tall clouds. This is not that kind of fire. It is the kind of fire that just barely puts out enough smoke to detonate the smoke alarms. And he is losing time for this shit.

The Deliverator holds the horn button down. The Abkhazian manager comes to the window. He is supposed to use the intercom to talk to drivers, he could say anything he wanted and it would be piped straight into the Deliverator's car, but no, he has to talk face to face, like the Deliverator is some kind of fucking ox cart driver. He is red-faced, sweating, his eyes roll as he tries to think of the English words.

"A fire, a little one," he says.

The Deliverator says nothing. Because he knows that all of this is going onto videotape. The tape is being pipelined, as it happens, to CosaNostra Pizza University, where it will be analyzed in a pizza management science laboratory. It will be shown to Pizza University students, perhaps to the very students who will replace this man when he gets fired, as a textbook example of how to screw up your life.

"New employee—put his dinner in the microwave—had foil in it—boom!" the manager says.

Abkhazia had been part of the Soviet fucking Union. A new immigrant from Abkhazia trying to operate a microwave was like a deep-sea tube worm doing brain surgery. Where did they get these guys? Weren't there any Americans who could bake a fucking pizza?

"Just give me one pie," the Deliverator says.

Talking about pies snaps the guy into the current century. He gets a grip. He slams the window shut, strangling the relentless keening of the smoke alarm.

A Nipponese robot arm shoves the pizza out and into the top slot. The hatch folds shut to protect it.

As the Deliverator is pulling out of the chute, building up speed, checking the address that is flashed across his windshield, deciding whether to turn right or left, it happens. His stereo cuts out again—on command of the onboard system. The cockpit lights go red. *Red.* A repetitive buzzer begins to sound. The LED readout on his windshield, which echoes the one on the pizza box, flashes up: 20:00.

They have just given the Deliverator a twenty-minute-old pizza. He checks the address; it is twelve miles away.

2

The Deliverator lets out an involuntary roar and puts the hammer down. His emotions tell him to go back and kill that manager, get his swords out of the trunk, dive in through the little sliding window like a ninja, track him down through the moiling chaos of the microwaved franchise and confront him in a climactic thick-crust apocalypse. But he thinks the same thing when someone cuts him off on the freeway, and he's never done it—yet.

He can handle this. This is doable. He cranks up the orange warning lights to maximum brilliance, puts his headlights on autoflash. He overrides the warning buzzer, jams the stereo over to Taxiscan, which cruises all the taxi-driver frequencies listening for interesting traffic. Can't understand a fucking word. You could buy tapes, learn-while-you-drive, and learn to speak Taxilinga. It was essential, to get a job in that business. They said it was based on English but not one word in a hundred was recognizable. Still, you could get an idea. If there was trouble on this road, they'd be babbling about it in Taxilinga, give him some warning, let him take an alternate route so he wouldn't get

he grips the wheel

stuck in traffic

his eyes get big, he can feel the pressure driving them back into his skull

or caught behind a mobile home

his bladder is very full

and deliver the pizza

Oh, God oh, God

late

22:06 hangs on the windshield; all he can see, all he can think about is 30:01.

The taxi drivers are buzzing about something. Taxilinga is mellifluous babble with a few harsh foreign sounds, like butter spiced with broken glass. He keeps hearing "fare." They are always jabbering about their fucking fares. Big deal. What happens if you deliver your fare *late*

you don't get as much of a tip? Big deal.

Big slowdown at the intersection of CSV-5 and Oahu Road, per usual, only way to avoid it is to cut through The Mews at Windsor Heights.

TMAWHs all have the same layout. When creating a new Burbclave, TMAWH Development Corporation will chop down any mountain ranges and divert the course of any mighty rivers that threaten to interrupt this street plan—ergonomically designed to encourage driving safety. A Deliverator can go into a Mews at Windsor Heights anywhere from Fairbanks to Yaroslavl to the Shenzhen special economic zone and find his way around.

But once you've delivered a pie to every single house in a TMAWH a few times, you get to know its little secrets. The Deliverator is such a man. He knows that in a standard TMAWH there is only one yard—one yard—that prevents you from driving straight in one entrance, across the Burbclave, and out the other. If you are squeamish about driving on grass, it might take you ten minutes to meander through TMAWH. But if you have the balls to lay tracks across that one yard, you have a straight shot through the center.

The Deliverator knows that yard. He has delivered pizzas there. He has looked at it, scoped it out, memorized the location of the shed and the picnic table, can find them even in the dark—knows that if it ever came to this, a twenty-three-minute pizza, miles to go, and a slowdown at CSV-5 and Oahu—he could enter The Mews at Windsor Heights (his electronic delivery-man's visa would raise the gate automatically), scream down Heritage Boulevard, rip the turn onto Strawbridge Place (ignoring the DEAD END sign and the speed limit and the CHILDREN PLAYING ideograms that are strung so liberally throughout TMAWH), thrash the speed bumps with his mighty radials, blast up the driveway of Number 15 Strawbridge Circle, cut a hard left around the backyard shed, careen into the backyard of Number 84 Mayapple Place, avoid its picnic table (tricky), get into their driveway and out onto Mayapple, which takes him to Bellewoode Valley Road, which runs straight to the exit of the Burbclave. TMAWH security police might be waiting for him at the exit, but their STDs, Severe Tire Damage devices, only point one way—they can keep people out, but not keep them in.

This car can go so fucking fast that if a cop took a bite of a doughnut as the Deliverator was entering Heritage Boulevard, he probably wouldn't be able to swallow it until about the time the Deliverator was shrieking out onto Oahu.

Thunk. And more red lights come up on the windshield: the perimeter security of the Deliverator's vehicle has been breached.

No. It can't be.

Someone is shadowing him. Right off his left flank. A person on a skateboard, rolling down the highway right behind him, just as he is laying in his approach vectors to Heritage Boulevard.

The Deliverator, in his distracted state, has allowed himself to get pooned. As in harpooned. It is a big round padded electromagnet on the end of an arachnofiber cable. It has just thunked onto the back of the Deliverator's car, and stuck. Ten feet behind him, the owner of this cursed device is surfing, taking him for a ride, skateboarding along like a water skier behind a boat.

In the rearview, flashes of orange and blue. The parasite is not just a punk out having a good time. It is a businessman making money. The orange and blue coverall, bulging all over with sintered armorgel padding, is the uniform of a Kourier. A Kourier from RadiKS, Radikal Kourier Systems. Like a bicycle messenger, but a hundred times more irritating because they don't pedal under their own power—they just latch on and slow you down.

Naturally. The Deliverator was in a hurry, flashing his lights, squealing his contact patches. The fastest thing on the road. Naturally, the Kourier would choose him to latch onto.

No need to get rattled. With the shortcut through TMAWH, he will have plenty of time. He passes a slower car in the middle lane, then cuts right in front of him. The Kourier will have to unpoon or else be slammed sideways into the slower vehicle.

Done. The Kourier isn't ten feet behind him anymore—he is right there, peering in the rear window. Anticipating the maneuver, the Kourier reeled in his cord, which is attached to a handle with a power reel in it, and is now right on top of the pizza mobile, the front wheel of his skateboard actually underneath the Deliverator's rear bumper.

An orange-and-blue-gloved hand reaches forward, a transparent sheet of plastic draped over it, and slaps his driver's side window. The Deliverator has just been stickered. The sticker is a foot across and reads, in big orange block letters, printed backward so that he can read it from the inside.

THAT WAS STALE

He almost misses the turnoff for The Mews at Windsor Heights. He has to jam the brakes, let traffic clear, cut across the curb lane to enter the Burbclave. The border post is well lighted, the customs agents ready to frisk all comers—cavity-search them if they are the wrong kind of people—but the gate flies open as if by magic as the security system senses that this is a CosaNostra Pizza vehicle, just making a delivery, sir. And as he goes through, the Kourier—that tick on his ass—waves to the border police! What a prick! Like he comes in here all the time!

He probably does come in here all the time. Picking up important shit for important TMAWH people, delivering it to other FOQNEs, Franchise-Organized Quasi-National Entities, getting it through customs. That's what Kouriers do. Still.

He's going too slow, lost all his momentum, his timing is off. Where's the Kourier? Ah, reeled out some line, is following behind again. The Deliverator knows that this jerk is in for a big surprise. Can he stay on his fucking skateboard while he's being hauled over the flattened remains of some kid's plastic tricycle at a hundred kilometers? We're going to find out.

The Kourier leans back—the Deliverator can't help watching in the rearview—leans back like a water skier, pushes off against his board, and swings around beside him, now traveling abreast with him up Heritage Boulevard and *slap* another sticker goes up, this one on the windshield! It says

SMOOTH MOVE, EX-LAX

The Deliverator has heard of these stickers. It takes hours to get them off. Have to take the car into a detailing place, pay trillions of dollars. The Deliverator has two things on his agenda now: He is going to shake this street scum, whatever it takes, and deliver the fucking pizza all in the space of

24:23

the next five minutes and thirty-seven seconds.

This is it—got to pay more attention to the road—he swings into the side street, no warning, hoping maybe to whipsaw the Kourier into the street sign on the corner. Doesn't work. The smart ones watch your front tires, they see when you're turning, can't surprise them. Down Strawbridge Place! It seems so long, longer than he remembered—natural when you're in a hurry. Sees the glint of cars up ahead, cars parked sideways to the road—these must be parked in the circle. And there's the house. Light blue vinyl clapboard two-story with one-story garage to the side. He makes that driveway the center of his universe, puts the Kourier out of his mind, tries not to think about Uncle Enzo, what he's doing right now—in the bath, maybe, or taking a crap, or making love to some actress, or teaching Sicilian songs to one of his twenty-six granddaughters.

The slope of the driveway slams his front suspension halfway up into the engine compartment, but that's what suspensions are for. He evades the car in the driveway—must have visitors tonight, didn't remember that these people drove a Lexus—cuts through the hedge, into the side yard, looks for that shed, that shed he absolutely must not run into

it's not there, they took it down

next problem, the picnic table in the next yard

hang on, there's a fence, when did they put up a fence?

This is no time to put on the brakes. Got to build up some speed, knock it down without blowing all this momentum. It's just a four-foot wooden thing.

The fence goes down easy, he loses maybe ten percent of his speed. But strangely, it looked like an *old* fence, maybe he made a wrong turn somewhere—he realizes, as he catapults into an empty backyard swimming pool.

————

_____ If it had been full of water, that wouldn't have been so bad, maybe the car would have been saved, he wouldn't owe CosaNostra Pizza a new car. But no, he does a Stuka into the far wall of the pool, it sounds more like an explosion than a crash. The airbag inflates, comes back down a second later like a curtain revealing the structure of his new life: he is stuck in a dead car in an empty pool in a TMAWH, the sirens of the Burbclave's security police are approaching, and there's a pizza behind his head, resting there like the blade of a guillotine, with 25:17 on it.

"Where's it going?" someone says. A woman.

He looks up through the distorted frame of the window, now rimmed with a fractal pattern of crystallized safety glass. It is the Kourier talking to him. The Kourier is not a man, it is a young woman. A fucking teenaged girl. She is pristine, unhurt. She has skated right down into the pool, she's now oscillating back and forth from one side of the pool to the other, skating up one bank, almost to the lip, turning around, skating down and across and up the opposite side. She is holding her poon in her right hand, the electromagnet reeled up against the handle so it looks like some kind of a strange wide-angle intergalactic death ray. Her chest glitters like a general's with a hundred little ribbons and medals, except each rectangle is not a ribbon, it is a bar code. A bar code with an ID number that gets her into a different business, highway, or FOQNE.

"Yo!" she says. "Where's the pizza going?"

He's going to die and she's *gamboling*.

"White Columns. 5 Oglethorpe Circle," he says.

"I can do that. Open the hatch."

His heart expands to twice its normal size. Tears come to his eyes. He may live. He presses a button and the hatch opens.

On her next orbit across the bottom of the pool, the Kourier yanks the pizza out of its slot. The Deliverator winces, imagining the garlicky topping accordioning into the back wall of the box. Then she puts it sideways under her arm. It's more than a Deliverator can stand to watch.

But she'll get it there. Uncle Enzo doesn't have to apologize for ugly, ruined, cold pizzas, just late ones.

"Hey," he says, "take this."

The Deliverator sticks his black-clad arm out the shattered

window. A white rectangle glows in the dim backyard light: a business card. The Kourier snatches it from him on her next orbit, reads it. It says

HIRO PROTAGONIST

Last of the freelance hackers
Greatest sword fighter in the world
Stringer, Central Intelligence Corporation
Specializing in software-related intel
(music, movies & microcode)

On the back is gibberish explaining how he may be reached: a telephone number. A universal voice phone locator code. A P.O. box. His address on half a dozen electronic communications nets. And an address in the Metaverse.

"Stupid name," she says, shoving the card into one of a hundred little pockets on her coverall.

"But you'll never forget it," Hiro says.

"If you're a hacker . . . "

"How come I'm delivering pizzas?"

"Right."

"Because I'm a freelance hacker. Look, whatever your name is—I owe you one."

"Name's Y.T.," she says, shoving at the pool a few times with one foot, building up more energy. She flies out of the pool as if catapulted, and she's gone. The smartwheels of her skateboard, many, many spokes extending and retracting to fit the shape of the ground, take her across the lawn like a pat of butter skidding across hot Teflon.

Hiro, who as of thirty seconds ago is no longer the Deliverator, gets out of the car and pulls his swords out of the trunk, straps them around his body, prepares for a breathtaking nighttime escape run across TMAWH territory. The border with Oakwood Estates is only minutes away, he has the layout memorized (sort of), and he knows how these Burbclave cops operate, because he used to be one. So he has a good chance of making it. But it's going to be interesting.

Above him, in the house that owns the pool, a light has come on, and children are looking down at him through their bedroom windows, all warm and fuzzy in their Li'l Crips and Ninja Raft Warrior pajamas, which can either be flameproof or noncarcinogenic but not both at the same time. Dad is emerging from the back door, pulling on a jacket. It is a nice family, a safe family in a house full of light, like the family he was a part of until thirty seconds ago.

3

Hiro Protagonist and Vitaly Chernobyl, roommates, are chilling out in their home, a spacious 20-by-30 in a U-Stor-It in Inglewood, California. The room has a concrete slab floor, corrugated steel walls separating it from the neighboring units, and—this is a mark of distinction and luxury—a roll-up steel door that faces northwest, giving them a few red rays at times like this, when the sun is setting over LAX. From time to time, a 777 or a Sukhoi/Kawasaki Hypersonic Transport will taxi in front of the sun and block the sunset with its rudder, or just mangle the red light with its jet exhaust, braiding the parallel rays into a dappled pattern on the wall.

But there are worse places to live. There are much worse places right here in this U-Stor-It. Only the big units like this one have their own doors. Most of them are accessed via a communal loading dock that leads to a maze of wide corrugated-steel hallways and freight elevators. These are slum housing, 5-by-10s and 10-by-10s where Yanoama tribespersons cook beans and parboil fistfuls of coca leaves over heaps of burning lottery tickets.

It is whispered that in the old days, when the U-Stor-It was actually used for its intended purpose (namely, providing cheap extra storage space to Californians with too many material goods), certain entrepreneurs came to the front office, rented out 10-by-10s using fake IDs, filled them up with steel drums full of toxic chemical waste, and then abandoned them, leaving the problem for the U-Stor-It Corporation to handle. According to these rumors, U-Stor-It just padlocked those units and wrote them off. Now, the immigrants claim, certain units remain haunted by this chemical specter. It is a story they tell their children, to keep them from trying to break into padlocked units.

No one has ever tried to break into Hiro and Vitaly's unit because there's nothing in there to steal, and at this point in their lives, neither one of them is important enough to kill, kidnap, or interrogate. Hiro owns a couple of nice Nipponese swords, but he always wears them, and the whole idea of stealing fantastically dangerous weapons presents the would-be perp with inherent dangers and contradictions: When you are wrestling for possession of a sword, the man with the handle always wins. Hiro also has a pretty nice computer that he usually takes with him when he goes anywhere. Vitaly owns half a carton of Lucky Strikes, an electric guitar, and a hangover.

At the moment, Vitaly Chernobyl is stretched out on a futon, quiescent, and Hiro Protagonist is sitting crosslegged at a low table, Nipponese style, consisting of a cargo pallet set on cinderblocks.

As the sun sets, its red light is supplanted by the light of many neon logos emanating from the franchise ghetto that constitutes this U-Stor-It's natural habitat. This light, known as loglo, fills in the shadowy corners of the unit with seedy, oversaturated colors.

Hiro has cappuccino skin and spiky, truncated dreadlocks. His hair does not cover as much of his head as it used to, but he is a young man, by no means bald or balding, and the slight retreat of his hairline only makes more of his high cheekbones. He is wearing shiny goggles that wrap halfway around his head; the bows of the goggles have little earphones that are plugged into his outer ears.

The earphones have some built-in noise cancellation features. This sort of thing works best on steady noise. When jumbo jets make their takeoff runs on the runway across the street, the sound is reduced to a low doodling hum. But when Vitaly Chernobyl thrashes out an experimental guitar solo, it still hurts Hiro's ears.

The goggles throw a light, smoky haze across his eyes and reflect a distorted wide-angle view of a brilliantly lit boulevard that stretches off into an infinite blackness. This boulevard does not really exist; it is a computer-rendered view of an imaginary place.

Beneath this image, it is possible to see Hiro's eyes, which look Asian. They are from his mother, who is Korean by way of Nippon. The rest of him looks more like his father, who was African by way of Texas by way of the Army—back in the days before it got split up into a number of competing organizations such as General Jim's Defense System and Admiral Bob's National Security.

Four things are on the cargo pallet: a bottle of expensive beer from the Puget Sound area, which Hiro cannot really afford; a long sword known in Nippon as a *katana* and a short sword known as a *wakizashi*—Hiro's father looted these from Japan after World War II went atomic—and a computer.

The computer is a featureless black wedge. It does not have a power cord, but there is a narrow translucent plastic tube emerging from a hatch on the rear, spiraling across the cargo pallet and the floor, and plugged into a crudely installed fiber-optics socket above the head of the sleeping Vitaly Chernobyl. In the center of the plastic tube is a hair-thin fiber-optic cable. The cable is carrying a lot of information back and forth between Hiro's computer and the rest of the world. In order to transmit the same amount of information on paper, they would have to arrange for a 747 cargo freighter packed with telephone books and encyclopedias to power-dive into their unit every couple of minutes, forever.

Hiro can't really afford the computer either, but he has to have one. It is a tool of his trade. In the worldwide community of hackers, Hiro is a talented drifter. This is the kind of lifestyle that sounded romantic to him as recently as five years ago. But in the bleak light of full adulthood, which is to one's early twenties as Sunday morning is to Saturday night, he can clearly see what it really amounts to: He's broke and unemployed. And a few short weeks ago, his tenure as a pizza deliverer—the only pointless dead-end job he really enjoys—came to an end. Since then, he's been putting a lot more emphasis on his auxiliary emergency backup job: freelance stringer for the CIC, the Central Intelligence Corporation of Langley, Virginia.

The business is a simple one. Hiro gets information. It may be gossip, videotape, audiotape, a fragment of a computer disk, a xerox of a document. It can even be a joke based on the latest highly publicized disaster.

He uploads it to the CIC database—the Library, formerly the Library of Congress, but no one calls it that anymore. Most people are not entirely clear on what the word "congress" means.

And even the word "library" is getting hazy. It used to be a place full of books, mostly old ones. Then they began to include videotapes, records, and magazines. Then all of the information got converted into machine-readable form, which is to say, ones and zeroes. And as the number of media grew, the material became more up to date, and the methods for searching the Library became more and more sophisticated, it approached the point where there was no substantive difference between the Library of Congress and the Central Intelligence Agency. Fortuitously, this happened just as the government was falling apart anyway. So they merged and kicked out a big fat stock offering.

Millions of other CIC stringers are uploading millions of other fragments at the same time. CIC's clients, mostly large corporations and Sovereigns, rifle through the Library looking for useful information, and if they find a use for something that Hiro put into it, Hiro gets paid.

A year ago, he uploaded an entire first-draft film script that he stole from an agent's wastebasket in Burbank. Half a dozen studios wanted to see it. He ate and vacationed off of that one for six months.

Since then, times have been leaner. He has been learning the hard way that 99 percent of the information in the Library never gets used at all.

Case in point: After a certain Kourier tipped him off to the existence of Vitaly Chernobyl, he put a few intensive weeks into researching a new musical phenomenon—the rise of Ukrainian nuclear fuzz-grunge collectives in L.A. He has planted exhaustive notes on this trend in the Library, including video and audio. Not one single record label, agent, or rock critic has bothered to access it.

The top surface of the computer is smooth except for a fisheye lens, a polished glass dome with a purplish optical coating. Whenever Hiro is using the machine, this lens emerges and clicks into place, its base flush with the surface of the computer. The neighborhood loglo is curved and foreshortened on its surface.

Hiro finds it erotic. This is partly because he hasn't been properly laid in several weeks. But there's more to it. Hiro's father, who was stationed in Japan for many years, was obsessed with cameras. He kept bringing them back from his stints in the Far

East, encased in many protective layers, so that when he took them out to show Hiro, it was like watching an exquisite striptease as they emerged from all that black leather and nylon, zippers and straps. And once the lens was finally exposed, pure geometric equation made real, so powerful and vulnerable at once, Hiro could only think it was like nuzzling through skirts and lingerie and outer labia and inner labia. . . . It made him feel naked and weak and brave.

The lens can see half of the universe—the half that is above the computer, which includes most of Hiro. In this way, it can generally keep track of where Hiro is and what direction he's looking in.

Down inside the computer are three lasers—a red one, a green one, and a blue one. They are powerful enough to make a bright light but not powerful enough to burn through the back of your eyeball and broil your brain, fry your frontals, lase your lobes. As everyone learned in elementary school, these three colors of light can be combined, with different intensities, to produce any color that Hiro's eye is capable of seeing.

In this way, a narrow beam of any color can be shot out of the innards of the computer, up through that fisheye lens, in any direction. Through the use of electronic mirrors inside the computer, this beam is made to sweep back and forth across the lenses of Hiro's goggles, in much the same way as the electron beam in a television paints the inner surface of the eponymous Tube. The resulting image hangs in space in front of Hiro's view of Reality.

By drawing a slightly different image in front of each eye, the image can be made three-dimensional. By changing the image seventy-two times a second, it can be made to move. By drawing the moving three-dimensional image at a resolution of 2K pixels on a side, it can be as sharp as the eye can perceive, and by pumping stereo digital sound through the little earphones, the moving 3-D pictures can have a perfectly realistic soundtrack.

So Hiro's not actually here at all. He's in a computer-generated universe that his computer is drawing onto his goggles and pumping into his earphones. In the lingo, this imaginary place is known as the Metaverse. Hiro spends a lot of time in the Metaverse. It beats the shit out of the U-Stor-It.

—————————— Hiro is approaching the Street. It is the Broadway, the Champs Élysées of the Metaverse. It is the brilliantly lit boulevard that can be seen, miniaturized and backward, reflected in the lenses of his goggles. It does not really exist. But right now, millions of people are walking up and down it.

The dimensions of the Street are fixed by a protocol, hammered out by the computer-graphics ninja overlords of the Association for Computing Machinery's Global Multimedia Protocol Group. The Street seems to be a grand boulevard going all the way around the equator of a black sphere with a radius of a bit more than ten thousand kilometers. That makes it 65,536 kilometers around, which is considerably bigger than Earth.

The number 65,536 is an awkward figure to everyone except a hacker, who recognizes it more readily than his own mother's date of birth: It happens to be a power of 2—2^{16} power to be exact—and even the exponent 16 is equal to 2^4, and 4 is equal to 2^2. Along with 256; 32,768; and 2,147,483,648; 65,536 is one of the foundation stones of the hacker universe, in which 2 is the only really important number because that's how many digits a computer can recognize. One of those digits is 0, and the other is 1. Any number that can be created by fetishistically multiplying 2s by each other, and subtracting the occasional 1, will be instantly recognizable to a hacker.

Like any place in Reality, the Street is subject to development. Developers can build their own small streets feeding off of the main one. They can build buildings, parks, signs, as well as things that do not exist in Reality, such as vast hovering overhead light shows, special neighborhoods where the rules of three-dimensional spacetime are ignored, and free-combat zones where people can go to hunt and kill each other.

The only difference is that since the Street does not really exist—it's just a computer-graphics protocol written down on a piece of paper somewhere—none of these things is being physically built. They are, rather, pieces of software, made available to the public over the worldwide fiber-optics network. When Hiro goes into the Metaverse and looks down the Street and sees buildings and electric signs stretching off into the darkness, disappearing over the curve of the globe, he is actually staring at the

graphic representations—the user interfaces—of a myriad different pieces of software that have been engineered by major corporations. In order to place these things on the Street, they have
had to get approval from the Global Multimedia Protocol Group,
have had to buy frontage on the Street, get zoning approval,
obtain permits, bribe inspectors, the whole bit. The money these
corporations pay to build things on the Street all goes into a trust
fund owned and operated by the GMPG, which pays for developing and expanding the machinery that enables the Street to exist.

Hiro has a house in a neighborhood just off the busiest part of
the Street. It is a very old neighborhood by Street standards.
About ten years ago, when the Street protocol was first written,
Hiro and some of his buddies pooled their money and bought one
of the first development licenses, created a little neighborhood of
hackers. At the time, it was just a little patchwork of light amid
a vast blackness. Back then, the Street was just a necklace of
streetlights around a black ball in space.

Since then, the neighborhood hasn't changed much, but the
Street has. By getting in on it early, Hiro's buddies got a head
start on the whole business. Some of them even got very rich off
of it.

That's why Hiro has a nice big house in the Metaverse but has
to share a 20-by-30 in Reality. Real estate acumen does not always
extend across universes.

The sky and the ground are black, like a computer screen that
hasn't had anything drawn into it yet; it is always nighttime in the
Metaverse, and the Street is always garish and brilliant, like Las
Vegas freed from constraints of physics and finance. But people
in Hiro's neighborhood are very good programmers, so it's tasteful. The houses look like real houses. There are a couple of Frank
Lloyd Wright reproductions and some fancy Victoriana.

So it's always a shock to step out onto the Street, where everything seems to be a mile high. This is Downtown, the most
heavily developed area. If you go a couple of hundred kilometers
in either direction, the development will taper down to almost
nothing, just a thin chain of streetlights casting white pools on
the black velvet ground. But Downtown is a dozen Manhattans,
embroidered with neon and stacked on top of each other.

In the real world—planet Earth, Reality—there are somewhere between six and ten billion people. At any given time, most of them are making mud bricks or field-stripping their AK-47s. Perhaps a billion of them have enough money to own a computer; these people have more money than all of the others put together. Of these billion potential computer owners, maybe a quarter of them actually bother to own computers, and a quarter of these have machines that are powerful enough to handle the Street protocol. That makes for about sixty million people who can be on the Street at any given time. Add in another sixty million or so who can't really afford it but go there anyway, by using public machines, or machines owned by their school or their employer, and at any given time the Street is occupied by twice the population of New York City.

That's why the damn place is so overdeveloped. Put in a sign or a building on the Street and the hundred million richest, hippest, best-connected people on earth will see it every day of their lives.

It is a hundred meters wide, with a narrow monorail track running down the middle. The monorail is a free piece of public utility software that enables users to change their location on the Street rapidly and smoothly. A lot of people just ride back and forth on it, looking at the sights. When Hiro first saw this place, ten years ago, the monorail hadn't been written yet; he and his buddies had to write car and motorcycle software in order to get around. They would take their software out and race it in the black desert of the electronic night.

4

Y.T. has been privileged to watch many a young Clint plant his sweet face in an empty Burbclave pool during an unauthorized night run, but always on a skateboard, never ever in a car. The landscape of the suburban night has much weird beauty if you just look.

Back on the paddle again. It rolls across the yard on a set of RadiKS Mark IV Smartwheels. She upgraded to said magical sprockets after the following ad appeared in *Thrasher* magazine:

CHISELED SPAM

is what you will see in the mirror if you surf on a weak plank with dumb, fixed wheels and interface with a muffler, retread, snow turd, road kill, driveshaft, railroad tie, or unconscious pedestrian.

If you think this is unlikely, you've been surfing too many ghost malls. All of these obstacles and more were recently observed on a one-mile stretch of the New Jersey Turnpike. Any surfer who tried to groove that 'vard on a stock plank would have been sneezing brains.

Don't listen to so-called purists who claim any obstacle can be jumped. Professional Kouriers know: If you have pooned a vehicle moving fast enough for fun and profit, your reaction time is cut to tenths of a second—even less if you are way spooled.

Buy a set of RadiKS Mark II Smartwheels—it's cheaper than a total face retread and a lot more fun. Smartwheels use sonar, laser rangefinding, and millimeter-wave radar to identify mufflers and other debris before you even get honed about them.

Don't get Midasized—upgrade today!

These were words of wisdom. Y.T. bought the wheels. Each one consists of a hub with many stout spokes. Each spoke telescopes in five sections. On the end is a squat foot, rubber tread on the bottom, swiveling on a ball joint. As the wheels roll, the feet plant themselves one at a time, almost glomming into one continuous tire. If you surf over a bump, the spokes retract to pass over it. If you surf over a chuckhole, the robo-prongs plumb its asphalty depths. Either way, the shock is thereby absorbed, no thuds, smacks, vibrations, or clunks will make their way into the plank or the Converse high-tops with which you tread it. The ad was right—you cannot be a professional road surfer without smartwheels.

Prompt delivery of the pizza will be a trivial matter. She glides from the dewy turf over the lip of the driveway without a bump, picks up speed on the 'crete, surfs down its slope into the street. A twitch of the butt reorients the plank, now she is cruising down Homedale Mews looking for a victim. A black car, alive with nasty lights, whines past her the other way, closing in on the hapless

Hiro Protagonist. Her RadiKS Knight Vision goggles darken strategically to cut the noxious glaring of same, her pupils feel safe to remain wide open, scanning the road for signs of movement. The swimming pool was at the crest of this Burbclave, it's downhill from here, but not downhill enough.

Half a block away, on a side street, a bimbo box, a minivan, grinds its four pathetic cylinders into action. She sees it cater-corner from her present coordinates. The white backup lights flash instantly as the driver shifts into D by way of R and N. Y.T. aims herself at the curb, hits it at a fast running velocity, the spokes of the smartwheels see it coming and retract in the right way so that she glides from street to lawn without a hitch. Across the lawn, the feet leave a trail of hexagonal padmarks. A stray dog turd, red with meaty undigestible food coloring, is embossed with the RadiKS logo, a mirror image of which is printed on the tread of each spoke.

The bimbo box is pulling away from the curb, across the street. Squirrelly scrubbing noises squirm from its sidewalls as they grind against the curb; we are in the Burbs, where it is better to take a thousand clicks off the lifespan of your Goodyears by invariably grinding them up against curbs than to risk social ostracism and outbreaks of mass hysteria by parking several inches away, out in the middle of the street (*That's okay, Mom, I can walk to the curb from here*), a menace to traffic, a deadly obstacle to uncertain young bicyclists. Y.T. has pressed the release button on her poon's reel/handle unit, allowing a meter of cord to unwind. She whips it up and around her head like a bolo on the austral range. She is about to lambada this trite conveyance. The head of the poon, salad-bowl size, whistles as it orbits around; this is unnecessary but sounds cool.

Pooning a bimbo box takes more skill than a ped would ever imagine, because of their very road-unworthiness, their congenital lack of steel or other ferrous matter for the MagnaPoon to bite down on. Now they have superconducting poons that stick to aluminum bodywork by inducing eddy currents in the actual flesh of the car, turning it into an unwilling electromagnet, but Y.T. does not have one of these. They are the trademark of the hardcore Burbclave surfer, which, despite this evening's entertainment, she is not. Her poon will only stick to steel, iron, or (slightly) to nickel. The only steel in a bimbo box of this make is in the frame.

She makes a low-slung approach. Her poon's orbital plane is nearly vertical, it almost grinds on the twinkly suburban macadam on the forward limb of each orbit. When she pounds the release button, it takes off from an altitude of about one centimeter, angling slightly upward, across the street, under the floor of the bimbo box, and sucks steel. It's a solid hit, as solid as you can get on this nebula of air, upholstery, paint, and marketing known as the family minivan.

The reaction is instantaneous, quick-witted by Burb standards. This person wants Y.T. gone. The van takes off like a hormone-pumped bull who has just been nailed in the ass by the barbed probe of a picador. It's not Mom at the wheel. It's young Studley, the teenaged boy, who like every other boy in this Burbclave has been taking intravenous shots of horse testosterone every afternoon in the high school locker room since he was fourteen years old. Now he's bulky, stupid, thoroughly predictable.

He steers erratically, artificially pumped muscles not fully under his control. The molded, leather-grained, maroon-colored steering wheel smells like his mother's hand lotion; this drives him into a rage. The bimbo box surges and slows, surges and slows, because he is pumping the gas pedal, because holding it to the floor doesn't seem to have any effect. He wants this car to be like his muscles: more power than he knows what to do with. Instead, it hampers him. As a compromise, he hits the button that says POWER. Another button that says ECONOMY pops out and goes dead, reminding him, like an educational demonstration, that the two are mutually exclusive. The van's tiny engine downshifts, which makes it feel more powerful. He holds his foot steady on the gas and, making the run down Cottage Heights Road, the minivan's speed approaches one hundred kilometers.

Approaching the terminus of Cottage Heights Road, where it tees into Bellewoode Valley Road, he espies a fire hydrant. TMAWH fire hydrants are numerous, for safety, and highly designed, for property values, not the squat iron things imprinted with the name of some godforsaken Industrial Revolution foundry and furry from a hundred variously flaked layers of cheap city paint. They are brass, robot-polished every Thursday morning, dignified pipes rising straight up from the perfect, chemically induced turf of the Burbclave lawns, flaring out to present potential firefighters with a menu of three possible hose connections. They were designed on a computer screen by the same aesthetes who designed the DynaVictorian houses and the tasteful mailboxes and the immense marble street signs that sit at each intersection like headstones. Designed on a computer screen, but with an eye toward the elegance of things past and forgotten about. Fire hydrants that tasteful people are proud to have on their front lawns. Fire hydrants that the real estate people don't feel the need to airbrush out of pictures.

This fucking Kourier is about to die, knotted around one of those fire hydrants. Studley the Testosterone Boy will see to it. It is a maneuver he has witnessed on television—which tells no lies—a trick he has practiced many times in his head. Building up maximum speed on Cottage Heights, he will yank the hand brake while swinging the wheel. The ass end of the minivan will snap around. The pesky Kourier will be cracked like a whip at the end of her unbreakable cable. Into the fire hydrant she will go. Studley the Teenager will be victorious, free to cruise in triumph down Bellewoode Valley and out into the greater world of adult men in cool cars, free to go return his overdue videotape, *Raft Warriors IV: The Final Battle.*

Y.T. does not know any of this for a fact, but she suspects it. None of this is real. It is her reconstruction of the psychological environment inside of that bimbo box. She sees the hydrant coming a mile away, sees Studley reaching down to rest one hand on the parking brake. It is all so obvious. She feels sorry for Studley and his ilk. She reels out, gives herself lots of slack. He whips the wheel, jerks the brake. The minivan goes sideways, overshooting its mark, and doesn't quite snap her around the way he wanted; she has to help it. As its ass is rotating around, she reels in hard, converting that gift of angular momentum into forward velocity, and ends up shooting right past the van going well over a mile a minute. She is headed for a marble gravestone that says BELLEWOODE VALLEY ROAD. She leans away from it, leans into a vicious turn, her spokes grip the pavement and push her away from that gravestone, she can touch the pavement with one hand she is heeled over so hard, the spokes push her onto the desired street. Meanwhile, she has clicked off the electromagnetic force that held her pooned to the van. The poon head comes loose, caroms off the pavement behind her as it is automatically reeled in to reunite with the handle. She is headed straight for the exit of the Burbclave at fantastic speed.

Behind her, an explosive crash sounds, resonating in her gut, as the minivan slides sideways into the gravestone.

She ducks under the security gate and plunges into traffic on Oahu. She cuts between two veering, blaring, and screeching BMWs. BMW drivers take evasive action at the drop of a hat, emulating the drivers in the BMW advertisements—this is how they convince themselves they didn't get ripped off. She drops into a fetal position to pass underneath a semi, headed for the Jersey barrier in the median strip like she's going to die, but Jersey barriers are easy for the smartwheels. That lower limb of the barrier has such a nice bank to it, like they designed it for road surfers. She rides halfway up the barrier, angles gently back down to the lane for a smooth landing, and she's in traffic. There's a car right there and she doesn't even have to throw the poon, just reaches out and plants it right on the lid of the trunk.

This driver's resigned to his fate, doesn't care, doesn't hassle her. He takes her as far as the entrance to the next Burbclave, which is a White Columns. Very southern, traditional, one of the Apartheid Burbclaves. Big ornate sign above the main gate: WHITE PEOPLE ONLY. NON-CAUCASIANS MUST BE PROCESSED.

She's got a White Columns visa. Y.T. has a visa to everywhere. It's right there on her chest, a little bar code. A laser scans it as she careens toward the entrance and the immigration gate swings open for her. It's an ornate ironwork number, but harried White Columns residents don't have time to sit idling at the Burbclave entrance watching the gate slowly roll aside in Old South majestic turpitude, so it's mounted on some kind of electromagnetic railgun.

She is gliding down the antebellum tree-lined lanes of White Columns, one microplantation after another, still coasting on the residual kinetic energy boost that originated in the fuel in Studley the Teenager's gas tank.

The world is full of power and energy and a person can go far by just skimming off a tiny bit of it.

The LEDs on the pizza box say: 29:32, and the guy who ordered it—Mr. Pudgely and his neighbors, the Pinkhearts and the Roundass clan—are all gathered on the front lawn of their microplantation, prematurely celebrating. Like they had just bought the winning lottery ticket. From their front door they have a clear view all the way down to Oahu Road, and they can see that nothing is on its way that looks like a CosaNostra delivery car. Oh, there is curiosity—sniffing interest—at this Kourier with the big square thing under her arm—maybe a portfolio, a new ad layout for some Caucasian supremacist marketing honcho in the next plat over, but—

The Pudgelys and the Pinkhearts and the Roundasses are all staring at her, slackjawed. She has just enough residual energy to swing into their driveway. Her momentum carries her to the top. She stops next to Mr. Pudgely's Acura and Mrs. Pudgely's bimbo box and steps off her plank. The spokes, noting her departure, even themselves out, plant themselves on the top of the driveway, refuse to roll backward.

A blinding light from the heavens shines down upon them. Her Knight Visions keep her from being blinded, but the customers bend their knees and hunch their shoulders as though the light were heavy. The men hold their hairy forearms up against their brows, swivel their great tubular bodies to and fro, trying to find the source of the illumination, muttering clipped notations to each other, brief theories about its source, fully in control of the unknown phenomenon. The women coo and flutter. Because of the magical influence of the Knight Visions, Y.T. can still see the LEDs: 29:54, and that's what it says when she drops the pizza on Mr. Pudgely's wing tips.

The mystery light goes off.

_____ The others are still blinded, but Y.T. sees into the night with her Knight Visions, sees all the way into near infrared, and she sees the source of it, a double-bladed stealth helicopter thirty feet above the neighbor's house. It is tastefully black and unadorned, not a news crew—though another helicopter, an old-fashioned audible one, brightly festooned with up-to-the-minute logos, is thumping and whacking its way across White Columns airspace at this very moment, goosing the plantations with its own spotlight, hoping to be the first to obtain this major scoop: a pizza was delivered late tonight, film at eleven. Later, our personality journalist speculates on where Uncle Enzo will stay when he makes his compulsory trip to our Standard Metropolitan Statistical Area. But the black chopper is running dark, would be nearly invisible if not for the infrared trail coming out of its twin turbojets.

It is a Mafia chopper, and all they wanted to do was to record the event on videotape so that Mr. Pudgely would not have a leg to hop around on in court, should he decide to take his case down to Judge Bob's Judicial System and argue for a free pizza.

One more thing. There's a lot of shit in the air tonight, a few megatons of topsoil blowing down from Fresno, and so when the laser beam comes on it is startlingly visible, a tiny geometric line, a million blazing red grains strung on a fiber-optic thread, snapping into life instantly between the chopper and Y.T.'s chest. It appears to widen into a narrow fan, an acute triangle of red light whose base encompasses all of Y.T.'s torso.

It takes half a second. They are scanning the many bar codes mounted on her chest. They are finding out who she is. The Mafia now knows everything about Y.T.—where she lives, what she does, her eye color, credit record, ancestry, and blood type.

That done, the chopper tilts and vanishes into the night like a hockey puck sliding into a bowl of India ink. Mr. Pudgely is saying something, making a joke about how close they came, the others eke out a laugh, but Y.T. cannot hear them because they are buried under the thunderwhack of the news chopper, then flash-frozen and crystalized under its spotlight. The night air is full of bugs, and now Y.T. can see all of them, swirling in mysterious formations, hitching rides on people and on currents of air. There is one on her wrist, but she doesn't slap at it.

The spotlight lingers for a minute. The broad square of the pizza box, bearing the CosaNostra logo, is mute testimony. They hover, shoot a little tape just in case.

Y.T. is bored. She gets on her plank. The wheels blossom and become circular. She guides a tight wobbly course around the cars, coasts down into the street. The spotlight follows her for a moment, maybe picking up some stock footage. Videotape is cheap. You never know when something will be useful, so you might as well videotape it.

People make their living that way—people in the intel business. People like Hiro Protagonist. They just know stuff, or they just go around and videotape stuff. They put it in the Library. When people want to know the particular things that they know or watch their videotapes, they pay them money and check it out of the Library, or just buy it outright. This is a weird racket, but Y.T. likes the idea of it. Usually, the CIC won't pay any attention to a Kourier. But apparently Hiro has a deal with them. Maybe she can make a deal with Hiro. Because Y.T. knows a lot of interesting little things.

One little thing she knows is that the Mafia owes her a favor.

5

As Hiro approaches the Street, he sees two young couples, probably using their parents' computers for a double date in the Metaverse, climbing down out of Port Zero, which is the local port of entry and monorail stop.

He is not seeing real people, of course. This is all a part of the moving illustration drawn by his computer according to specifications coming down the fiber-optic cable. The people are pieces of software called avatars. They are the audiovisual bodies that people use to communicate with each other in the Metaverse. Hiro's avatar is now on the Street, too, and if the couples coming off the monorail look over in his direction, they can see him, just as he's seeing them. They could strike up a conversation: Hiro in the U-Stor-It in L.A. and the four teenagers probably on a couch in a suburb of Chicago, each with their own laptop. But they probably won't talk to each other, any more than they would in Reality. These are nice kids, and they don't want to talk to a solitary crossbreed with a slick custom avatar who's packing a couple of swords.

Your avatar can look any way you want it to, up to the limitations of your equipment. If you're ugly, you can make your avatar beautiful. If you've just gotten out of bed, your avatar can still be wearing beautiful clothes and professionally applied makeup. You can look like a gorilla or a dragon or a giant talking penis in the Metaverse. Spend five minutes walking down the Street and you will see all of these.

Hiro's avatar just looks like Hiro, with the difference that no matter what Hiro is wearing in Reality, his avatar always wears a black leather kimono. Most hacker types don't go in for garish avatars, because they know that it takes a lot more sophistication to render a realistic human face than a talking penis. Kind of the way people who really know clothing can appreciate the fine details that separate a cheap gray wool suit from an expensive hand-tailored gray wool suit.

You can't just materialize anywhere in the Metaverse, like Captain Kirk beaming down from on high. This would be confusing and irritating to the people around you. It would break the metaphor. Materializing out of nowhere (or vanishing back into Reality) is considered to be a private function best done in the confines of your own House. Most avatars nowadays are anatomically correct, and naked as a babe when they are first created, so in any case, you have to make yourself decent before you emerge onto the Street. Unless you're something intrinsically indecent and you don't care.

If you are some peon who does not own a House, for example, a person who is coming in from a public terminal, then you materialize in a Port. There are 256 Express Ports on the street, evenly spaced around its circumference at intervals of 256 kilometers. Each of these intervals is further subdivided 256 times with Local Ports, spaced exactly one kilometer apart (astute students of hacker semiotics will note the obsessive repetition of the number 256, which is 2^8 power—and even that 8 looks pretty juicy, dripping with 2^2 additional 2s). The Ports serve a function analogous to airports: This is where you drop into the Metaverse from somewhere else. Once you have materialized in a Port, you can walk down the Street or hop on the monorail or whatever.

The couples coming off the monorail can't afford to have custom avatars made and don't know how to write their own. They have to buy off-the-shelf avatars. One of the girls has a pretty nice one. It would be considered quite the fashion statement among the K-Tel set. Looks like she has bought the Avatar Construction Set™ and put together her own, customized model out of miscellaneous parts. It might even look something like its owner. Her date doesn't look half bad himself.

The other girl is a Brandy. Her date is a Clint. Brandy and Clint are both popular, off-the-shelf models. When white-trash high school girls are going on a date in the Metaverse, they invariably run down to the computer-games section of the local Wal-Mart and buy a copy of Brandy. The user can select three breast sizes: improbable, impossible, and ludicrous. Brandy has a limited repertoire of facial expressions: cute and pouty; cute and sultry; perky and interested; smiling and receptive; cute and spacy. Her eyelashes are half an inch long, and the software is so cheap that they are rendered as solid ebony chips. When a Brandy flutters her eyelashes, you can almost feel the breeze.

Clint is just the male counterpart of Brandy. He is craggy and handsome and has an extremely limited range of facial expressions.

Hiro wonders, idly, how these two couples got together. They are clearly from disparate social classes. Perhaps older and younger siblings. But then they come down the escalator and disappear into the crowd and become part of the Street, where there are enough Clints and Brandys to found a new ethnic group.

_____ The Street is fairly busy. Most of the people here are Americans and Asians—it's early morning in Europe right now. Because of the preponderance of Americans, the crowd has a garish and surreal look about it. For the Asians, it's the middle of the day, and they are in their dark blue suits. For the Americans, it's party time, and they are looking like just about anything a computer can render.

The moment Hiro steps across the line separating his neighborhood from the Street, colored shapes begin to swoop down on him from all directions, like buzzards on fresh road kill. Animercials are not allowed in Hiro's neighborhood. But almost anything is allowed in the Street.

A passing fighter plane bursts into flames, falls out of its trajectory, and zooms directly toward him at twice the speed of sound. It plows into the Street fifty feet in front of him, disintegrates, and explodes, blooming into a tangled cloud of wreckage and flame that skids across the pavement toward him, growing to envelop him so that all he can see is turbulent flame, perfectly simulated and rendered.

Then the display freezes, and a man materializes in front of Hiro. He is a classic bearded, pale, skinny hacker, trying to beef himself up by wearing a bulky silk windbreaker blazoned with the logo of one of the big Metaverse amusement parks. Hiro knows the guy; they used to run into each other at trade conventions all the time. He's been trying to hire Hiro for the last two months.

"Hiro, I can't understand why you're holding out on me. We're making bucks here—Kongbucks and yen—and we can be flexible on pay and bennies. We're putting together a swords-and-sorcery thing, and we can use a hacker with your skills. Come on down and talk to me, okay?"

Hiro walks straight through the display, and it vanishes. Amusement parks in the Metaverse can be fantastic, offering a wide selection of interactive three-dimensional movies. But in the end, they're still nothing more than video games. Hiro's not so poor, yet, that he would go and write video games for this company. It's owned by the Nipponese, which is no big deal. But it's also managed by the Nipponese, which means that all the programmers have to wear white shirts and show up at eight in the morning and sit in cubicles and go to meetings.

When Hiro learned how to do this, way back fifteen years ago, a hacker could sit down and write an entire piece of software by himself. Now, that's no longer possible. Software comes out of factories, and hackers are, to a greater or lesser extent, assembly-line workers. Worse yet, they may become managers who never get to write any code themselves.

The prospect of becoming an assembly-line worker gives Hiro some incentive to go out and find some really good intel tonight. He tries to get himself psyched up, tries to break out of the lethargy of the long-term underemployed. This intel thing can be a great racket, once you get yourself jacked into the grid. And with his connections, it shouldn't be any problem. He just has to get serious about it. *Get serious. Get serious.* But it's so hard to get serious about anything.

He owes the Mafia the cost of a new car. That's a good reason to get serious.

He cuts straight across the Street and under the monorail line, headed for a large, low-slung black building. It is extraordinarily somber for the Street, like a parcel that someone forgot to develop. It's a squat black pyramid with the top cut off. It has one single door—since this is all imaginary, there are no regulations dictating the number of emergency exits. There are no guards, no signs, nothing to bar people from going in, yet thousands of avatars mill around, peering inside, looking for a glimpse of something. These people can't pass through the door because they haven't been invited.

Above the door is a matte black hemisphere about a meter in diameter, set into the front wall of the building. It is the closest thing the place has to decoration. Underneath it, in letters carved into the wall's black substance, is the name of the place: THE BLACK SUN.

So it's not an architectural masterpiece. When Da5id and Hiro and the other hackers wrote The Black Sun, they didn't have enough money to hire architects or designers, so they just went in for simple geometric shapes. The avatars milling around the entrance don't seem to care.

If these avatars were real people in a real street, Hiro wouldn't be able to reach the entrance. It's way too crowded. But the computer system that operates the Street has better things to do than to monitor every single one of the millions of people there, trying to prevent them from running into each other. It doesn't bother trying to solve this incredibly difficult problem. On the Street, avatars just walk right through each other.

So when Hiro cuts through the crowd, headed for the entrance, he really is cutting through the crowd. When things get this jammed together, the computer simplifies things by drawing all of the avatars ghostly and translucent so you can see where you're going. Hiro appears solid to himself, but everyone else looks like a ghost. He walks through the crowd as if it's a fogbank, clearly seeing The Black Sun in front of him.

He steps over the property line, and he's in the doorway. And in that instant he becomes solid and visible to all the avatars milling outside. As one, they all begin screaming. Not that they have any idea who the hell he is—Hiro is just a starving CIC stringer who lives in a U-Stor-It by the airport. But in the entire world there are only a couple of thousand people who can step over the line into The Black Sun.

He turns and looks back at ten thousand shrieking groupies. Now that he's all by himself in the entryway, no longer immersed in a flood of avatars, he can see all of the people in the front row of the crowd with perfect clarity. They are all done up in their wildest and fanciest avatars, hoping that Da5id—The Black Sun's owner and hacker-in-chief—will invite them inside. They flicker and merge together into a hysterical wall. Stunningly beautiful women, computer-airbrushed and retouched at seventy-two frames a second, like *Playboy* pinups turned three-dimensional—these are would-be actresses hoping to be discovered. Wild-looking abstracts, tornadoes of gyrating light—hackers who are hoping that Da5id will notice their talent, invite them inside, give them a job. A liberal sprinkling of black-and-white people—persons who are accessing the Metaverse through cheap public terminals, and who are rendered in jerky, grainy black and white. A lot of these are run-of-the-mill psycho fans, devoted to the fantasy of stabbing some particular actress to death; they can't even get close in Reality, so they goggle into the Metaverse to stalk their prey. There are would-be rock stars done up in laser light, as though they just stepped off the concert stage, and the avatars of Nipponese businessmen, exquisitely rendered by their fancy equipment, but utterly reserved and boring in their suits.

There's one black-and-white who stands out because he's taller than the rest. The Street protocol states that your avatar can't be any taller than you are. This is to prevent people from walking around a mile high. Besides, if this guy's using a pay terminal—which he must be, to judge from the image quality—it can't jazz up his avatar. It just shows him the way he is, except not as well. Talking to a black-and-white on the Street is like talking to a person who has his face stuck in a xerox machine, repeatedly pounding the copy button, while you stand by the output tray pulling the sheets out one at a time and looking at them.

He has long hair, parted in the middle like a curtain to reveal a tattoo on his forehead. Given the shitty resolution, there's no way to see the tattoo clearly, but it appears to consist of words. He has a wispy Fu Manchu mustache.

Hiro realizes that the guy has noticed him and is staring back, looking him up and down, paying particular attention to the swords.

A grin spreads across the black-and-white guy's face. It is a satisfied grin. A grin of recognition. The grin of a man who knows something Hiro doesn't. The black-and-white guy has been standing with his arms folded across his chest, like a man who is bored, who's been waiting for something, and now his arms drop to his sides, swing loosely at the shoulders, like an athlete limbering up. He steps as close as he can and leans forward; he's so tall that the only thing behind him is empty black sky, torn with the glowing vapor trails of passing animercials.

"Hey, Hiro," the black-and-white guy says, "you want to try some Snow Crash?"

_____ A lot of people hang around in front of The Black Sun saying weird things. You ignore them. But this gets Hiro's attention.

Oddity the first: The guy knows Hiro's name. But people have ways of getting that information. It's probably nothing.

The second: This sounds like an offer from a drug pusher. Which would be normal in front of a Reality bar. But this is the Metaverse. And you can't sell drugs in the Metaverse, because you can't get high by looking at something.

The third: The name of the drug. Hiro's never heard of a drug called Snow Crash before. That's not unusual—a thousand new drugs get invented each year, and each of them sells under half a dozen brand names.

But "snow crash" is computer lingo. It means a system crash—a bug—at such a fundamental level that it frags the part of the computer that controls the electron beam in the monitor, making it spray wildly across the screen, turning the perfect gridwork of pixels into a gyrating blizzard. Hiro has seen it happen a million times. But it's a very peculiar name for a drug.

The thing that really gets Hiro's attention is his confidence. He has an utterly calm, stolid presence. It's like talking to an asteroid. Which would be okay if he were doing something that made the tiniest little bit of sense. Hiro's trying to read some clues in the guy's face, but the closer he looks, the more his shitty black-and-white avatar seems to break up into jittering, hard-edged pixels. It's like putting his nose against the glass of a busted TV. It makes his teeth hurt.

"Excuse me," Hiro says. "What did you say?"

"You want to try some Snow Crash?"

He has a crisp accent that Hiro can't quite place. His audio is as bad as his video. Hiro can hear cars going past the guy in the background. He must be goggled in from a public terminal alongside some freeway.

"I don't get this," Hiro says. "What is Snow Crash?"

"It's a drug, asshole," the guy says. "What do you think?"

"Wait a minute. This is a new one on me," Hiro says. "You honestly think I'm going to give you some money here? And then what do I do, wait for you to mail me the stuff?"

"I said try, not buy," the guy says. "You don't have to give me any money. Free sample. And you don't have to wait for no mail. You can have it now."

He reaches into his pocket and pulls out a hypercard.

It looks like a business card. The hypercard is an avatar of sorts. It is used in the Metaverse to represent a chunk of data. It might be text, audio, video, a still image, or any other information that can be represented digitally.

Think of a baseball card, which carries a picture, some text, and some numerical data. A baseball *hypercard* could contain a highlight film of the player in action, shown in perfect high-def television; a complete biography, read by the player himself, in stereo digital sound; and a complete statistical database along with specialized software to help you look up the numbers you want.

A hypercard can carry a virtually infinite amount of information. For all Hiro knows, this hypercard might contain all the books in the Library of Congress, or every episode of *Hawaii*

Five-O that was ever filmed, or the complete recordings of Jimi Hendrix, or the 1950 Census.

Or—more likely—a wide variety of nasty computer viruses. If Hiro reaches out and takes the hypercard, then the data it represents will be transferred from this guy's system into Hiro's computer. Hiro, naturally, wouldn't touch it under any circumstances, any more than you would take a free syringe from a stranger in Times Square and jab it into your neck.

And it doesn't make sense anyway. "That's a hypercard. I thought you said Snow Crash was a drug," Hiro says, now totally nonplussed.

"It is," the guy says. "Try it."

"Does it fuck up your brain?" Hiro says. "Or your computer?"

"Both. Neither. What's the difference?"

Hiro finally realizes that he has just wasted sixty seconds of his life having a meaningless conversation with a paranoid schizophrenic. He turns around and goes into The Black Sun.

6

At the exit of White Columns sits a black car, curled up like a panther, a burnished steel lens reflecting the loglo of Oahu Road. It is a Unit. It is a Mobile Unit of MetaCops Unlimited. A silvery badge is embossed on its door, a chrome-plated cop badge the size of a dinner plate, bearing the name of said private peace organization and emblazoned

DIAL 1-800-THE COPS
All Major Credit Cards

MetaCops Unlimited is the official peacekeeping force of White Columns, and also of The Mews at Windsor Heights, The Heights at Bear Run, Cinnamon Grove, and The Farms of Cloverdelle. They also enforce traffic regulations on all highways and byways operated by Fairlanes, Inc. A few different FOQNEs also use them: Caymans Plus and The Alps, for example. But franchise nations prefer to have their own security force. You can bet that Metazania and New South Africa handle their own security; that's the only reason people become citizens, so they can get drafted. Obviously, Nova Sicilia has its own security, too. Narcolombia doesn't need security because people are scared just to drive past the franchise at less than a hundred miles an hour (Y.T. always snags a nifty power boost in neighborhoods thick with Narcolombia consulates), and Mr. Lee's Greater Hong Kong, the grandaddy of all FOQNEs, handles it in a typically Hong Kong way, with robots.

MetaCops' main competitor, WorldBeat Security, handles all roads belonging to Cruiseways, plus has worldwide contracts with Dixie Traditionals, Pickett's Plantation, Rainbow Heights (check it out—two apartheid Burbclaves and one for black suits), Meadowvale on the [insert name of river] and Brickyard Station. WorldBeat is smaller than MetaCops, handles more upscale contracts, supposedly has a bigger espionage arm—though if that's what people want, they just talk to an account rep at the Central Intelligence Corporation.

And then there's The Enforcers—but they cost a lot and don't take well to supervision. It is rumored that, under their uniforms, they wear T-shirts bearing the unofficial Enforcer coat of arms: a fist holding a nightstick, emblazoned with the words SUE ME.

So Y.T. is coasting down a gradual slope toward the heavy iron gate of White Columns, waiting for it to roll aside, waiting, waiting—but the gate does not seem to be opening. No laser pulse has shot out of the guard shack to find out who Y.T. is. The system has been overridden. If Y.T. was a stupid ped she would go up to the MetaCop and ask him why. The MetaCop would say, "The security of the city-state," and nothing more. These Burbclaves! These city-states! So small, so insecure, that just about everything, like not mowing your lawn, or playing your stereo too loud, becomes a national security issue.

No way to skate around the fence; White Columns has eight-foot iron, robo-wrought, all the way around. She rolls up to the gate, grabs the bars, rattles it, but it's too big and solid to rattle.

MetaCops aren't allowed to lean against their Unit—makes them look lazy and weak. They can almost lean, look like they're leaning, they can even brandish a big leaning-against-the-car 'tude like this particular individual, but they can't lean. Besides, with the complete, glinting majesty of their Personal Portable

Equipment Suite hanging on their Personal Modular Equipment Harness, they would scratch the finish of the Unit.

"Jack this barrier to commerce, man, I got deliveries to make," Y.T. announces to the MetaCop.

A wet, smacking burst, not loud enough to be an explosion, sounds from the back of the Mobile Unit. It is the soft thup of a thick wrestler's loogie being propelled through a rolled-up tongue. It is the distant, muffled splurt of a baby having a big one. Y.T.'s hand, still gripping the bars of the gate, stings for a moment, then feels cold and hot at the same time. She can barely move it. She smells vinyl.

The MetaCop's partner climbs out of the back seat of the Mobile Unit. The window of the back door is open, but everything on the Mobile Unit is so black and shiny you can't tell that until the door moves. Both MetaCops, under their glossy black helmets and night-vision goggles, are grinning. The one getting out of the Mobile Unit is carrying a Short-Range Chemical Restraint Projector—a loogie gun. Their little plan has worked. Y.T. didn't think to aim her Knight Visions into the back seat to check for a goo-firing sniper.

The loogie, when expanded into the air like this, is about the size of a football. Miles and miles of eensy but strong fibers, like spaghetti. The sauce on the spaghetti is sticky, goopy stuff that stays fluid for an instant, when the loogie gun is fired, then sets quickly.

MetaCops have to tote this kind of gear because when each franchulate is so small, you can't be chasing people around. The perp—almost always an innocent thrasher—is always a three-second skateboard ride away from asylum in the neighboring franchulate. Also, the incredible bulk of the Personal Modular Equipment Harness—the chandelier o' gear—and all that is clipped onto it slows them down so bad that whenever they try to run, people just start laughing at them. So instead of losing some pounds, they just clip more stuff onto their harnesses, like the loogie gun.

The snotty, fibrous drop of stuff has wrapped all the way around her hand and forearm and lashed them onto the bar of the gate. Excess goo has sagged and run down the bar a short ways, but is setting now, turning into rubber. A few loose strands have also whipped forward and gained footholds on her shoulder, chest, and lower face. She backs away and the adhesive separates from the fibers, stretching out into long, infinitely thin strands, like hot mozzarella. These set instantly, become solid, and then break, curling away like smoke. It is not quite so grotendous, now that the loogie is off her face, but her hand is still perfectly immobilized.

"You are hereby warned that any movement on your part not explicitly endorsed by verbal authorization on my part may pose a direct physical risk to you, as well as consequential psychological and possibly, depending on your personal belief system, spiritual risks ensuing from your personal reaction to said physical risk. Any movement on your part constitutes an implicit and irrevocable acceptance of such risk," the first MetaCop says. There is a little speaker on his belt, simultaneously translating all of this into Spanish and Japanese.

"Or as we used to say," the other MetaCop says, "freeze, sucker!"

The untranslatable word resonates from the little speaker, pronounced "esucker" and "saka" respectively.

"We are authorized Deputies of MetaCops Unlimited. Under Section 24.5.2 of the White Columns Code, we are authorized to carry out the actions of a police force on this territory."

"Such as hassling innocent thrashers," Y.T. says.

The MetaCop turns off the translator. "By speaking English you implicitly and irrevocably agree for all our future conversation to take place in the English language," he says.

"You can't even rez what Y.T. says," Y.T. says.

"You have been identified as an Investigatory Focus of a Registered Criminal Event that is alleged to have taken place on another territory, namely, The Mews at Windsor Heights."

"That's another country, man. This is White Columns!"

"Under provisions of the The Mews at Windsor Heights Code, we are authorized to enforce law, national security concerns, and societal harmony on said territory also. A treaty between The Mews at Windsor Heights and White Columns authorizes us to place you in temporary custody until your status as an Investigatory Focus has been resolved."

"Your ass is busted," the second MetaCop says.

"As your demeanor has been nonaggressive and you carry no visible weapons, we are not authorized to employ heroic measures to ensure your cooperation," the first MetaCop says.

"You stay cool and we'll stay cool," the second MetaCop says.

"However, we are equipped with devices, including but not limited to projectile weapons, which, if used, may pose an extreme and immediate threat to your health and well-being."

"Make one funny move and we'll blow your head off," the second MetaCop says.

"Just unglom my fuckin' hand," Y.T. says. She has heard all this a million times before.

—————————— White Columns, like most Burbclaves, has no jail, no police station. So unsightly. Property values. Think of the liability exposure. MetaCops has a franchise just down the road that serves as headquarters. As for a jail, some place to habeas the occasional stray corpus, any half-decent franchise strip has one.

They are cruising in the Mobile Unit. Y.T.'s hands are cuffed together in front of her. One hand is still half-encased in rubbery goo, smelling so intensely of vinyl fumes that both MetaCops have rolled down their windows. Six feet of loose fibers trail into her lap, across the floor of the Unit, out the door, and drag on the pavement. The MetaCops are taking it easy, cruising down the middle lane, not above issuing a speeding ticket here and there as long as they're in their jurisdiction. Motorists around them drive slowly and sanely, appalled by the thought of having to pull over and listen to half an hour of disclaimers, advisements, and tangled justifications from the likes of these. The occasional CosaNostra delivery boy whips past them in the left lane, orange lights aflame, and they pretend not to notice.

"What's it gonna be, the Hoosegow or The Clink?" the first MetaCop says. From the way he is talking, he must be talking to the other MetaCop.

"The Hoosegow, please," Y.T. says.

"The Clink!" the other MetaCop says, turning around, sneering at her through the antiballistic glass, wallowing in power.

The whole interior of the car lights up as they drive past a Buy 'n' Fly. Loiter in the parking lot of a Buy 'n' Fly and you'd get a suntan. Then WorldBeat Security would come and arrest you. All that security-inducing light makes the Visa and MasterCard stickers on the driver's-side window glow for a moment.

"Y.T. is card-carrying," Y.T. says. "What does it cost to get off?"

"How come you keep calling yourself Whitey?" the second MetaCop says. Like many people of color, he has misconstrued her name.

"Not whitey. Y.T.," The first MetaCop says.

"That's what Y.T. is called," Y.T. says.

"That's what I said," the second MetaCop says. "Whitey."

"Y.T.," the first one says, accenting the T so brutally that he throws a glittering burst of saliva against the windshield. "Let me guess—Yolanda Truman?"

"No."

"Yvonne Thomas?"

"No."

"Whatsit stand for?"

"Nothing."

Actually, it stands for Yours Truly, but if they can't figure that out, fuck 'em.

"You can't afford it," the first MetaCop says. "You're going up against TMAWH here."

"I don't have to officially get off. I could just escape."

"This is a class Unit. We don't support escapes," the first MetaCop says.

"Tell you what," the second one says. "You pay us a trillion bucks and we'll take you to a Hoosegow. Then you can bargain with them."

"Half a trillion," Y.T. says.

"Seven hundred and fifty billion," the MetaCop says. "Final. Shit, you're wearing cuffs, you can't be bargaining with us."

Y.T. unzips a pocket on the thigh of her coverall, pulls out the card with her clean hand, runs it through a slot on the back of the front seat, puts it back in her pocket.

————————— The Hoosegow looks like a nice new one. Y.T. has seen hotels that were worse places to sleep. Its logo sign, a saguaro cactus with a black cowboy hat resting on top of it at a jaunty angle, is brand-new and clean.

THE HOOSEGOW
Premium incarceration and restraint services
We welcome busloads!

There are a couple of other MetaCop cars in the lot, and an Enforcer paddybus parked across the back, taking up ten consecutive spaces. This draws much attention from the MetaCops. The Enforcers are to the MetaCops what the Delta Force is to the Peace Corps.

"One to check in," says the second MetaCop. They are standing in the reception area. The walls are lined with illuminated signs, each one bearing the image of some Old West desperado. Annie Oakley stares down blankly at Y.T., providing a role model. The check-in counter is faux rustic; the employees all wear cowboy hats and five-pointed stars with their names embossed on them. In back is a door made of hokey, old-fashioned iron bars. Once you got through there, it would look like an operating room. A whole line of little cells, curvy and white like prefab shower stalls—in fact, they double as shower stalls, you bathe in the middle of the room. Bright lights that turn themselves off at eleven o'clock. Coin-operated TV. Private phone line. Y.T. can hardly wait.

The cowboy behind the desk aims a scanner at Y.T., zaps her bar code. Hundreds of pages about Y.T.'s personal life zoom up on a graphics screen.

"Huh," he says. "Female."

The two MetaCops look at each other like, what a genius—this guy could never be a MetaCop.

"Sorry, boys, we're full up. No space for females tonight."

"Aw, c'mon."

"See that bus in back? There was a riot at Snooze 'n' Cruise. Some Narcolombians were selling a bad batch of Vertigo. Place went nuts. Enforcers sent in a half dozen squads, brought in about thirty. So we're full up. Try The Clink, down the street."

Y.T. does not like the looks of this.

They put her back in the car, turn on the noise cancellation in the back seat, so she can't hear anything except squirts and gurgles coming from her own empty tummy, and the glistening crackle whenever she moves her glommed-up hand. She was really looking forward to a Hoosegow meal—Campfire Chili or Bandit Burgers.

In the front seat, the two MetaCops are talking to each other. They pull out into traffic. Up in front of them is a square illuminated logo, a giant Universal Product Code in black-on-white with BUY 'N' FLY underneath it.

Stuck onto the same signpost, beneath the Buy 'n' Fly sign, is a smaller one, a narrow strip in generic lettering: THE CLINK.

They are taking her to The Clink. The bastards. She pounds on the glass with cuffed-together hands, leaving sticky handprints. Let these bastards try to wash the stuff off. They turn around and look right through her, the guilty scum, like they heard something but they can't imagine what.

They enter the Buy 'n' Fly's nimbus of radioactive blue security light. Second MetaCop goes in, talks to the guy behind the counter. There's a fat white boy purchasing a monster trucks magazine, wearing a New South Africa baseball cap with a Confederate flag, and overhearing them he peers out the window, wanting to lay his eyes on a real perp. A second man comes out from back, same ethnicity as the guy behind the counter, another dark man with burning eyes and a bony neck. This one is carrying a three-ring binder with the Buy 'n' Fly logo. To find the manager of a franchise, don't strain to read his title off the name tag, just look for the one with the binder.

The manager talks to the MetaCop, nods his head, pulls a keychain out of a drawer.

Second MetaCop comes out, saunters to the car, suddenly whips open the back door.

"Shut up," he says, "or next time I fire the loogie gun into your mouth."

"Good thing you like The Clink," Y.T. says, "cause that is where you will be tomorrow night, loogie-man."

" 'Zat right?"

"Yeah. For credit card fraud."

"Me cop, you thrasher. How you gonna make a case at Judge Bob's Judicial System?"

"I work for RadiKS. We protect our own."

"Not tonight you don't. Tonight you took a pizza from the scene of a car wreck. Left the scene of an accident. RadiKS tell you to deliver that pizza?"

Y.T. does not return fire. The MetaCop is right; RadiKS did not tell her to deliver that pizza. She was doing it on a whim.

"So RadiKS ain't gonna help you. So shut up."

He jerks her arm, and the rest of her follows. The three-ringer gives her a quick look, just long enough to make sure she is really a person, not a sack of flour or an engine block or a tree stump. He leads them around to the fetid rump of the Buy 'n' Fly, dark realm of wretched refuse in teeming dumpsters. He unlocks the back door, a boring steel number with jimmy marks around the edges like steel-clawed beasts have been trying to get in.

Y.T. is taken downstairs into the basement. First MetaCop follows, carrying her plank, banging it heedlessly against doorways and stained polycarbonate bottle racks.

"Better take her uniform—all that gear," the second MetaCop suggests, not unlewdly.

The manager looks at Y.T., trying not to let his gaze travel sinfully up and down her body. For thousands of years his people have survived on alertness: waiting for Mongols to come galloping over the horizon, waiting for repeat offenders to swing sawed-off shotguns across their check-out counters. His alertness right now is palpable and painful; he's like a goblet of hot nitroglycerin. The added question of sexual misconduct makes it even worse. To him it's no joke.

Y.T. shrugs, trying to think of something unnerving and wacky. At this point, she is supposed to squeal and shrink, wriggle and whine, swoon and beg. They are threatening to take her clothes. How awful. But she does not get upset because she knows that they are expecting her to.

A Kourier has to establish space on the pavement. Predictable law-abiding behavior lulls drivers. They mentally assign you to a little box in the lane, assume you will stay there, can't handle it when you leave that little box.

Y.T. is not fond of boxes. Y.T. establishes her space on the pavement by zagging mightily from lane to lane, establishing a precedent of scary randomness. Keeps people on their toes, makes them react to her, instead of the other way round. Now these men are trying to put her in a box, make her follow rules.

She unzips her coverall all the way down below her navel. Underneath is naught but billowing pale flesh.

The MetaCops raise their eyebrows.

The manager jumps back, raises both hands up to form a visual shield, protecting himself from the damaging input. "No, no, no!" he says.

Y.T. shrugs, zips herself back up.

She's not afraid; she's wearing a dentata.

The manager handcuffs her to a cold-water pipe. Second MetaCop removes his newer, more cybernetic brand of handcuffs, snaps them back onto his harness. First MetaCop leans her plank against the wall, just out of her reach. Manager kicks a rusty coffee can across the floor, caroming it expertly off her skin, so she can go to the bathroom.

"Where you from?" Y.T. asks.

"Tadzhikistan," he says.

A jeek. She should have known.

"Well, shitcan soccer must be your national pastime."

The manager doesn't get it. The MetaCops emit rote, shallow laughter.

Papers are signed. Everyone else goes upstairs. On his way out the door, the manager turns off the lights; in Tadzhikistan, electricity is quite the big deal.

Y.T. is in The Clink.

7

The Black Sun is as big as a couple of football fields laid side by side. The decor consists of black, square tabletops hovering in the air (it would be pointless to draw in legs), evenly spaced across the floor in a grid. Like pixels. The only exception is in the middle, where the bar's four quadrants come together ($4 = 2^2$). This part is occupied by a circular bar sixteen meters across. Everything is matte black, which makes it a lot easier for the computer system to draw things in on top of it—no worries about filling in a complicated background. And that way all attention can be focused on the avatars, which is the way people like it.

It doesn't pay to have a nice avatar on the Street, where it's so crowded and all the avatars merge and flow into one another. But The Black Sun is a much classier piece of software. In The Black Sun, avatars are not allowed to collide. Only so many people can be here at once, and they can't walk through each other. Everything is solid and opaque and realistic. And the clientele has a lot more class—no talking penises in here. The avatars look like real people. For the most part, so do the daemons.

"Daemon" is an old piece of jargon from the UNIX operating system, where it referred to a piece of low-level utility software, a fundamental part of the operating system. In The Black Sun, a daemon is like an avatar, but it does not represent a human being. It's a robot that lives in the Metaverse. A piece of software, a kind of spirit that inhabits the machine, usually with some particular role to carry out. The Black Sun has a number of daemons that serve imaginary drinks to the patrons and run little errands for people.

It even has bouncer daemons that get rid of undesirables—grab their avatars and throw them out the door, applying certain basic principles of avatar physics. Da5id has even enhanced the physics of The Black Sun to make it a little cartoonish, so that particularly obnoxious people can be hit over the head with giant mallets or crushed under plummeting safes before they are ejected. This happens to people who are being disruptive, to anyone who is pestering or taping a celebrity, and to anyone who seems contagious. That is, if your personal computer is infected with viruses, and attempts to spread them via The Black Sun, you had better keep one eye on the ceiling.

Hiro mumbles the word "Bigboard." This is the name of a piece of software he wrote, a power tool for a CIC stringer. It digs into The Black Sun's operating system, rifles it for information, and then throws up a flat square map in front of his face, giving him a quick overview of who's here and whom they're talking to. It's all unauthorized data that Hiro is not supposed to have. But Hiro is not some bimbo actor coming here to network. He is a hacker. If he wants some information, he steals it right out of the guts of the system—gossip ex machina.

Bigboard shows him that Da5id is ensconced in his usual place, a table in the Hacker Quadrant near the bar. The Movie Star Quadrant has the usual scattering of Sovereigns and wannabes. The Rock Star Quadrant is very busy tonight; Hiro can see that a Nipponese rap star named Sushi K has stopped in for a visit. And there are a lot of record-industry types hanging around in the Nipponese Quadrant—which looks like the other quadrants except that it's quieter, the tables are closer to the floor, and it's full of bowing and fluttering geisha daemons. Many of these people probably belong to Sushi K's retinue of managers, flacks, and lawyers.

Hiro cuts across the Hacker Quadrant, headed for Da5id's table. He recognizes many of the people in here, but as usual, he's surprised and disturbed by the number he doesn't recognize—all those sharp, perceptive twenty-one-year-old faces. Software development, like professional sports, has a way of making thirty-year-old men feel decrepit.

Looking up the aisle toward Da5id's table, he sees Da5id talking to a black-and-white person. Despite her lack of color and shitty resolution, Hiro recognizes her by the way she folds her arms when she's talking, the way she tosses her hair when she's listening to Da5id. Hiro's avatar stops moving and stares at her, adopting just the same facial expression with which he used to stare at this woman years ago. In Reality, he reaches out with one hand, picks up his beer, takes a pull on the bottle, and lets it roll around in his mouth, a bundle of waves clashing inside a small space.

_____ Her name is Juanita Marquez. Hiro has known her ever since they were freshmen together at Berkeley, and they were in the same lab section in a freshman physics class. The first time he saw her, he formed an impression that did not change for many years: She was a dour, bookish, geeky type who dressed like she was interviewing for a job as an accountant at a funeral parlor. At the same time, she had a flamethrower tongue that she would turn on people at the oddest times, usually in some grandiose, earth-scorching retaliation for a slight or breach of etiquette that none of the other freshmen had even perceived.

It wasn't until a number of years later, when they both wound up working at Black Sun Systems, Inc., that he put the other half of the equation together. At the time, both of them were working on avatars. He was working on bodies, she was working on faces. She *was* the face department, because nobody thought that faces were all that important—they were just flesh-toned busts on top of the avatars. She was just in the process of proving them all desperately wrong. But at this phase, the all-male society of bit-heads that made up the power structure of Black Sun Systems said that the face problem was trivial and superficial. It was, of course, nothing more than sexism, the especially virulent type espoused by male techies who sincerely believe that they are too smart to be sexists.

That first impression, back at the age of seventeen, was nothing more than that—the gut reaction of a post-adolescent Army brat who had been on his own for about three weeks. His mind was good, but he only understood one or two things in the whole world—samurai movies and the Macintosh—and he understood them far, far too well. It was a worldview with no room for someone like Juanita.

There is a certain kind of small town that grows like a boil on the ass of every Army base in the world. In a long series of such places, Hiro Protagonist was speed-raised like a mutant hothouse orchid flourishing under the glow of a thousand Buy 'n' Fly security spotlights. Hiro's father had joined the army in 1944, at the age of sixteen, and spent a year in the Pacific, most of it as a prisoner of war. Hiro was born when his father was in his late middle age. By that time, Dad could long since have quit and taken his pension, but he wouldn't have known what to do with himself outside of the service, and so he stayed in until they finally kicked him out in the late eighties. By the time Hiro made it out to Berkeley, he had lived in Wrightstown, New Jersey; Tacoma, Washington; Fayetteville, North Carolina; Hinesville, Georgia; Killeen, Texas; Grafenwehr, Germany; Seoul, Korea; Ogden, Kansas; and Watertown, New York. All of these places were basically the same, with the same franchise ghettos, the same strip joints, and even the same people—he kept running into school chums he'd known years before, other Army brats who happened to wind up at the same base at the same time.

Their skins were different colors but they all belonged to the same ethnic group: Military. Black kids didn't talk like black kids. Asian kids didn't bust their asses to excel in school. White kids, by and large, didn't have any problem getting along with the black and Asian kids. And girls knew their place. They all had the same moms with the same generous buttocks in stretchy slacks and the same frosted-and-curling-ironed hairdos, and they were all basically sweet and endearing and conforming and, if they happened to be smart, they went out of their way to hide it.

So the first time Hiro saw Juanita, or any other girl like her, his perspectives were bent all out of shape. She had long, glossy black hair that had never been subjected to any chemical process other than regular shampooing. She didn't wear blue stuff on her eyelids. Her clothing was dark, tailored, restrained. And she didn't take shit from anyone, not even her professors, which seemed shrewish and threatening to him at the time.

When he saw her again after an absence of several years—a period spent mostly in Japan, working among real grown-ups from a higher social class than he was used to, people of substance who wore real clothes and did real things with their lives— he was startled to realize that Juanita was an elegant, stylish knockout. He thought at first that she had undergone some kind of radical changes since their first year in college.

But then he went back to visit his father in one of those Army towns and ran into the high school prom queen. She had grown up shockingly fast into an overweight dame with loud hair and loud clothes who speed-read the tabloids at the check-out line in the commissary because she didn't have the spare money to buy them, who popped her gum and had two kids that she didn't have the energy or the foresight to discipline.

Seeing this woman at the commissary, he finally went through a belated, dim-witted epiphany, not a brilliant light shining down from heaven, more like the brown glimmer of a half-dead flashlight from the top of a stepladder: Juanita hadn't really changed much at all since those days, just grown into herself. It was he who had changed. Radically.

He came into her office once, strictly on a business matter. Until this point, they had seen each other around the office a lot but acted like they had never met before. But when he came into her office that day, she told him to close the door behind him, and she blacked out the screen on her computer and started twiddling a pencil between her hands and eyed him like a plate of day-old sushi. Behind her on the wall was an amateurish paint-ing of an old lady, set in an ornate antique frame. It was the only decoration in Juanita's office. All the other hackers had color photographs of the space shuttle lifting off, or posters of the starship *Enterprise*.

"It's my late grandmother, may God have mercy on her soul," she said, watching him look at the painting. "My role model."

"Why? Was she a programmer?"

She just looked at him over the rotating pencil like, how slow can a mammal be and still have respiratory functions? But in-stead of lowering the boom on him, she just gave a simple answer: "No." Then she gave a more complicated answer. "When I was fifteen years old, I missed a period. My boyfriend and I were using a diaphragm, but I knew it was fallible. I was good at math, I had the failure rate memorized, burnt into my subconscious. Or maybe it was my conscious, I can never keep them straight. Anyway, I was terrified. Our family dog started treating me dif-ferently—supposedly, they can smell a pregnant woman. Or a pregnant bitch, for that matter."

By this point, Hiro's face was frozen in a wary, astonished position that Juanita later made extensive use of in her work. Because, as she was talking to him, she was watching his face, analyzing the way the little muscles in his forehead pulled his brows up and made his eyes change shape.

"My mother was clueless. My boyfriend was worse than clue-less—in fact, I ditched him on the spot, because it made me realize what an alien the guy was—like many members of your species." By this, she was referring to males.

"Anyway, my grandmother came to visit," she continued, glancing back over her shoulder at the painting. "I avoided her until we all sat down for dinner. And then she figured out the whole situation in, maybe, ten minutes, just by watching my face across the dinner table. I didn't say more than ten words—'Pass the tortillas.' I don't know how my face conveyed that informa-tion, or what kind of internal wiring in my grandmother's mind enabled her to accomplish this incredible feat. To condense fact from the vapor of nuance."

Condense fact from the vapor of nuance. Hiro has never forgotten the sound of her speaking those words, the feeling that came over him as he realized for the first time how smart Juanita was.

She continued. "I didn't even really appreciate all of this until about ten years later, as a grad student, trying to build a user interface that would convey a lot of data very quickly, for one of these baby-killer grants." This was her term for anything related to the Defense Department. "I was coming up with all kinds of elaborate technical fixes like trying to implant electrodes directly into the brain. Then I remembered my grandmother and realized, my God, the human mind can absorb and process an incredible amount of information—if it comes in the right format. The right interface. If you put the right face on it. Want some coffee?"

Then he had an alarming thought: What had he been like back in college? How much of an asshole had he been? Had he left Juanita with a bad impression?

Another young man would have worried about it in silence, but Hiro has never been restrained by thinking about things too hard, and so he asked her out for dinner and, after having a couple of drinks (she drank club sodas), just popped the question: Do you think I'm an asshole?

She laughed. He smiled, believing that he had come up with a good, endearing, flirtatious bit of patter.

He did not realize until a couple of years later that this question was, in effect, the cornerstone of their relationship. Did Juanita think that Hiro was an asshole? He always had some reason to think that the answer was yes, but nine times out of ten she insisted the answer was no. It made for some great arguments and some great sex, some dramatic fallings out and some passionate reconciliations, but in the end the wildness was just too much for them—they were exhausted by work—and they backed away from each other. He was emotionally worn out from wondering what she really thought of him, and confused by the fact that he cared so deeply about her opinion. And she, maybe, was beginning to think that if Hiro was so convinced in his own mind that he was unworthy of her, maybe he knew something she didn't.

Hiro would have chalked it all up to class differences, except that her parents lived in a house in Mexicali with a dirt floor, and his father made more money than many college professors. But the class idea still held sway in his mind, because class is more than income—it has to do with knowing where you stand in a web of social relationships. Juanita and her folks knew where they stood with a certitude that bordered on dementia. Hiro never knew. His father was a sergeant major, his mother was a Korean woman whose people had been mine slaves in Nippon, and Hiro didn't know whether he was black or Asian or just plain Army, whether he was rich or poor, educated or ignorant, talented or lucky. He didn't even have a part of the country to call home until he moved to California, which is about as specific as saying that you live in the Northern Hemisphere. In the end, it was probably his general disorientation that did them in.

After the breakup, Hiro went out with a long succession of essentially bimbos who (unlike Juanita) were impressed that he worked for a high-tech Silicon Valley firm. More recently, he has had to go searching for women who are even easier to impress.

Juanita went celibate for a while and then started going out with Da5id and eventually got married to him. Da5id had no doubts whatsoever about his standing in the world. His folks were Russian Jews from Brooklyn and had lived in the same brownstone for seventy years after coming from a village in Latvia where they had lived for five hundred years; with a Torah on his lap, he could trace his bloodlines all the way back to Adam and Eve. He was an only child who had always been first in his class in everything, and when he got his master's in computer science from Stanford, he went out and started his own company with about as much fuss as Hiro's dad used to exhibit in renting out a new P. O. box when they moved. Then he got rich, and now he runs The Black Sun. Da5id has always been certain of everything.

Even when he's totally wrong. Which is why Hiro quit his job at Black Sun Systems, despite the promise of future riches, and why Juanita divorced Da5id two years after she married him.

Hiro did not attend Juanita and Da5id's wedding; he was languishing in jail, into which he had been thrown a few hours before the rehearsal. He had been found in Golden Gate Park,

lovesick, wearing nothing but a thong, taking long pulls from a
jumbo bottle of Courvoisier and practicing *kendo* attacks with a
genuine samurai sword, floating across the grass on powerfully
muscled thighs to slice other picnickers' hurtling Frisbees and
baseballs in twain. Catching a long fly ball with the edge of your
blade, neatly halving it like a grapefruit, is not an insignificant
feat. The only drawback is that the owners of the baseball may
misinterpret your intentions and summon the police.

He got out of it by paying for all the baseballs and Frisbees, but
since that episode, he has never even bothered to ask Juanita
whether or not she thinks he's an asshole. Even Hiro knows the
answer now.

Since then, they've gone very different ways. In the early years
of The Black Sun project, the only way the hackers ever got paid
was by issuing stock to themselves. Hiro tended to sell his off
almost as quickly as he got it. Juanita didn't. Now she's rich, and
he isn't. It would be easy to say that Hiro is a stupid investor and
Juanita a smart one, but the facts are a little more complicated
than that: Juanita put her eggs in one basket, keeping all her
money in Black Sun stock; as it turns out, she made a lot of
money that way, but she could have gone broke, too. And Hiro
didn't have a lot of choice in some ways. When his father got sick,
the Army and the V.A. took care of most of his medical bills, but
they ran into a lot of expenses anyway, and Hiro's mother—who
could barely speak English—wasn't equipped to make or handle
money on her own. When Hiro's father died, he cashed in all of
his Black Sun stock to put Mom in a nice community in Korea.
She loves it there. Goes golfing every day. He could have kept his
money in The Black Sun and made ten million dollars about a
year later when it went public, but his mother would have been
a street person. So when his mother visits him in the Metaverse,
looking tan and happy in her golfing duds, Hiro views that as his
personal fortune. It won't pay the rent, but that's okay—when
you live in a shithole, there's always the Metaverse, and in the
Metaverse, Hiro Protagonist is a warrior prince.

8

His tongue is stinging; he realizes that, back in Reality, he has forgotten to swallow his beer.

It's ironic that Juanita has come into this place in a low-tech, black-and-white avatar. She was the one who figured out a way to make avatars show something close to real emotion. That is a fact Hiro has never forgotten, because she did most of her work when they were together, and whenever an avatar looks surprised or angry or passionate in the Metaverse, he sees an echo of himself or Juanita—the Adam and Eve of the Metaverse. Makes it hard to forget.

Shortly after Juanita and Da5id got divorced, The Black Sun really took off. And once they got done counting their money, marketing the spinoffs, soaking up the adulation of others in the hacker community, they all came to the realization that what made this place a success was not the collision-avoidance algorithms or the bouncer daemons or any of that other stuff. It was Juanita's faces.

Just ask the businessmen in the Nipponese Quadrant. They come here to talk turkey with suits from around the world, and they consider it just as good as a face-to-face. They more or less ignore what is being said—a lot gets lost in translation, after all. They pay attention to the facial expressions and body language of the people they are talking to. And that's how they know what's going on inside a person's head—by condensing fact from the vapor of nuance.

Juanita refused to analyze this process, insisted that it was something ineffable, something you couldn't explain with words. A radical, rosary-toting Catholic, she has no problem with that kind of thing. But the bitheads didn't like it. Said it was irrational mysticism. So she quit and took a job with some Nipponese company. They don't have any problem with irrational mysticism as long as it makes money.

But Juanita never comes to The Black Sun anymore. Partly, she's pissed at Da5id and the other hackers who never appreciated her work. But she has also decided that the whole thing is bogus. That no matter how good it is, the Metaverse is distorting the way people talk to each other, and she wants no such distortion in her relationships.

Da5id notices Hiro, indicates with a flick of his eyes that this is not a good time. Normally, such subtle gestures are lost in the system's noise, but Da5id has a very good personal computer, and Juanita helped design his avatar—so the message comes through like a shot fired into the ceiling.

Hiro turns away, saunters around the big circular bar in a slow orbit. Most of the sixty-four bar stools are filled with lower-level Industry people, getting together in twos and threes, doing what they do best: gossip and intrigue.

"So I get together with the director for a story conference. He's got this beach house—"

"Incredible?"

"Don't get me started."

"I heard. Debi was there for a party when Frank and Mitzi owned it."

"Anyway, there's this scene, early, where the main character wakes up in a dumpster. The idea is to show how, you know, despondent he is—"

"That crazy energy—"

"Exactly."

"Fabulous."

"I like it. Well, he wants to replace it with a scene where the guy is out in the desert with a bazooka, blowing up old cars in an abandoned junkyard."

"You're kidding!"

"So we're sitting there on his fucking patio over the beach and he's going, like, *whoom! whoom!* imitating this goddamn bazooka. He's thrilled by the idea. I mean, this is a man who wants to put a bazooka in a movie. So I think I talked him out of it."

"Nice scene. But you're right. A bazooka doesn't do the same thing as a dumpster."

Hiro pauses long enough to get this down, then keeps walking. He mumbles "Bigboard" again, recalls the magic map, pinpoints his own location, and then reads off the name of this nearby screenwriter. Later on, he can do a search of industry publications to find out what script this guy is working on, hence the name of this mystery director with a fetish for bazookas. Since this whole conversation has come to him via his computer, he's just taken an audio tape of the whole thing. Later, he can process it to disguise the voices, then upload it to the Library, cross-referenced under the director's name. A hundred struggling screenwriters will call this conversation up, listen to it over and over until they've got it memorized, paying Hiro for the privilege, and within a few weeks, bazooka scripts will flood the director's office. *Whoom!*

The Rock Star Quadrant is almost too bright to look at. Rock star avatars have the hairdos that rock stars can only wear in their dreams. Hiro scans it briefly to see if any of his friends are in there, but it's mostly parasites and has-beens. Most of the people Hiro knows are will-bes or wannabes.

The Movie Star Quadrant is easier to look at. Actors love to come here because in The Black Sun, they always look as good as they do in the movies. And unlike a bar or club in Reality, they can get into this place without physically having to leave their mansion, hotel suite, ski lodge, private airline cabin, or whatever. They can strut their stuff and visit with their friends without any exposure to kidnappers, paparazzi, script-flingers, assassins, ex-spouses, autograph brokers, process servers, psycho fans, marriage proposals, or gossip columnists.

He gets up off the bar stool and resumes his slow orbit, scanning the Nipponese Quadrant. It's a lot of guys in suits, as usual. Some of them are talking to gringos from the Industry. And a large part of the quadrant, in the back corner, has been screened off by a temporary partition.

Bigboard again. Hiro figures out which tables are behind the partition, starts reading off the names. The only one he recognizes immediately is an American: L. Bob Rife, the cable-television monopolist. A very big name to the Industry, though he's rarely seen. He seems to be meeting with a whole raft of big Nipponese honchos. Hiro has his computer memorize their names so that, later, he can check them against the CIC database and find out who they are. It has the look of a big and important meeting.

"Secret Agent Hiro! How are you doing?"

Hiro turns around. Juanita is right behind him, standing out in her black-and-white avatar, looking good anyway. "How are you?" she asks.

"Fine. How are you?"

"Great. I hope you don't mind talking to me in this ugly fax-of-life avatar."

"Juanita, I would rather look at a fax of you than most other women in the flesh."

"Thanks, you sly bastard. It's been a long time since we've talked!" she observes, as though there's something remarkable about this.

Something's going on.

"I hope *you're* not going to mess around with Snow Crash," she says. "Da5id won't listen to me."

"What am I, a model of self-restraint? I'm exactly the kind of guy who *would* mess around with it."

"I know you better than that. You're impulsive. But you're very clever. You have those sword-fighting reflexes."

"What does that have to do with drug abuse?"

"It means you can see bad things coming and deflect them. It's an instinct, not a learned thing. As soon as you turned around and saw me, that look came over your face, like, what's going on? What the hell is Juanita up to?"

"I didn't think you talked to people in the Metaverse."

"I do if I want to get through to someone in a hurry," she says. "And I'll always talk to you."

"Why me?"

"You know. Because of us. Remember? Because of our relationship—when I was writing this thing—you and I are the only two people who can ever have an honest conversation in the Metaverse."

"You're just the same mystical crank you always were," he says, smiling so as to make this a charming statement.

"You can't imagine how mystical and cranky I am now, Hiro."

"How mystical and cranky are you?"

She eyes him warily. Exactly the same way she did when he came into her office years ago.

It comes into his mind to wonder why she is always so alert in his presence. In college, he used to think that she was afraid of his intellect, but he's known for years that this is the last of her worries. At Black Sun Systems, he figured that it was just typical female guardedness—Juanita was afraid he was trying to get her into the sack. But this, too, is pretty much out of the question.

At this late date in his romantic career, he is just canny enough to come up with a new theory: She's being careful because she likes him. She likes him in spite of herself. He is exactly the kind of tempting but utterly wrong romantic choice that a smart girl like Juanita must learn to avoid.

That's definitely it. There's something to be said for getting older.

By way of answering his question, she says, "I have an associate I'd like you to meet. A gentleman and a scholar named Lagos. He's a fascinating guy to talk to."

"Is he your boyfriend?"

She thinks this one over rather than lashing out instantaneously. "My behavior at The Black Sun to the contrary, I don't fuck every male I work with. And even if I did, Lagos is out of the question."

"Not your type?"

"Not by a long shot."

"What is your type, anyway?"

"Old, rich, unimaginative blonds with steady careers."

This one almost slips by him. Then he catches it. "Well, I could dye my hair. And I'll get old eventually."

She actually laughs. It's a tension-releasing kind of outburst. "Believe me, Hiro, I'm the last person you want to be involved with at this point."

"Is this part of your church thing?" he asks. Juanita has been using her excess money to start her own branch of the Catholic church—she considers herself a missionary to the intelligent atheists of the world.

"Don't be condescending," she says. "That's exactly the attitude I'm fighting. Religion is not for simpletons."

"Sorry. This is unfair, you know—you can read every expression on my face, and I'm looking at you through a fucking blizzard."

"It's definitely related to religion," she says. "But this is so complex, and your background in that area is so deficient, I don't know where to begin."

"Hey, I went to church every week in high school. I sang in the choir."

"I know. That's exactly the problem. Ninety-nine percent of everything that goes on in most Christian churches has nothing whatsoever to do with the actual religion. Intelligent people all notice this sooner or later, and they conclude that the entire one hundred percent is bullshit, which is why atheism is connected with being intelligent in people's minds."

"So none of that stuff I learned in church has anything to do with what you're talking about?"

Juanita thinks for a while, eyeing him. Then she pulls a hypercard out of her pocket. "Here. Take this."

As Hiro pulls it from her hand, the hypercard changes from a jittery two-dimensional figment into a realistic, cream-colored, finely textured piece of stationery. Printed across its face in glossy black ink is a pair of words

---

B A B E L

(Infocalypse)

9

The world freezes and grows dim for a second. The Black Sun loses its smooth animation and begins to move in fuzzy stop-action. Clearly, his computer has just taken a major hit; all of its circuits are busy processing a huge bolus of data—the contents of the hypercard—and don't have time to redraw the image of The Black Sun in its full, breathtaking fidelity.

"Holy shit!" he says, when The Black Sun pops back into full animation again. "What the hell is in this card? You must have half of the Library in here!"

"And a librarian to boot," Juanita says, "to help you sort

through it. And lots of videotapes of L. Bob Rife—which accounts for most of the bytes."

"Well, I'll try to have a look at it," he says dubiously.

"Do. Unlike Da5id, you're just smart enough to benefit from this. And in the meantime, stay away from Raven. And stay away from Snow Crash. Okay?"

"Who's Raven?" he asks. But Juanita is already on her way out the door. The fancy avatars all turn around to watch her as she goes past them; the movie stars give her drop-dead looks, and the hackers purse their lips and stare reverently.

——————— Hiro orbits back around to the Hacker Quadrant. Da5id's shuffling hypercards around on his table—business stats on The Black Sun, film and video clips, hunks of software, scrawled telephone numbers.

"There's a little blip in the operating system that hits me right in the gut every time you come in the door," Da5id says. "I always have this premonition that The Black Sun is headed for a crash."

"Must be Bigboard," Hiro says. "It has one routine that patches some of the traps in low memory, for a moment."

"Ah, that's it. Please, please throw that thing away," Da5id says.

"What, Bigboard?"

"Yeah. It was totally rad at one point, but now it's like trying to work on a fusion reactor with a stone ax."

"Thanks."

"I'll give you all the headers you need if you want to update it to something a little less dangerous," Da5id says. "I wasn't impugning your abilities. I'm just saying you need to keep up with the times."

"It's fucking hard," Hiro says. "There's no place for a freelance hacker anymore. You have to have a big corporation behind you."

"I'm aware of that. And I'm aware that you can't stand to work for a big corporation. That's why I'm saying, I'll give you the stuff you need. You're always a part of The Black Sun to me, Hiro, even since we parted ways."

It is classic Da5id. He's talking with his heart again, bypassing his head. If Da5id weren't a hacker, Hiro would despair of his ever having enough brains to do anything.

"Let's talk about something else," Hiro says. "Was I just hallucinating, or are you and Juanita on speaking terms again?"

Da5id gives him an indulgent smile. He has been very kind to Hiro ever since The Conversation, several years back. It was a conversation that started out as a friendly chat over beer and oysters between a couple of longtime comrades-in-arms. It was not until three-quarters of the way through The Conversation that it dawned on Hiro that he was, in fact, being fired, at this very moment. Since The Conversation, Da5id has been known to feed Hiro useful bits of intel and gossip from time to time.

"Fishing for something useful?" Da5id asks knowingly. Like many bitheads, Da5id is utterly guileless, but at times like this, he thinks he's the reincarnation of Machiavelli.

"I got news for you, man," Hiro says. "Most of the stuff you give me, I never put into the Library."

"Why not? Hell, I give you all my best gossip. I thought you were making money off that stuff."

"I just can't stand it," Hiro says, "taking parts of my private conversations and whoring them out. Why do you think I'm broke?"

There's another thing he doesn't mention, which is that he's always considered himself to be Da5id's equal, and he can't stand the idea of feeding off Da5id's little crumbs and tidbits, like a dog curled up under his table.

"I was glad to see Juanita come in here—even as a black-and-white," Da5id says. "For her not to use The Black Sun—it's like Alexander Graham Bell refusing to use the telephone."

"Why did she come in tonight?"

"Something's bugging her," Da5id says. "She wanted to know if I'd seen certain people on the Street."

"Anyone in particular?"

"She's worried about a really large guy with long black hair," Da5id says. "Peddling something called—get this—Snow Crash."

"Has she tried the Library?"

"Yeah. I assume so, anyway."

"Have you seen this guy?"

"Oh, yeah. It's not hard to find him," Da5id says. "He's right outside the door. I got this from him."

Da5id scans the table, picks up one of the hypercards, and shows it to Hiro.

SNOW CRASH

tear this card in half to
release your free sample

"Da5id," Hiro says, "I can't believe you took a hypercard from a black-and-white person."

Da5id laughs. "This is not the old days, my friend. I've got so much antiviral medicine in my system that nothing could get through. I get so much contaminated shit from all the hackers who come through here, it's like working in a plague ward. So I'm not afraid of whatever's in this hypercard."

"Well, in that case, I'm curious," Hiro says.

"Yeah. Me, too." Da5id laughs.

"It's probably something very disappointing."

"Probably an animercial," Da5id agrees. "Think I should do it?"

"Yeah. Go for it. It's not every day you get to try out a new drug," Hiro says.

"Well, you can try one every day if you want to," Da5id says, "but it's not every day you find one that can't hurt you." He picks up the hypercard and tears it in half.

For a second, nothing happens. "I'm waiting," Da5id says.

An avatar materializes on the table in front of Da5id, starting out ghostly and transparent, gradually becoming solid and three-dimensional. It's a really trite effect; Hiro and Da5id are already laughing.

The avatar is a stark naked Brandy. It doesn't even look like the standard Brandy; this looks like one of the cheap Taiwanese Brandy knockoffs. Clearly, it's just a daemon. She is holding a pair of tubes in her hands, about the size of paper-towel rolls.

Da5id is leaning back in his chair, enjoying this. There is something hilariously tawdry about the entire scene.

The Brandy leans forward, beckoning Da5id toward her. Da5id leans into her face, grinning broadly. She puts her crude, ruby-red lips up by his ear and mumbles something that Hiro can't hear.

When she leans back away from Da5id, his face has changed. He looks dazed and expressionless. Maybe Da5id really looks that way; maybe Snow Crash has messed up his avatar somehow so that it's no longer tracking Da5id's true facial expressions. But he's staring straight ahead, eyes frozen in their sockets.

The Brandy holds the pair of tubes up in front of Da5id's immobilized face and spreads them apart. It's actually a scroll. She's unrolling it right in front of Da5id's face, spreading it apart like a flat two-dimensional screen in front of his eyes. Da5id's paralyzed face has taken on a bluish tinge as it reflects light coming out of the scroll.

Hiro walks around the table to look. He gets a brief glimpse of the scroll before the Brandy snaps it shut again. It is a living wall of light, like a flexible, flat-screened television set, and it's not showing anything at all. Just static. White noise. Snow.

Then she's gone, leaving no trace behind. Desultory, sarcastic applause sounds from a few tables in the Hacker Quadrant.

Da5id's back to normal, wearing a grin that's part snide and part embarrassed.

"What was it?" Hiro says. "I just glimpsed some snow at the very end."

"You saw the whole thing," Da5id says. "A fixed pattern of black-and-white pixels, fairly high-resolution. Just a few hundred thousand ones and zeroes for me to look at."

"So in other words, someone just exposed your optic nerve to, what, maybe a hundred thousand bytes of information," Hiro says.

"Noise, is more like it."

"Well, all information looks like noise until you break the code," Hiro says.

"Why would anyone show me information in binary code? I'm not a computer. I can't read a bitmap."

"Relax, Da5id, I'm just shitting you," Hiro says.

"You know what it was? You know how hackers are always trying to show me samples of their work?"

"Yeah."

"Some hacker came up with this scheme to show me his stuff. And everything worked fine until the moment the Brandy opened the scroll—but his code was buggy, and it snow-crashed at the wrong moment, so instead of seeing his output, all I saw was snow."

"Then why did he *call* the thing Snow Crash?"

"Gallows humor. He knew it was buggy."

"What did the Brandy whisper in your ear?"

"Some language I didn't recognize," Da5id says. "Just a bunch of babble."

Babble. Babel.

"Afterward, you looked sort of stunned."

Da5id looks resentful. "I wasn't stunned. I just found the whole experience so weird, I guess I just was taken aback for a second."

Hiro is giving him an extremely dubious look. Da5id notices it and stands up. "Want to go see what your competitors in Nippon are up to?"

"What competitors?"

"You used to design avatars for rock stars, right?"

"Still do."

"Well, Sushi K is here tonight."

"Oh, yeah. The hairdo the size of a galaxy."

"You can see the rays from here," Da5id says, waving toward the next quadrant, "but I want to see the whole getup."

It does look as though the sun is rising somewhere in the middle of the Rock Star Quadrant. Above the heads of the milling avatars, Hiro can see a fan of orange beams radiating outward from some point in the middle of the crowd. It keeps moving, turning around, shaking from side to side, and the whole universe seems to move with it. On the Street, the full radiance of Sushi K's Rising Sun hairdo is suppressed by the height and width regulations. But Da5id allows free expression inside The Black Sun, so the orange rays extend all the way to the property lines.

"I wonder if anyone's told him yet that Americans won't buy

rap music from a Japanese person," Hiro says as they stroll over there.

"Maybe you should tell him," Da5id suggests, "charge him for the service. He's in L.A. right now, you know."

"Probably staying in a hotel full of bootlickers telling him what a big star he's going to be. He needs to be exposed to some actual biomass."

They inject themselves into a stream of traffic, winding a narrow channel through a rift in the crowd.

"Biomass?" Da5id says.

"A body of living stuff. It's an ecology term. If you take an acre of rain forest or a cubic mile of ocean or a square block of Compton and strain out all the nonliving stuff—dirt and water—you get the biomass."

Da5id, ever the bithead, says, "I do not understand." His voice sounds funny; there's a lot of white noise creeping into his audio.

"Industry expression," Hiro says. "The Industry feeds off the human biomass of America. Like a whale straining krill from the sea."

Hiro wedges himself between a couple of Nipponese businessmen. One is wearing uniform blue, but the other is a neo-traditional, wearing a dark kimono. And, like Hiro, he's wearing two swords—the long katana on his left hip and the one-handed wakizashi stuck diagonally in his waistband. He and Hiro glance cursorily at each other's armaments. Then Hiro looks away and pretends not to notice, while the neo-traditional is freezing solid, except for the corners of his mouth, which are curling downward. Hiro has seen this kind of thing before. He knows he's about to get into a fight.

People are moving out of the way; something big and inexorable is plunging through the crowd, shoving avatars this way and that. Only one thing has the ability to shove people around like that inside The Black Sun, and that's a bouncer daemon.

As they get closer, Hiro sees that it's a whole flying wedge of them, gorillas in tuxedos. Real gorillas. And they seem to be headed toward Hiro.

He tries to back away, but he quickly runs into something. Looks like Bigboard finally got him in trouble; he's on his way out of the bar.

"Da5id," Hiro says. "Call them off, man, I'll stop using it."

All of the people in his vicinity are staring over Hiro's shoulder, their faces illuminated by a stew of brilliant colored lights.

Hiro turns around to look at Da5id. But Da5id's not there anymore.

Instead of Da5id, there is just a jittering cloud of bad digital karma. It's so bright and fast and meaningless that it hurts to look at. It flashes back and forth from color to black and white, and when it's in color, it rolls wildly around the color wheel as though being strafed with high-powered disco lights. And it's not staying within its own body space; hair-thin pixel lines keep shooting off to one side, passing all the way across The Black Sun and out through the wall. It is not so much an organized body as it is a centrifugal cloud of lines and polygons whose center cannot hold, throwing bright bits of body shrapnel all over the room, interfering with people's avatars, flickering and disappearing.

The gorillas don't mind. They shove their long furry fingers into the midst of the disintegrating cloud and latch onto it somehow and carry it past Hiro, toward the exit. Hiro looks down as it goes past him and sees what looks very much like Da5id's face as viewed through a pile of shattered glass. It's just a momentary glimpse. Then the avatar is gone, expertly drop-kicked out the front door, soaring out over the Street in a long flat arc that takes it over the horizon. Hiro looks up the aisle to see Da5id's table, empty, surrounded by stunned hackers. Some of them are shocked, some are trying to stifle grins.

Da5id Meier, supreme hacker overlord, founding father of the Metaverse protocol, creator and proprietor of the world-famous Black Sun, has just suffered a system crash. He's been thrown out of his own bar by his own daemons.

10

About the second or third thing they learned how to do when studying to become Kouriers was how to shiv open a pair of handcuffs. Handcuffs are not intended as long-term restraint devices, millions of Clink franchisees to the contrary. And the longtime status of skateboarders as an oppressed ethnic group means that by now all of them are escape artists of some degree.

First things first. Y.T. has many a thing hanging off her uniform. The uniform has a hundred pockets, big flat pockets for deliveries and eensy narrow pockets for gear, pockets sewn into sleeves, thighs, shins. The equipment stuck into these multifarious pockets tends to be small, tricky, lightweight: pens, markers, penlights, penknives, lock picks, bar-code scanners, flares, screwdrivers, Liquid Knuckles, bundy stunners, and lightsticks. A calculator is stuck upside-down to her right thigh, doubling as a taxi meter and a stopwatch.

On the other thigh is a personal phone. As the manager is locking the door upstairs, it begins to ring. Y.T. offhooks it with her free hand. It is her mother.

"Hi, Mom. Fine, how are you? I'm at Tracy's house. Yeah, we went to the Metaverse. We were just fooling around at this arcade on the Street. Pretty bumpin'. Yes, I used a nice avatar. Nah, Tracy's mom said she'd give me a ride home later. But we might stop off at the Joyride on Victory for a while, okay? Okay, well, sleep tight, Mom. I will. I love you, too. See you later."

She punches the flash button, killing the chat with Mom and giving her a fresh dial tone in the space of about half a second. "Roadkill," she says.

The telephone remembers and dials Roadkill's number.

Roaring sounds. This is the sound of air peeling over the microphone of Roadkill's personal phone at some terrifying velocity. Also the competing whooshes of many vehicles' tires on pavement, broken by chuckhole percussion; sounds like the crumbling Ventura.

"Yo, Y.T.," Roadkill says, " 'sup?"

" 'Sup with you?"

"Surfing the Tura. 'Sup with you?"

"Maxing The Clink."

"Whoa! Who popped you?"

"MetaCops. Affixed me to the gate of White Columns with a loogie gun."

"Whoa, how very! When you leaving?"

"Soon. Can you swing by and give me a hand?"

"What do you mean?"

Men. "You know, *give me a hand.* You're my boyfriend," she says, speaking very simply and plainly. "If I get popped, you're supposed to come around and help bust me out." Isn't everyone supposed to know this stuff? Don't parents teach their kids anything anymore?

"Well, uh, where are you?"

"Buy 'n' Fly number 501,762."

"I'm on my way to Bernie with a super-ultra."

As in San Bernardino. As in super-ultra-high-priority delivery. As in, you're out of luck.

"Okay, thanks for nothing."

"Sorry."

"Surfing safety," Y.T. says, in the traditional sarcastic sign off.

"Keep breathing," Roadkill says. The roaring noise snaps off.

What a jerk. Next date, he's really going to have to grovel. But in the meantime, there's one other person who owes her one. The only problem is that he might be a spaz. But it's worth a try.

"Hello?" he says into his personal phone. He's breathing hard and a couple of sirens are dueling in the background.

"Hiro Protagonist?"

"Yeah, who's this?"

"Y.T. Where are you?"

"In the parking lot of a Safeway on Oahu," he says. And he's telling the truth; in the background she can hear the shopping carts performing their clashy, anal copulations.

"I'm kind of busy now, Whitey—but what can I do for you?"

"It's Y.T., " she says, "and you can help bust me out of The Clink." She gives him the details.

"How long ago did he put you there?"

"Ten minutes."

"Okay, the three-ring binder for Clink franchises states that the manager is supposed to check on the detainee half an hour after admission."

"How do you know this stuff?" she says accusingly.

"Use your imagination. As soon as the manager pulls his half-hour check, wait for another five minutes, and then make your move. I'll try to give you a hand. Okay?"

"Got it."

_____ At half an hour on the dot, she hears the back door being unlocked. The lights come on. Her Knight Visions save her from wracking eyeball pains. The manager thunks down a couple of steps, glares at her, glares at her for rather a long time. The manager, clearly, is tempted. That momentary glimpse of flesh has been ricocheting around in his brain for half an hour. He is wracking his mind with vast cosmological dilemmas. Y.T. hopes that he does not try anything, because the dentata's effects can be unpredictable.

"Make up your fucking mind," she says.

It works. This fresh burst of culture shock rattles the jeek out of his ethical conundrum. He gives Y.T. a disapproving glower—she, after all, forced him to be attracted to her, forced him to get horny, made his head swim—she didn't have to get arrested, did she?—and so on top of everything else he's angry with her. As if he has a right to be.

This is the gender that invented the polio vaccine?

He turns, goes back up the steps, kills the light, locks the door.

She notes the time, sets her alarm watch for five minutes from now—the only North American who actually knows how to set the alarm on her digital wristwatch—pulls her shiv kit from one of the narrow pockets on her sleeve. She also hauls out a light-stick and snaps it so she can see 'sup. She finds one piece of narrow, flat spring steel, slides it up into the manacle's innards, depresses the spring-loaded pawl. The cuff, formerly a one-way ratchet that could only get tighter, springs loose from the cold-water pipe.

She could take it off her wrist, but she has decided she likes the look of it. She cuffs the loose manacle onto her wrist, right next to the other one, forming a double bracelet. The kind of thing her mom used to do, back when she was a punk.

The steel door is locked, but Buy 'n' Fly safety regs mandate an emergency exit from the basement in case of fire. Here, it's a basement window with mondo bars and a big red multilingual fire alarm bolted onto it. The red looks black in the green glow of the lightstick. She reads the instructions that are in English, runs through it once or twice in her mind, then waits for the alarm to go off. She whiles away the time by reading the instructions in all the other languages, wondering which is which. It all looks like Taxilinga to Y.T.

The window is almost too grungy to see through, but she sees something black walking past it. Hiro.

About ten seconds later, her wristwatch goes off. She punches the emergency exit. The bell rings. The bars are trickier than she thought—good thing it's not a real fire—but eventually she gets them open. She throws her plank outside onto the parking lot, drags her body through just as she hears the rear door being unlocked. By the time the three-ringer has found that all-important light switch, she is banking a sharp turn into the front lot—which has turned into a jeek festival!

Every jeek in Southern Cal is here, it seems, driving their giant, wrecked taxicabs with alien livestock in the back seat, reeking of incense and sloshing neon-hued Airwicks! They have set up a giant eight-tubed hookah on the trunk of one of the cabs and are slurping up great mountain-man lungfuls of choking smoke.

And they're all staring at Hiro Protagonist, who is just staring back at them. Everyone in the parking lot looks completely astounded.

He must have made his approach from the rear—didn't realize that the front lot was full of jeeks. Whatever he was planning isn't going to work. The plan is screwed.

The manager comes running around from the back of the Buy 'n' Fly, sounding a bloodcurdling Taxilinga tocsin. He's got missile lock on Y.T.'s ass.

But the jeeks around the hookah don't care about Y.T. They've got missile lock on Hiro. They carefully hang the ornate silver nozzles on a rack built into the neck of the mega-bong. Then they start moving toward him, reaching into the folds of their robes, the inner pockets of their windbreakers.

Y.T. is distracted by a sharp hissing noise. Her eyes glance back at Hiro, and she sees that he has withdrawn a three-foot, curved sword from a scabbard, which she did not notice before. He has dropped into a squat. The blade of the sword glitters painfully under the killer security lights of the Buy 'n' Fly.

How sweet!

It would be an understatement to say that the hookah boys are taken aback. But they are not scared so much as they are confused. Almost undoubtedly, most of them have guns. So why is this guy trying to bother them with a sword?

She remembers that one of the multiple professions on Hiro's business card is *Greatest sword fighter in the world.* Can he really take out a whole clan of armed jeeks?

The manager's hand clenches her upper arm—like this is really going to stop her. She reaches across her body with the other hand and lets him have it with a brief squirt of Liquid Knuckles. He makes a muffled, distant grunt, his head snaps back, he lets go of her arm and staggers back wildly until he sprawls against another taxi, jamming the heels of both hands into his eye sockets.

Wait a sec. There's nobody in that particular taxi. But she can see a two-foot-long macramé keychain dangling from the ignition.

She tosses her plank through the window of the taxi, dives in after it (she's small, opening the door is optional), climbs in behind the driver's seat, sinking into a deep nest of wooden beads and air fresheners, grinds the motor, and takes off. Backward. Headed for the rear parking lot. The car was pointed outward, in taxicab style, ready for a quick getaway, which would be fine if she were by herself—but there is Hiro to think of. The radio is screaming, alive with hollered bursts of Taxilinga. She backs all the way around behind the Buy 'n' Fly. The back lot is strangely quiet and empty.

She shifts into drive and blasts back the way she came. The jeeks haven't quite had time to react, were expecting her to come out the other way. She screams it to a halt right next to Hiro, who has already had the presence of mind to put his sword back in its scabbard. He dives in the passenger-side window. Then she stops paying attention to him. She's got other stuff to look at, such as whether she's going to get broadsided as she pulls out onto the road.

She doesn't get broadsided, though a car has to squeal around her. She guns it out onto the highway. It responds as only an ancient taxicab will.

The only problem being that half a dozen other ancient taxicabs are now following them.

Something is pressing against Y.T.'s left thigh. She looks down. It is a remarkably huge revolver in a net bag hanging on the door panel.

She has to find someplace to pull into. If she could find a Nova Sicilia franchulate, that would do it—the Mafia owes her one. Or a New South Africa, which she hates. But the New South Africans hate jeeks even more.

Scratch that; Hiro is black, or at least part black. Can't take him into New South Africa. And because Y.T. is a Cauc, they can't go to Metazania.

"Mr. Lee's Greater Hong Kong," Hiro says. "Half mile ahead on the right."

"Nice thinking—but they won't let you in with your swords, will they?"

"Yes," he says, "because I'm a citizen."

Then she sees it. The sign stands out because it is a rare one. Don't see many of these. It is a green-and-blue sign, soothing and calm in a glare-torn franchise ghetto. It says:

MR. LEE'S GREATER HONG KONG

Explosive noise from in back. Her head smacks into the whiplash arrestor. Another taxi rear-ended them.

And she screams into the parking lot of Mr. Lee's doing seventy-five. The security system doesn't even have time to rez her visa and drop the STD, so it's Severe Tire Damage all the way, those bald radials are left behind on the spikes. Sparking along on four naked rims, she shrieks to a stop on the lawngrid, which doubles as carbon dioxide–eating turf and impervious parking lot.

She and Hiro climb out of the car.

Hiro is grinning wildly, pinioned in the crossfire of a dozen red laser beams scanning him from every direction at once. The Hong Kong robot security system is checking him out. Her, too; she looks down to see the lasers scribbling across her chest.

"Welcome to Mr. Lee's Greater Hong Kong, Mr. Protagonist," the security system says through a P.A. speaker. "And welcome to your guest, Ms. Y.T."

The other taxis have stopped in formation along the curb.

Several of them overshot the Hong Kong franchise and had to back up a block or so. A barrage of doors thunking shut. Some of them don't bother, just leave the engines running and the doors wide open. Three jeeks linger on the sidewalk, eyeing the tire shreds impaled on spikes: long streaks of neoprene sprouting steel and fiberglass hairs, like ruined toupées. One of them has a revolver in his hand, pointed straight down at the sidewalk.

Four more jeeks run up to join them. Y.T. counts two more revolvers and a pump shotgun. Any more of these guys and they'll be able to form a government.

They step carefully over the spikes and onto the lush Hong Kong lawngrid. As they do, the lasers appear once more. The jeeks turn all red and grainy for a second.

Then something different happens. Lights come on. The security system wants better illumination on these people.

Hong Kong franchulates are famous for their lawngrids—whoever heard of a lawn you could park on?—and for their antennas. They all look like NASA research facilities with their antennas. Some of them are satellite uplinks, pointed at the sky. But some of them, tiny little antennas, are pointed at the ground, at the lawngrid.

Y.T. does not really get this, but these small antennas are millimeter-wave radar transceivers. Like any other radar, they are good at picking up metallic objects. Unlike the radar in an air traffic control center, they can rez fine details. The rez of a system is only as fine as its wavelength; since the wavelength of this radar is about a millimeter, it can see the fillings in your teeth, the grommets in your Converse high-tops, the rivets in your Levi's. It can calculate the value of your pocket change.

Seeing guns is not a problem. This thing can even tell if the guns are loaded, and with what sort of ammunition. That is an important function, because guns are illegal in Mr. Lee's Greater Hong Kong.

11

It doesn't seem polite to hang around and gawk over the fact that Da5id's computer crashed. A lot of the younger hackers are doing just that, as a way of showing all the other hackers how knowledgeable they are. Hiro shrugs it off and turns back in the direction of the Rock Star Quadrant. He still wants to see Sushi K's hairdo.

But his path is being blocked by the Nipponese man—the neo-traditional. The guy with the swords. He's facing off against Hiro, about two sword-lengths apart, and it doesn't look like he intends to move.

Hiro does the polite thing. He bows at the waist, straightens up.

The businessman does the much less polite thing. He looks Hiro rather carefully up and down, then returns the bow. Sort of.

"These—" the businessman says. "Very nice."

"Thank you, sir. Please feel free to converse in Nipponese if you prefer."

"This is what your avatar wears. You do not carry such weapons in Reality," the businessman says. In English.

"I'm sorry to be difficult, but in fact, I do carry such weapons in Reality," Hiro says.

"Exactly like these?"

"Exactly."

"These are ancient weapons, then," the businessman says.

"Yes, I believe they are."

"How did you come to be in possession of such important family heirlooms from Nippon?" the businessman says.

Hiro knows the subtext here: *What do you use those swords for, boy, slicing watermelon?*

"They are now my family heirlooms," Hiro says. "My father won them."

"Won them? Gambling?"

"Single combat. It was a struggle between my father and a Nipponese officer. The story is quite complicated."

"Please excuse me if I have misinterpreted your story," the businessman says, "but I was under the impression that men of your race were not allowed to fight during that war."

"Your impression is correct," Hiro says. "My father was a truck driver."

"Then how did he come to be in hand-to-hand combat with a Nipponese officer?"

"The incident took place outside a prisoner-of-war camp," Hiro says. "My father and another prisoner tried to escape. They were pursued by a number of Nipponese soldiers and the officer who owned these swords."

"Your story is very difficult to believe," the businessman says, "because your father could not have survived such an escape long enough to pass the swords on to his son. Nippon is an island nation. There is nowhere he could have escaped to."

"This happened very late in the war," Hiro says, "and this camp was just outside of Nagasaki."

The businessman chokes, reddens, nearly loses it. His left hand reaches up to grip the scabbard of his sword. Hiro looks around; suddenly they are in the center of an open circle of people some ten yards across.

"Do you think that the manner in which you came to possess these swords was honorable?" the businessman says.

"If I did not, I would long since have returned them," Hiro says.

"Then you will not object to losing them in the same fashion," the businessman says.

"Nor will you object to losing yours," Hiro says.

The businessman reaches across his body with his right hand, grips the handle of his sword just below the guard, draws it out, snaps it forward so it's pointing at Hiro, then places his left hand on the grip just below the right.

Hiro does the same.

Both of them bend their knees, dropping into a low squat while keeping the torso bolt upright, then stand up again and shuffle their feet into the proper stance—feet parallel, both pointed straight ahead, right foot in front of the left foot.

The businessman turns out to have a lot of *zanshin*. Translating this concept into English is like translating "fuckface" into Nipponese, but it might translate into "emotional intensity" in football lingo. He charges directly at Hiro, hollering at the top of his lungs. The movement actually consists of a very rapid shuffling motion of the feet, so that he stays balanced at all times. At the last moment, he draws the sword up over his head and snaps it down toward Hiro. Hiro brings his own sword up, rotating it around sideways so that the handle is up high, above and to the left of his face, and the blade slopes down and to the right, providing a roof above him. The businessman's blow bounces off this roof like rain, and then Hiro sidesteps to let him go by and snaps the sword down toward his unprotected shoulder. But the businessman is moving too fast, and Hiro's timing is off. The blade cuts behind and to the side of the businessman.

Both men wheel to face each other, back up, get back into the stance.

"Emotional intensity" doesn't convey the half of it, of course. It is the kind of coarse and disappointing translation that makes the dismembered bodies of samurai warriors spin in their graves. The word "zanshin" is larded down with a lot of other folderol that you have to be Nipponese to understand.

And Hiro thinks, frankly, that most of it is pseudomystical crap, on the same level as his old high school football coach exhorting his men to play at 110 percent.

The businessman makes another attack. This one is pretty straightforward: a quick shuffling approach and then a snapping cut in the direction of Hiro's ribcage. Hiro parries it.

Now Hiro knows something about this businessman, namely, that like most Nipponese sword fighters, all he knows is *kendo*.

Kendo is to real samurai sword fighting what fencing is to real swashbuckling: an attempt to take a highly disorganized, chaotic, violent, and brutal conflict and turn it into a cute game. As in fencing, you're only supposed to attack certain parts of the body—the parts that are protected by armor. As in fencing, you're not allowed to kick your opponent in the kneecaps or break a chair over his head. And the judging is totally subjective. In kendo, you can get a good solid hit on your opponent and still not get credit for it, because the judges feel you didn't possess the right amount of zanshin.

Hiro doesn't have any zanshin at all. He just wants this over with. The next time the businessman sets up his ear-splitting screech and shuffles toward Hiro, cutting and snapping his blade, Hiro parries the attack, turns around, and cuts both of his legs off just above the knees.

The businessman collapses to the floor.

It takes a lot of practice to make your avatar move through the Metaverse like a real person. When your avatar has just lost its legs, all that skill goes out the window.

"Well, land sakes!" Hiro says. "Lookee here!" He whips his blade sideways, cutting off both of the businessman's forearms, causing the sword to clatter onto the floor.

"Better fire up the ol' barbecue, Jemima!" Hiro continues, whipping the sword around sideways, cutting the businessman's body in half just above the navel. Then he leans down so he's looking right into the businessman's face. "Didn't anyone tell you," he says, losing the dialect, "that I was a hacker?"

Then he hacks the guy's head off. It falls to the floor, does a half-roll, and comes to rest staring straight up at the ceiling. So Hiro steps back a couple of paces and mumbles, "Safe."

A largish safe, about a meter on a side, materializes just below the ceiling, plummets, and lands directly on the businessman's head. The impact drives both the safe and the head straight down through the floor of The Black Sun, leaving a square hole in the floor, exposing the tunnel system underneath. The rest of the dismembered body is still strewn around the floor.

At this moment, a Nipponese businessman somewhere, in a nice hotel in London or an office in Tokyo or even in the first-class lounge of the LATH, the Los Angeles/Tokyo Hypersonic, is sitting in front of his computer, red-faced and sweating, looking at The Black Sun Hall of Fame. He has been cut off from contact with The Black Sun itself, disconnected as it were from the Metaverse, and is just seeing a two-dimensional display. The top ten swordsmen of all time are shown along with their photographs. Beneath is a scrolling list of numbers and names, starting with #11. He can scroll down the list if he wants to find his own ranking. The screen helpfully informs him that he is currently ranked number 863 out of 890 people who have ever participated in a sword fight in The Black Sun.

Number One, the name and the photograph on the top of the list, belongs to Hiroaki Protagonist.

12

Ng Security Industries Semi-Autonomous Guard Unit #A-367 lives in a pleasant black-and-white Metaverse where porterhouse steaks grow on trees, dangling at head level from low branches, and blood-drenched Frisbees fly through the crisp, cool air for no reason at all, until you catch them.

He has a little yard all to himself. It has a fence around it. He knows he can't jump over the fence. He's never actually tried to jump it, because he knows he can't. He doesn't go into the yard unless he has to. It's hot out there.

He has an important job: Protect the yard. Sometimes people come in and out of the yard. Most of the time, they are good people, and he doesn't bother them. He doesn't know why they are good people. He just knows it. Sometimes they are bad people, and he has to do bad things to them to make them go away. This is fitting and proper.

Out in the world beyond his yard, there are other yards with other doggies just like him. These aren't nasty dogs. They are all his friends.

The closest neighbor doggie is far away, farther than he can see. But he can hear this doggie bark sometimes, when a bad person approaches his yard. He can hear other neighbor doggies, too, a whole pack of them stretching off into the distance, in all directions. He belongs to a big pack of nice doggies.

He and the other nice doggies bark whenever a stranger comes into their yard, or even near it. The stranger doesn't hear him, but all the other doggies in the pack do. If they live nearby, they get excited. They wake up and get ready to do bad things to that stranger if he should try to come into their yard.

When a neighbor doggie barks at a stranger, pictures and sounds and smells come into his mind along with the bark. He suddenly knows what that stranger looks like. What he smells

like. How he sounds. Then, if that stranger should come anywhere near his yard, he will recognize him. He will help spread
the bark along to other nice doggies so that the entire pack can
all be prepared to fight the stranger.

Tonight, Semi-Autonomous Guard Unit #A-367 is barking. He
is not just passing some other doggie's bark to the pack. He is
barking because he feels very excited about things that are happening in his yard.

First, two people came in. This made him excited because
they came in very fast. Their hearts are beating quickly and they
are sweating and they smell scared. He looked at these two people to see if they were carrying bad things.

The little one is carrying things that are a little naughty, but
not really bad. The big one is carrying some pretty bad things.
But he knows, somehow, that the big one is okay. He belongs in
this yard. He is not a stranger; he lives here. And the little one is
his guest.

Still, he senses there is something exciting happening. He
starts to bark. The people in the yard don't hear him barking. But
all the other nice doggies in the pack, far away, hear him, and
when they do, they see these two scared, nice people, smell them,
and hear them.

Then more people come into his yard. They are also excited;
he can hear their hearts beating. Saliva floods his mouth as he
smells the hot salty blood pumping through their arteries. These
people are excited and angry and just a little bit scared. They
don't live here; they are strangers. He doesn't like strangers very
much.

He looks at them and sees that they are carrying three revolvers, a .38 and two .357 magnums; that the .38 is loaded with
hollow-points, one of the .357s is loaded with Teflon bullets and
has also been cocked; and that the pump shotgun is loaded with
buckshot and already has a shell chambered, plus four more
shells in its magazine.

The things that the strangers are carrying are bad. Scary
things. He gets excited. He gets angry. He gets a little bit scared,
but he likes being scared, to him it is the same thing as being
excited. Really, he has only two emotions: sleeping and
adrenaline overdrive.

The bad stranger with the shotgun is raising his weapon!

It is an utterly terrible thing. A lot of bad, excited strangers are invading his yard with evil things, come to hurt the nice visitors.

He barely has time to bark out a warning to the other nice doggies before he launches himself from his doghouse, propelled on a white-hot jet of pure, feral emotion.

_____ In Y.T.'s peripheral vision she sees a brief flash, hears a clunking noise. She looks over in that direction to see that the source of the light is a sort of doggie door built into the side of the Hong Kong franchise. The doggie door has in the very recent past been slammed open by something coming from the inside, headed for the lawngrid with the speed and determination of a howitzer shell.

As all of this registers on Y.T.'s mind, she begins to hear the shouting of the jeeks. This shouting is not angry and not scared either. No one has had time to get scared yet. It is the shouting of someone who has just had a bucket of ice water dumped over his head.

This shouting is still getting underway, she is still turning her head to look at the jeeks, when the doggie door emits another burst of light. Her eyes flick that-a-way; she thinks that she saw something, a long round shadow cross-sectioned in the light for a blurry instant as the door was being slammed inward. But when her eyes focus on it, she sees nothing except the oscillating door, same as before. These are the only impressions left on her mind, except for one more detail: a train of sparks that danced across the lawngrid from the doggie door to the jeeks and back again during this one-second event, like a skyrocket glancing across the lot.

People say that the Rat Thing runs on four legs. Perhaps the claws on its robot legs made those sparks as they were digging into the lawngrid for traction.

The jeeks are all in motion. Some of them have just been body-slammed into the lawngrid and are still bouncing and rolling. Others are still in mid-collapse. They are unarmed. They are reaching to grip their gun hands with the opposite hands, still hollering, though now their voices are tinged with a certain amount of fear. One of them has had his trousers torn from the waistband all the way down to the ankle, and a strip of fabric is trailing out across the lot, as though he had his pocket picked by something that was in too much of a hurry to let go of the actual pocket before it left. Maybe this guy had a knife in his pocket.

There is no blood anywhere. The Rat Thing is precise. Still they hold their hands and holler. Maybe it's true what they say, that the Rat Thing gives you an electrical shock when it wants you to let go of something.

"Look out," she hears herself saying, "they got guns."

Hiro turns and grins at her. His teeth are very white and straight; he has a sharp grin, a carnivore's grin. "No, they don't. Guns are illegal in Hong Kong, remember?"

"They had guns just a second ago," Y.T. says, bulging her eyes and shaking her head.

"The Rat Thing has them now," Hiro says.

The jeeks all decide they better leave. They run out and get into their taxis and take off, tires asqueal.

Y.T. backs the taxi on its rims out over the STD and into the street, where she grindingly parallel parks it. She goes back into the Hong Kong franchise, a nebula of aromatic freshness trailing behind her like the tail of a comet. She is thinking, oddly enough, about what it would be like to climb into the back of the car with Hiro Protagonist for a while. Pretty nice, probably. But she'd have to take out the dentata, and this isn't the place. Besides, anyone decent enough to come help her escape from The Clink probably has some kind of scruples about boffing fifteen-year-old girls.

"That was nice of you," he says, nodding at the parked taxi. "Are you going to pay for his tires, too?"

"No. Are you?"

"I'm having some cash flow problems."

She stands there in the middle of the Hong Kong lawngrid. They look each other up and down, carefully.

"I called my boyfriend. But he flaked out on me," she says.

"Another thrasher?"

"The same."

"You made the same mistake I made once," he says.

"What's that?"

"Mixing business with pleasure. Going out with a colleague. It gets very confusing."

"Yeah. I see what you mean." She's not exactly sure what a colleague is.

"I was thinking that we should be partners," she says.

She's expecting him to laugh at her. But instead he grins and nods his head slightly. "The same thing occurred to me. But I'd have to think about how it would work."

She is astounded that he would actually be thinking this. Then she gets the sap factor under control and realizes: He's waffling. Which means he's probably lying. This is probably going to end with him trying to get her into bed.

"I gotta go," she says. "Gotta get home."

Now we'll see how fast he loses interest in the partnership concept. She turns her back on him.

Suddenly, they are impaled on Hong Kong robot spotlights one more time.

Y.T. feels a sharp bruising pain in her ribs, as though someone punched her. But it wasn't Hiro. He is an unpredictable freak who carries swords, but she can smell chick-punchers a mile off.

"Ow!" she says, twisting away from the impact. She looks down to see a small heavy object bouncing on the ground at their feet. Out in the street, an ancient taxi squeals its tires, getting the hell out of there. A jeek is hanging out the rear window, shaking his fist at them. He must have thrown a rock at her.

Except it's not a rock. The heavy thing at her feet, the thing that just bounced off of Y.T.'s ribcage, is a hand grenade. She stares for a second, recognizing it, a well-known cartoon icon made real.

Then her feet get knocked out from under her, too fast really to hurt. And just when she's getting reoriented to that, there is a painfully loud bang from another part of the parking lot.

And then everything finally stops long enough to be seen and understood.

The Rat Thing has stopped. Which they never do. It's part of their mystery that you never get to see them, they move so fast. No one knows what they look like.

No one except for Y.T. and Hiro, now.

It's bigger than she imagined. The body is Rottweiler-sized, segmented into overlapping hard plates like those of a rhinoceros. The legs are long, curled way up to deliver power, like a cheetah's. It must be the tail that makes people refer to it as a Rat Thing, because that's the only ratlike part—incredibly long and flexible. But it looks like a rat's tail with the flesh eaten away by acid, because it just consists of segments, hundreds of them neatly plugged together, like vertebrae.

"Jesus H. Christ!" Hiro says. And she knows, from that, that he's never seen one either.

Right now, the tail is coiled and piled around on top of the Rat Thing's body like a rope that has fallen out of a tree. Parts of it are trying to move, other parts of it look dead and inert. The legs are moving one by one, spasmodically, not acting in concert. The whole thing just looks terribly wrong, like footage of an airplane that has had its tail blown off, trying to maneuver for a landing. Even someone who is not an engineer can see that it has gone all perverse and twisted.

The tail writhes and lashes like a snake, uncoils itself, rises up off the Rat Thing's body, gets out of the way of its legs. But still the legs have problems; it can't get itself up.

"Y.T.," Hiro is saying, "don't."

She does. One footstep at a time, she approaches the Rat Thing.

"It's dangerous, in case you hadn't noticed," Hiro says, following her a few paces behind. "They say it has biological components."

"Biological components?"

"Animal parts. So it might be unpredictable."

She likes animals. She keeps walking.

She's seeing it better now. It's not all armor and muscle. A lot of it actually looks kind of flimsy. It has short stubby winglike things projecting from its body: A big one from each shoulder and a row of smaller ones down the length of its spine, like on a stegosaurus. Her Knight Visions tell her that these things are hot enough to bake pizzas on. As she approaches, they seem to unfold and grow.

They are blooming like flowers in an educational film, spreading and unfolding to reveal a fine complicated internal structure that has been all collapsed together inside. Each stubby wing splits off into little miniature copies of itself, and each of those in turn splits off into more smaller copies and so on forever. The smallest ones are just tiny bits of foil, so small that, from a distance, the edges look fuzzy.

It is continuing to get hotter. The little wings are almost red hot now. Y.T. slides her goggles up onto her forehead and cups her hands around her face to block out the surrounding lights, and sure enough she can see them beginning to make a dull brownish glow, like an electric stove element that has just been turned on. The grass underneath the Rat Thing is beginning to smoke.

"Careful. Supposedly they have really nasty isotopes inside," Hiro says behind her. He has come up a little closer now, but he's still hanging way back.

"What's an isotope?"

"A radioactive substance that makes heat. That's its energy source."

"How do you turn it off?"

"You don't. It keeps making heat until it melts."

Y.T. is only a few feet away from the Rat Thing now, and she can feel the heat on her cheeks. The wings have unfolded as far as they can go. At their roots they are a bright yellow-orange, fading out through red and brown to their delicate edges, which are still dark. The acrid smoke of the burning grass obscures some of the details.

She thinks: The edges of the wings look like something I've seen before. They look like the thin metal vanes that run up the outside of a window air conditioner, the ones that you can write your name in by mashing them down with your finger.

Or like the radiator on a car. The fan blows air over the radiator to cool off the engine.

"It's got radiators," she says. "The Rat Thing has got radiators to cool off." She's gathering intel right at this very moment.

But it's not cooling off. It's just getting hotter.

Y.T. surfs through traffic jams for a living. That's her economic niche: beating the traffic. And she knows that a car doesn't boil over when it is speeding down an open freeway. It boils over when it is stopped in traffic. Because when it sits still, not enough air is being blown over the radiator.

That's what's happening to the Rat Thing right now. It has to keep moving, keep forcing air over its radiators, or else it overheats and melts down.

"Cool," she says. "I wonder if it's going to blow up or what."

The body converges to a sharp nose. In the front it bends down sharply, and there is a black glass canopy, raked sharply like the windshield of a fighter plane. If the Rat Thing has eyes, this is where it looks out.

Under that, where the jaw should be are the remains of some kind of mechanical stuff that has been mostly blown off by the explosion of the grenade.

The black glass windshield—or facemask, or whatever you call it—has a hole blown through it. Big enough that Y.T. could put her hand through. On the other side of that hole, it's dark and she can't see much, especially so close to the bright orange glare coming from the radiators. But she can see that red stuff is coming out from inside. And it ain't no Dexron II. The Rat Thing is hurt and it's bleeding.

"This thing is real," she says. "It's got blood in its veins." She's thinking: This is intel. *This is intel.* I can make money off this with my pardner—my pod—Hiro.

Then she thinks: The poor thing is burning itself alive.

"Don't do it. Don't touch it, Y.T.," Hiro says.

She steps right up to it, flips her goggles down to protect her face from the heat. The Rat Thing's legs stop their spasmodic movements, as though waiting for her.

She bends down and grabs its front legs. They react, tightening their pushrod muscles against the pull of her hands. It's exactly like grabbing a dog by the front legs and asking it to dance. This thing is alive. It reacts to her. She knows.

She looks up at Hiro, just to make sure he's taking this all in. He is.

"Jerk!" she says. "I stick my neck out and say I want to be your partner, and you say you want to think about it? What's your problem, I'm not good enough to work with you?"

She leans back and begins dragging the Rat Thing backward across the lawngrid. It's incredibly light. No wonder it can run so fast. She could pick it up, if she felt like burning herself alive.

As she drags it backward toward the doggie door, it brands a blackened, smoking trail into the lawngrid. She can see steam rising up out of her coverall, old sweat and stuff boiling out of the fabric. She's small enough to fit through the doggie door—another thing she can do and Hiro can't. Usually these things are locked, she's tried to mess with them. But this one is opened.

Inside, the franchise is bright, white, robot-polished floors. A few feet from the doggie door is what looks like a black washing machine. This is the Rat Thing's hutch, where it lurks in darkness and privacy, waiting for a job to do. It is wired into the franchise by a thick cable coming out of the wall. Right now, the hutch's door is hanging open, which is another thing she's never seen before. And steam is rolling out from inside of it.

Not steam. Cold stuff. Like when you open your freezer door on a humid day.

She pushes the Rat Thing into its hutch. Some kind of cold liquid sprays out of all the walls and bursts into steam before it even reaches the Rat Thing's body, and the steam comes blasting out the front of the hutch so powerfully that it knocks her on her ass.

The long tail is strung out the front of the hutch, across the floor, and out through the doggie door. She picks up part of it, the sharp machine-tooled edges of its vertebrae pinching her gloves.

Suddenly it tenses, comes alive, vibrates for a second. She jerks her hands back. The tail shoots back inside the hutch like a rubber band snapping. She can't even see it move. Then the hutch door slams shut. A janitor robot, a Hoover with a brain, hums out of another doorway to clean the long streaks of blood off the floor.

Above her, hanging on the foyer wall facing the main entrance, is a framed poster with a garland of well-browned jasmine blossoms hung around it. It consists of a photo of the wildly grinning Mr. Lee, with the usual statement underneath:

WELCOME!
It is my pleasure to welcome all quality folks to visiting of Hong Kong. Whether seriously in business or on a fun-loving

hijink, make yourself totally homely in this meager environment. If any aspect is not utterly harmonious, gratefully bring it to my notice and I shall strive to earn your satisfaction.

We of Greater Hong Kong take many prides in our tiny nation's extravagant growth. The ones who saw our isle as a morsel of Red China's pleasure have struck their faces in keen astonishment to see many great so-called powers of the olden guard reel in dismay before our leaping strides and charged-up hustling, freewheeling idiom of high-tech personal accomplishment and betterment of all peoples. The potentials of all ethnic races and anthropologies to merge under a banner of the Three Principles to follow

1. Information, information, information!
2. Totally fair marketeering!
3. Strict ecology!

have been peerless in the history of economic strife.

Who would disdain to subscribe under this flowing banner? If you have not attained your Hong Kong citizenship, apply for a passport now! In this month, the usual fee of HK$100 will be kindly neglected. Fill out a coupon (below) now. If coupons are lacking, dial 1-800-HONG KONG instantly to apply from the help of our wizened operators.

Mr. Lee's Greater Hong Kong is a private, wholly extraterritorial, sovereign, quasi-national entity not recognized by any other nationalities and in no way affiliated with the former Crown Colony of Hong Kong, which is part of the People's Republic of China. The People's Republic of China admits or accepts no responsibility for Mr. Lee, the Government of Greater Hong Kong, or any of the citizens thereof, or for any violations of local law, personal injury, or property damage occurring in territories, buildings, municipalities, institutions, or real estate owned, occupied, or claimed by Mr. Lee's Greater Hong Kong.

Join us instantly!

Your enterprising partner,

Mr. Lee

Back in his cool little house, Semi-Autonomous Guard Unit #A-367 is howling.

Outside in the yard, it was very hot and he felt bad. Whenever he is out in the yard, he gets hot unless he keeps running. When he got hurt and had to lie down for a long time, he felt hotter than he had ever been before.

Now he doesn't feel hot anymore. But he is still hurt. He is howling his injured howl. He is telling all the neighbor doggies that he needs help. They feel sad and upset and repeat his howl and pass it along to all the rest of the doggies.

Soon he hears the vet's car approaching. The nice vet will come and make him feel better.

He starts barking again. He is telling all the other doggies about how the bad strangers came and hurt him. And how hot it was out in the yard when he had to lie down. And how the nice girl helped him and took him back to his cool house.

_____ Right in front of the Hong Kong franchise, Y.T. notices a black Town Car that has been sitting there for a while. She doesn't have to see the plates to know it's Mafia. Only the Mafia drives cars like that. The windows are blackened, but she knows someone's in there keeping an eye on her. How do they do it? You see these Town Cars everywhere, but you never see them move, never see them get anyplace. She's not even sure they have engines in them.

"Okay. Sorry," Hiro says. "I keep my own thing going, but we have a partnership for any intel you can dig up. Fifty-fifty split."

"Deal," she says, climbing onto her plank.

"Call me anytime. You have my card."

"Hey, that reminds me. Your card said you're into the three Ms of software."

"Yeah. Music, movies, and microcode."

"You heard of Vitaly Chernobyl and the Meltdowns?"

"No. Is that a band?"

"Yeah. It's the greatest band. You should check it out, homeboy, it's going to be the next big thing."

She coasts out onto the road and poons an Audi with Blooming Greens license plates. It ought to take her home. Mom's probably in bed, pretending to sleep, being worried.

Half a block from the entrance to Blooming Greens, she unpoons the Audi and coasts into a McDonald's. She goes into the ladies'. It has a hung ceiling. She stands on the seat of the third toilet, pushes up one of the ceiling tiles, moves it aside. A cotton sleeve tumbles out, bearing a delicate floral print. She pulls on it and hauls down the whole ensemble, the blouse, the pleated skirt, underwear from Vicky's, the leather shoes, the necklace and earrings, even a fucking purse. She takes off her RadiKS coverall, wads it up, sticks it into the ceiling, replaces the loose tile. Then she puts on the ensemble.

Now she looks just like she did when she had breakfast with Mom this morning.

She carries her plank down the street to Blooming Greens, where it's legal to carry them but not to put them on the 'crete. She flashes her passport at the border post, walks a quarter of a mile down crisp new sidewalks, and up to the house where the porch light is on.

Mom's sitting in the den, in front of her computer, as usual. Mom works for the Feds. Feds don't make much money, but they have to work hard, to show their loyalty.

Y.T. goes in and looks at her mother, who has slumped down in her chair, put her hands around her face almost like she's vogueing, put bare stockinged feet up. She wears these awful cheap Fed stockings that are like scouring cloth, and when she walks, her thighs rub together underneath her skirt and make a rasping noise. There is a heavy-duty Ziploc bag on the table, full of water that used to be ice a couple of hours ago. Y.T. looks at Mom's left arm. She has rolled up her sleeve to expose the fresh bruise, just above her elbow, where they put the blood-pressure cuff. Weekly Fed polygraph test.

"Is that you?" Mom shouts, not realizing that Y.T.'s in the room.

Y.T. retreats into the kitchen so she won't surprise her mother. "Yeah, Mom," she shouts back. "How was your day?"

"I'm tired," Mom says. It's what she always says.

Y.T. pinches a beer from the fridge and starts running a hot bath. It makes a roaring sound that relaxes her, like the white-noise generator on Mom's nightstand.

13

The Nipponese businessman lies cut in segments on The Black Sun's floor. Surprisingly (he looks so real when he's in one piece), no flesh, blood, or organs are visible through the new cross-sections that Hiro's sword made through his body. He is nothing more than a thin shell of epidermis, an incredibly complex inflatable doll. But the air does not rush out of him, he fails to collapse, and you can look into the aperture of a sword cut and see, instead of bones and meat, the back of the skin on the other side.

It breaks the metaphor. The avatar is not acting like a real body. It reminds all The Black Sun's patrons that they are living in a fantasy world. People hate to be reminded of this.

When Hiro wrote The Black Sun's sword-fighting algorithms —code that was later picked up and adopted by the entire Metaverse—he discovered that there was no good way to handle the aftermath. Avatars are not supposed to die. Not supposed to fall apart. The creators of the Metaverse had not been morbid enough to foresee a demand for this kind of thing. But the whole point of a sword fight is to cut someone up and kill them. So Hiro had to kludge something together, in order that the Metaverse would not, over time, become littered with inert, dismembered avatars that never decayed.

So the first thing that happens, when someone loses a sword fight, is that his computer gets disconnected from the global network that is the Metaverse. He gets chucked right out of the system. It is the closest simulation of death that the Metaverse can offer, but all it really does is cause the user a lot of annoyance.

Furthermore, the user finds that he can't get back into the Metaverse for a few minutes. He can't log back on. This is because his avatar, dismembered, is still in the Metaverse, and it's a rule that your avatar can't exist in two places at once. So the user can't get back in until his avatar has been disposed of.

Disposal of hacked-up avatars is taken care of by Graveyard Daemons, a new Metaverse feature that Hiro had to invent. They are small lithe persons swathed in black, like ninjas, not even their eyes showing. They are quiet and efficient. Even as Hiro is stepping back from the hacked-up body of his former opponent, they are emerging from invisible trapdoors in The Black Sun's floor, climbing up out of the netherworld, converging on the fallen businessman. Within seconds, they have stashed the body parts into black bags. Then they climb back down through their secret trapdoors and vanish into hidden tunnels beneath The Black Sun's floor. A couple of curious patrons try to follow them, try to pry open the trapdoors, but their avatars' fingers find nothing but smooth matte black. The tunnel system is accessible only to the Graveyard Daemons.

And, incidentally, to Hiro. But he rarely uses it.

The Graveyard Daemons will take the avatar to the Pyre, an eternal, underground bonfire beneath the center of The Black Sun, and burn it. As soon as the flames consume the avatar, it will vanish from the Metaverse, and then its owner will be able to sign on as usual, creating a new avatar to run around in. But, hopefully, he will be more cautious and polite the next time around.

_____ Hiro looks up into the circle of applauding, whistling, and cheering avatars and notes that they are fading out. The entire Black Sun now looks like it is being projected on gauze. On the other side of that gauze, bright lights shine through, overwhelming the image. Then it disappears entirely.

He peels off his goggles and finds himself standing in the parking lot of the U-Stor-It, holding a naked katana.

The sun has just gone down. A couple of dozen people are standing around him at a great distance, shielding themselves behind parked cars, awaiting his next move. Most of them are pretty scared, but a few of them are just plain excited.

Vitaly Chernobyl is standing in the open door of their 20-by-30. His hairdo is backlighted. It has been petrified by means of egg whites and other proteins. These substances refract the light and throw off tiny little spectral fragments, a cluster-bombed rainbow. Right now, a miniature image of The Black Sun is being projected onto Vitaly's ass by Hiro's computer. He is rocking unsteadily from foot to foot, as though standing on both of them at the same time is too complicated to deal with this early in the day, and he hasn't decided which one to use.

"You're blocking me," Hiro says.

"It's time to go," Vitaly says.

"You're telling me it's time to go? I've been waiting for you to wake up for an hour."

As Hiro approaches, Vitaly watches his sword uncertainly. Vitaly's eyes are dry and red, and on his lower lip he is sporting a chancre the size of a tangerine.

"Did you win your sword fight?"

"Of course I won the fucking sword fight," Hiro says. "I'm the greatest sword fighter in the world."

"And you wrote the software."

"Yeah. That, too," Hiro says.

_____ After Vitaly Chernobyl and the Meltdowns arrived in Long Beach on one of those hijacked ex-Soviet refugee freighters, they fanned out across southern California looking for expanses of reinforced concrete that were as vast and barren as the ones they had left behind in Kiev. They weren't homesick. They needed such environments in order to practice their art.

The L.A. River was a natural site. And there were plenty of nice overpasses. All they had to do was follow skateboarders to the secret places they had long since discovered. Thrashers and nuclear fuzz-grunge collectives thrive in the same environment. That's where Vitaly and Hiro are going right now.

Vitaly has a really old VW Vanagon, the kind with a pop-top that turns it into a makeshift camper. He used to live in it, staying on the street or in various Snooze 'n' Cruise franchises, until he met up with Hiro Protagonist. Now, the ownership of the Vanagon is subject to dispute, because Vitaly owes Hiro more money than it is technically worth. So they share it.

They drive the Vanagon around to the other side of the U-Stor-It, honking the horn and flashing the lights in order to shoo a hundred little kids away from the loading dock. It's not a playground, kids.

They pick their way down a broad corridor, excusing themselves every inch of the way as they step over little Mayan encampments and Buddhist shrines and white trash stoned on Vertigo, Apple Pie, Fuzzy Buzzy, Narthex, Mustard, and the like. The floor needs sweeping: used syringes, crack vials, charred spoons, pipe stems. There are also many little tubes, about thumb sized, transparent plastic with a red cap on one end. They might be crack vials, but the caps are still on them, and pipeheads wouldn't be so fastidious as to replace the lid on an empty vial. It must be something new Hiro hasn't heard of before, the McDonald's styrofoam burger box of drug containers.

They push through a fire door into another section of the U-Stor-It, which looks the same as the last one (everything looks the same in America, there are no transitions now). Vitaly owns the third locker on the right, a puny 5-by-10 that he is actually using for its intended purpose: storage.

Vitaly steps up to the door and commences trying to remember the combination to the padlock, which involves a certain amount of random guessing. Finally, the lock snaps and pops open. Vitaly shoots the bolt and swings the door open, sweeping a clean half-circle through the drug paraphernalia. Most of the 5-by-10 is occupied by a couple of large four-wheeled flatbed handcarts piled high with speakers and amps.

Hiro and Vitaly wheel the carts down to the loading dock, put the stuff into the Vanagon, and then return the empty carts to the 5-by-10. Technically, the carts are community property, but no one believes that.

The drive to the scene of the concert is long, made longer by the fact that Vitaly, rejecting the technocentric L.A. view of the universe in which Speed is God, likes to stay on the surface and drive at about thirty-five miles per hour. Traffic is not great, either. So Hiro jacks his computer into the cigarette lighter and goggles into the Metaverse.

He is no longer connected to the network by a fiber-optic cable, and so all his communication with the outside world has to take place via radio waves, which are much slower and less reliable. Going into The Black Sun would not be practical—it would look and sound terrible, and the other patrons would look at him as if he were some kind of black-and-white person. But there's no problem with going into his office, because that's generated within the guts of his computer, which is sitting on his lap; he doesn't need any communication with the outside world for that.

He materializes in his office, in his nice little house in the old hacker neighborhood just off the Street. It is all quite Nipponese: tatami mats cover the floor. His desk is a great, ruddy slab of rough-sawn mahogany. Silvery cloud-light filters through rice-paper walls. A panel in front of him slides open to reveal a garden, complete with babbling brook and steelhead trout jumping out from time to time to grab flies. Technically speaking, the pond should be full of carp, but Hiro is American enough to think of carp as inedible dinosaurs that sit on the bottom and eat sewage.

There is something new: A globe about the size of a grapefruit, a perfectly detailed rendition of Planet Earth, hanging in space at arm's length in front of his eyes. Hiro has heard about this but never seen it. It is a piece of CIC software called, simply, Earth. It is the user interface that CIC uses to keep track of every bit of spatial information that it owns—all the maps, weather data, architectural plans, and satellite surveillance stuff.

Hiro has been thinking that in a few years, if he does really well in the intel biz, maybe he will make enough money to subscribe to Earth and get this thing in his office. Now it is suddenly here, free of charge. The only explanation he can come up with is that Juanita must have given it to him.

But first things first. The Babel/Infocalypse card is still in his avatar's pocket. He takes it out.

One of the rice-paper panels that make up the walls of his office slides open. On the other side of it, Hiro can see a large, dimly lit room that wasn't there before; apparently Juanita came in and made a major addition to his house as well. A man walks into the office.

The Librarian daemon looks like a pleasant, fiftyish, silver-haired, bearded man with bright blue eyes, wearing a V-neck sweater over a work shirt, with a coarsely woven, tweedy-looking wool tie. The tie is loosened, the sleeves pushed up. Even though he's just a piece of software, he has reason to be cheerful; he can move through the nearly infinite stacks of information in the Library with the agility of a spider dancing across a vast web of cross-references. The Librarian is the only piece of CIC software that costs even more than Earth; the only thing he can't do is think.

"Yes, sir," the Librarian says. He is eager without being obnoxiously chipper; he clasps his hands behind his back, rocks forward slightly on the balls of his feet, raises his eyebrows expectantly over his half-glasses.

"Babel's a city in Babylon, right?"

"It *was* a *legendary* city," the Librarian says. "Babel is a Biblical term for Babylon. The word is Semitic; Bab means gate and El means God, so Babel means 'Gate of God.' But it is probably also somewhat onomatopoeic, imitating someone who speaks in an incomprehensible tongue. The Bible is full of puns."

"They built a tower to Heaven and God knocked it down."

"This is an anthology of common misconceptions. God did not do anything to the Tower itself. 'And the LORD said, "Behold, they are one people, and they have all one language; and this is only the beginning of what they will do; and nothing that they propose to do will now be impossible for them. Come, let us go down, and there confuse their language, that they may not understand one another's speech." So the LORD scattered them abroad from there over the face of all the earth, and they left off building the city. Therefore its name was called Babel, because there the LORD confused the language of all the earth.' Genesis 11:6–9, Revised Standard Version."

"So the tower wasn't knocked down. It just went on hiatus."

"Correct. It was not knocked down."

"But that's bogus."

"Bogus?"

"Provably false. Juanita believes that nothing is provably true or provably false in the Bible. Because if it's provably false, then the Bible is a lie, and if it's provably true, then the existence of God is proven and there's no room for faith. The Babel story is provably false, because if they built a tower to Heaven and God *didn't* knock it down, then it would still be around somewhere, or at least a visible remnant of it."

"In assuming that it was very tall, you are relying on an obsolete reading. The tower is described, literally, as 'its top with the heavens.' For many centuries, this was interpreted to mean that its top was so high that it was in the heavens. But in the last century or so, as actual Babylonian ziggurats have been excavated, astrological diagrams—pictures of the heavens—have been found inscribed into their tops."

"Oh. Okay, so the *real* story is that a tower was built with heavenly diagrams carved into its top. Which is far more plausible than a tower that reaches to the heavens."

"More than plausible," the Librarian reminds him. "Such structures have actually been found."

"Anyway, you're saying that when God got angry and came down on them, the tower itself wasn't affected. But they had to stop building the tower because of an informational disaster— they couldn't talk to each other."

" 'Disaster' is an astrological term meaning 'bad star,' " the Librarian points out. "Sorry—but due to my internal structure, I'm a sucker for non sequiturs."

"That's okay, really," Hiro says. "You're a pretty decent piece of ware. Who wrote you, anyway?"

"For the most part I write myself," the Librarian says. "That is, I have the innate ability to learn from experience. But this ability was originally coded into me by my creator."

"Who wrote you? Maybe I know him," Hiro says. "I know a lot of hackers."

"I was not coded by a professional hacker, per se, but by a researcher at the Library of Congress who taught himself how to code," the Librarian says. "He devoted himself to the common problem of sifting through vast amounts of irrelevant detail in order to find significant gems of information. His name was Dr. Emanuel Lagos."

"I've heard the name," Hiro says. "So he was kind of a meta-librarian. That's funny, I guessed he was one of those old CIA spooks who hangs around in the CIC."

"He never worked with the CIA."

"Okay. Let's get some work done. Look up every piece of free information in the Library that contains L. Bob Rife and arrange it in chronological order. The emphasis here is on *free.*"

"Television and newspapers, yes, sir. One moment, sir," the Librarian says. He turns around and exits on crepe soles. Hiro turns his attention to Earth.

The level of detail is fantastic. The resolution, the clarity, just the look of it, tells Hiro, or anyone else who knows computers, that this piece of software is some heavy shit.

It's not just continents and oceans. It looks exactly like the earth would look from a point in geosynchronous orbit directly above L.A., complete with weather systems—vast spinning galaxies of clouds, hovering just above the surface of the globe, casting gray shadows on the oceans—and polar ice caps, fading and fragmenting into the sea. Half of the globe is illuminated by sunlight, and half is dark. The terminator—the line between night and day—has just swept across L.A. and is now creeping across the Pacific, off to the west.

Everything is going in slow motion. Hiro can see the clouds change shape if he watches them long enough. Looks like a clear night on the East Coast.

Something catches his attention, moving rapidly over the surface of the globe. He thinks it must be a gnat. But there are no gnats in the Metaverse. He tries to focus on it. The computer, bouncing low-powered lasers off his cornea, senses this change in emphasis, and then Hiro gasps as he seems to plunge downward toward the globe, like a space-walking astronaut who has just fallen out of his orbital groove. When he finally gets it under control, he's just a few hundred miles above the earth, looking down at a solid bank of clouds, and he can see the gnat gliding along below him. It's a low-flying CIC satellite, swinging north to south in a polar orbit.

"Your information, sir," the Librarian says.

Hiro startles and glances up. Earth swings down and out of his field of view and there is the Librarian, standing in front of the desk, holding out a hypercard. Like any librarian in Reality, this daemon can move around without audible footfalls.

"Can you make a little more noise when you walk? I'm easily startled," Hiro says.

"It is done, sir. My apologies."

Hiro reaches out for the hypercard. The Librarian takes half a step forward and leans toward him. This time, his foot makes a soft noise on the tatami mat, and Hiro can hear the white noise of his trousers sliding over his leg.

Hiro takes the hypercard and looks at it. The front is labeled

> *Results of Library search on:*
> *Rife, Lawrence Robert, 1948–*

He flips the card over. The back is divided into several dozen fingernail-sized icons. Some of them are little snapshots of the front pages of newspapers. Many of them are colorful, glowing rectangles: miniature television screens showing live video.

"That's impossible," Hiro says. "I'm sitting in a VW van, okay? I'm jacked in over a cellular link. You couldn't have moved that much video into my system that fast."

"It was not necessary to move anything," the Librarian says. "All existing video on L. Bob Rife was collected by Dr. Lagos and placed in the Babel/Infocalypse stack, which you have in your system."

"Oh."

14

Hiro stares at the miniature TV in the upper left corner of the card. It zooms toward him until it's about the size of a twelve-inch low-def television set at arm's length. Then the video image begins to play. It's very poor eight-millimeter film footage of a high school football game in the sixties. No soundtrack.

"What is this game?"

The Librarian says, "Odessa, Texas, 1965. L. Bob Rife is a fullback, number eight in the dark uniform."

"This is more detail than I need. Can you summarize some of these things?"

"No. But I can list the contents briefly. The stack contains eleven high school football games. Rife was on the second-string Texas all-state team in his senior year. Then he proceeded to Rice on an academic scholarship and walked onto the football team, so there are also fourteen tapes of college games. Rife majored in communications."

"Logically enough, considering what he became."

"He became a television sports reporter in the Houston market, so there are fifty hours of footage from this period—mostly outtakes, of course. After two years in this line of work, Rife went into business with his great-uncle, a financier with roots in the oil business. The stack contains a few newspaper stories to that effect, which, as I note from reading them, are all textually related—implying that they came from the same source."

"A press release."

"Then there are no stories for five years."

"He was up to something."

"Then we begin to see more stories, mostly from the Religion sections of Houston newspapers, detailing Rife's contributions to various organizations."

"That sounded like summary to me. I thought you couldn't summarize."

"I can't really. I was quoting a summary that Dr. Lagos made to Juanita Marquez recently, in my presence, when they were reviewing the same data."

"Go on."

"Rife contributed $500 to the Highlands Church of the Baptism by Fire, Reverend Wayne Bedford, head minister; $2,500 to the Pentecostal Youth League of Bayside, Reverend Wayne Bedford, president; $150,000 to the Pentecostal Church of the New Trinity, Reverend Wayne Bedford, founder and patriarch; $2.3 million to Rife Bible College, Reverend Wayne Bedford, President and chairman of the theology department; $20 million to the archaeology department of Rife Bible College, plus $45 million to the astronomy department and $100 million to the computer science department."

"Did these donations take place before hyperinflation?"

"Yes, sir. They were, as the expression goes, real money."

"That Wayne Bedford guy—is this the same Reverend Wayne who runs the Reverend Wayne's Pearly Gates?"

"The same."

"Are you telling me that Rife owns the Reverend Wayne?"

"He owns a majority share in Pearlgate Associates, which is the multinational that runs the Reverend Wayne's Pearly Gates chain."

"Okay, let's keep sifting through this," Hiro says.

Hiro peeps out over his goggles to confirm that Vitaly is still nowhere near the concert. Then he dives back in and continues to go over the video and the news stories that Lagos has compiled.

During the same years that Rife makes his contributions to the Reverend Wayne, he's showing up with increasing frequency in the business section, first in the local papers and later in *The Wall Street Journal* and *The New York Times*. There is a big flurry of publicity—obvious PR plants—after the Nipponese tried to use their old-boy network to shut him out of the telecommunications market there, and he took it to the American public, spending $10 million of his own money on a campaign to convince Americans that the Nipponese were duplicitous schemers. A triumphal cover on *The Economist* after the Nipponese finally knuckled under and let him corner the fiber-optics market in that country and, by extension, most of East Asia.

Finally, then, the lifestyle pieces start coming in. L. Bob Rife has let his publicist know that he wants to show a more human side. There is a personality journalism program that does a puff piece on Rife after he buys a new yacht, surplus, from the U.S. Government.

L. Bob Rife, last of the nineteenth-century monopolists, is shown consulting with his decorator in the captain's quarters. It looks nice as it is, considering that Rife bought this ship from the Navy, but it's not Texan enough for him. He wants it gutted and rebuilt. Then, shots of Rife maneuvering his steerlike body through the narrow passages and steep staircase of the ship's interior—typical boring gray steel Navy scape, which, he assures the interviewer, he is going to have spruced up considerably.

"Y'know, there's a story that when Rockefeller bought himself a yacht, he bought a pretty small one, like a seventy-footer or something. Small by the standards of the day. And when someone asked him why he went and bought himself such a dinky little yacht, he just looked at the guy and said, 'What do you think I am, a Vanderbilt?' Haw! Well, anyway, welcome aboard my yacht."

L. Bob Rife says this while standing on a huge open-air platform elevator along with the interviewer and the whole camera crew. The elevator is going up. In the background is the Pacific Ocean. As Rife is speaking the last part of the line, suddenly the elevator rises up to the top and the camera turns around, and we are looking out across the deck of the aircraft carrier *Enterprise*, formerly of the U.S. Navy, now the personal yacht of L. Bob Rife, who beat out both General Jim's Defense System and Admiral Bob's Global Security in a furious bidding war. L. Bob Rife proceeds to admire the vast, flat open spaces of the carrier's flight deck, likening it to certain parts of Texas. He suggests that it would be amusing to cover part of it with dirt and raise cattle there.

Another profile, this one shot for a business network, apparently made somewhat later: Back on the *Enterprise*, where the captain's office has been massively reworked. L. Bob Rife, Lord of Bandwidth, is sitting behind his desk, having his mustache waxed. Not in the sense that women have their legs waxed. He's having the curl smoothed out and restored. The waxer is a very short Asian woman who does it so delicately that it doesn't even interfere with his talking, mostly about his efforts to extend his cable TV network throughout Korea and into China and link it up with his big fiber-optic trunk line that runs across Siberia and over the Urals.

"Yeah, you know, a monopolist's work is never done. No such thing as a perfect monopoly. Seems like you can never get that last one-tenth of one percent."

"Isn't the government still strong in Korea? You must have more trouble with regulations there."

L. Bob Rife laughs. "Y'know, watching government regulators trying to keep up with the world is my favorite sport. Remember when they busted up Ma Bell?"

"Just barely." The reporter is a woman in her twenties.

"You know what it was, right?"

"Voice communications monopoly."

"Right. They were in the same business as me. The information business. Moving phone conversations around on little tiny copper wires, one at a time. Government busted them up—at the same time when I was starting cable TV franchises in thirty states. Haw! Can you believe that? It's like if they figured out a way to regulate horses at the same time the Model T and the airplane were being introduced."

"But a cable TV system isn't the same as a phone system."

"At that stage it wasn't, cause it was just a local system. But once you get local systems all over the world, all you got to do is hook 'em together and it's a global network. Just as big as the phone system. Except this one carries information ten thousand times faster. It carries images, sound, data, you name it."

——————— A naked PR plant, a half-hour television commercial with no purpose whatsoever other than to let L. Bob Rife tell his side of a particular issue. It seems that a number of Rife's programmers, the people who made his systems run, got together and formed a union—unheard of, for hackers—and filed a suit against Rife, claiming that he had placed audio and video bugs in their homes, in fact placed all of them under twenty-four-hour surveillance, and harassed and threatened some programmers who were making what he called "unacceptable lifestyle choices." For example, when one of his programmers and her husband engaged in oral sex in their own bedroom one night, the next morning she was called into Rife's office, where he called her a slut and a sodomite and told her to clean out her desk. The bad publicity from this so annoyed Rife that he felt the need to blow a few million on some more PR.

"I deal in information," he says to the smarmy, toadying pseudojournalist who "interviews" him. He's sitting in his office in Houston, looking slicker than normal. "All television going out to consumers throughout the world goes through me. Most of the information transmitted to and from the CIC database passes through my networks. The Metaverse—the entire Street—exists by virtue of a network that I own and control.

"But that means, if you'll just follow my reasoning for a bit, that when I have a programmer working under me who is working with that information, he is wielding enormous power. Information is going into his brain. And it's staying there. It travels with him when he goes home at night. It gets all tangled up into his *dreams,* for Christ's sake. He talks to his wife about it. And, goddamn it, he doesn't have any right to that information. If I was running a car factory, I wouldn't let workers drive the cars home or borrow tools. But that's what I do at five o'clock each day, all over the world, when my hackers go home from work.

"When they used to hang rustlers in the old days, the last thing they would do is piss their pants. That was the ultimate sign, you see, that they had lost control over their own bodies, that they were about to die. See, it's the first function of any organization to control its own sphincters. We're not even doing that. So we're working on refining our management techniques so that we can control that information no matter where it is—on our hard disks or even inside the programmers' heads. Now, I can't say more because I got competition to worry about. But it is my fervent hope that in five or ten years, this kind of thing won't even be an issue."

——————— A half-hour episode of a science news program, this one on the controversial new subject of infoastronomy, the search for radio signals coming from other solar systems. L. Bob Rife has taken a personal interest in the subject; as various national governments auction off their possessions, he has purchased a string of radio observatories and hooked them together, using his fabled fiber-optic net, to turn them into a single giant antenna as big as the whole earth. He is scanning the skies twenty-four hours a day, looking for radio waves that mean something—radio waves carrying information from other civilizations. And why, asks the interviewer—a celebrity professor from MIT—why would a simple oilman be interested in such a high-flown, abstract pursuit?

"I just about got this planet all sewn up."

Rife delivers this line with an incredibly sardonic and contemptuous twang, the exaggerated accent of a cowboy who suspects that some Yankee pencilneck is looking down his nose at him.

——————— Another news piece, this one apparently done a few years later. Again we are on the *Enterprise,* but this time the atmosphere is different again. The top deck has been turned into an open-air refugee camp. It is swarming with Bangladeshis that L. Bob Rife plucked out of the Bay of Bengal after their country washed into the ocean in a series of massive floods, caused by deforestation farther upstream in India—hydrological warfare. The camera pans to look out over the edge of the flight deck, and down below, we see the first beginnings of the Raft: a relatively small collection of a few hundred boats that have glommed onto the *Enterprise*, hoping for a free ride across to America.

Rife's walking among the people, handing out Bible comics and kisses to little kids. They cluster around with broad smiles, pressing their palms together and bowing. Rife bows back, very awkwardly, but there's no gaiety on his face. He's deadly serious.

"Mr. Rife, what's your opinion of the people who say you're just doing this as a self-aggrandizing publicity stunt?" This interviewer is trying to be more of a Bad Cop.

"Shit, if I took time out to have an opinion about everything, I wouldn't get any work done," L. Bob Rife says. "You should ask these people what they think."

"You're telling me that this refugee assistance program has nothing to do with your public image?"

"Nope. L—"

There's an edit and they cut away to the journalist, pontificating into the camera. Rife was on the verge of delivering a sermon, Hiro senses, but they cut him off.

But one of the true glories of the Library is that it has so many outtakes. Just because a piece of videotape never got edited into a broadcast program doesn't mean it's devoid of intel value. CIC long ago stuck its fingers into the networks' videotape libraries. All of those outtakes—millions of hours of footage—have not actually been uploaded to the Library in digital form yet. But you can send in a request, and CIC will go and pull that videotape off the shelf for you and play it back.

Lagos has already done it. The tape is right there.

"Nope. Look. The Raft is a media event. But in a much more profound, general sense than you can possibly imagine."

"Oh."

"It's created by the media in that without the media, people wouldn't know it was here, Refus wouldn't come out and glom onto it the way they do. And it sustains the media. It creates a lot of information flow—movies, news reports—you know."

"So you're creating your own news event to make money off the information flow that it creates?" says the journalist, desperately trying to follow. His tone of voice says that this is all a waste of videotape. His weary attitude suggests that this is not the first time Rife has flown off on a bizarre tangent.

"Partly. But that's only a very crude explanation. It really goes a lot deeper than that. You've probably heard the expression that the Industry feeds off of biomass, like a whale straining krill from the ocean."

"I've heard the expression, yes."

"That's my expression. I made it up. An expression like that is just like a virus, you know—it's a piece of information—data— that spreads from one person to the next. Well, the function of the Raft is to bring more biomass. To renew America. Most countries are static, all they need to do is keep having babies. But America's like this big old clanking, smoking machine that just lumbers across the landscape scooping up and eating everything in sight. Leaves behind a trail of garbage a mile wide. Always needs more fuel. Ever read the story about the labyrinth and the minotaur?"

"Sure. That was on Crete, right?" The journalist only answers out of sarcasm; he can't believe he's here listening to this, he wants to fly back to L.A. yesterday.

"Yeah. Every year, the Greeks had to pony up a few virgins and send them to Crete as tribute. Then the king put them into the labyrinth, and the minotaur ate them up. I used to read that story when I was a kid and wonder who the hell these guys were, on Crete, that everyone else was so scared of them that they would just meekly give up their children to be eaten, every year. They must have been some mean sons of bitches.

"Now I have a different perspective on it. America must look, to those poor little buggers down there, about the same as Crete looked to those poor Greek suckers. Except that there's no coercion involved. Those people down there give up their children willingly. Send them into the labyrinth by the millions to be eaten up. The Industry feeds on them and spits back images, sends out movies and TV programs, over my networks, images of wealth and exotic things beyond their wildest dreams, back to those people, and it gives them something to dream about, something to aspire to. And that is the function of the Raft. It's just a big old krill carrier."

Finally the journalist gives up on being a journalist, just starts to slag L. Bob Rife openly. He's had it with this guy. "That's disgusting. I can't believe you can think about people that way."

"Shit, boy, get down off your high horse. Nobody really gets eaten. It's just a figure of speech. They come here, they get decent jobs, find Christ, buy a Weber grill, and live happily ever after. What's wrong with that?"

Rife is pissed. He's yelling. Behind him, the Bangladeshis are picking up on his emotional vibes and becoming upset themselves. Suddenly, one of them, an incredibly gaunt man with a long drooping mustache, runs in front of the camera and begins to shout: "a ma la ge zen ba dam gal nun ka aria su su na an da . . . " The sounds spread from him to his neighbors, spreading across the flight deck like a wave.

"Cut," the journalist says, turning into the camera. "Just cut. The Babble Brigade has started up again."

The soundtrack now consists of a thousand people speaking in tongues under the high-pitched, shit-eating chuckles of L. Bob Rife.

"This is the miracle of tongues," Rife shouts above the tumult. "I can understand every word these people are saying. Can you, brother?"

_____ "Yo! Snap out of it, pod!"

Hiro looks up from the card. No one is in his office except for the Librarian.

The image loses focus and veers upward and out of his field of view. Hiro is looking out the windshield of the Vanagon. Someone has just yanked his goggles off his face—not Vitaly.

"I'm out here, gogglehead!"

Hiro looks out the window. It's Y.T., hanging onto the side of the van with one hand, holding his goggles in the other.

"You spend too much time goggled in," she says. "Try a little Reality, man."

"Where we are going," Hiro says, "we're going to get more Reality than I can handle."

_____ As Hiro and Vitaly approach the vast freeway overpass where tonight's concert is to take place, the solid ferrous quality of the Vanagon attracts MagnaPoons like a Twinkie draws cockroaches. If they knew that Vitaly Chernobyl himself was in the van, they'd go crazy, they'd stall the van's engine. But right now, they'll poon anything that might be headed toward the concert.

When they get closer to the overpass, it becomes a lost cause trying to drive at all, the thrashers are so thick and numerous. It's like putting on crampons and trying to walk through a room full of puppies. They have to nose their way along, tapping the horn, flashing the lights.

Finally, they get to the flatbed semi that constitutes the stage for tonight's concert. Next to it is another semi, full of amps and other sound gear. The drivers of the trucks, an oppressed minority of two, have retreated into the cab of the sound truck to smoke cigarettes and glare balefully at the swarm of thrashers, their sworn enemies in the food chain of the highways. They will not voluntarily come out until five in the morning, when the way has been made plain.

A couple of the other Meltdowns are standing around smoking cigarettes, holding them between two fingers in the Slavic style, like darts. They stomp the cigarettes out on the concrete with their cheap vinyl shoes, run up to the Vanagon, and begin to haul out the sound equipment. Vitaly puts on goggles, hooks himself into a computer on the sound truck, and begins tuning the system. There's a 3-D model of the overpass already in memory. He has to figure out how to sync the delays on all the different speaker clusters to maximize the number of nasty, clashing echoes.

15

The warm-up band, Blunt Force Trauma, gets rolling at about 9:00 P.M. On the first power chord, a whole stack of cheap pre-owned speakers shorts out; its wires throw sparks into the air, sending an arc of chaos through the massed skateboarders. The sound truck's electronics isolate the bad circuit and shut it off before anything or anyone gets hurt. Blunt Force Trauma play a kind of speed reggae heavily influenced by the antitechnological ideas of the Meltdowns.

These guys will probably play for an hour, then there will be a couple of hours of Vitaly Chernobyl and the Meltdowns to look forward to. And if Sushi K shows up, he's welcome to make a guest appearance at the mike.

Just in case that actually happens, Hiro pulls back from the delirious center of the crowd and begins to orbit back and forth along its fringes. Y.T.'s in there somewhere, but no point in trying to track her down. She would be embarrassed, anyway, to be seen with an oldster like Hiro.

Now that the concert is up and running, it will take care of itself. There's not much more for Hiro to do. Besides, interesting things happen along borders—transitions—not in the middle where everything is the same. There may be something happening along the border of the crowd, back where the lights fade into the shade of the overpass.

The fringe crowd looks pretty typical for the wrong side of an L.A. overpass in the middle of the night. There's a good-sized shantytown of hardcore Third World unemployables, plus a scattering of schizophrenic first worlders who have long ago burned their brains to ash in the radiant heat of their own imaginings. A lot of them have emerged from their overturned dumpsters and refrigerator boxes to stand on tiptoe at the edge of the crowd and peer into the noise and light. Some of them look sleepy and awed, and some—stocky Latino men—look amused by the whole thing, passing cigarettes back and forth and shaking their heads in disbelief.

This is Crips turf. The Crips wanted to provide security, but Hiro, a student of Altamont, decided to take the risk of snubbing them. He hired The Enforcers to do it instead.

So every few dozen feet there's a large man with erect posture wearing an acid green windbreaker with ENFORCER spelled out across the back. Very conspicuous, which is how they like it. But it's all done with electropigment, so if there's trouble, these guys can turn themselves black by flipping a lapel switch. And they can make themselves bulletproof just by zipping the wind-breakers up the front. Right now, it's a warm night, and most of them are leaving their uniforms open to the cool breezes. Some of them are just coasting, but most of them are attentive, keeping their eyes on the crowd, not the band.

Seeing all of those soldiers, Hiro looks for the general and soon finds him: a small, stout black guy, a pint-sized weightlifter type. He's wearing the same windbreaker as the others, but there's an additional layer of bulletproof vest underneath, and clipped onto that he's got a nice assortment of communications gear and small, clever devices for hurting people. He's doing a lot of jog-ging back and forth, swiveling his head from side to side, mum-bling quick bursts into his headset like a football coach on the sidelines.

Hiro notices a tall man in his late thirties, distinguished goatee, wearing a very nice charcoal gray suit. Hiro can see the diamonds in his tie pin flashing from a hundred feet away. He knows that if he gets up closer he will be able to see the word "Crips" spelled out in blue sapphires, nestled among those diamonds. He's got his own security detail of half a dozen other guys in suits. Even though they aren't doing security, they couldn't help sending along a token delegation to show the colors.

——————— This is a non sequitur that has been nibbling on the edges of Hiro's mind for the last ten minutes: Laser light has a particular kind of gritty intensity, a molecular purity reflecting its origins. Your eye notices this, somehow knows that it's unnat-ural. It stands out anywhere, but especially under a dirty overpass in the middle of the night. Hiro keeps getting flashes of it in his peripheral vision, keeps glancing over to track down its source. It's obvious to him, but no one else seems to notice.

Someone in this overpass, somewhere, is bouncing a laser beam off Hiro's face.

It's annoying. Without being too obvious about it, he changes his course slightly, wanders over to a point downwind of a trash fire that's burning in a steel drum. Now he's standing in the middle of a plume of diluted smoke that he can smell but can't quite see.

But the next time the laser darts into his face, it scatters off a million tiny, ashy particulates and reveals itself as a pure geometric line in space, pointing straight back to its source.

It's a gargoyle, standing in the dimness next to a shanty. Just in case he's not already conspicuous enough, he's wearing a suit. Hiro starts walking toward him.

Gargoyles represent the embarrassing side of the Central Intelligence Corporation. Instead of using laptops, they wear their computers on their bodies, broken up into separate modules that hang on the waist, on the back, on the headset. They serve as human surveillance devices, recording everything that happens around them. Nothing looks stupider; these getups are the modern-day equivalent of the slide-rule scabbard or the calculator pouch on the belt, marking the user as belonging to a class that is at once above and far below human society. They are a boon to Hiro because they embody the worst stereotype of the CIC stringer. They draw all of the attention. The payoff for this self-imposed ostracism is that you can be in the Metaverse all the time, and gather intelligence all the time.

The CIC brass can't stand these guys because they upload staggering quantities of useless information to the database, on the off chance that some of it will eventually be useful. It's like writing down the license number of every car you see on your way to work each morning, just in case one of them will be involved in a hit-and-run accident. Even the CIC database can only hold so much garbage. So, usually, these habitual gargoyles get kicked out of CIC before too long.

This guy hasn't been kicked out yet. And to judge from the

quality of his equipment—which is very expensive—he's been at it for a while. So he must be pretty good.

If so, what's he doing hanging around this place?

"Hiro Protagonist," the gargoyle says as Hiro finally tracks him down in the darkness beside a shanty. "CIC stringer for eleven months. Specializing in the Industry. Former hacker, security guard, pizza deliverer, concert promoter." He sort of mumbles it, not wanting Hiro to waste his time reciting a bunch of known facts.

The laser that kept jabbing Hiro in the eye was shot out of this guy's computer, from a peripheral device that sits above his goggles in the middle of his forehead. A long-range retinal scanner. If you turn toward him with your eyes open, the laser shoots out, penetrates your iris, tenderest of sphincters, and scans your retina. The results are shot back to CIC, which has a database of several tens of millions of scanned retinas. Within a few seconds, if you're in the database already, the owner finds out who you are. If you're not already in the database, well, you are now.

Of course, the user has to have access privileges. And once he gets your identity, he has to have more access privileges to find out personal information about you. This guy, apparently, has a lot of access privileges. A lot more than Hiro.

"Name's Lagos," the gargoyle says.

So this is the guy. Hiro considers asking him what the hell he's doing here. He'd love to take him out for a drink, talk to him about how the Librarian was coded. But he's pissed off. Lagos is being rude to him (gargoyles are rude by definition).

"You here on the Raven thing? Or just that fuzz-grunge tip you've been working on for the last, uh, thirty-six days approximately?" Lagos says.

Gargoyles are no fun to talk to. They never finish a sentence. They are adrift in a laser-drawn world, scanning retinas in all directions, doing background checks on everyone within a thousand yards, seeing everything in visual light, infrared, millimeter-wave radar, and ultrasound all at once. You think they're talking to you, but they're actually poring over the credit record of some stranger on the other side of the room, or identifying the make and model of airplanes flying overhead. For all he knows, Lagos is standing there measuring the length of Hiro's cock through his trousers while they pretend to make conversation.

"You're the guy who's working with Juanita, right?" Hiro says.

"Or she's working with me. Or something like that."

"She said she wanted me to meet you."

For several seconds Lagos is frozen. He's ransacking more data. Hiro wants to throw a bucket of water on him.

"Makes sense," he says. "You're as familiar with the Metaverse as anyone. Freelance hacker—that's exactly right."

"Exactly right for what? No one wants freelance hackers anymore."

"The corporate assembly-line hackers are suckers for infection. They're going to go down by the thousands, just like Sennacherib's army before the walls of Jerusalem," Lagos says.

"Infection? Sennacherib?"

"And you can defend yourself in Reality, too—that'll be good if you ever go up against Raven. Remember, his knives are as sharp as a molecule. They'll go through a bulletproof jacket like lingerie."

"Raven?"

"You'll probably see him tonight. Don't mess with him."

"Okay," Hiro says. "I'll look out for him."

"That's not what I said," Lagos says. "I said, don't mess with him."

"Why not?"

"It's a dangerous world," Lagos says. "Getting more dangerous all the time. So we don't want to upset the balance of terror. Just think about the Cold War."

"Yup." All Hiro wants to do now is walk away and never see this guy again, but he won't wind up the conversation.

"You're a hacker. That means you have deep structures to worry about, too."

"Deep structures?"

"Neurolinguistic pathways in your brain. Remember the first time you learned binary code?"

"Sure."

"You were forming pathways in your brain. Deep structures. Your nerves grow new connections as you use them—the axons split and push their way between the dividing glial cells—your bioware self-modifies—the software becomes part of the hardware. So now you're vulnerable—all hackers are vulnerable—to a *nam-shub*. We have to look out for each other."

"What's a nam-shub? Why am I vulnerable to it?"

"Just don't stare into any bitmaps. Anyone try to show you a raw bitmap lately? Like, in the Metaverse?"

Interesting. "Not to me personally, but now that you mention it, this Brandy came up to my friend—"

"A cult prostitute of Asherah. Trying to spread the disease. Which is synonymous with evil. Sound melodramatic? Not really. You know, to the Mesopotamians, there was no independent concept of evil. Just disease and ill health. Evil was a synonym for disease. So what does that tell you?"

Hiro walks away, the same way he walks away from psychotic street people who follow him down the street.

"It tells you that evil is a virus!" Lagos calls after him. "Don't let the nam-shub into your operating system!"

Juanita's working with this alien?

_____ Blunt Force Trauma play for a solid hour, segueing from one song into the next with no chink or crevice in the wall of noise. All a part of the aesthetic. When the music stops, their set is over. For the first time, Hiro can hear the exaltation of the crowd. It's a blast of high-pitched noise that he feels in his head, ringing his ears.

But there's a low thudding sound, too, like someone pummeling a bass drum, and for a minute he thinks maybe it's a truck rolling by on the overpass above them. But it's too steady for that, it doesn't die away.

It's behind him. Other people have noticed it, turned to look toward the sound, are scurrying out of the way. Hiro sidesteps, turning to see what it is.

Big and black, to begin with. It does not seem as though such a large man could perch on a motorcycle, even a big chortling Harley like this one.

Correction. It's a Harley with some kind of a sidecar added, a sleek black projectile hanging off to the right, supported on its own wheel. But no one is sitting in the sidecar.

It does not seem as though a man could be this bulky without being fat. But he's not fat at all, he's wearing tight stretchy clothes—like leather, but not quite—that show bones and muscles, but nothing else.

He is riding the Harley so slowly that he would certainly fall over if not for the sidecar. Occasionally he gooses it forward with a flick of the fingers on his clutch hand.

Maybe one reason he looks so big—other than the fact that he really is big—is the fact that he appears totally neckless. His head starts out wide and just keeps getting wider until it merges with his shoulders. At first Hiro thinks it must be some kind of avant-garde helmet. But when the man rolls past him, this great shroud moves and flutters and Hiro sees that it is just his hair, a thick mane of black hair tossed back over his shoulders, trailing down his back almost to his waist.

As he is marveling at this, he realizes that the man has turned his head to look back at him. Or to look in his general direction, anyway. It's impossible to tell exactly what he's looking at because of his goggles, a smooth convex shell over the eyes, interrupted by a narrow horizontal slit.

He is looking at Hiro. He gives him the same fuck-you smile that he sported earlier tonight, when Hiro was standing in the entryway to The Black Sun, and he was in a public terminal somewhere.

This is the guy. Raven. This is the guy that Juanita is looking for. The guy Lagos told him not to mess with. And Hiro has seen him before, outside the entrance to The Black Sun. This is the guy who gave the Snow Crash card to Da5id.

The tattoo on his forehead consists of three words, written in block letters: POOR IMPULSE CONTROL.

Hiro startles and actually jumps into the air as Vitaly Chernobyl and the Meltdowns launch into their opening number, "Radiation Burn." It is a tornado of mostly high-pitched noise and distortion, like being flung bodily through a wall of fishhooks.

These days, most states are franchulates or Burbclaves, much too small to have anything like a jail, or even a judicial system. So when someone does something bad, they try to find quick and dirty punishments, like flogging, confiscation of property, public humiliation, or, in the case of people who have a high potential of going on to hurt others, a warning tattoo on a prominent body part. POOR IMPULSE CONTROL. Apparently, this guy went to such a place and lost his temper real bad.

For an instant, a glowing red gridwork is plotted against the side of Raven's face. It rapidly shrinks, all sides converging inward toward the right pupil. Raven shakes his head, turns to look for the source of the laser light, but it's already gone. Lagos has already got his retinal scan.

That's why Lagos is here. He's not interested in Hiro or Vitaly Chernobyl. He's interested in Raven. And somehow, Lagos knew that he was going to be here. And Lagos is somewhere nearby, right now, videotaping the guy, probing the contents of his pockets with radar, recording his pulse and respiration.

Hiro picks up his personal phone. "Y.T.," he says, and it dials Y.T.'s number.

It rings for a long time before she picks it up. It's almost impossible to hear anything over the sound of the concert.

"What the fuck do you want?"

"Y.T., I'm sorry about this. But something's going on. Something big time. I'm keeping one eye on a big biker named Raven."

"The problem with you hackers is you never stop working."

"That's what a hacker is," Hiro says.

"I'll keep an eye on this Raven guy, too," she says, "sometime when I *am* working." Then she hangs up.

16

Raven makes a couple of broad, lazy sweeps along the perimeter of the crowd, going very slowly, looking in all directions. He is annoyingly calm and unhurried.

Then he cuts farther out into the darkness, away from the crowd. He does a little more looking around, checking out the perimeter of the shantytown. And finally, he swings the big Harley around in a trajectory that brings him back to the big important Crip. The guy with the sapphire tie clip and the personal security detail.

Hiro begins weaving through the crowd in that direction, trying not to be too obvious about it. This looks like it's going to be interesting.

As Raven approaches, the bodyguards converge on the head Crip, form a loose protective ring around him. As he comes nearer, all of them back away a step or two, as though the man is surrounded by an invisible force field. He finally comes to a stop, deigns to put his feet on the ground. He flicks a few switches on the handlebars before he steps away from his Harley. Then, anticipating what's next, he stands with his feet apart and his arms up.

One Crip approaches from each side. They don't look real happy about this particular duty, they keep casting sidelong glances at the motorcycle. The head Crip keeps goading them forward with his voice, shooing them toward Raven with his hands. Each one of them has a hand-held metal-detecting wand. They swirl the wands around his body and find nothing at all, not even the tiniest speck of metal, not even coins in his pocket. The man is 100 percent organic. So if nothing else, Lagos's warning about Raven's knife has turned out to be bullshit.

These two Crips walk rapidly back to the main group. Raven begins to follow them. But the head Crip takes a step back, holds both of his hands up in a "stop" motion. Raven stops, stands there, the grin returning to his face.

The head Crip turns away and gestures back toward his black BMW. The rear door of the BMW opens up and a man gets out, a younger, smaller black man in round wire-rims, wearing jeans and big white athletic shoes and typical studentish gear.

The student walks slowly toward Raven, pulling something from his pocket. It's a hand-held device, but much too bulky to be a calculator. It's got a keypad on the top and a sort of window on one end, which the student keeps aiming toward Raven. There's an LED readout above the keypad and a red flashing light underneath that. The student is wearing a pair of headphones that are jacked into a socket on the butt of the device.

For starters, the student aims the window at the ground, then at the sky, then at Raven, keeping his eye on the flashing red light and the LED readout. It has the feel of some kind of religious rite, accepting digital input from the sky spirit and then the ground spirit and then from the black biker angel.

Then he begins to walk slowly toward Raven, one step at a time. Hiro can see the red light flashing intermittently, not following any particular pattern or rhythm.

The student gets to within a yard of Raven and then orbits him a couple of times, always keeping the device aimed inward. When he's finished, he steps back briskly, turns, and aims it toward the motorcycle. When the device is aimed at the motorcycle, the red light flashes much more quickly.

The student walks up to the head Crip, pulling off his headphones, and has a short conversation with him. The Crip listens to the student but keeps his eyes fixed on Raven, nods his head a few times, finally pats the student on his shoulder and sends him back to the BMW.

It was a Geiger counter.

_____ Raven strolls up to the big Crip. They shake hands, a standard plain old Euro-shake, no fancy variations. It's not a real friendly get-together. The Crip has his eyes a little too wide open, Hiro can see the furrows in his brow, everything about his posture and his face screaming out: Get me away from this Martian.

Raven goes back to his radioactive hog, releases a few bungee cords, and picks up a metal briefcase. He hands it to the head Crip, and they shake hands again. Then he turns away, walks slowly and calmly back to the motorcycle, gets on, and putt-putts away.

Hiro would love to stick around and watch some more, but he has the feeling that Lagos has this particular event covered. And besides, he has other business. Two limousines are fighting their way through the crowd, headed for the stage.

_____ The limousines stop, and Nipponese people start to climb out. Dark-clad, unfunky, they stand around awkwardly in the middle of the party/riot, like a handful of broken nails suspended in a colorful jello mold. Finally, Hiro makes bold enough to go up and look into one of the windows to find out if this is who he thinks it is.

Can't see through the smoked glass. He bends down, puts his face right near the window, trying to make it real obvious.

Still no response. Finally, he knocks on the window.

Silence. He looks up at the entourage. They are all watching him. But when he looks up they glance away, suddenly remember to drag on their cigarettes or rub their eyebrows.

There is only one source of light inside the limousine that's bright enough to be visible through the smoked glass, and that is the distinctive inflated rectangle of a television screen.

What the hell. This is America, Hiro is half American, and there's no reason to take this politeness thing to an unhealthy extreme. He hauls the door open and looks into the back of the limousine.

Sushi K is sitting there wedged in between a couple of other young Nipponese men, programmers on his imageering team. His hairdo is turned off, so it just looks like an orange Afro. He is wearing a partly assembled stage costume, apparently expecting to be performing tonight. Looks like he's taking Hiro up on his offer.

He's watching a well-known television program called *Eye Spy*. It is produced by CIC and syndicated through one of the major studios. It is reality television: CIC picks out one of their agents who is involved in a wet operation—doing some actual cloak-and-dagger work—and has him put on a gargoyle rig so that everything he sees and hears is transmitted back to the home base in Langley. This material is then edited into a weekly hour-long program.

Hiro never watches it. Now that he works for CIC, he finds it kind of annoying. But he hears a lot of gossip about the show, and he knows that tonight they are showing the second-to-last episode in a five-part arc. CIC has smuggled a guy onto the Raft, where he is trying to infiltrate one of its many colorful and sadistic pirate bands: the Bruce Lee organization.

Hiro enters the limousine and gets a look at the TV just in time to see Bruce Lee himself, as seen from the point of view of the hapless gargoyle spy, approaching down some dank corridor on a Raft ghost ship. Condensation is dripping from the blade of Bruce Lee's samurai sword.

"Bruce Lee's men have trapped the spy in an old Korean

factory ship in the Core," one of Sushi K's henchmen says, a rapid hissing explanation. "They are looking for him now."

Suddenly, Bruce Lee is pinioned under a brilliant spotlight that makes his trademark diamond grin flash like the arm of a galaxy. In the middle of the screen, a pair of cross hairs swing into place, centered on Bruce Lee's forehead. Apparently, the spy has decided he must fight his way out of this mess and is bringing some powerful CIC weapons system to bear on Bruce Lee's skull. But then a blur comes in from the side, a mysterious dark shape blocking our view of Bruce Lee. The cross hairs are now centered on—what, exactly?

We'll have to wait until next week to find out.

Hiro sits down across from Sushi K and the programmers, next to the television set, so that he can get a TV's-eye view of the man.

"I'm Hiro Protagonist. You got my message, I take it."

"Fabu!" Sushi K cries, using the Nipponese abbreviation of the all-purpose Hollywood adjective "fabulous."

He continues, "Hiro-san, I am deeply indebted to you for this once-in-a-lifetime chance to perform my small works before such an audience." He says the whole thing in Nipponese except for "once-in-a-lifetime chance."

"I must humbly apologize for arranging the whole thing so hastily and haphazardly," Hiro says.

"It pains me deeply that you should feel the need to apologize when you have given me an opportunity that any Nipponese rapper would give anything for—to perform my humble works before actual homeboys from the ghettos of L.A."

"I am profoundly embarrassed to reveal that these fans are not exactly ghetto homeboys, as I must have carelessly led you to believe. They are thrashers. Skateboarders who like both rap music and heavy metal."

"Ah. This is fine, then," Sushi K says. But his tone of voice suggests that it's not really fine at all.

"But there are representatives of the Crips here," Hiro says, thinking very, very fast even by his standards, "and if your performance is well received, as I'm quite certain it will be, they will spread the word throughout their community."

Sushi K rolls down the window. The decibel level quintuples

in an instant. He stares at the crowd, five thousand potential market shares, young people with funkiness on their minds. They've never heard any music before that wasn't perfect. It's either studio-perfect digital sound from their CD players or performance-perfect fuzz-grunge from the best people in the business, the groups that have come to L.A. to make a name for themselves and have actually survived the gladiatorial combat environment of the clubs. Sushi K's face lights up with a combination of joy and terror. Now he actually has to go up there and do it. In front of the seething biomass.

Hiro goes out and paves the way for him. That's easy enough. Then he bails. He's done his bit. No point in wasting time on this puny Sushi K thing when Raven is out there, representing a much larger source of income. So he wanders back out toward the periphery.

"Yo! Dude with the swords," someone says.

Hiro turns around, sees a green-jacketed Enforcer motioning to him. It's the short, powerful guy with the headset, the guy in charge of the security detail.

"Squeaky," he says, extending his hand.

"Hiro," Hiro says, shaking it, and handing over his business card. No particular reason to be coy with these guys. "What can I do for you, Squeaky?"

Squeaky reads the card. He has a kind of exaggerated politeness that is kind of like a military man. He's calm, mature, rolemodelesque, like a high school football coach. "You in charge of this thing?"

"To the extent anyone is."

"Mr. Protagonist, we got a call a few minutes ago from a friend of yours named Y.T."

"What's wrong? Is she okay?"

"Oh, yes, sir, she's just fine. But you know that bug you were talking to earlier?"

Hiro's never heard the term "bug" used this way, but he reckons that Squeaky is referring to the gargoyle, Lagos.

"Yeah."

"Well, there's a situation involving that gentleman that Y.T. sort of tipped us off to. We thought you might want to have a look."

"What's going on?"

"Uh, why don't you come with me. You know, some things are easier to show than to explain verbally."

As Squeaky turns, Sushi K's first rap song begins. His voice sounds tight and tense.

I'm Sushi K and I'm here to say
I like to rap in a different way

Look out Number One in every city
Sushi K rap has all most pretty

My special talking of remarkable words
Is not the stereotyped bucktooth nerd

My hair is big as a galaxy
Cause I attain greater technology

Hiro follows Squeaky away from the crowd, into the dimly lit area on the edge of the shantytown. Up above them on the overpass embankment, he can dimly make out phosphorescent shapes—green-jacketed Enforcers orbiting some strange attractor.

"Watch your step," Squeaky says as they begin to climb up the embankment. "It's slippery in places."

I like to rap about sweetened romance
My fond ambition is of your pants

So here is of special remarkable way
Of this fellow raps named Sushi K

The Nipponese talking phenomenon
Like samurai sword his sharpened tongue

Who raps the East Asia and the Pacific
Prosperity Sphere, to be specific

It's a typical loose slope of dirt and stones that looks like it would wash away in the first rainfall. Sage and cactus and tumbleweeds here and there, all looking scraggly and half-dead from air pollution.

It's hard to see anything clearly, because Sushi K is jumping around down below them on the stage, the brilliant orange rays of his sunburst hairdo are sweeping back and forth across the embankment at a speed that seems to be supersonic, washing grainy, gritty light over the weeds and the rocks and throwing everything into weird, discolored, high-contrast freeze frames.

Sarariman on subway listen
For Sushi K like nuclear fission

Fire-breathing lizard Gojiro
He my always big-time hero

His mutant rap burn down whole block
Start investing now Sushi K stock

It on Nikkei stock exchange
Waxes; other rappers wane

Best investment, make my day
Corporation Sushi K

Squeaky is walking straight uphill, paralleling a fresh motorcycle track that has cut deeply into the loose yellow soil. It consists of a deep, wide track with a narrower one that runs parallel, a couple of feet to the right.

The track gets deeper the farther up they go. Deeper and darker. It looks less and less like a motorcycle rut in loose dirt and more like a drainage ditch for some sinister black effluent.

Coming to America now
Rappers trying to start a row

Say "Stay in Japan, please, listen!
We can't handle competition!"

U.S. rappers booing and hissin'
Ask for rap protectionism

They afraid of Sushi K
Cause their audience go away

He got chill financial backin'
Give those U.S. rappers a smackin'

Sushi K concert machine
Fast efficient super clean

Run like clockwork in a watch
Kick old rappers in the crotch

One of The Enforcers up the hill is carrying a flashlight. As he moves, it sweeps across the ground at a flat angle, briefly illuminating the ground like a searchlight. For an instant, the light shines into the motorcycle rut, and Hiro perceives that it has become a river of bright red, oxygenated blood.

He learn English total immersion
English/Japanese be mergin'

Into super combination
So can have fans in every nation

Hong Kong they speak English, too
Yearn of rappers just like you

Anglophones who live down under
Sooner later start to wonder

When they get they own rap star
Tired of rappers from afar

Lagos is lying on the ground, sprawled across the tire track. He has been slit open like a salmon, with a single smooth-edged cut that begins at his anus and runs up his belly, through the middle of his sternum, all the way up to the point of his jaw. It's not just a superficial slash. It appears to go all the way to his spine in some places. The black nylon straps that hold his computer system to his body have been neatly cut where they cross the midline, and half of the stuff has fallen off into the dust.

So I will get big radio traffic
When you look at demographic

Sushi K research statistic
Make big future look ballistic

Speed of Sushi K growth stock
Put U.S. rappers into shock

17

Jason Breckinridge wears a terracotta blazer. It is the color of Sicily. Jason Breckinridge has never been to Sicily. He may get to go there someday, as a premium. In order to get the free cruise to Sicily, Jason has to accumulate 10,000 Goombata Points.

He begins this quest in a favorable position. By opening up his own Nova Sicilia franchise, he started out with an automatic 3,333 points in the Goombata Point bank. Add to that a one-time-only Citizenship Bonus of 500 points and the balance is starting to look pretty good. The number is stored in the big computer in Brooklyn.

Jason grew up in the western suburbs of Chicago, one of the most highly franchised regions in the country. He attended the University of Illinois business school, racking up a GPA of 2.9567, and did a senior thesis called "The Interaction of the Ethnographic, Financial, and Paramilitary Dimensions of Competition in Certain Markets." This was a case study of turf struggle between Nova Sicilia and Narcolombia franchises in his old neighborhood in Aurora.

Enrique Cortazar ran the failing Narcolombia franchise upon which Jason had hinged his argument. Jason interviewed him several times over the phone, briefly, but never saw Mr. Cortazar face to face.

Mr. Cortazar celebrated Jason's graduation by firebombing the Breckinridges' Omni Horizon van in a parking lot and then firing eleven clips of automatic rifle ammunition through the front wall of their house.

Fortunately, Mr. Caruso, who ran the local string of Nova Sicilia franchulates that was in the process of beating the pants off of Enrique Cortazar, got wind of these attacks before they happened, probably by intercepting signal intelligence from Mr. Cortazar's fleet of poorly secured cellular phones and CB radios. He was able to warn Jason's family in time, so that when all of those bullets flew through their house in the middle of the night, they were enjoying complimentary champagne in an Old Sicilia Inn five miles down Highway 96.

Naturally, when the B-school held its end-of-the-year job fair, Jason made a point of swinging by the Nova Sicilia booth to thank Mr. Caruso for saving everyone in his family from certain death.

"Hey, y'know, it was just, like a neighbor kinda thing, y'know, Jasie boy?" Mr. Caruso said, whacking Jason across the shoulder blades and squeezing his deltoids, which were the size of cantaloupes. Jason did not hit the steroids as hard as he had when he was fifteen, but he was still in great shape.

Mr. Caruso was from New York. He had one of the most popular booths at the job fair. It was being held in a big exhibition space in the Union. The hall had been done up with an imaginary street pattern. Two "highways" divided it up into quadrants, and all the franchise companies and nationalities had their booths along the highways. Burbclaves and other companies had booths hidden among the suburban "streets" within the quadrants. Mr. Caruso's Nova Sicilia booth was right at the intersection of the two highways. Dozens of scrubby B-school grads were lined up there waiting to interview, but Mr. Caruso noticed Jason standing in line and went right up and plucked him out of line and grabbed his deltoids. All the other B-school grads stared at Jason enviously. That made Jason feel good, really special. That was the feeling he got about Nova Sicilia: personalized attention.

"Well, I was going to interview here, of course, and at Mr. Lee's Greater Hong Kong, because I'm real interested in high tech," Jason said, in response to Mr. Caruso's fatherly questioning.

Mr. Caruso gave him an especially hard squeeze. His voice said that he was painfully surprised, but that he didn't necessarily think any less of Jason for it, not yet anyway. "Hong Kong? What would a smart white kid like you want with a fuckin' Nip operation?"

"Well, technically they're not Nips—which is short for Nipponese," Jason said. "Hong Kong is a predominantly Cantonese—"

"They're all Nips," Mr. Caruso said, "and y'know why I say that? Not because I'm a fuckin' racist, because I'm not. Because to them—to those people, y'know, the Nips—we're all foreign devils. That's what they call us. Foreign devils. How d'ya like that?"

Jason just laughed appreciatively.

"After all the good things we did for them. But here in America, Jasie boy, we're all foreign devils, ain't we? We all came from someplace—'cept for the fuckin' Indians. You ain't gonna interview over at the Lakota Nation, are ya?"

"No, sir, Mr. Caruso," Jason said.

"Good thinkin'. I agree with that. I'm gettin' away from my main point, which is that since we all have our own unique ethnic and cultural identities, we have to get a job with an organization that uniquely respects and seeks to preserve those distinctive identities—forging them together into a functionin' whole, y'know?"

"Yes, I see your point, Mr. Caruso," Jason said.

By this point, Mr. Caruso had led him some distance away and was strolling with him down one of the metaphorical Highways o' Opportunity. "Now, can you think of some business organizations that fill that fuckin' bill, Jasie boy?"

"Well . . ."

"Not fuckin' Hong Kong. That's for white people who want to be Japs but can't, didja know that? You don't wanta be a Jap, do ya?"

"Ha ha. No, sir, Mr. Caruso."

"Y'know what I heard?" Mr. Caruso let go of Jason, turned, and stood close to him, chest to chest, his cigar zinging past Jason's ear like a flaming arrow as he gesticulated. This was a confidential portion of the chat, a little anecdote between the two men. "In Japan, if you screw up? You gotta cut off one a your fingers. Chop. Just like that. Honest to God. You don't believe me?"

"I believe you. But that's not all of Japan, sir. Just in the *Yakuza*. The Japanese Mafia."

Mr. Caruso threw back his head and laughed, put his arm around Jason's shoulders again. "Y'know, I like you, Jason, I really do," he said. "The Japanese Mafia. Tell me something, Jason, you ever hear anyone describe our thing as 'The Sicilian Yakuza'? Huh?"

Jason laughed. "No, sir."

"Y'know why that is? Y'know?" Mr. Caruso had come to the serious, meaningful part of his speech.

"Why is that, sir?"

Mr. Caruso wheeled Jason around so that both of them were staring down the length of the highway to the tall effigy of Uncle Enzo, standing above the intersection like the Statue of Liberty.

"Cause there's only one, son. Only one. And you could be a part of it."

"But it's so competitive—"

"What? Listen to this! You got a three-point grade average! You're gonna kick butt, son!"

Mr. Caruso, like any other franchisee, had access to Turfnet, the multiple listing service that Nova Sicilia used to keep track of what it called "opportunity zones." He took Jason back to the booth—right past all of those poor dorks waiting in line, Jason really liked that—and signed onto the network. All Jason had to do was pick out a region.

"I have an uncle who owns a car dealership in southern California," Jason said, "and I know that's a rapidly expanding area, and—"

"Plenty of opportunity zones!" Mr. Caruso said, pounding away on the keyboard with a flourish. He wheeled the monitor around to show Jason a map of the L.A. area blazing with red splotches that represented unclaimed turf sectors. "Take your pick, Jasie boy!"

_____ Now Jason Breckinridge is the manager of Nova Sicilia #5328 in the Valley. He puts on his smart terracotta blazer every morning and drives to work in his Oldsmobile. Lots of young entrepreneurs would be driving BMWs or Acuras, but the organization of which Jason is now a part puts a premium on tradition and family values and does not go in for flashy foreign imports. "If an American car is good enough for Uncle Enzo..."

Jason's blazer has the Mafia logo embroidered on the breast pocket. A letter "G" is worked into the logo, signifying Gambino, which is the division that handles accounts for the L.A. Basin. His name is written underneath: "Jason (The Iron Pumper) Breckinridge." That is the nickname that he and Mr. Caruso came up with a year ago at the job fair in Illinois. Everyone gets to have a nickname, it is a tradition and a mark of pride, and they like you to pick something that says something about you.

As manager of a local office, Jason's job is to portion work out to local contractors. Every morning, he parks his Oldsmobile out front and goes into the office, ducking quickly into the armored doorway to foil possible Narcolombian snipers. This does not prevent them from taking occasional potshots at the big Uncle Enzo that rises up above the franchise, but those signs can take an amazing amount of abuse before they start looking seedy.

Safely inside, Jason signs onto Turfnet. A job list scrolls automatically onto the screen. All Jason has to do is find contractors to handle all of those jobs before he goes home that night, or else he has to take care of them himself. One way or another, they have to get done. The great majority of the jobs are simple deliveries, which he portions out to Kouriers. Then there are collections from delinquent borrowers and from franchisees who depend on Nova Sicilia for their plant security. If it's a first notice, Jason likes to drop by in person, just to show the flag, to emphasize that his organization takes a personal, one-to-one, hands-on, micromanaged approach to debt-related issues. If it's a second or third notice, he usually writes a contract with Deadbeaters International, a high-impact collection agency with whose work he has always been very happy. Then there is the occasional Code H. Jason hates to deal with Code Hs, views them as symptoms of a breakdown in the system of mutual trust that makes society work. But usually these are handled directly from the regional level, and all Jason has to do is aftermath management and spin control.

This morning, Jason is looking especially crisp, his Oldsmobile freshly waxed and polished. Before he goes inside, he plucks a couple of burger wrappers off the parking lot, snipers be damned. He has heard that Uncle Enzo is in the area, and you never knew when he might pull his fleet of limousines and war wagons into a neighborhood franchise and pop in to shake hands with the rank and file. Yes, Jason is going to be working late tonight, burning the oil until he receives word that Uncle Enzo's plane is safely out of the area.

He signs onto Turfnet. A list of jobs scrolls up as usual, not a very long list. Interfranchise activity is way down today, as all the local managers gird, polish, and inspect for the possible arrival of Uncle Enzo. But one of the jobs scrolls up in red letters, a priority job.

Priority jobs are a little unusual. A symptom of bad morale and general slipshoddity. Every job should be a priority job. But every so often, there is something that absolutely can't be delayed or screwed up. A local manager like Jason can't order up a priority job; it has to come from a higher echelon.

Usually, a priority job is a Code H. But Jason notes with relief that this one is a simple delivery. Certain documents are to be hand carried from his office to Nova Sicilia #4649, which is south of downtown.

Way south. Compton. A war zone, longtime stronghold of Narcolombians and Rastafarian gunslingers.

Compton. Why the hell would an office in Compton need a personally signed copy of his financial records? They should be spending all of their time doing Code Hs on the competition, out there.

As a matter of fact, there is a very active Young Mafia group on a certain block in Compton that has just succeeded in driving away all of the Narcolombians and turning the whole area into a Mafia Watch neighborhood. Old ladies are walking the streets again. Children are waiting for schoolbuses and playing hopscotch on sidewalks that recently were stained with blood. It's a fine example; if it can be done on this block, it can be done anywhere.

As a matter of fact, Uncle Enzo is coming to congratulate them in person.

This afternoon.

And #4649 is going to be his temporary headquarters.

The implications are stunning.

Jason has been given a priority job to deliver his records to the very franchise where Uncle Enzo will be taking his espresso this afternoon!

Uncle Enzo is interested in him.

Mr. Caruso claimed he had connections higher up, but could they really go this high?

Jason sits back in his color-coordinated earth-tone swivel chair to consider the very real possibility that in a few days, he's going to be managing a whole region—or even better.

One thing's for sure—this is not a delivery to be entrusted to any Kourier, any punk on a skateboard. Jason is going to trundle his Oldsmobile into Compton personally to drop this stuff off.

18

He's there an hour ahead of schedule. He was shooting for half an hour early, but once he gets a load of Compton—he's heard stories about the place, of course, but my God—he starts driving like a maniac. Cheap, nasty franchises all tend to adopt logos with a lot of bright, hideous yellow in them, and so Alameda Street is clearly marked out before him, a gout of radioactive urine ejected south from the dead center of L.A. Jason aims himself right down the middle, ignoring lane markings and red lights, and puts the hammer down.

Most of the franchises are yellow-logoed, wrong-side-of-the-tracks operations like Uptown, Narcolombia, Caymans Plus, Metazania, and The Clink. But standing out like rocky islands in this swamp are the Nova Sicilia franchulates—beachheads for the Mafia's effort to outduel the overwhelmingly strong Narcolombia.

Shitty lots that even The Clink wouldn't buy always tend to get picked up by economy-minded three-ringers who have just shelled out a million yen for a Narcolombia license and who need some real estate, any real estate, that they can throw a fence around and extraterritorialize. These local franchulates send most of their gross to Medellín in franchising fees and keep barely enough to pay overhead.

Some of them try to scam, to sneak a few bills into their pocket when they think the security camera isn't watching, and run down the street to the nearest Caymans Plus or The Alps franchulate, which hover in these areas like flies on road kill. But these people rapidly find out that in Narcolombia, just about everything is a capital offense, and there is no judicial system to speak of, just flying justice squads that have the right to blow into your franchulate any time of day or night and fax your records back to the notoriously picky computer in Medellín. Nothing sucks more than being hauled in front of a firing squad against the back wall of the business that you built with your own two hands.

Uncle Enzo reckons that with the Mafia's emphasis on loyalty and traditional family values, they can sign up a lot of these entrepreneurs before they become Narcolombian citizens.

And that explains the billboards that Jason sees with growing frequency as he drives into Compton. The smiling face of Uncle Enzo seems to beam down from every corner. Typically, he's got his arm around the shoulders of a young wholesome-looking black kid, and there's a catch phrase above: THE MAFIA—YOU'VE GOT A FRIEND IN THE FAMILY! and RELAX—YOU ARE ENTERING A MAFIA WATCH NEIGHBORHOOD! and UNCLE ENZO FORGIVES AND FORGETS.

This last one usually accompanies a picture of Uncle Enzo with his arm around some teenager's shoulders, giving him a stern avuncular talking-to. It is an allusion to the fact that the Colombians and Jamaicans kill just about everyone.

NO WAY, JOSÉ! Uncle Enzo holding up one hand to stop an Uzi-toting Hispanic scumbag; behind him stands a pan-ethnic phalanx of kids and grannies, resolutely gripping baseball bats and frying pans.

Oh, sure, the Narcolombians still have a lock on coca leaves, but now that Nippon Pharmaceuticals has its big cocaine-synthesis facility in Mexicali nearly complete, that will cease to be a factor. The Mafia is betting that any smart youngster going into the business these days will take note of these billboards and think twice. Why end up suffocating on your own entrails out in back of some Buy 'n' Fly when you can put on a crisp terracotta blazer instead and become part of a jovial familia? Especially now that they have black, Hispanic, and Asian capos who will respect your cultural identity? In the long term, Jason is bullish on the Mob.

His black Oldsmobile is a fucking bullseye in a place like this. It's the worst thing he has ever seen, Compton. Lepers roasting dogs on spits over tubs of flaming kerosene. Street people push-ing wheelbarrows piled high with dripping clots of million- and billion-dollar bills that they have raked up out of storm sewers. Road kills—enormous road kills—road kills so big that they could only be human beings, smeared out into chunky swaths a block long. Burning roadblocks across major avenues. No franchises anywhere. The Oldsmobile keeps popping. Jason can't think of what it is until he realizes that people are shooting at him. Good thing he let his uncle talk him into springing for full armor! When he figures that one out, he actually gets psyched. This is the real thing, man! He's driving around in his Olds and the bastards are shooting at him, and it just don't matter!

Every street for three blocks around the franchise is blocked off by Mafia war wagons. Men lurk on top of burned tenements carrying six-foot-long rifles and wearing black windbreakers with MAFIA across the back in five-inch fluorescent letters.

This is it, man, this is the real shit.

Pulling up to the checkpoint, he notes that his Olds is now straddling a portable claymore mine. If he's the wrong guy, it'll turn the car into a steel doughnut. But he's not the wrong guy. He's the right guy. He's got a priority job, a heap of documents on the seat next to him, wrapped up tight and pretty.

He rolls the window down and a top-echelon Mafia guardsman nails him with the retinal scanner. None of this ID card nonsense. They know who he is in a microsecond. He sits back against his whiplash arrestor, turns the rearview mirror to face himself, checks his hairstyle. It's not half bad.

"Bud," the guard says, "you ain't on the list."

"Yes, I am," Jason says. "This is a priority delivery. Got the papers right here."

He hands a hard copy of the Turfnet job order to the guard, who looks at it, grunts, and goes into his war wagon, which is richly festooned with antennas.

There is a very, very long wait.

A man is approaching on foot, walking across the emptiness between the Mafia franchise and the perimeter. The vacant lot is a wilderness of charred bricks and twisted electrical conduit, but this gentleman is walking across it like Christ on the Sea of Galilee. His suit is perfectly black. So is his hair. He doesn't have any guards with him. The perimeter security is that good.

Jason notices that all the guards at this checkpoint are standing a little straighter, adjusting their ties, shooting their cuffs. Jason wants to climb out of his bullet-pocked Oldsmobile to show proper respect to whoever this guy is, but he can't get the door open because a big guard is standing right there, using the roof as a mirror.

All too quickly, he's there.

"Is this him?" he says to a guard.

The guard looks at Jason for a couple of seconds, as though he can't quite believe it, then looks at the important man in the black suit and nods.

The man in the black suit nods back, tugs on his cuffs a little bit, squints around him for a few moments, looking at the snipers up on the roofs, looking everywhere but at Jason. Then he steps forward one pace. One of his eyes is made of glass and doesn't point in the same direction as the other one. Jason thinks he's looking elsewhere. But he's looking at Jason with his good eye. Or maybe he isn't. Jason can't tell which eye is the real one. He shudders and stiffens like a puppy in a deep freeze.

"Jason Breckinridge," the man says.

"The Iron Pumper," Jason reminds him.

"Shut up. For the rest of this conversation, you don't say anything. When I tell you what you did wrong, you don't say you're sorry, because I already know you're sorry. And when you drive outta here alive, you don't thank me for being alive. And you don't even say good-bye to me."

Jason nods.

"I don't even want you to nod, that's how much you annoy me. Just freeze and shut up. Okay, here we go. We gave you a priority job this morning. It was real easy. All you had to do was read the fucking job sheet. But you didn't read it. You just took it upon yourself to make the fuckin' delivery on your own. Which the job sheet explicitly tells you not to do."

Jason's eyes flick in the direction of the bundle of documents on the seat.

"That's crap," the man says. "We don't want your fucking documents. We don't care about you and your fucking franchise out in the middle a nowhere. All we wanted was the Kourier. The job sheet said that this delivery was supposed to be made by one particular Kourier who works your area, name of Y.T. Uncle

Enzo happens to like Y.T. He wants to meet her. Now, because you screwed up, Uncle Enzo don't get his wish. Oh, what a terrible outcome. What an embarrassment. What an incredible fuckup, is what it is. It's too late to save your franchise, Jason The Iron Pumper, but it might not be too late to keep the sewer rats from eating your nipples for dinner."

19

"This wasn't done with a sword," Hiro says. He is beyond astonishment as he stands and stares at Lagos's corpse. All the emotions will probably come piling in on him later, when he goes home and tries to sleep. For now, the thinking part of his brain seems cut loose from his body, as if he has just ingested a great deal of drugs, and he's just as cool as Squeaky.

"Oh, yeah? How can you tell?" Squeaky says.

"Swords make quick cuts, all the way through. Like, you cut off a head or an arm. A person who's been killed with a sword doesn't look like this."

"Really? Have you killed a lot of people with swords, Mr. Protagonist?"

"Yes. In the Metaverse."

They stand for a while longer, looking at it.

"This doesn't look like a speed move. This looks like a strength move," Squeaky says.

"Raven looks strong enough."

"That he does."

"But I don't think he was carrying a weapon. The Crips frisked him earlier, and he was clean."

"Well, then he must have borrowed one," Squeaky says. "This bug was all over the place, you know. We were keeping an eye on him, because we were afraid he was going to piss Raven off. He kept going around looking for a vantage point."

"He's loaded with surveillance gear," Hiro says. "The higher he gets, the better it works."

"So he ended up here on this embankment. And apparently the perpetrator knew where he was."

"The dust," Hiro says. "Watch the lasers."

Down below, Sushi K pirouettes spastically as a beer bottle caroms off his forehead. A bundle of lasers sweeps across the embankment, clearly visible in the fine dust being drawn out of it by the wind.

"This guy—this bug—was using lasers. As soon as he came up here—"

"They betrayed his position," Squeaky says.

"And then Raven came after him."

"Well, we're not saying it's him," Squeaky says. "But I need to know if this character"—he nods at the corpse—"might have done anything that would have made Raven feel threatened."

"What is this, group therapy? Who cares if Raven felt threatened?"

"I do," Squeaky says with great finality.

"Lagos was just a gargoyle. A big hoover for intel. I don't think he did wet operations—and if he did, he wouldn't do it in that get-up."

"So why do you think Raven was feeling so jumpy?"

"I guess he doesn't like being under surveillance," Hiro says.

"Yeah." Squeaky says. "You should remember that."

Then Squeaky puts one hand over his ear, the better to hear voices on his headset radio.

"Did Y.T. see this happen?" Hiro says.

"No," Squeaky mumbles, a few seconds later. "But she saw him leaving the scene. She's following him."

"Why would she want to do that!?"

"I guess you told her to, or something."

"I didn't think she'd take off after him."

"Well, she doesn't know that he killed the guy," Squeaky says. "She just phoned in a sighting—he's riding his Harley into Chinatown." And he begins running up the embankment. A couple of Enforcers' cars are parked on the shoulder of the highway up there, waiting.

Hiro tags along. His legs are in incredible shape from sword fighting, and he manages to catch up to Squeaky by the time he reaches his car. When the driver undoes the electric door locks, Hiro scoots into the back seat as Squeaky is going into the front. Squeaky turns around and gives him a tired look.

"I'll behave," Hiro says.

"Just one thing—"

"I know. Don't fuck around with Raven."

"That's right."

Squeaky holds his glare for another second and then turns around, motions the driver to drive. He impatiently rips ten feet of hard copy out of the dashboard printer and begins sifting through it.

On this long strip of paper, Hiro glimpses multiple renditions of the important Crip, the guy with the goatee whom Raven was dealing with earlier. On the printout, he is labeled as "T-Bone Murphy."

There's also a picture of Raven. It's an action shot, not a mug shot. It is terrible output. It has been caught through some kind of light-amplifying optics that wash out the color and make everything incredibly grainy and low contrast. It looks like some image processing has been done to make it sharper; this also makes it grainier. The license plate is just an oblate blur, overwhelmed by the glow of the taillight. It is heeled over sharply, the sidecar wheel several inches off the ground. But the rider doesn't have any visible neck; his head, or rather the dark splotch that is there, just keeps getting wider until it merges into his shoulders. Definitely Raven.

"How come you have pictures of T-Bone Murphy in there?" Hiro says.

"He's chasing him," Squeaky says.

"Who's chasing whom?"

"Well, your friend Y.T. ain't no Edward R. Murrow. But as far as we can tell from her reports, they've been sighted in the same area, trying to kill each other," Squeaky says. He's speaking with the slow, distant tones of someone who is getting live updates over his headphones.

"They were doing some kind of a deal earlier," Hiro says.

"Then I ain't hardly surprised they're trying to kill each other now."

_____ Once they get to a certain part of town, following the T-Bone and Raven show becomes a matter of connect-the-ambulances. Every couple of blocks there is a cluster of cops and medics, lights sparkling, radios coughing. All they have to do is go from one to the next.

At the first one, there is a dead Crip lying on the pavement. A six-foot-wide blood slick runs from his body, diagonally down the street to a storm drain. The ambulance people are standing around, smoking and drinking coffee from go cups, waiting for The Enforcers to get finished measuring and photographing so that they can haul the corpse to the morgue. There are no IV lines set up, no bits of medical trash strewn around the area, no open doc boxes; they didn't even try.

They proceed around a couple of corners to the next constellation of flashing lights. Here, the ambulance drivers are inflating a cast around the leg of a MetaCop.

"Run over by the motorcycle," Squeaky says, shaking his head with the traditional Enforcer's disdain for their pathetic junior relations, the MetaCops.

Finally, he patches the radio feed into the dashboard so they can all hear it.

The motorcyclist's trail is now cold, and it sounds like most of the local cops are dealing with aftermath problems. But a citizen has just called in to complain that a man on a motorcycle, and several other persons, are trashing a field of hops on her block.

"Three blocks from here," Squeaky says to the driver.

"Hops?" Hiro says.

"I know the place. Local microbrewery," Squeaky says. "They grow their own hops. Contract it out to some urban gardeners. Chinese peasants who do the grunt work for 'em."

_____ When they arrive, the first authority figures on the scene, it is obvious why Raven decided to let himself get chased into a hop field: It is great cover. The hops are heavy, flowering vines that grow on trellises lashed together out of long bamboo poles. The trellises are eight feet high; you can't see a thing.

They all get out of the car.

"T-Bone?" Squeaky hollers.

They hear someone yelling in English from the middle of the field. "Over here!" But he isn't responding to Squeaky.

They walk into the hop field. Carefully. There is an enveloping smell, a resiny odor not unlike marijuana, the sharp smell that comes off an expensive beer. Squeaky motions for Hiro to stay behind him.

In other circumstances, Hiro would do so. He is half Japanese, and under certain circumstances, totally respectful of authority.

This is not one of those circumstances. If Raven comes anywhere near Hiro, Hiro is going to be talking to him with his katana. And if it comes to that, Hiro doesn't want Squeaky anywhere near him, because he could lose a limb on the backswing.

"Yo, T-Bone!" Squeaky yells. "It's The Enforcers, and we're pissed! Get the fuck out of there, man. Let's go home!"

T-Bone, or Hiro assumes it is T-Bone, responds only by firing a short burst from a machine pistol. The muzzle flash lights up the hop vines like a strobe light. Hiro aims one shoulder at the ground, buries himself in soft earth and foliage for a few seconds.

"Fuck!" T-Bone says. It is a disappointed fuck, but a fuck with a heavy undertone of overwhelming frustration and not a little fear.

Hiro gets up into a conservative squat, looks around. Squeaky and the other Enforcer are nowhere to be seen.

Hiro forces his way through one of the trellises and into a row that is closer to the action.

The other Enforcer—the driver—is in the same row, about ten meters away, his back turned to Hiro. He glances over his shoulder in Hiro's direction, then looks in the other direction and sees someone else—Hiro can't quite see who, because The Enforcer is in the way.

"What the fuck," The Enforcer says.

Then he jumps a little, as though startled, and something happens to the back of his jacket.

"Who is it?" Hiro says.

The Enforcer doesn't say anything. He is trying to turn back around, but something prevents it. Something is shaking the vines around him.

The Enforcer shudders, careens sideways from foot to foot. "Got to get loose," he says, speaking loudly to no one in particular. He breaks into a trot, running away from Hiro. The other person who was in the row is gone now. The Enforcer is running in a strange stiff upright gait with his arms down to his sides. His bright green windbreaker isn't hanging correctly.

Hiro runs after him. The Enforcer is trotting toward the end of the row, where the lights of the street are visible.

The Enforcer exits the field a couple of seconds ahead of him, and, when Hiro gets to the curb, is in the middle of the road, illuminated mostly by flashing blue light from a giant overhead video screen. He is turning around and around with strange little stomping footsteps, not keeping his balance very well. He is saying, "Aaah, aaah" in a low, calm voice that gurgles as though he badly needs to clear his throat.

As The Enforcer revolves, Hiro perceives that he has been impaled on an eight-foot-long bamboo spear. Half sticks out the front, half out the back. The back half is dark with blood and black fecal clumps, the front half is greenish-yellow and clean. The Enforcer can only see the front half and his hands are playing up and down it, trying to verify what his eyes are seeing. Then the back half whacks into a parked car, spraying a narrow fan of head cheese across the waxed and polished trunk lid. The car's alarm goes off. The Enforcer hears the sound and turns around to see what it is.

When Hiro last sees him, he is running down the center of the pulsating neon street toward the center of Chinatown, wailing a terrible, random song that clashes with the bleating of the car alarm. Hiro feels even at this moment that something has been torn open in the world and that he is dangling above the gap, staring into a place where he does not want to be. Lost in the biomass.

Hiro draws his katana.

"Squeaky!" Hiro hollers. "He's throwing spears! He's pretty good at it! Your driver is hit!"

"Got it!" Squeaky hollers.

Hiro goes back into the closest row. He hears a sound off to the right and uses the katana to cut his way through into that row. This is not a nice place to be at the moment, but it is safer than standing in the street under the plutonic light of the video screen.

Down the row is a man. Hiro recognizes him by the strange shape of his head, which just gets wider until it reaches his shoulders. He is holding a freshly cut bamboo pole in one hand, torn from the trellis.

Raven strokes one end of it with his other hand, and a chunk falls off. Something flickers in that hand, the blade of a knife apparently. He has just cut off the end of the pole at an acute angle to make it into a spear.

He throws it fluidly. The motion is calm and beautiful. The spear disappears because it is coming straight at Hiro.

Hiro does not have time to adopt the proper stance, but this is fine since he has already adopted it. Whenever he has a katana in his hands he adopts it automatically, otherwise he fears that he may lose his balance and carelessly lop off one of his extremities. Feet parallel and pointed straight ahead, right foot in front of the left foot, katana held down at groin level like an extension of the phallus. Hiro raises the tip and slaps at the spear with the side of the blade, diverting it just enough; it goes into a slow sideways spin, the point missing Hiro just barely and entangling itself in a vine on Hiro's right. The butt end swings around and gets hung up on the left, tearing out a number of vines as it comes to a stop. It is heavy, and traveling very fast.

Raven is gone.

Mental note: Whether or not Raven intended to take on a bunch of Crips and Enforcers singlehandedly tonight, he didn't even bother to pack a gun.

Another burst of gunfire sounds from several rows over.

Hiro has been standing here for rather a long time, thinking about what just happened. He cuts through the next row of vines and heads in the direction of the muzzle flash, running his mouth: "Don't shoot this way, T-Bone, I'm on your side, man."

"Motherfucker threw a stick into my chest, man!" T-Bone complains.

When you're wearing armor, getting hit by a spear just isn't such a big deal anymore.

"Maybe you should just forget it," Hiro says. He is having to cut his way through a lot of rows to reach T-Bone, but as long as T-Bone keeps talking, Hiro can find him.

"I'm a Crip. We don't forget nothing," T-Bone says. "Is that you?"

"No," Hiro says. "I'm not there yet."

A very brief burst of gunfire, rapidly cut off. Suddenly, no one is talking. Hiro cuts his way into the next row and almost steps on T-Bone's hand, which has been amputated at the wrist. Its finger is still tangled in the trigger guard of a MAC-11.

The remainder of T-Bone is two rows away. Hiro stops and watches through the vines.

Raven is one of the largest men Hiro has seen outside of a professional sporting event. T-Bone is backing away from him down the row. Raven, moving with long confident strides, catches up with T-Bone and swings one hand up into T-Bone's body; Hiro doesn't have to see the knife to know it is there.

It looks as though T-Bone is going to get out of this with nothing worse than a sewn-on hand and some rehab work, because you can't stab a person to death that way, not if he is wearing armor.

T-Bone screams.

He is bouncing up and down on Raven's hand. The knife has gone all the way through the bulletproof fabric and now Raven is trying to gut T-Bone the same way he did Lagos. But his knife—whatever the hell it is—won't cut through the fabric that way. It is sharp enough to penetrate—which should be impossible—but not sharp enough to slash.

Raven pulls it out, drops to one knee, and swings his knife hand around in a long ellipse between T-Bone's thighs. Then he jumps over T-Bone's collapsing body and runs.

Hiro gets the sense that T-Bone is a dead man, so he follows Raven. His intention is not to hunt the man down, but rather to maintain a very clear picture of where he is.

He has to cut through a number of rows. He rapidly loses Raven. He considers running as fast as he can in the opposite direction.

Then he hears the deep, lung-stretching rumble of a motorcycle engine. Hiro runs for the nearest street exit, just hoping to catch a glimpse.

He does, though it is a quick one, not a hell of a lot better than the graphic in the cop car. Raven turns to look at Hiro, just as he is blowing out of there. He's right under a streetlight, so Hiro gets a clear look at his face for the first time. He is Asian. He has a wispy mustache that trails down past his chin.

Another Crip comes running out into the street half a second after Hiro, as Raven is pulling away. He slows for a moment to take stock of the situation, then charges the motorcycle like a linebacker. He is crying out as he does so, a war cry.

Squeaky emerges about the same time as the Crip, starts chasing both of them down the street.

Raven seems to be unaware of the Crip running behind him, but in hindsight it seems apparent that he has been watching his approach in the rearview mirror of the motorcycle. As the Crip comes in range, Raven's hand lets go of the throttle for a moment, snaps back as if he is throwing away a piece of litter. His fist strikes the middle of the Crip's face like a frozen ham shot out of a cannon. The Crip's head snaps back, his feet are lifted off the ground, he does most of a backflip and strikes the pavement, hitting first with the nape of his neck, both arms slamming out straight onto the road as he does so. It looks a lot like a controlled fall, though if so, it has to be more reflex than anything.

Squeaky decelerates, turns, and kneels down next to the fallen Crip, ignoring Raven.

Hiro watches the large, radioactive, spear-throwing killer drug lord ride his motorcycle into Chinatown. Which is the same as riding it into China, as far as chasing him down is concerned.

He runs up to the Crip, who is lying crucified in the center of the street. The lower half of the Crip's face is pretty hard to make out. His eyes are half open, and he looks quite relaxed. He speaks quietly. "He's a fucking Indian or something."

Interesting idea. But Hiro still thinks he's Asian.

"What the fuck did you think you were doing, asshole?" Squeaky says. He sounds so pissed that Hiro steps away from him.

"That fucker ripped us off—the suitcase burned," the Crip mumbles through a mashed jaw.

"So why didn't you just write it off? Are you crazy, fucking with Raven like that?"

"He ripped us off. Nobody does that and lives."

"Well, Raven just did," Squeaky says. Finally, he's calming down a little. He rocks back on his heels, looks up at Hiro.

"T-Bone and your driver are not likely to be alive," Hiro says. "This guy better not move—he could have a neck fracture."

"He's lucky I don't fracture his fucking neck," Squeaky says.

The ambulance people get there fast enough to slap an inflatable cervical collar around the Crip's neck before he gets ambitious enough to stand up. They haul him away within a few minutes.

Hiro goes back into the hops and finds T-Bone. T-Bone is dead, slumped in a kneeling position against a trellis. The stab wound through his bulletproof vest probably would have been fatal, but Raven wasn't satisfied with that. He went down low and slashed up and down the insides of T-Bone's thighs, which are now laid open all the way to the bone. In doing so, he put great lengthwise rents into both of T-Bone's femoral arteries, and his entire blood supply dropped out of him. Like slicing the bottom off a styrofoam cup.

20

The Enforcers turn the entire block into a mobile cop headquarters with cars and paddy wagons and satellite links on flatbed trucks. Dudes with white coats are walking up and down through the hop field with Geiger counters. Squeaky is wandering around with his headset, staring into space, carrying on conversations with people who aren't there. A tow truck shows up, towing T-Bone's black BMW behind it.

"Yo, pod." Hiro turns around and looks. It's Y.T. She's just come out of a Hunan place across the street. She hands Hiro a little white box and a pair of chopsticks. "Spicy chicken with black bean sauce, no MSG. You know how to use chopsticks?"

Hiro shrugs off this insult.

"I got a double order," Y.T. continues, "cause I figure we got some good intel tonight."

"Are you aware of what happened here?"

"No. I mean, some people obviously got hurt."

"But you weren't an eyewitness."

"No, I couldn't keep up with them."

"That's good," Hiro says.

"What did happen?"

Hiro just shakes his head. The spicy chicken is glistening darkly under the lights; he has never been less hungry in his life. "If I had known, I wouldn't have gotten you involved. I just thought it was a surveillance job."

"What happened?"

"I don't want to get into it. Look. Stay away from Raven, okay?"

"Sure," she says. She says it in the chirpy tone of voice that she uses when she's lying and she wants to make sure you know it.

Squeaky hauls open the back door of the BMW and looks into the back seat. Hiro steps a little closer, gets a nasty whiff of cold smoke. It is the smell of burnt plastic.

The aluminum briefcase that Raven earlier gave to T-Bone is sitting in the middle of the seat. It looks like it has been thrown into a fire; it has black smoke stains splaying out around the locks, and its plastic handle is partially melted. The buttery leather that covers the BMW's seats has burn marks on it. No wonder T-Bone was pissed.

Squeaky pulls on a pair of latex gloves. He hauls the briefcase out, sets it on the trunk lid, and rips the latches open with a small prybar.

Whatever it is, it is complicated and highly designed. The top half of the case has several rows of the small red-capped tubes that Hiro saw at the U-Stor-It. There are five rows with maybe twenty tubes in each row.

The bottom half of the case appears to be some kind of miniaturized, old-fashioned computer terminal. Most of it is occupied by a keyboard. There is a small liquid-crystal display screen that can probably handle about five lines of text at a time. There is a penlike object attached to the case by a cable, maybe three feet long uncoiled. It looks like it might be a light pen or a bar-code scanner. Above the keyboard is a lens, set at an angle so that it is aimed at whoever is typing on the keyboard. There are other features whose purpose is not so obvious: a slot, which might be a place to insert a credit or ID card, and a cylindrical socket that is about the size of one of those little tubes.

This is Hiro's reconstruction of how the thing looked at one time. When Hiro sees it, it is melted together. Judging from the pattern of smoke marks on the outside of the case—which appear to be jetting outward from the crack between the top and bottom—the source of the flame was inside, not outside.

Squeaky reaches down and unsnaps one of the tubes from the bracket, holds it up in front of the bright lights of Chinatown. It had been transparent but was now smirched by heat and smoke. From a distance, it looks like a simple vial, but stepping up to look at it more closely Hiro can see at least half a dozen tiny individual compartments inside the thing, all connected to each other by capillary tubes. It has a red plastic cap on one end of it. The cap has a black rectangular window, and as Squeaky rotates it, Hiro can see the dark red glint of an inactive LED display inside, like looking at the display on a turned-off calculator. Underneath this is a small perforation. It isn't just a simple drilled hole. It is wide at the surface, rapidly narrowing to a nearly invisible pinpoint opening, like the bell of a trumpet.

The compartments inside the vial are all partially filled with liquids. Some of them are transparent and some are blackish brown. The brown ones have to be organics of some kind, now reduced by the heat into chicken soup. The transparent ones could be anything.

"He got out to go into a bar and have a drink," Squeaky mumbles. "What an asshole."

"Who did?"

"T-Bone. See, T-Bone was, like, the registered owner of this unit. The suitcase. And as soon as he got more than about ten feet away from it—*foosh*—it self-destructed."

"Why?"

Squeaky looks at Hiro like he's stupid. "Well, it's not like I work for Central Intelligence or anything. But I would guess that whoever makes this drug—they call it Countdown, or Redcap, or Snow Crash—has a real thing about trade secrets. So if the pusher abandons the suitcase, or loses it, or tries to transfer ownership to someone else—*foosh*."

"You think the Crips are going to catch up with Raven?"

"Not in Chinatown. Shit," Squeaky says, getting pissed again in retrospect, "I can't believe that guy. I could have killed him."

"Raven?"

"No. That Crip. Chasing Raven. He's lucky Raven got to him first, not me."

"You were chasing the Crip?"

"Yeah, I was chasing the Crip. What, did you think I was trying to catch Raven?"

"Sort of, yeah. I mean, he's the bad guy, right?"

"Definitely. So I'd be chasing Raven if I was a cop and it was my job to catch bad guys. But I'm an Enforcer, and it's my job to enforce order. So I'm doing everything I can—and so is every other Enforcer in town—to protect Raven. And if you have any ideas about trying to go and find Raven yourself and get revenge for that colleague of yours that he offed, you can forget it."

"Offed? What colleague?" Y.T. breaks in. She didn't see what happened with Lagos.

Hiro is mortified by this idea. "Is that why everyone was telling me not to fuck with Raven? They were afraid I was going to *attack* him?"

Squeaky eyes the swords. "You got the means."

"Why should anyone protect Raven?"

Squeaky smiles, as though we have just crossed the border into the realm of kidding around. "He's a Sovereign."

"So declare war on him."

"It's not a good idea to declare war on a nuclear power."

"Huh?"

"Christ," Squeaky says, shaking his head, "if I had any idea how little you knew about this shit, I never would have let you into my car. I thought you were some kind of a serious CIC wet-operations guy. Are you telling me you really didn't know about Raven?"

"Yes, that's what I'm telling you."

"Okay. I'm gonna tell you this so you don't go out and cause any more trouble. Raven's packing a torpedo warhead that he boosted from an old Soviet nuke sub. It was a torpedo that was designed to take out a carrier battle group with one shot. A nuclear torpedo. You know that funny-looking sidecar that Raven has on his Harley? Well, it's a hydrogen bomb, man.

Armed and ready. The trigger's hooked up to EEG trodes embedded in his skull. If Raven dies, the bomb goes off. So when Raven comes into town, we do everything in our power to make the man feel welcome."

Hiro's just gaping. Y.T. has to step in on his behalf. "Okay," she says. "Speaking for my partner and myself, we'll stay away from him."

21

Y.T. reckons she is going to spend all afternoon being a ramp turd. The surf is always up on the Harbor Freeway, which gets her from Downtown into Compton, but the off-ramps into that neighborhood are so rarely used that three-foot tumbleweeds grow in their potholes. And she's definitely not going to travel into Compton under her own power. She wants to poon something big and fast.

She can't use the standard trick of ordering a pizza to her destination and then pooning the delivery boy as he roars past, because none of the pizza chains deliver to this neighborhood. So she'll have to stop at the off-ramp and wait hours and hours for a ride. A ramp turd.

She does not want to do this delivery at all. But the franchisee wants her to do it bad. Really bad. The amount of money he has offered her is so high, it's stupid. The package must be full of some kind of intense new drug.

But that's not as weird as what happens next. She is cruising down the Harbor Freeway, approaching the desired off-ramp, having pooned a southbound semi. A quarter-mile from the off-ramp, a bullet-pocked black Oldsmobile cruises past her, right-turn signal flashing. He's going to exit. It's too good to be true. She poons the Oldsmobile.

As she cruises down the ramp behind this flatulent sedan, she checks out the driver in his rearview mirror. It is the franchisee himself, the one who is paying her a totally stupid amount of money to do this job.

By this point, she's more afraid of him than she is of Compton.

He must be a psycho. He must be in love with her. This is all a twisted psycho love plot.

But it's a little late now. She stays with him, looking for a way out of this burning and rotting neighborhood.

They are approaching a big, nasty-looking Mafia roadblock. He guns the gas pedal, headed straight for death. She can see the destination franchise ahead. At the last second, he whips the car around and squeals sideways to a halt.

He couldn't have been more helpful. She unpoons as he's giving her this last little kick of energy and sails through the checkpoint at a safe and sane speed. The guards keep their guns pointed at the sky, swivel their heads to look at her butt as she rolls past them.

———————— The Compton Nova Sicilia franchise is a grisly scene. It is a jamboree of Young Mafia. These youths are even duller than the ones from the all-Mormon Deseret Burbclave. The boys are wearing tedious black suits. The girls are encrusted with pointless femininity. Girls can't even be in the Young Mafia; they have to be in the Girls' Auxiliary and serve macaroons on silver plates. "Girls" is too fine a word for these organisms, too high up the evolutionary scale. They aren't even chicks.

She's going way too fast, so she kicks the board around sideways, plants pads, leans into it, skids to a halt, roiling up a wave of dust and grit that dulls the glossy shoes of several Young Mafia who are milling out front, nibbling dinky Italo-treats and playing grown-up. It condenses on the white lace stockings of the Young Mafia proto-chicks. She falls off the board, appearing to catch her balance at the last moment. She stomps on the edge of the plank with one foot, and it bounces four feet into the air, spinning rapidly around its long axis, up into her armpit, where she clamps it tight under one arm. The spokes of the smartwheels all retract so that the wheels are barely larger than their hubs. She slaps the MagnaPoon into a handy socket on the bottom of the plank so that her gear is all in one handy package.

"Y.T.," she says. "Young, fast, and female. Where the fuck's Enzo?"

The boys decide to get all "mature" on Y.T. Males of this age are preoccupied with snapping each other's underwear and drinking until they are in a coma. But around a female, they do the "mature" thing. It is hilarious. One of them steps forward slightly, interposing himself between Y.T. and the nearest proto-chick. "Welcome to Nova Sicilia," he says. "Can I assist you in some way?"

Y.T. sighs deeply. She is a fully independent businessperson, and these people are trying to do a peer thing on her.

"Delivery for one Enzo? Y'know, I can't wait to get out of this neighborhood."

"It's a good neighborhood, now," the YoMa says. "You should stick around for a few minutes. Maybe you could learn some manners."

"You should try surfing the Ventura at rush hour. Maybe you could learn your limitations."

The YoMa laughs like, okay, if that's how you want it. He gestures toward the door. "The man you want to talk to is in there. Whether he wants to talk to you or not, I'm not sure."

"He fucking asked for me," Y.T. says.

"He came across the country to be with us," the guy says, "and he seems pretty happy with us."

All the other YoMas mumble and nod supportively.

"Then why are you standing outside?" Y.T. asks, going inside.

Inside the franchise, things are startlingly relaxed. Uncle Enzo is in there, looking just like he does in the pictures, except big-ger than Y.T. expected. He is sitting at a desk playing cards with some other guys in funeral garb. He is smoking a cigar and nursing an espresso. Can't get too much stimulation, ap-parently.

There's a whole Uncle Enzo portable support system in here. A traveling espresso machine has been set up on another desk. A cabinet sits next to it, doors open to reveal a big foil bag of Italian Roast Water-Process Decaf and a box of Havana cigars. There's also a gargoyle in one corner, patched into a bigger-than-normal laptop, mumbling to himself.

Y.T. lifts her arm, allows the plank to fall into her hand. She slaps it down on top of an empty desk and approaches Uncle Enzo, unslinging the delivery from her shoulder.

"Gino, please," Uncle Enzo says, nodding at the delivery. Gino steps forward to take it from her.

"Need your signature on that," Y.T. says. For some reason she does not refer to him as "pal" or "bub."

She's momentarily distracted by Gino. Suddenly, Uncle Enzo has come rather close to her, caught her right hand in his left hand. Her Kourier gloves have an opening on the back of the hand just big enough for his lips. He plants a kiss on Y.T.'s hand. It's warm and wet. Not slobbery and gross, not antiseptic and dry either. Interesting. The guy has confidence going for him. Christ, he's slick. Nice lips. Sort of firm muscular lips, not gelatinous and blubbery like fifteen-year-old lips can be. Uncle Enzo has a very faint citrus-and-aged-tobacco smell to him. Fully smelling it would involve standing pretty close to him. He is towering over her, standing at a respectable distance now, glinting at her through crinkly old-guy eyes.

Seems pretty nice.

"I can't tell you how much I've been looking forward to meeting you, Y.T.," he says.

"Hi," she says. Her voice sounds chirpier than she likes it to be. So she adds, "What's in that bag that's so fucking valuable, anyway?"

"Absolutely nothing," Uncle Enzo says. His smile is not exactly smug. More embarrassed, like what an awkward way to meet someone. "It all has to do with imageering," he says, spreading one hand dismissively. "There are not many ways for a man like me to meet with a young girl that do not generate incorrect images in the media. It's stupid. But we pay attention to these things."

"So, what did you want to meet with me about? Got a delivery for me to make?"

All the guys in the room laugh.

The sound startles Y.T. a little, reminds her that she is performing in front of a crowd. Her eyes flick away from Uncle Enzo for a moment.

Uncle Enzo notices this. His smile gets infinitesimally narrower, and he hesitates for a moment. In that moment, all the other guys in the room stand up and head for the exit.

"You may not believe me," he says, "but I simply wanted to thank you for delivering that pizza a few weeks ago."

"Why shouldn't I believe you?" she asks. She is amazed to hear nice, sweet things coming out of her mouth.

So is Uncle Enzo. "I'm sure you of all people can come up with a reason."

"So," she says, "you having a nice day with all the Young Mafia?"

Uncle Enzo gives her a look that says, watch it, child. A second after she gets scared, she starts laughing, because it's a put-on, he's just giving her a hard time. He smiles, indicating that it's okay for her to laugh.

Y.T. can't remember when she's been so involved in a conversation. Why can't all people be like Uncle Enzo?

"Let me see," Uncle Enzo says, looking at the ceiling, scanning his memory banks. "I know a few things about you. That you are fifteen years old, you live in a Burbclave in the Valley with your mother."

"I know a few things about you, too," Y.T. hazards.

Uncle Enzo laughs. "Not nearly as much as you think, I promise. Tell me, what does your mother think of your career?"

Nice of him to use the word "career." "She's not totally aware of it—or doesn't want to know."

"You're probably wrong," Uncle Enzo says. He says it cheerfully enough, not trying to cut her down or anything. "You might be shocked at how well-informed she is. This is my experience, anyway. What does your mother do for a living?"

"She works for the Feds."

Uncle Enzo finds that richly amusing. "And her daughter is delivering pizzas for Nova Sicilia. What does she do for the Feds?"

"Some kind of thing where she can't really tell me in case I blab it. She has to take a lot of polygraph tests."

Uncle Enzo seems to understand this very well. "Yes, a lot of Fed jobs are that way."

There is an opportune silence.

"It kind of freaks me out," Y.T. says.

"The fact that she works for the Feds?"

"The polygraph tests. They put a thing around her arm—to measure the blood pressure."

"A sphygmomanometer," Uncle Enzo says crisply.

"It leaves a bruise around her arm. For some reason, that kind of bothers me."

"It should bother you."

"And the house is bugged. So when I'm home—no matter what I'm doing—someone else is probably listening."

"Well, I can certainly relate to that," Uncle Enzo says.

They both laugh.

"I'm going to ask you a question that I've always wanted to ask a Kourier," Uncle Enzo says. "I always watch you people through the windows of my limousine. In fact, when a Kourier poons me, I always tell Peter, my driver, not to give them a hard time. My question is, you are covered from head to toe in protective padding. So why don't you wear a helmet?"

"The suit's got a cervical airbag that blows up when you fall off the board, so you can bounce on your head. Besides, helmets feel weird. They say it doesn't affect your hearing, but it does."

"You use your hearing quite a bit in your line of work?"

"Definitely, yeah."

Uncle Enzo is nodding. "That's what I suspected. We felt the same way, the boys in my unit in Vietnam."

"I heard you went to Vietnam, but—" She stops, sensing danger.

"You thought it was hype. No, I went there. Could have stayed out, if I'd wanted. But I volunteered."

"You volunteered to go to Vietnam?"

Uncle Enzo laughs. "Yes, I did. The only boy in my family to do so."

"Why?"

"I thought it would be safer than Brooklyn."

Y.T. laughs.

"A bad joke," he says. "I volunteered because my father didn't want me to. And I wanted to piss him off."

"Really?"

"Definitely. I spent years and years finding ways to piss him off. Dated black girls. Grew my hair long. Smoked marijuana. But the capstone, my ultimate achievement—even better than having my ear pierced—was volunteering for service in Vietnam. But I had to take extreme measures even then."

Y.T.'s eyes dart back and forth between Uncle Enzo's creased and leathery earlobes. In the left one she just barely sees a tiny diamond stud.

"What do you mean, extreme measures?"

"Everyone knew who I was. Word gets around, you know. If I had volunteered for the regular Army, I would have ended up stateside, filling out forms—maybe even at Fort Hamilton, right there in Bensonhurst. To prevent that, I volunteered for Special Forces, did everything I could to get into a front-line unit." He laughs. "And it worked. Anyway, I'm rambling like an old man. I was trying to make a point about helmets."

"Oh, yeah."

"Our job was to go through the jungle making trouble for some slippery gentlemen carrying guns bigger than they were. Stealthy guys. And we depended on our hearing, too—just like you do. And you know what? We never wore helmets."

"Same reason?"

"Exactly. Even though they didn't cover the ears, really, they did something to your sense of hearing. I still think I owe my life to going bareheaded."

"That's really cool. That's really interesting."

"You'd think they would have solved the problem by now."

"Yeah," Y.T. volunteers, "some things never change, I guess."

Uncle Enzo throws back his head and belly laughs. Usually, Y.T. finds this kind of thing pretty annoying, but Uncle Enzo just seems like he's having a good time, not putting her down.

Y.T. wants to ask him how he went from the ultimate rebellion to running the family beeswax. She doesn't. But Uncle Enzo senses that it is the next, natural subject of the conversation.

"Sometimes I wonder who'll come after me," he says. "Oh, we have plenty of excellent people in the next generation. But after that—well, I don't know. I guess all old people feel like the world is coming to an end."

"You got millions of those Young Mafia types," Y.T. says.

"All destined to wear blazers and shuffle papers in suburbia. You don't respect those people very much, Y.T., because you're young and arrogant. But I don't respect them much either, because I'm old and wise."

This is a fairly shocking thing for Uncle Enzo to be saying, but Y.T. doesn't feel shocked. It just seems like a reasonable statement coming from her reasonable pal, Uncle Enzo.

"None of them would ever volunteer to go get his legs shot off in the jungle, just to piss off his old man. They lack a certain fiber. They are lifeless and beaten down."

"That's sad," Y.T. says. It feels better to say this than to trash them, which was her first inclination.

"Well," says Uncle Enzo. It is the "well" that begins the end of a conversation. "I was going to send you some roses, but you wouldn't really be interested in that, would you?"

"Oh, I wouldn't mind," she says, sounding pathetically weak to herself.

"Here's something better, since we are comrades in arms," he says. He loosens his tie and collar, reaches down into his shirt, pulls out an amazingly cheap steel chain with a couple of stamped silver tags dangling from it. "These are my old dog tags," he says. "Been carrying them around for years, just for the hell of it. I would be amused if you would wear them."

Trying to keep her knees steady, she puts the dog tags on. They dangle down onto her coverall.

"Better put them inside," Uncle Enzo says.

She drops them down into the secret place between her breasts. They are still warm from Uncle Enzo.

"Thanks."

"It's just for fun," he says, "but if you ever get into trouble, and you show those dog tags to whoever it is that's giving you a bad time, then things will probably change very quickly."

"Thanks, Uncle Enzo."

"Take care of yourself. Be good to your mother. She loves you."

22

As she steps out of the Nova Sicilia franchulate, a guy is waiting for her. He smiles, not without irony, and makes just a hint of a bow, sort of to get her attention. It's pretty ridiculous, but after being with Uncle Enzo for a while, she's definitely into it. So she doesn't laugh in his face or anything, just looks the other way and blows him off.

"Y.T. Got a job for ya," he says.

"I'm busy," she says, "got other deliveries to make."

"You lie like a mattress," he says appreciatively. "Y'know that gargoyle in there? He's patched in to the RadiKS computer even as we speak. So we all know for a fact you don't got no jobs to do."

"Well, I can't take jobs from a customer," Y.T. says. "We're centrally dispatched. You have to go through the 1-800 number."

"Jeez, what kind of a fucking dickhead do you think I am?" the guy says.

Y.T. stops walking, turns, finally looks at the guy. He's tall, lean. Black suit, black hair. And he's got a gnarly-looking glass eye.

"What happened to your eye?" she says.

"Ice pick, Bayonne, 1985," he says. "Any other questions?"

"Sorry, man, I was just asking."

"Now back to business. Because I don't have my head totally up my asshole, like you seem to assume, I am aware that all Kouriers are centrally dispatched through the 1-800 number. Now, we don't like 1-800 numbers and central dispatching. It's just a thing with us. We like to go person-to-person, the old-fashioned way. Like, on my momma's birthday, I don't pick up the phone and dial 1-800-CALL-MOM. I go there in person and give her a kiss on the cheek, okay? Now in this case, we want you in particular."

"How come?"

"Because we just love to deal with difficult little chicks who ask too many fucking questions. So our gargoyle has already patched himself in to the computer that RadiKS uses to dispatch Kouriers."

The man with the glass eye turns, rotating his head way, way around like an owl, and nods in the direction of the gargoyle. A second later, Y.T.'s personal phone rings.

"Fucking pick it up," he says.

"What?" she says into the phone.

A computer voice tells her that she is supposed to make a pickup in Griffith Park and deliver it to a Reverend Wayne's Pearly Gates franchise in Van Nuys.

"If you want something delivered from point A to point B, why don't you just drive it down there yourselves?" Y.T. asks. "Put it in one of those black Lincoln Town Cars and just get it done."

"Because in this case, the something doesn't exactly belong to us, and the people at point A and point B, well, we aren't necessarily on the best of terms, mutually speaking."

"You want me to steal something," Y.T. says.

The man with the glass eye is pained, wounded. "No, no, no. Kid, listen. We're the fucking Mafia. We want to steal something, we already know how to do that, okay? We don't need a fifteen-year-old girl's help to get something stolen. What we are doing here is more of a covert operation."

"A spy thing." *Intel.*

"Yeah. A spy thing," the man says, his tone of voice suggesting that he is trying to humor someone. "And the only way to get this operation to work is if we have a Kourier who can cooperate with us a little bit."

"So all that stuff with Uncle Enzo was fake," Y.T. says. "You're just trying to get all friendly with a Kourier."

"Oh, ho, listen to this," says the man with the glass eye, genuinely amused. "Yeah, like we have to go all the way to the top to impress a fifteen-year-old. Look, kid, there's a million Kouriers out there we could bribe to do this. We're going with you, again, because you have a personal relationship with our outfit."

"Well, what do you want me to do?"

"Exactly what you would normally do at this juncture," the man says. "Go to Griffith Park and make the pickup."

"That's it?"

"Yeah. Then make the delivery. But do us a favor and take I-5, okay?"

"That's not the best way to do it—"

"Do it anyway."

"Okay."

"Now come on, we'll give you an escort out of this hellhole."

_____ Sometimes, if the wind is going the right way, and you get into the pocket of air behind a speeding eighteen-wheeler, you don't even have to poon it. The vacuum, like a mighty hoover, sucks you in. You can stay there all day. But if you screw up, you suddenly find yourself alone and powerless in the left lane of a highway with a convoy of semis right behind you. Just as bad, if you give in to its power, it will suck you right into its mudflaps, you will become axle dressing, and no one will ever know. This is called the Magic Hoover Poon. It reminds Y.T. of the way her life has been since the fateful night of the Hiro Protagonist pizza adventure.

Her poon cannot miss as she slingshots her way up the San Diego Freeway. She can get a solid yank off even the lightest, trashiest plastic-and-aluminum Chinese econobox. People don't fuck with her. She has established her space on the pavement.

She is going to get so much business now. She will have to sub a lot of work out to Roadkill. And sometimes, just to make important business arrangements, they will have to check into a motel somewhere—which is exactly what real business people do. Lately, Y.T. has been trying to teach Roadkill how to give her a massage. But Roadkill can never get past her shoulder blades before he loses it and starts being Mr. Macho. Which anyway is kind of sweet. And anyway, you take what you can get.

This is not the most direct route to Griffith Park by a longshot, but this is what the Mafia wants her to do: Take 405 all the way up into the Valley, and then approach from that direction, which is the direction she'd normally come from. They're so paranoid. So professional.

LAX goes by on her left. On her right, she gets a glimpse of the U-Stor-It where that dweeb, her partner, is probably goggled into his computer. She weaves through complex traffic flows around

Hughes Airport, which is now a private outpost of Mr. Lee's Greater Hong Kong. Continues past the Santa Monica Airport, which just got bought out by Admiral Bob's Global Security. Cuts through the middle of Fedland, where her mother goes to work every day.

Fedland used to be the VA Hospital and a bunch of other Federal buildings; now it has condensed into a kidney-shaped lozenge that wraps around 405. It has a barrier around it, a perimeter fence put up by stringing chain link fabric, concertina wire, heaps of rubble, and Jersey barriers from one building to the next. All of the buildings in Fedland are big and ugly. Human beings mill around their plinths, wearing wool clothing the color of damp granite. They are scrawny and dark underneath the white majesty of the buildings.

On the far side of the Fedland barrier, off to the right, she can see UCLA, which is now being jointly run by the Japanese and Mr. Lee's Greater Hong Kong and a few big American corporations.

People say that over there to the left, in Pacific Palisades, is a big building above the ocean where the Central Intelligence Corporation has its West Coast headquarters. Soon—like maybe tomorrow—she'll go up there, find that building, maybe just cruise past it and wave. She has great stuff to tell Hiro now. Great intel on Uncle Enzo. People would pay millions for it.

But in her heart, she's already feeling the pangs of conscience. She knows that she cannot kiss and tell on the Mafia. Not because she's afraid of them. Because they trust her. They were nice to her. And who knows, it might turn into something. A better career than she could get with CIC.

Not many cars are taking the off-ramp into Fedland. Her mother does it every morning, as do a bunch of other Feds. But all Feds go to work early and stay late. It's a loyalty thing with them. The Feds have a fetish for loyalty—since they don't make a lot of money or get a lot of respect, you have to prove you're personally committed and that you don't care about those trappings.

Case in point: Y.T. has been pooned onto the same cab all the way from LAX. It's got an Arab in the back seat. His burnous flutters in the wind from the open window; the air conditioning doesn't work, an L.A. cabbie doesn't make enough money to buy Chill—Freon—on the underground market. This is typical: only the Feds would make a visitor take a dirty, un–air conditioned cab. Sure enough, the cab pulls onto the ramp marked UNITED STATES. Y.T. disengages and slaps her poon onto a Valley-bound delivery truck.

On top of the huge Federal Building, a bunch of Feds with walkie-talkies and dark glasses and FEDS windbreakers lurk, aiming long lenses into the windshields of the vehicles coming up Wilshire Boulevard. If this were nighttime, she'd probably see a laser scanner playing over the bar-code license plate of the taxi as it veers onto the U.S. exit.

Y.T.'s mom has told her all about these guys. They are the Executive Branch General Operational Command, EBGOC. The FBI, Federal Marshalls, Secret Service, and Special Forces all claim some separate identity still, like the Army, Navy, and Air Force used to, but they're all under the command of EBGOC, they all do the same things, and they are more or less interchangeable. Outside of Fedland, everyone just knows them as the Feds. EBGOC claims the right to go anywhere, anytime, within the original borders of the United States of America, without a warrant or even a good excuse. But they only really feel at home here, in Fedland, staring down the barrel of a telephoto lens, shotgun microphone, or sniper rifle. The longer the better.

Down below them, the taxicab with the Arab in the back slows down to sublight speed and winds its way down a twisting slalom course of Jersey barriers with .50-caliber machine gun nests strategically placed here and there. It comes to a stop in front of an STD device, straddling an open pit where EBGOC boys stand with dogs and high-powered spotlights to look up its skirt for bombs or NBCI (nuclear-biological-chemical-informational) agents in the undercarriage. Meanwhile, the driver gets out and pops the hood and trunk so that more Feds can inspect them; another Fed leans against the window next to the Arab and grills him through the window.

They say that in D.C., all the museums and the monuments have been concessioned out and turned into a tourist park that now generates about 10 percent of the Government's revenue.

The Feds could run the concession themselves and probably keep more of the gross, but that's not the point. It's a philosophical thing. A back-to-basics thing. Government should govern. It's not in the entertainment industry, is it? Leave entertaining to Industry weirdos—people who majored in tap dancing. Feds aren't like that. Feds are serious people. Poli sci majors. Student council presidents. Debate club chairpersons. The kinds of people who have the grit to wear a dark wool suit and a tightly buttoned collar even when the temperature has greenhoused up to a hundred and ten degrees and the humidity is thick enough to stall a jumbo jet. The kinds of people who feel most at home on the dark side of a one-way mirror.

23

Sometimes, to prove their manhood, boys of about Y.T.'s age will drive to the eastern end of the Hollywood Hills, into Griffith Park, pick the road of their choosing, and simply drive through it. Making it through there unscathed is a lot like counting coup on a High Plains battlefield; simply having come that close to danger makes you more of a man.

By definition, all they ever see are the through streets. If you are driving into Griffith Park for some highjinks and you see a NO OUTLET sign, you know that it is time to shift your dad's Accord into reverse and drive it backward all the way back home, revving the engine way past the end of the tachometer.

Naturally, as soon as Y.T. enters the park, following the road she was told to follow, she sees a NO OUTLET sign.

Y.T.'s not the first Kourier to take a job like this, and so she has heard about the place she is going. It is a narrow canyon, accessed only by this one road, and down in the bottom of the canyon a new gang lives. Everyone calls them the Falabalas, because that's how they talk to each other. They have their own language and it sounds like babble.

Right now, the important thing is not to think about how stupid this is. Making the right decision is, priority-wise, down there along with getting enough niacin and writing a thank-you letter to grandma for the nice pearl earrings. The only important thing is not to back down.

A row of machine-gun nests marks the border of Falabala territory. It seems like overkill to Y.T. But then she's never been in a conflict with the Mafia, either. She plays it cool, idles toward the barrier at maybe ten miles an hour. This is where she'll freak out and get scared if she's going to. She is holding aloft a color-faxed RadiKS document, featuring the cybernetic radish logo, proclaiming that she really is here to pick up an important delivery, honest. It'll never work with these guys.

But it does. A big gnarled-up coil of razor ribbon is pulled out of her way, just like that, and she glides through without slowing down. And that's when she knows that it's going to be fine. These people are just doing business here, just like anyone else.

She doesn't have to skate far into the canyon. Thank God. She goes around a few turns, into kind of an open flat area surrounded by trees, and finds herself in what looks like an open-air insane asylum.

Or a Moonie festival or something.

A couple of dozen people are here. None of them have been taking care of themselves at all. They are all wearing the ragged remains of what used to be pretty decent clothing. Half a dozen of them are kneeling on the pavement with their hands clenched tightly together, mumbling to unseen entities.

On the trunk lid of a dead car, they've set up an old junked computer terminal, just a dark monitor screen with a big spider-web crack in it, like someone bounced a coffee mug off the glass. A fat man with red suspenders dangling around his knees is sliding his hands up and down the keyboard, whacking the keys randomly, talking out loud in a meaningless babble. A couple of the others stand behind him, peeking over his shoulder and around his body, and sometimes they try to horn in on it, but he shoves them out of the way.

There's also a crowd of people clapping their hands, swaying their bodies, and singing "The Happy Wanderer." They're really into it, too. Y.T. hasn't seen such childlike glee on anyone's face since the first time she let Roadkill take her clothes off. But this is a different kind of childlike glee that does not look right on a bunch of thirty-something people with dirty hair.

And finally, there is a guy that Y.T. dubs the High Priest. He's wearing a formerly white lab coat, bearing the logo of some company in the Bay Area. He's sacked out in the back of a dead station wagon, but when Y.T. enters the area he jumps up and runs toward her in a way that she can't help but find a little threatening. But compared to these others, he seems almost like a regular, healthy, fit, demented bush-dwelling psychotic.

"You're here to pick up a suitcase, right?"

"I'm here to pick up something. I don't know what it is," she says.

He goes over to one of the dead cars, unlocks the hood, pulls out an aluminum briefcase. It looks exactly like the one that Squeaky took out of the BMW last night. "Here's your delivery," he says, striding toward her. She backs away from him instinctively.

"I understand, I understand," he says. "I'm a scary creep."

He puts it on the ground, puts his foot on it, gives it a shove. It slides across the pavement to Y.T., bouncing off the occasional rock.

"There's no big hurry on this delivery," he says. "Would you like to stay and have a drink? We've got Kool-Aid."

"I'd love to," Y.T. says, "but my diabetes is acting up real bad."

"Well, then you can just stay and be a guest of our community. We have a lot of wonderful things to tell you about. Things that could really change your life."

"Do you have anything in writing? Something I could take with me?"

"Gee, I'm afraid we don't. Why don't you stay. You seem like a really nice person."

"Sorry, Jack, but you must be confusing me with a bimbo," Y.T. says. "Thanks for the suitcase. I'm out of here."

Y.T. starts digging at the pavement with one foot, building up speed as fast as she can. On her way out, she passes by a young woman with a shaved head, dressed in the dirty and haggard remains of a Chanel knockoff. As Y.T. goes by her, she smiles vacantly, sticks out her hand, and waves. "Hi," she says. "ba ma zu na la amu pa go lu ne me a ba du."

"Yo," Y.T. says.

_____ A couple of minutes later, she's pooning her way up I-5, headed up into Valley-land. She's a little freaked-out, her timing is off, she's taking it easy. A tune keeps running through her head: "The Happy Wanderer." It's driving her crazy.

A large black blur keeps pulling alongside her. It would be a tempting target, so large and ferrous, if it were going a little faster. But she can make better time than this barge, even when she's taking it slow.

The driver's side window of the black car rolls down. It's the guy. Jason. He's sticking his whole head out the window to look back at her, driving blind. The wind at fifty miles per hour does not ruffle his firmly gelled razor cut.

He smiles. He has an imploring look about him, the same look that Roadkill gets. He points suggestively at his rear quarter-panel.

What the hell. The last time she pooned this guy, he took her exactly where she was going. Y.T. detaches from the Acura she's been hitched to for the last half mile, swings it over to Jason's fat Olds. And Jason takes her off the freeway and onto Victory Boulevard, headed for Van Nuys, which is exactly right.

But after a couple of miles, he swings the wheel sharply right and screeches into the parking lot of a ghost mall, which is wrong. Right now, nothing's parked in the lot but an eighteen-wheeler, motor running, SALDUCCI BROS. MOVING & STORAGE painted on the sides.

"Come on," Jason says, getting out of his Oldsmobile. "You don't want to waste any time."

"Screw you, asshole," she says, reeling in her poon, looking back toward the boulevard for some promising westbound traffic. Whatever this guy has in mind, it is probably unprofessional.

"Young lady," says another voice, an older and more arresting sort of voice, "it's fine if you don't like Jason. But your pal, Uncle Enzo, needs your help."

A door on the back of the semi has opened up. A man in a black suit is standing there. Behind him, the interior of the semi is brightly lit up. Halogen light glares off the man's slick hairdo.

Even with this backlighting, she can tell it is the man with the glass eye.

"What do you want?" she says.

"What I want," he says, looking her up and down, "and what I need are different things. Right now I'm working, see, which means that what I want is not important. What I need is for you to get into this truck along with your skateboard and that suitcase."

Then he adds, "Am I getting through to you?" He asks the question almost rhetorically, like he presumes the answer is no.

"He's for real," Jason says, as though Y.T. must be hanging on his opinion.

"Well, there you have it," the man with the glass eye says.

Y.T. is supposed to be on her way to a Reverend Wayne's Pearly Gates franchise. If she screws up this delivery, that means she's double-crossing God, who may or may not exist, and in any case who is capable of forgiveness. The Mafia definitely exists and hews to a higher standard of obedience.

She hands her stuff—the plank and the aluminum case—up to the man with the glass eye, then vaults up into the back of the semi, ignoring his proffered hand. He recoils, holds up his hand, looks at it to see if there's something wrong with it. By the time her feet leave the ground, the truck is already moving. By the time the door is pulled shut behind her, they have already pulled onto the boulevard.

"Just gotta run a few tests on this delivery of yours," the man with the glass eye says.

"Ever think of introducing yourself?" Y.T. says.

"Nah," he says, "people always forget names. You can just think of me as that one guy, y'know?"

Y.T. is not really listening. She is checking out the inside of the truck.

The trailer of this rig consists of a single long skinny room. Y.T. has just come in through its only entrance. At this end of the room, a couple of Mafia guys are lounging around, the way they always do.

Most of the room is taken up by electronics. Big electronics.

"Going to just do some computer stuff, y'know," he says, handing the briefcase over to a computer guy. Y.T. knows he's a computer guy because he has long hair in a ponytail and he's wearing jeans and he seems gentle.

"Hey, if anything happens to that, my ass is grass," Y.T. says. She's trying to sound tough and brave, but it's a hollow act in these circumstances.

The man with the glass eye is, like, shocked. "What do you think I am, some kind of incredibly stupid dickhead?" he says. "Shit, that's just what I need, trying to explain to Uncle Enzo how I managed to get his little bunny rabbit shot in the kneecaps."

"It's a noninvasive procedure," the computer guy says in a placid, liquid voice.

The computer guy rotates the case around in his hand a few times, just to get a feel for it. Then he slides it into a large open-ended cylinder that is resting on the top of a table. The walls of the cylinder are a couple of inches thick. Frost appears to be growing on this thing. Mystery gases continuously slide off of it, like teaspoons of milk dropped into turbulent water. The gases plunge out across the table and drop to the floor, where they make a little carpet of fog that flows and blooms around their shoes. When the computer guy has it in place, he yanks his hand back from the cold.

Then he puts on a pair of computer goggles.

That's all there is to it. He just sits there for a few minutes. Y.T. is not a computer person, but she knows that somewhere behind the cabinets and doors in the back of this truck there is a big computer doing a lot of things right now.

"It's like a CAT scanner," the man with the glass eye says, using the same hushed tone of voice as a sportscaster in a golfing tournament. "But it reads everything, you know," he says, rotating his hands impatiently in all-encompassing circles.

"How much does it cost?"

"I don't know."

"What's it called?"

"Doesn't really have a name yet."

"Well, who makes it?"

"We made the goddamn thing," the man with the glass eye says. "Just, like in the last couple weeks."

"What for?"

"You're asking too many questions. Look. You're a cute kid. I mean, you're a hell of a chick. You're a knockout. But don't go thinking you're too important at this stage."

At this stage. Hmm.

24

Hiro is in his 20-by-30 at the U-Stor-It. He is spending a little time in Reality, as per the suggestion of his partner. The door is open so that ocean breezes and jet exhaust can blow through. All the furniture—the futons, the cargo pallet, the experimental cinderblock furniture—has been pushed up against the walls. He is holding a one-meter-long piece of heavy rebar with tape wrapped around one end to make a handle. The rebar approximates a katana, but it is very much heavier. He calls it the redneck katana.

He is in the kendo stance, barefoot. He should be wearing voluminous ankle-length culottes and a heavy indigo tunic, which is the traditional uniform, but instead he is wearing jockey shorts. Sweat is running down his smoothly muscled cappuccino back and exploring his cleavage. Blisters the size of green grapes are forming on the ball of his left foot. Hiro's heart and lungs are well developed, and he has been blessed with unusually quick reflexes, but he is not intrinsically strong, the way his father was. Even if he were intrinsically strong, working with the redneck katana would be very difficult.

He is full of adrenaline, his nerves are shot, and his mind is cluttered up with free-floating anxiety—floating around on an ocean of generalized terror.

He is shuffling back and forth down the thirty-foot axis of the room. From time to time he will accelerate, raise the redneck katana up over his head until it is pointed backward, then bring it swiftly down, snapping his wrists at the last moment so that it comes to a stop in midair. Then he says, "Next!"

Theoretically. In fact, the redneck katana is difficult to stop once it gets moving. But it's good exercise. His forearms look like bundles of steel cables. Almost. Well, they will soon, anyway.

The Nipponese don't go in for this nonsense about follow-through. If you strike a man on the top of his head with a katana and do not make any effort to stop the blade, it will divide his skull and probably get hung up in his collarbone or his pelvis, and then you will be out there in the middle of the medieval bat-tlefield with a foot on your late opponent's face, trying to work the blade loose as his best friend comes running up to you with a certain vengeful gleam in his eye. So the plan is to snap the blade to a full stop just after the impact, maybe crease his brain-pan an inch or two, then whip it out and look for another samu-rai, hence: "Next!"

He has been thinking about what happened earlier tonight with Raven, which pretty much rules out sleep, and this is why he is practicing with the redneck katana at three in the morning.

He knows he was totally unprepared. The spear just came at him. He slapped at it with the blade. He happened to slap it at the right time, and it missed him. But he did this almost absentmind-edly.

Maybe that's how great warriors do it. Carelessly, not wracking their minds with the consequences.

Maybe he's flattering himself.

_____ The sound of a helicopter has been getting louder for some minutes now. Even though Hiro lives right next to the airport, this is unusual. They're not supposed to fly right near LAX, it raises evident safety questions.

It doesn't stop getting louder until it is very loud, and at that point, the helicopter is hovering a few feet above the parking lot, right out in front of Hiro and Vitaly's 20-by-30. It's a nice one, a corporate jet chopper, dark green, with subdued markings. Hiro suspects that in brighter light, he would be able to make out the logo of a defense contractor, most likely General Jim's Defense System.

A pale-faced white man with a very high forehead-cum-bald spot jumps out of the chopper, looking a lot more athletic than his face and general demeanor would lead you to expect, and jogs across the parking lot directly toward Hiro. This is the kind of guy

Hiro remembers from when his dad was in the Army—not the gristly veterans of legends and movies, just sort of regular thirty-five-year-old guys rattling around in bulky uniforms. He's a major. His name, sewn onto his BDUs, is Clem.

"Hiro Protagonist?"

"The same."

"Juanita sent me to pick you up. She said you'd recognize the name."

"I recognize the name. But I don't really work for Juanita."

"She says you do now."

"Well, that's nice," Hiro says. "So I guess it's kind of urgent?"

"I think that would be a fair assumption," Major Clem says.

"Can I spare a few minutes? Because I've been working out, and I need to run next door."

Major Clem looks next door. The next logo down the strip is THE REST STOP.

"The situation is fairly static. You could spare five minutes," Major Clem says.

Hiro has an account with The Rest Stop. To live at the U-Stor-It, you sort of have to have an account. So he gets to bypass the front office where the attendant waits by the cash register. He shoves his membership card into a slot, and a computer screen lights up with three choices:

M

F

NURSERY (UNISEX)

Hiro slaps the "M" button. Then the screen changes to a menu of four choices:

OUR SPECIAL LIMITED FACILITIES—THRIFTY BUT
   SANITARY

STANDARD FACILITIES—JUST LIKE HOME—MAYBE JUST
   A LITTLE BETTER

PRIME FACILITIES—A GRACIOUS PLACE FOR THE
   DISCRIMINATING PATRON

THE LAVATORY GRANDE ROYALE

He has to override a well-worn reflex to stop himself from automatically punching SPECIAL LIMITED FACILITIES, which is what he and all the other U-Stor-It residents always use. Almost impossible to go in there and not come in contact with someone else's bodily fluids. Not a pretty sight. Not at all gracious. Instead—what the fuck, Juanita's going to hire him, right?—he slams the button for LAVATORY GRANDE ROYALE.

Never been here before. It's like something on the top floor of a luxury high-rise casino in Atlantic City, where they put semi-retarded adults from South Philly after they've blundered into the mega-jackpot. It's got everything that a dimwitted pathological gambler would identify with luxury: gold-plated fixtures, lots of injection-molded pseudomarble, velvet drapes, and a butler.

None of the U-Stor-It residents ever use The Lavatory Grande Royale. The only reason it's here is that this place happens to be across the street from LAX. Singaporean CEOs who want to have a shower and take a nice, leisurely crap, with all the sound effects, without having to hear and smell other travelers doing the same, can come here and put it all on their corporate travel card.

The butler is a thirty-year-old Centroamerican whose eyes look a little funny, like they've been closed for the last several hours. He is just throwing some improbably thick towels over his arm as Hiro bursts in.

"Gotta get in and out in five minutes," Hiro says.

"You want shave?" the butler says. He paws at his own cheeks suggestively, unable to peg Hiro's ethnic group.

"Love to. No time."

He peels off his jockey shorts, tosses his swords onto the crushed-velvet sofa, and steps into the marbleized amphitheatre of the shower stall. Hot water hits him from all directions at once. There's a knob on the wall so you can choose your favorite temperature.

Afterward, he'd like to take a dump, read some of those glossy phone book–sized magazines next to the high-tech shitter, but he's got to get going. He dries himself off with a fresh towel the size of a circus tent, yanks on some loose drawstring slacks and a

T-shirt, throws some Kongbucks at the butler, and runs out, girding himself with the swords.

———————— It's a short flight, mostly because the military pilot is happy to eschew comfort in favor of speed. The chopper takes off at a shallow angle, keeping low so it won't get sucked into any jumbo jets, and as soon as the pilot gets room to maneuver, he whips the tail around, drops the nose, and lets the rotor yank them onward and upward across the basin, toward the sparsely lit mass of the Hollywood Hills.

But they stop short of the Hills, and end up on the roof of a hospital. Part of the Mercy chain, which technically makes this Vatican airspace. So far, this has Juanita written all over it.

"Neurology ward," Major Clem says, delivering this string of nouns like an order. "Fifth floor, east wing, room 564."

———————— The man in the hospital bed is Da5id.

Extremely thick, wide leather straps have been stretched across the head and foot of the bed. Leather cuffs, lined with fluffy sheepskin, are attached to the straps. These cuffs have been fastened around Da5id's wrists and ankles. He's wearing a hospital gown that has mostly fallen off.

The worst thing is that his eyes don't always point in the same direction. He's hooked up to an EKG that's charting his heartbeat, and even though Hiro's not a doctor, he can see it's not a regular pattern. It beats too fast, then it doesn't beat at all, then an alarm sounds, then it starts beating again.

He has gone completely blank. His eyes are not seeing anything. At first, Hiro thinks that his body is limp and relaxed. Getting closer, he sees that Da5id is taut and shivering, slick with perspiration.

"We put in a temporary pacemaker," a woman says.

Hiro turns. It's a nun who also appears to be a surgeon.

"How long has he been in convulsions?"

"His ex-wife called us in, said she was worried."

"Juanita."

"Yes. When the paramedics arrived, he had fallen out of his

chair at home and was convulsing on the floor. You can see a
bruise, here, where we think his computer fell off the table and
hit him in the ribs. So to protect him from further damage, we
put him in four-points. But for the last half hour he's been like
this—like his whole body is in fibrillation. If he stays this way,
we'll take the restraints off."

"Was he wearing goggles?"

"I don't know. I can check for you."

"But you think this happened while he was goggled into his
computer?"

"I really don't know, sir. All I know is, he's got such bad cardiac
arrhythmia that we had to implant a temporary pacemaker right
there on his office floor. We gave him some seizure medication,
which didn't work. Put him on some downers to calm him, which
worked slightly. Put his head into various pieces of imaging machinery to find out what the problem was. The jury is still out on
that."

"Well, I'm going to go look at his house," Hiro says.

The doctor shrugs.

"Let me know when he comes out of it," Hiro says.

The doctor doesn't say anything to this. For the first time,
Hiro realizes that Da5id's condition may not be temporary.

As Hiro is stepping out into the hallway, Da5id speaks, "e ne
em ma ni a gi a gi ni mu ma ma dam e ne em am an ki ga a gi a
gi . . . "

Hiro turns around and looks. Da5id has gone limp in the restraints, seems relaxed, half asleep. He is looking at Hiro through
half-closed eyes. "e ne em dam gal nun na a gi agi e ne em u mu
un abzu ka a gi a agi . . . "

Da5id's voice is deep and placid, with no trace of stress. The
syllables roll off his tongue like drool. As Hiro walks down the
hallway he can hear Da5id talking all the way.

"i ge en i ge en nu ge en nu ge en us sa tur ra lu ra ze em
men . . . "

_____ Hiro gets back into the chopper. They cruise up
the middle of Beachwood Canyon, headed straight for the Hollywood sign.

Da5id's house has been transfigured by light. It's at the end of its own little road, at the summit of a hill. The road has been blocked off by a squat froglike Jeep-thing from General Jim's, saturated red and blue light sweeping and pulsing out of it. Another helicopter is above the house, supported on a swirling column of radiance. Soldiers creep up and down the property, carrying hand-held searchlights.

"We took the precaution of securing the area," Major Clem says.

At the fringes of all this light, Hiro can see the dead organic colors of the hillside. The soldiers are trying to push it back with their searchlights, trying to burn it away. He is about to bury himself in it, become a single muddy pixel in some airline passenger's window. Plunging into the biomass.

Da5id's laptop is on the floor next to the table where he liked to work. It is surrounded by medical debris. In the middle of this, Hiro finds Da5id's goggles, which either fell off when he hit the floor, or were stripped off by the paramedics.

Hiro picks up the goggles. As he brings them up toward his eyes, he sees the image: a wall of black-and-white static. Da5id's computer has snow-crashed.

He closes his eyes and drops the goggles. You can't get hurt by looking at a bitmap. Or can you?

_____ The house is sort of a modernist castle with a high turret on one end. Da5id and Hiro and the rest of the hackers used to go up there with a case of beer and a hibachi and just spend a whole night, eating jumbo shrimp and crab legs and oysters and washing them down with beer. Now it's deserted, of course, just the hibachi, which is rusted and almost buried in gray ash, like an archaeological relic. Hiro has pinched one of Da5id's beers from the fridge, and he sits up here for a while, in what used to be his favorite place, drinking his beer slowly, like he used to, reading stories in the lights.

The old central neighborhoods are packed in tight below an eternal, organic haze. In other cities, you breathe industrial contaminants, but in L.A., you breathe amino acids. The hazy sprawl is ringed and netted with glowing lines, like hot wires in a toaster.

At the outlet of the canyon, it comes close enough that the light sharpens and breaks up into stars, arches, glowing letters. Streams of red and white corpuscles throb down highways to the fuzzy logic of intelligent traffic lights. Farther away, spreading across the basin, a million sprightly logos smear into solid arcs, like geometric points merging into curves. To either side of the franchise ghettos, the loglo dwindles across a few shallow layers of development and into a surrounding dimness that is burst here and there by the blaze of a security spotlight in someone's backyard.

The franchise and the virus work on the same principle: what thrives in one place will thrive in another. You just have to find a sufficiently virulent business plan, condense it into a three-ring binder—its DNA—xerox it, and embed it in the fertile lining of a well-traveled highway, preferably one with a left-turn lane. Then the growth will expand until it runs up against its property lines.

In olden times, you'd wander down to Mom's Cafe for a bite to eat and a cup of joe, and you would feel right at home. It worked just fine if you never left your hometown. But if you went to the next town over, everyone would look up and stare at you when you came in the door, and the Blue Plate Special would be something you didn't recognize. If you did enough traveling, you'd never feel at home anywhere.

But when a businessman from New Jersey goes to Dubuque, he knows he can walk into a McDonald's and no one will stare at him. He can order without having to look at the menu, and the food will always taste the same. McDonald's is Home, condensed into a three-ring binder and xeroxed. "No surprises" is the motto of the franchise ghetto, its *Good Housekeeping* seal, subliminally blazoned on every sign and logo that make up the curves and grids of light that outline the Basin.

The people of America, who live in the world's most surprising and terrible country, take comfort in that motto. Follow the loglo outward, to where the growth is enfolded into the valleys and the canyons, and you find the land of the refugees. They have fled from the true America, the America of atomic bombs, scalpings, hip-hop, chaos theory, cement overshoes, snake handlers, spree killers, space walks, buffalo jumps, drive-bys, cruise missiles, Sherman's March, gridlock, motorcycle gangs, and bungee jumping. They have parallel-parked their bimbo boxes in identical computer-designed Burbclave street patterns and secreted themselves in symmetrical sheetrock shitholes with vinyl floors and ill-fitting woodwork and no sidewalks, vast house farms out in the loglo wilderness, a culture medium for a medium culture.

The only ones left in the city are street people, feeding off debris; immigrants, thrown out like shrapnel from the destruction of the Asian powers; young bohos; and the technomedia priesthood of Mr. Lee's Greater Hong Kong. Young smart people like Da5id and Hiro, who take the risk of living in the city because they like stimulation and they know they can handle it.

25

Y.T. can't really tell where they are. It's clear that they're stuck in traffic. It's not like this is predictable or anything.

"Y.T. must get under way now," she announces.

No reaction for a sec. Then the hacker guy sits back in his chair, stares out through his goggles, ignoring the 3-D compu-display, taking in a nice view of the wall. "Okay," he says.

Quick as a mongoose, the man with the glass eye darts in, yanks the aluminum case out of the cryogenic cylinder, tosses it to Y.T. Meantime, one of the lounging-around Mafia guys is opening the back door of the truck, giving them all a nice view of a traffic jam on the boulevard.

"One other thing," the man with the glass eye says, and shoves an envelope into one of Y.T.'s multitudinous pockets.

"What's that?" Y.T. says.

He holds up his hands self-protectively. "Don't worry, it's just a little something. Now get going."

He motions at the guy who's holding her plank. The guy turns out to be fairly hip, because he just throws the plank. It lands at an odd angle on the floor between them. But the spokes have long ago seen the floor coming, calculated all the angles, extended and flexed themselves like the legs and feet of a basketball player coming back to earth from a monster dunk. The plank lands on its feet, banks this way, then that, as it regains its balance, then steers itself right up to Y.T. and stops beside her.

She stands on it, kicks a few times, flies out the back door of the semi, and onto the hood of a Pontiac that was following them much too closely. Its windshield makes a nice surface to bank off of, and she gets her direction neatly reversed by the time she hits the pavement. The owner of the Pontiac is honking self-righteously, but there's no way he can chase her down because traffic is totally stopped, Y.T. is the only thing for miles around that is actually capable of movement. Which is the whole point of Kouriers in the first place.

_____ The Reverend Wayne's Pearly Gates #1106 is a pretty big one. Its low serial number implies great age. It was built long ago, when land was cheap and lots were big. The parking lot is half full. Usually, all you see at a Reverend Wayne's are old beaters with wacky Spanish expressions nail-polished on the rear bumpers—the rides of CentroAmerican evangelicals who have come up north to get decent jobs and escape the relentlessly Catholic style of their homelands. This lot also has a lot of just plain old regular bimbo boxes with license plates from all the Burbclaves.

Traffic is moving a little better on this stretch of the boulevard, and so Y.T. comes into the lot at a pretty good clip, takes one or two orbits around the franchise to work off her speed. A smooth parking lot is hard to resist when you are going fast, and to look at it from a slightly less juvenile point of view, it's a good idea to scope things out, to be familiar with your environment. Y.T. learns that this parking lot is linked with that of a Chop Shop franchise next door ("We turn any vehicle into CASH in minutes!"), which in turn flows into the lot of a neighboring strip mall. A dedicated thrasher could probably navigate from L.A. to New York by coasting from one parking lot into the next.

This parking lot makes popping and skittering noises in some areas. Looking down, she sees that behind the franchise, near the dumpster, the asphalt is strewn with small glass vials, like the one that Squeaky was looking at last night. They are scattered about like cigarette butts behind a bar. When the footpads of her wheels pass over these vials, they tiddlywink out from underneath and skitter across the pavement.

People are lined up out the door, waiting to get in. Y.T. jumps the line and goes inside.

_____ The front room of the Reverend Wayne's Pearly Gates is, of course, like all the others. A row of padded vinyl chairs where worshippers can wait for their number to be called, with a potted plant at each end and a table strewn with primeval magazines. A toy corner where kids can kill time, reenacting imaginary, cosmic battles in injection-molded plastic. A counter done up in fake wood so it looks like something from an old church. Behind the counter, a pudgy high school babe, dishwater blond hair that has been worked over pretty good with a curling iron, blue metal-flake eyeshadow, an even coat of red makeup covering her broad, gelatinous cheeks, a flimsy sort of choir robe thrown over her T-shirt.

When Y.T. comes in, she is right in the middle of a transaction. She sees Y.T. right away, but no three-ring binder anywhere in the world allows you to flag or fail in the middle of a transaction.

Stymied, Y.T. sighs and crosses her arms to convey impatience. In any other business establishment, she'd already be raising hell and marching around behind the counter as if she owned the place. But this is a church, damn it.

There's a little rack along the front of the counter bearing religious tracts, free for the taking, donation requested. Several slots on the rack are occupied by the Reverend Wayne's famous bestseller, *How America Was Saved from Communism: ELVIS SHOT JFK.*

She pulls out the envelope that the man with the glass eye stuck into her pocket. It is not thick and soft enough to contain a lot of cash, unfortunately.

It contains half a dozen snapshots. All of them feature Uncle Enzo. He is on the broad, flat horseshoe driveway of a large house, larger than any house Y.T. has ever seen with her own two eyes. He is standing on a skateboard. Or falling off of a skateboard. Or coasting, slowly, arms splayed wildly out to the sides, chased by nervous security personnel.

A piece of paper is wrapped around the pictures. It says: "Y.T.—Thanks for your help. As you can see from these pictures, I tried to train for this assignment, but it's going to take some practice. Your friend, Uncle Enzo."

Y.T. wraps the pictures up just the way they were, puts them back in her pocket, stifles a smile, returns to business matters.

The girl in the robe is still performing her transaction behind the counter. The transactee is a stocky Spanish-speaking woman in an orange dress.

The girl types some stuff into the computer. The customer snaps her Visa card down on the fake wood altar top; it sounds like a rifle shot. The girl pries the card up using her inch-long fingernails, a dicey and complicated operation that makes Y.T. think of insects climbing out of their egg sacs. Then she performs the sacrament, swiping the card through its electromagnetic slot with a carefully modulated sweep of the arm, as though tearing back a veil, handing over the slip, mumbling that she needs a signature and daytime phone number. She might as well have been speaking Latin, but that's okay, since this customer is familiar with the liturgy and signs and numbers it before the words are fully spoken.

Then it just remains for the Word from On High. But computers and communications are awfully good these days, and it usually doesn't take longer than a couple of seconds to perform a charge-card verification. The little machine beeps out its approval code, heavenly tunes sing out from tinny speakers, and a wide pair of pearlescent doors in the back of the room swing majestically open.

"Thank you for your donation," the girl says, slurring the words together into a single syllable.

The customer stomps toward the double doors, drawn in by hypnotic organ strains. The interior of the chapel is weirdly colored, illuminated partly by fluorescent fixtures wedged into the ceiling and partly by large colored light boxes that simulate stained-glass windows. The largest of these, shaped like a fattened Gothic arch, is bolted to the back wall, above the altar, and features a blazing trinity: Jesus, Elvis, and the Reverend Wayne. Jesus gets top billing. The worshipper is not half a dozen steps into the place before she thuds down on her knees in the middle of the aisle and begins to speak in tongues: "ar ia ari ar isa ve na a mir ia i sa, ve na a mir ia a sar ia ... "

The doors swing shut again.

"Just a sec," the girl says, looking at Y.T. a little nervously. She goes around the corner and stands in the middle of the toy area, inadvertently getting the hem of her robe caught up in a Ninja Raft Warriors battle module, and knocks on the door to the potty.

"Busy!" says a man's voice from the other side of the door.

"The Kourier's here," the girl says.

"I'll be right out," the man says, more quietly.

And he really is right out. Y.T. does not perceive any waiting time, no zipping up of the fly or washing of the hands. He is wearing a black suit with a clerical collar, pulling a lightweight black robe on over that as he emerges into the toy area, crushing little action figures and fighter aircraft beneath his black shoes. His hair is black and well greased, with individual strands of gray, and he wears wire-rimmed bifocals with a subtle brownish tint. He has very large pores.

And by the time he gets close enough that Y.T. can see all of these details, she can also smell him. She smells Old Spice, plus a strong whiff of vomit on his breath. But it's not boozy vomit.

"Gimme that," he says, and yanks the aluminum briefcase from her hand.

Y.T. never lets people do that.

"You have to sign for it," she says. But she knows it's too late. If you don't get them to sign first, you're screwed. You have no power, no leverage. You're just a brat on a skateboard.

Which is why Y.T. never lets people yank deliveries out of her hand. But this guy is a minister, for God's sake. She just didn't reckon on it. He yanked it out of her hand—and now he runs with it back to his office.

"I can sign for it," the girl says. She looks scared. More than that, she looks sick.

"It has to be him personally," Y.T. says. "Reverend Dale T. Thorpe."

Now she's done being shocked and starting to be pissed. So she just follows him right into his office.

"You can't go in there," the girl says, but she says it dreamily, sadly, like this whole thing is already half forgotten. Y.T. opens the door.

The Reverend Dale T. Thorpe sits at his desk. The aluminum briefcase is open in front of him. It is filled with the same complicated bit of business that she saw the other night, after the Raven thing. The Reverend Dale T. Thorpe seems to be leashed by the neck to this device.

No, actually he is wearing something on a string around his neck. He was keeping it under his clothes, the way Y.T. keeps Uncle Enzo's dog tags. He has pulled it out now and shoved it into a slot inside the aluminum case. It appears to be a laminated ID card with a bar code on it.

Now he pulls the card out and lets it dangle down his front. Y.T. cannot tell whether he has noticed her. He is typing on the keyboard, punching away with two fingers, missing letters, doing it again.

Then motors and servos inside the aluminum case whir and shudder. The Reverend Dale T. Thorpe has unsnapped one of the little vials from its place in the lid and inserted it into a socket next to the keyboard. It is slowly drawn down inside the machine.

The vial pops back out again. The red plastic cap is emitting grainy red light. It has little LEDs built into it, and they are spelling out numbers, counting down seconds: 5,4,3,2,1 . . .

The Reverend Dale T. Thorpe holds the vial up to his left nostril. When the LED counter gets down to zero, it hisses, like air coming out of a tire valve. At the same time, he inhales deeply, sucking it all into his lungs. Then he shoots the vial expertly into his wastebasket.

"Reverend?" the girl says. Y.T. spins around to see her drifting toward the office. "Would you do mine now, please?"

The Reverend Dale T. Thorpe does not answer. He has slumped back in his leather swivel chair and is staring at a neon-framed blowup of Elvis, in his Army days, holding a rifle.

26

When he wakes up, it's the middle of the day and he is all dried out from the sun, and birds are circling overhead, trying to decide whether he's dead or alive. Hiro climbs down from the roof of the turret and, throwing caution to the wind, drinks three glasses of L.A. tap water. He gets some bacon out of Da5id's fridge and throws it in the microwave. Most of General Jim's people have left, and there is only a token guard of soldiers down on the road. Hiro locks all the doors that look out on the hillside, because he can't stop thinking about Raven. Then he sits at the kitchen table and goggles in.

The Black Sun is mostly full of Asians, including a lot of people from the Bombay film industry, glaring at each other, stroking their black mustaches, trying to figure out what kind of hyperviolent action film will play in Persepolis next year. It is nighttime there. Hiro is one of the few Americans in the joint.

Along the back wall of the bar is a row of private rooms, ranging from little tête-à-têtes to big conference rooms where a bunch of avatars can gather and have a meeting. Juanita is waiting for Hiro in one of the smaller ones. Her avatar just looks like Juanita. It is an honest representation, with no effort made to hide the early suggestions of crow's-feet at the corners of her big black eyes. Her glossy hair is so well resolved that Hiro can see individual strands refracting the light into tiny rainbows.

"I'm at Da5id's house. Where are you?" Hiro says.

"In an airplane—so I may break up," Juanita says.

"You on your way here?"

"To Oregon, actually."

"Portland?"

"Astoria."

"Why on earth would you go to Astoria, Oregon, at a time like this?"

Juanita takes a deep breath, lets it out shakily. "If I told you, we'd get into an argument."

"What's the latest word on Da5id?" Hiro says.

"The same."

"Any diagnosis?"

Juanita sighs, looks tired. "There won't be any diagnosis," she says. "It's a software, not a hardware, problem."

"Huh?"

"They're rounding up the usual suspects. CAT scans, NMR scans, PET scans, EEGs. Everything's fine. There's nothing wrong with his brain—his hardware."

"It just happens to be running the wrong program?"

"His software got poisoned. Da5id had a snow crash last night, inside his head."

"Are you trying to say it's a psychological problem?"

"It kind of goes beyond those established categories," Juanita says, "because it's a new phenomenon. A very old one, actually."

"Does this thing just happen spontaneously, or what?"

"You tell me," she says. "You were there last night. Did anything happen after I left?"

"He had a Snow Crash hypercard that he got from Raven outside The Black Sun."

"Shit. That bastard."

"Who's the bastard? Raven or Da5id?"

"Da5id. I tried to warn him."

"He used it." Hiro goes on to explain the Brandy with the magic scroll. "Then later he had computer trouble and got bounced."

"I heard about that part," she says. "That's why I called the paramedics."

"I don't see the connection between Da5id's computer having a crash, and you calling an ambulance."

"The Brandy's scroll wasn't just showing random static. It was flashing up a large amount of digital information, in binary form. That digital information was going straight into Da5id's optic nerve. Which is part of the brain, incidentally—if you stare into a person's pupil, you can see the terminal of the brain."

"Da5id's not a computer. He can't read binary code."

"He's a hacker. He messes with binary code for a living. That ability is firm-wired into the deep structures of his brain. So he's susceptible to that form of information. And so are you, homeboy."

"What kind of information are we talking about?"

"Bad news. A metavirus," Juanita says. "It's the atomic bomb of informational warfare—a virus that causes any system to infect itself with new viruses."

"And that's what made Da5id sick?"

"Yes."

"Why didn't I get sick?"

"Too far away. Your eyes couldn't resolve the bitmap. It has to be right up in your face."

"I'll think about that one," Hiro says. "But I have another question. Raven also distributes another drug—in Reality—called, among other things, Snow Crash. What is it?"

"It's not a drug," Juanita says. "They make it look like a drug and feel like a drug so that people will want to take it. It's laced with cocaine and some other stuff."

"If it's not a drug, what is it?"

"It's chemically processed blood serum taken from people who are infected with the metavirus," Juanita says. "That is, it's just another way of spreading the infection."

"Who's spreading it?"

"L. Bob Rife's private church. All of those people are infected."

Hiro puts his head in his hands. He's not exactly thinking about this; he's letting it ricochet around in his skull, waiting for it to come to rest. "Wait a minute, Juanita. Make up your mind. This Snow Crash thing—is it a virus, a drug, or a religion?"

Juanita shrugs. "What's the difference?"

—————————— That Juanita is talking this way does not make it any easier for Hiro to get back on his feet in this conversation. "How can you say that? You're a religious person yourself."

"Don't lump all religion together."

"Sorry."

"All people have religions. It's like we have religion receptors built into our brain cells, or something, and we'll latch onto anything that'll fill that niche for us. Now, religion used to be essentially viral—a piece of information that replicated inside the human mind, jumping from one person to the next. That's the way it used to be, and unfortunately, that's the way it's headed right now. But there have been several efforts to deliver us from the hands of primitive, irrational religion. The first was made by someone named Enki about four thousand years ago. The second was made by Hebrew scholars in the eighth century B.C., driven out of their homeland by the invasion of Sargon II, but eventually it just devolved into empty legalism. Another attempt was made by Jesus—that one was hijacked by viral influences within fifty days of his death. The virus was suppressed by the Catholic Church, but we're in the middle of a big epidemic that started in Kansas in 1900 and has been gathering momentum ever since."

"Do you believe in God or not?" Hiro says. First things first.

"Definitely."

"Do you believe in Jesus?"

"Yes. But not in the physical, bodily resurrection of Jesus."

"How can you be a Christian without believing in that?"

"I would say," Juanita says, "how can you be a Christian with it? Anyone who takes the trouble to study the gospels can see that the bodily resurrection is a myth that was tacked onto the real story several years after the real histories were written. It's so *National Enquirer*-esque, don't you think?"

_____ Beyond that, Juanita doesn't have much to say. She doesn't want to get into it now, she says. She doesn't want to prejudice Hiro's thinking "at this point."

"Does that imply that there's going to be some other point? Is this a continuing relationship?" Hiro says.

"Do you want to find the people who infected Da5id?"

"Yes. Hell, Juanita, even if it weren't for the fact that he is my friend, I'd want to find them before they infect me."

"Look at the Babel stack, Hiro, and then visit me if I get back from Astoria."

"If you get back? What are you doing there?"

"Research."

She's been putting on a businesslike front through this whole talk, spitting out information, telling Hiro the way it is. But she's tired and anxious, and Hiro gets the idea that she's deeply afraid.

"Good luck," he says. He was all ready to do some flirting with her during this meeting, picking up where they left off last night. But something has changed in Juanita's mind between then and now. Flirting is the last thing on her mind.

Juanita's going to do something dangerous in Oregon. She doesn't want Hiro to know about it so that he won't worry.

"There's some good stuff in the Babel stack about someone named Inanna," she says.

"Who's Inanna?"

"A Sumerian goddess. I'm sort of in love with her. Anyway, you can't understand what I'm about to do until you understand Inanna."

"Well, good luck," Hiro says. "Say hi to Inanna for me."

"Thanks."

"When you get back, I want to spend some time with you."

"The feeling is mutual," she says. "But we have to get out of this first."

"Oh. I didn't realize I was in something."

"Don't be a sap. We're all in it."

Hiro leaves, exiting into The Black Sun.

There is one guy wandering around the Hacker Quadrant who really stands out. His avatar doesn't look so hot. And he's having trouble controlling it. He looks like a guy who's just goggled into the Metaverse for the first time and doesn't know how to move around. He keeps bumping into tables, and when he wants to turn around, he spins around several times, not knowing how to stop himself.

Hiro walks toward him, because his face seems a little familiar. When the guy finally stops moving long enough for Hiro to resolve him clearly, he recognizes the avatar. It's a Clint. Most often seen in the company of a Brandy.

The Clint recognizes Hiro, and his surprised face comes on for a second, is then replaced by his usual stern, stiff-lipped, craggy appearance. He holds up his hands together in front of him, and Hiro sees that he is holding a scroll, just like Brandy's.

Hiro reaches for his katana, but the scroll is already up in his face, spreading open to reveal the blue glare of the bitmap inside. He sidesteps, gets over to one side of the Clint, raising the katana overhead, snaps the katana straight down and cuts the Clint's arms off.

As the scroll falls, it spreads open even wider. Hiro doesn't dare look at it now. The Clint has turned around and is awkwardly trying to escape from The Black Sun, bouncing from table to table like a pinball.

If Hiro could kill the guy—cut his head off—then his avatar would stay in The Black Sun, be carried away by the Graveyard Daemons. Hiro could do some hacking and maybe figure out who he is, where he's coming in from.

But a few dozen hackers are lounging around the bar, watching all of this, and if they come over and look at the scroll, they'll all end up like Da5id.

Hiro squats down, looking away from the scroll, and pulls up one of the hidden trapdoors that lead down into the tunnel system. He's the one who coded those tunnels into The Black Sun to begin with; he's the only person in the whole bar who can use them. He sweeps the scroll into the tunnel with one hand, then closes the door.

Hiro can see the Clint, way over near the exit, trying to get his avatar aimed out through the door. Hiro runs after him. If the guy reaches the Street, he's gone—he'll turn into a translucent ghost. With a fifty-foot head start in a crowd of a million other translucent ghosts, there's just no way. As usual, there's a crowd of wannabes gathered on the Street out front. Hiro can see the usual assortment, including a few black-and-white people.

One of those black-and-whites is Y.T. She's loitering out there waiting for Hiro to come out.

"Y.T.!" he shouts. "Chase that guy with no arms!"

Hiro gets out the door just a few seconds after the Clint does. Both the Clint and Y.T. are already gone.

He turns back into The Black Sun, pulls up a trapdoor, and drops down into the tunnel system, the realm of the Graveyard Daemons. One of them has already picked up the scroll and is trudging in toward the center to throw it on the fire.

"Hey, bud," Hiro says, "take a right turn at the next tunnel and leave that thing in my office, okay? But do me a favor and roll it up first."

He follows the Graveyard Daemon down the tunnel, under the Street, until they're under the neighborhood where Hiro and the other hackers have their houses. Hiro has the Graveyard Daemon deposit the rolled-up scroll in his workshop, down in the basement—the room where Hiro does his hacking. Then Hiro continues upstairs to his office.

27

His voice phone is ringing. Hiro picks it up.

"Pod," Y.T. says, "I was beginning to think you'd never come out of there."

"Where are you?" Hiro says.

"In Reality or the Metaverse?"

"Both."

"In the Metaverse, I'm on a plusbound monorail train. Just passed by Port 35."

"Already? It must be an express."

"Good thinking. That Clint you cut the arms off of is two cars ahead of me. I don't think he knows I'm following him."

"Where are you in Reality?"

"Public terminal across the street from a Reverend Wayne's," she says.

"Oh, yeah? How interesting."

"Just made a delivery there."

"What kind of delivery?"

"An aluminum suitcase."

He gets the whole story out of her, or what he thinks is the whole story—there's no real way to tell.

"You're sure that the babbling that the people did in the park was the same as the babbling that the woman did at the Reverend Wayne's?"

"Sure," she says. "I know a bunch of people who go there. Or their parents go there and drag them along, you know."

"To the Reverend Wayne's Pearly Gates?"

"Yeah. And they all do that speaking in tongues. So I've heard it before."

"I'll talk to you later, pod," Hiro says. "I've got some serious research to do."

"Later."

The Babel/Infocalypse card is resting in the middle of his desk. Hiro picks it up. The Librarian comes in.

Hiro is about to ask the Librarian whether he knows that Lagos is dead. But it's a pointless question. The Librarian knows it, but he doesn't. If he wanted to check the Library, he could find out in a few moments. But he wouldn't really retain the information. He doesn't have an independent memory. The Library is his memory, and he only uses small parts of it at once.

"What can you tell me about speaking in tongues?" Hiro says.

"The technical term is 'glossolalia,' " the Librarian says.

"Technical term? Why bother to have a technical term for a religious ritual?"

The Librarian raises his eyebrows. "Oh, there's a great deal of technical literature on the subject. It is a neurological phenomenon that is merely *exploited* in religious rituals."

"It's a Christian thing, right?"

"Pentecostal Christians think so, but they are deluding themselves. Pagan Greeks did it—Plato called it *theomania*. The Oriental cults of the Roman Empire did it. Hudson Bay Eskimos, Chukchi shamans, Lapps, Yakuts, Semang pygmies, the North Borneo cults, the Trhi-speaking priests of Ghana. The Zulu Amandiki cult and the Chinese religious sect of Shang-ti-hui. Spirit mediums of Tonga and the Brazilian Umbanda cult. The Tungus tribesmen of Siberia say that when the shaman goes into his trance and raves incoherent syllables, he learns the entire language of Nature."

"The language of Nature."

"Yes, sir. The Sukuma people of Africa say that the language is *kinaturu*, the tongue of the ancestors of all magicians, who are thought to have descended from one particular tribe."

"What causes it?"

"If mystical explanations are ruled out, then it seems that glossolalia comes from structures buried deep within the brain, common to all people."

"What does it look like? How do these people act?"

"C. W. Shumway observed the Los Angeles revival of 1906 and noted six basic symptoms: complete loss of rational control; dominance of emotion that leads to hysteria; absence of thought or will; automatic functioning of the speech organs; amnesia; and occasional sporadic physical manifestations such as jerking or twitching. Eusebius observed similar phenomena around the year 300, saying that the false prophet begins by a deliberate suppression of conscious thought, and ends in a delirium over which he has no control."

"What's the Christian justification for this? Is there anything in the Bible that backs this up?"

"Pentecost."

"You mentioned that word earlier—what is it?"

"From the Greek *pentekostos,* meaning fiftieth. It refers to the fiftieth day after the Crucifixion."

"Juanita just told me that Christianity was hijacked by viral influences when it was only fifty days old. She must have been talking about this. What is it?"

" 'And they were all filled with the Holy Spirit and began to speak in other tongues, as the Spirit gave them utterance. Now there were dwelling in Jerusalem Jews, devout men from every nation under heaven. And at this sound the multitude came together, and they were bewildered, because each one heard them speaking in his own language. And they were amazed and wondered, saying, "Are not all these who are speaking Galileans? And how is it that we hear, each of us in his own native language? Parthians and Medes and Elamites and residents of Mesopotamia, Judea and Cappadocia, Pontus and Asia, Phrygia and Pamphylia, Egypt and the parts of Libya belonging to Cyrene, and visitors from Rome, both Jews and proselytes, Cretans and Arabians, we hear them telling in our own tongues the mighty works of God." And all were amazed and perplexed, saying to one another, "What does this mean?" ' Acts 2:4–12."

"Damned if I know," Hiro says. "Sounds like Babel in reverse."

"Yes, sir. Many Pentecostal Christians believe that the gift of tongues was given to them so that they could spread their religion to other peoples without having to actually learn their language. The word for that is 'xenoglossy.' "

"That's what Rife was claiming in that piece of videotape, on top of the *Enterprise*. He said he could understand what those Bangladeshis were saying."

"Yes, sir."

"Does that really work?"

"In the sixteenth century, Saint Louis Bertrand allegedly used the gift of tongues to convert somewhere between thirty thousand and three hundred thousand South American Indians to Christianity," the Librarian says.

"Wow. Spread through that population even faster than smallpox."

—————————— "What did the Jews think of this Pentecost thing?" Hiro says. "They were still running the country, right?"

"The Romans were running the country," the Librarian says, "but there were a number of Jewish religious authorities. At this time, there were three groups of Jews: the Pharisees, the Sadducees, and the Essenes."

"I remember the Pharisees from *Jesus Christ, Superstar*. They were the ones with the deep voices who were always hassling Christ."

"They were hassling him," the Librarian says, "because they were religiously very strict. They adhered to a strong legalistic version of the religion; to them, the Law was everything. Clearly, Jesus was a threat to them because he was proposing, in effect, to do away with the Law."

"He wanted a contract renegotiation with God."

"This sounds like an analogy, which I am not very good at—but even if it is taken literally, it is true."

"Who were the other two groups?"

"The Sadducees were materialists."

"Meaning what? They drove BMWs?"

"No. Materialists in the philosophical sense. All philosophies are either monist or dualist. Monists believe that the material world is the only world—hence, materialists. Dualists believe in a binary universe, that there is a spiritual world in addition to the material world."

"Well, as a computer geek, I have to believe in the binary universe."

The Librarian raises his eyebrows. "How does that follow?"

"Sorry. It's a joke. A bad pun. See, computers use binary code to represent information. So I was joking that I have to believe in the binary universe, that I have to be a dualist."

"How droll," the Librarian says, not sounding very amused. "Your joke may not be without genuine merit, however."

"How's that? I was just kidding, really."

"Computers rely on the one and the zero to represent all things. This distinction between something and nothing—this pivotal separation between being and nonbeing—is quite fundamental and underlies many Creation myths."

Hiro feels his face getting slightly warm, feels himself getting annoyed. He suspects that the Librarian may be pulling his leg, playing him for a fool. But he knows that the Librarian, however convincingly rendered he may be, is just a piece of software and cannot actually do such things.

"Even the word 'science' comes from an Indo-European root meaning 'to cut' or 'to separate.' The same root led to the word 'shit,' which of course means to separate living flesh from nonliving waste. The same root gave us 'scythe' and 'scissors' and 'schism,' which have obvious connections to the concept of separation."

"How about 'sword'?"

"From a root with several meanings. One of those meanings is 'to cut or pierce.' One of them is 'post' or 'rod.' And the other is, simply, 'to speak.' "

"Let's stay on track," Hiro says.

"Fine. I can return to this potential conversation fork at a later time, if you desire."

"I don't want to get all forked up at this point. Tell me about the third group—the Essenes."

"They lived communally and believed that physical and spiritual cleanliness were intimately connected. They were constantly bathing themselves, lying naked under the sun, purging themselves with enemas, and going to extreme lengths to make sure that their food was pure and uncontaminated. They even had their own version of the Gospels in which Jesus healed possessed people, not with miracles, but by driving parasites, such as tapeworm, out of their body. These parasites are considered to be synonymous with demons."

"They sound kind of like hippies."

"The connection has been made before, but it is faulty in many ways. The Essenes were strictly religious and would never have taken drugs."

"So to them there was no difference between infection with a parasite, like tapeworm, and demonic possession."

"Correct."

"Interesting. I wonder what they would have thought about computer viruses?"

"Speculation is not in my ambit."

"Speaking of which—Lagos was babbling to me about viruses and infection and something called a nam-shub. What does that mean?"

"Nam-shub is a word from Sumerian."

"Sumerian?"

"Yes, sir. Used in Mesopotamia until roughly 2000 B.C. The oldest of all written languages."

"Oh. So all the other languages are descended from it?"

For a moment, the Librarian's eyes glance upward, as if he's thinking about something. This is a visual cue to inform Hiro that he's making a momentary raid on the Library.

"Actually, no," the Librarian says. "No languages whatsoever are descended from Sumerian. It is an agglutinative tongue, meaning that it is a collection of morphemes or syllables that are grouped into words—very unusual."

"You are saying," Hiro says, remembering Da5id in the hospital, "that if I could hear someone speaking Sumerian, it would sound like a long stream of short syllables strung together."

"Yes, sir."

"Would it sound anything like glossolalia?"

"Judgment call. Ask someone real," the Librarian says.

"Does it sound like any modern tongue?"

"There is no provable genetic relationship between Sumerian and any tongue that came afterward."

"That's odd. My Mesopotamian history is rusty," Hiro says. "What happened to the Sumerians? Genocide?"

"No, sir. They were conquered, but there's no evidence of genocide per se."

"Everyone gets conquered sooner or later," Hiro says. "But their languages don't die out. Why did Sumerian disappear?"

"Since I am just a piece of code, I would be on very thin ice to speculate," the Librarian says.

"Okay. Does anyone understand Sumerian?"

"Yes, at any given time, it appears that there are roughly ten people in the world who can read it."

"Where do they work?"

"One in Israel. One at the British Museum. One in Iraq. One at the University of Chicago. One at the University of Pennsylvania. And five at Rife Bible College in Houston, Texas."

"Nice distribution. And have any of these people figured out what the word 'nam-shub' means in Sumerian?"

"Yes. A nam-shub is a speech with magical force. The closest English equivalent would be 'incantation,' but this has a number of incorrect connotations."

"Did the Sumerians believe in magic?"

The Librarian shakes his head minutely. "This is the kind of seemingly precise question that is in fact very profound, and that pieces of software, such as myself, are notoriously clumsy at. Allow me to quote from Kramer, Samuel Noah, and Maier, John R. *Myths of Enki, the Crafty God.* New York, Oxford: Oxford University Press, 1989: 'Religion, magic, and medicine are so completely intertwined in Mesopotamia that separating them is frustrating and perhaps futile work. . . . [Sumerian incantations] demonstrate an intimate connection between the religious, the magical, and the esthetic so complete that any attempt to pull one away from the other will distort the whole.' There is more material in here that might help explain the subject."

"In where?"

"In the next room," the Librarian says, gesturing at the wall. He walks over and slides the rice-paper partition out of the way.

A *speech with magical force.* Nowadays, people don't believe in these kinds of things. Except in the Metaverse, that is, where magic is possible. The Metaverse is a fictional structure made out of code. And code is just a form of speech—the form that computers understand. The Metaverse in its entirety could be considered a single vast nam-shub, enacting itself on L. Bob Rife's fiber-optic network.

The voice phone rings. "Just a second," Hiro says.

"Take your time," the Librarian says, not adding the obvious reminder that he can wait for a million years if need be.

"Me again," Y.T. says. "I'm still on the train. Stumps got off at Express Port 127."

"Hmm. That's the antipode of Downtown. I mean, it's as far away from Downtown as you can get."

"It is?"

"Yeah. One-two-seven is two to the seventh power minus one—"

"Spare me, I take your word for it. It's definitely out in the middle of fucking nowhere," she says.

"You didn't get off and follow him?"

"Are you kidding? All the way out there? It's ten thousand miles from the nearest building, Hiro."

She has a point. The Metaverse was built with plenty of room to expand. Almost all of the development is within two or three Express Ports—five hundred kilometers or so—of Downtown. Port 127 is twenty thousand miles away.

"What is there?"

"A black cube exactly twenty miles on a side."

"Totally black?"

"Yeah."

"How can you measure a black cube that big?"

"I'm riding along looking at the stars, okay? Suddenly, I can't see them anymore on the right side of the train. I start counting local ports. I count sixteen of them. We get to Express Port 127, and Stumpy climbs off and goes toward the black thing. I count sixteen more local ports and then the stars come out. Then I take thirty-two kilometers and multiply it by point six and I get twenty miles—you asshole."

"That's good," Hiro says. "That's good intel."

"Who do you think owns a black cube twenty miles across?"

"Just going on pure, irrational bias, I'm guessing L. Bob Rife. Supposedly, he has a big hunk of real estate out in the middle of nowhere where he keeps all the guts of the Metaverse. Some of us used to smash into it occasionally when we were out racing motorcycles."

"Well, gotta go, pod."

28

Hiro hangs up and walks into the new room. The Librarian follows.

It is about fifty feet on a side. The center of the space is occupied by three large artifacts, or rather three-dimensional renderings of artifacts. In the center is a thick slab of baked clay, hanging in space, about the size of a coffee table, and about a foot thick. Hiro suspects that it is a magnified rendering of a smaller object. The broad surfaces of the slab are entirely covered with angular writing that Hiro recognizes as cuneiform. Around the edges are rounded, parallel depressions that appear to have been made by fingers as they shaped the slab.

To the right of the slab is a wooden pole with branches on top, sort of a stylized tree. To the left of the slab is an eight-foot-high obelisk, also covered with cuneiform, with a bas-relief figure chiseled into the top.

The room is filled with a three-dimensional constellation of hypercards, hanging weightlessly in the air. It looks like a high-speed photograph of a blizzard in progress. In some places, the hypercards are placed in precise geometric patterns, like atoms in a crystal. In other places, whole stacks of them are clumped together. Drifts of them have accumulated in the corners, as though Lagos tossed them away when he was finished. Hiro finds that his avatar can walk right through the hypercards without disturbing the arrangement. It is, in fact, the three-dimensional counterpart of a messy desktop, all the trash still remaining wherever Lagos left it. The cloud of hypercards extends to every corner of the 50-by-50-foot space, and from floor level all the way up to about eight feet, which is about as high as Lagos's avatar could reach.

"How many hypercards in here?"

"Ten thousand, four hundred and sixty-three," the Librarian says.

"I don't really have time to go through them," Hiro says. "Can you give me some idea of what Lagos was working on here?"

"Well, I can read back the names of all the cards if you'd like. Lagos grouped them into four broad categories: Biblical studies, Sumerian studies, neurolinguistic studies, and intel gathered on L. Bob Rife."

"Without going into that kind of detail—what did Lagos have on his mind? What was he getting at?"

"What do I look like, a psychologist?" the Librarian says. "I can't answer those kinds of questions."

"Let me try it again. How does this stuff connect, if at all, to the subject of viruses?"

"The connections are elaborate. Summarizing them would require both creativity and discretion. As a mechanical entity, I have neither."

"How old is this stuff?" Hiro says, gesturing to the three artifacts.

"The clay envelope is Sumerian. It is from the third millennium B.C. It was dug up from the city of Eridu in southern Iraq. The black stele or obelisk is the Code of Hammurabi, which dates from about 1750 B.C. The treelike structure is a Yahwistic cult totem from Palestine. It's called an asherah. It's from about 900 B.C."

"Did you call that slab an envelope?"

"Yes. It has a smaller clay slab wrapped up inside of it. This was how the Sumerians made tamper-proof documents."

"All these things are in a museum somewhere, I take it?"

"The asherah and the Code of Hammurabi are in museums. The clay envelope is in the personal collection of L. Bob Rife."

"L. Bob Rife is obviously interested in this stuff."

"Rife Bible College, which he founded, has the richest archaeology department in the world. They have been conducting a dig
in Eridu, which was the cult center of a Sumerian god named
Enki."

"How are these things related to each other?"

The Librarian raises his eyebrows. "I'm sorry?"

"Well, let's try process of elimination. Do you know why Lagos
found Sumerian writings interesting as opposed to, say, Greek or
Egyptian?"

"Egypt was a civilization of stone. They made their art and
architecture of stone, so it lasts forever. But you can't write on
stone. So they invented papyrus and wrote on that. But papyrus
is perishable. So even though their art and architecture have
survived, their written records—their data—have largely disappeared."

"What about all those hieroglyphic inscriptions?"

"Bumper stickers, Lagos called them. Corrupt political
speech. They had an unfortunate tendency to write inscriptions
praising their own military victories before the battles had actually taken place."

"And Sumer is different?"

"Sumer was a civilization of clay. They made their buildings of
it and wrote on it, too. Their statues were of gypsum, which
dissolves in water. So the buildings and statues have since fallen
apart under the elements. But the clay tablets were either baked
or else buried in jars. So all the *data* of the Sumerians have
survived. Egypt left a legacy of art and architecture; Sumer's
legacy is its megabytes."

"How many megabytes?"

"As many as archaeologists bother to dig up. The Sumerians
wrote on everything. When they built a building, they would
write in cuneiform on every brick. When the buildings fell down,
these bricks would remain, scattered across the desert. In the
Koran, the angels who are sent to destroy Sodom and Gomorrah
say, 'We are sent forth to a wicked nation, so that we may bring
down on them a shower of clay-stones marked by your Lord for
the destruction of the sinful.' Lagos found this interesting—this
promiscuous dispersal of information, written on a medium that

lasts forever. He spoke of pollen blowing in the wind—I gather that this was some kind of analogy."

"It was. Tell me—has the inscription on this clay envelope been translated?"

"Yes. It is a warning. It says, 'This envelope contains the nam-shub of Enki.'"

"I know what a nam-shub is. What is the nam-shub of Enki?"

The Librarian stares off into the distance and clears his throat dramatically.

"Once upon a time, there was no snake, there was no scorpion,
There was no hyena, there was no lion,
There was no wild dog, no wolf,
There was no fear, no terror,
Man had no rival.
In those days, the land Shubur-Hamazi,
Harmony-tongued Sumer, the great land of the *me* of princeship,
Uri, the land having all that is appropriate,
The land Martu, resting in security,
The whole universe, the people well cared for,
To Enlil in one tongue gave speech.
Then the lord defiant, the prince defiant, the king defiant,
Enki, the lord of abundance, whose commands are trustworthy,
The lord of wisdom, who scans the land,
The leader of the gods,
The lord of Eridu, endowed with wisdom,
Changed the speech in their mouths, put contention into it,
Into the speech of man that had been one.

That is Kramer's translation."

"That's a story," Hiro says. "I thought a nam-shub was an incantation."

"The nam-shub of Enki is both a story and an incantation," the Librarian says. "A self-fulfilling fiction. Lagos believed that in its original form, which this translation only hints at, it actually did what it describes."

"You mean, changed the speech in men's mouths."

"Yes," the Librarian says.

"This is a Babel story, isn't it?" Hiro says. "Everyone was

speaking the same language, and then Enki changed their speech so that they could no longer understand each other. This must be the basis for the Tower of Babel stuff in the Bible."

"This room contains a number of cards tracing that connection," the Librarian says.

"You mentioned before that at one point, everyone spoke Sumerian. Then, nobody did. It just vanished, like the dinosaurs. And there's no genocide to explain how that happened. Which is consistent with the Tower of Babel story, and the nam-shub of Enki. Did Lagos think that Babel really happened?"

"He was sure of it. He was quite concerned about the vast number of human languages. He felt there were simply too many of them."

"How many?"

"Tens of thousands. In many parts of the world, you will find people of the same ethnic group, living a few miles apart in similar valleys under similar conditions, speaking languages that have absolutely nothing in common with each other. This sort of thing is not an oddity—it is ubiquitous. Many linguists have tried to understand Babel, the question of why human language tends to fragment, rather than converging on a common tongue."

"Has anyone come up with an answer yet?"

"The question is difficult and profound," the Librarian says. "Lagos had a theory."

"Yes?"

"He believed that Babel was an actual historical event. That it happened in a particular time and place, coinciding with the disappearance of the Sumerian language. That prior to Babel/ Infocalypse, languages tended to converge. And that afterward, languages have always had an innate tendency to diverge and become mutually incomprehensible—that this tendency is, as he put it, coiled like a serpent around the human brainstem."

"The only thing that could explain that is—"

Hiro stops, not wanting to say it.

"Yes?" the Librarian says.

"If there was some *phenomenon* that moved through the population, altering their minds in such a way that they couldn't process the Sumerian language anymore. Kind of in the same way that a virus moves from one computer to another, damaging each computer in the same way. Coiling around the brainstem."

"Lagos devoted much time and effort to this idea," the Librarian says. "He felt that the nam-shub of Enki was a neurolinguistic virus."

"And that this Enki character was a real personage?"

"Possibly."

"And that Enki invented this virus and spread it throughout Sumer, using tablets like this one?"

"Yes. A tablet has been discovered containing a letter to Enki, in which the writer complains about it."

"A letter to a god?"

"Yes. It is from Sin-samuh, the Scribe. He begins by praising Enki and emphasizing his devotion to him. Then he complains:

> 'Like a young . . . (line broken)
> I am paralyzed at the wrist.
>
> Like a wagon on the road when its yoke has split,
> I stand immobile on the road.
>
> I lay on a bed called "O! and O No!"
> I let out a wail.
>
> My graceful figure is stretched neck to ground,
> I am paralyzed of foot.
>
> My . . . has been carried off into the earth.
> My frame has changed.
>
> At night I cannot sleep,
> my strength has been struck down,
> my life is ebbing away.
>
> The bright day is made a dark day for me.
> I have slipped into my own grave.
>
> I, a writer who knows many things, am made a fool.
> My hand has stopped writing
> There is no talk in my mouth.'

"After more description of his woes, the scribe ends with,

'My god, it is you I fear.

I have written you a letter.
Take pity on me.

The heart of my god: have it given back to me.' "

29

Y.T. is maxing at a Mom's Truck Stop on 405, waiting for her ride. Not that she would ever be caught dead at a Mom's Truck Stop. If, like, a semi ran her over with all eighteen of its wheels in front of a Mom's Truck Stop, she would drag herself down the shoulder of the highway using her eyelid muscles until she reached a Snooze 'n' Cruise full of horny derelicts rather than go into a Mom's Truck Stop. But sometimes when you're a professional, they give you a job that you don't like, and you just have to be very cool and put up with it.

For purposes of this evening's job, the man with the glass eye has already supplied her with a "driver and security person," as he put it. A totally unknown quantity. Y.T. isn't sure she likes putting up with some mystery guy. She has this image in her mind that he's going to be like the wrestling coach at the high school. That would be so grotendous. Anyway, this is where she's supposed to meet him.

Y.T. orders a coffee and a slice of cherry pie à la mode. She carries them over to the public Street terminal back in the corner. It is sort of a wraparound stainless steel booth stuck between a phone booth, which has a homesick truck driver poured into it, and a pinball machine, which features a chick with big boobs that light up when you shoot the ball up the magic Fallopians.

She's not that good at the Metaverse, but she knows her way around, and she's got an address. And finding an address in the Metaverse shouldn't be any more difficult than doing it in Reality, at least if you're not a totally retarded ped.

As soon as she steps out into the Street, people start giving her these looks. The same kind of looks that people give her when she walks through the worsted-wool desolation of the Westlake Corporate Park in her dynamic blue-and-orange Kourier gear. She knows that the people in the Street are giving her dirty looks because she's just coming in from a shitty public terminal. She's a trashy black-and-white person.

The built-up part of the Street, around Port Zero, forms a luminescent thunderhead off to her right. She puts her back to it and climbs onto the monorail. She'd like to go into town, but that's an expensive part of the Street to visit, and she'd be dumping money into the coin slot about every one-tenth of a millisecond.

The guy's name is Ng. In Reality, he is somewhere in Southern California. Y.T. isn't sure exactly what he is driving; some kind of a van full of what the man with the glass eye described as "stuff, really incredible stuff that you don't need to know about." In the Metaverse, he lives outside of town, around Port 2, where things really start to spread out.

_____ Ng's Metaverse home is a French colonial villa in the prewar village of My Tho in the Mekong Delta. Visiting him is like going to Vietnam in about 1955, except that you don't have to get all sweaty. In order to make room for this creation, he has laid claim to a patch of Metaverse space a couple of miles off the Street. There's no monorail service in this low-rent development, so Y.T.'s avatar has to walk the entire way.

He has a large office with French doors and a balcony looking out over endless rice paddies where little Vietnamese people work. Clearly, this guy is a fairly hardcore techie, because Y.T. counts hundreds of people out in his rice paddies, plus dozens more running around the village, all of them fairly well rendered and all of them doing different things. She's not a bithead, but she knows that this guy is throwing a lot of computer time into the task of creating a realistic view out his office window. And the fact that it's Vietnam makes it twisted and spooky. Y.T. can't wait to tell Roadkill about this place. She wonders if it has bombings and strafings and napalm drops. That would be the best.

Ng himself, or at least, Ng's avatar, is a small, very dapper Vietnamese man in his fifties, hair plastered to his head, wearing military-style khakis. At the time Y.T. comes into his office, he is leaning forward in his chair, getting his shoulders rubbed by a geisha.

A geisha in Vietnam?

Y.T.'s grandpa, who was there for a while, told her that the Nipponese took over Vietnam during the war and treated it with the cruelty that was their trademark before we nuked them and they discovered that they were pacifists. The Vietnamese, like most other Asians, hate the Japanese. And apparently this Ng character gets a kick out of the idea of having a Japanese geisha around to rub his back.

But it is a very strange thing to do, for one reason: The geisha is just a picture on Ng's goggles, and on Y.T.'s. And you can't get a massage from a picture. So why bother?

When Y.T. comes in, Ng stands up and bows. This is how hardcore Street wackos greet each other. They don't like to shake hands because you can't actually feel the contact and it reminds you that you're not even really there.

"Yeah, hi," Y.T. says.

Ng sits back down and the geisha goes right back to it. Ng's desk is a nice French antique with a row of small television monitors along the back edge, facing toward him. He spends most of his time watching the monitors, even when he is talking.

"They told me a little bit about you," Ng says.

"Shouldn't listen to nasty rumors," Y.T. says.

Ng picks up a glass from his desk and takes a drink from it. It looks like a mint julep. Globes of condensation form on its surface, break loose, and trickle down the side. The rendering is so perfect that Y.T. can see a miniaturized reflection of the office windows in each drop of condensation. It's just totally ostentatious. What a bithead.

He is looking at her with a totally emotionless face, but Y.T. imagines that it is a face of hate and disgust. To spend all this money on the coolest house in the Metaverse and then have some skater come in done up in grainy black-and-white. It must be a real kick in the metaphorical nuts.

Somewhere in this house a radio is going, playing a mix of Vietnamese loungy type stuff and Yank wheelchair rock.

"Are you a Nova Sicilia citizen?" Ng says.

"No. I just chill sometimes with Uncle Enzo and the other Mafia dudes."

"Ah. Very unusual."

Ng is not a man in a hurry. He has soaked up the languid pace of the Mekong Delta and is content to sit there and watch his TV sets and fire off a sentence every few minutes.

Another thing: He apparently has Tourette's syndrome or some other brain woes because from time to time, for no apparent reason, he makes strange noises with his mouth. They have the twangy sound that you always hear from Vietnamese when they are in the back rooms of stores and restaurants carrying on family disputes in the mother tongue, but as far as Y.T. can tell, they aren't real words, just sound effects.

"Do you work a lot for these guys?" Y.T. asks.

"Occasional small security jobs. Unlike most large corporations, the Mafia has a strong tradition of handling its own security arrangements. But when something especially technical is called for—"

He pauses in the middle of this sentence to make an incredible zooming sound in his nose.

"Is that your thing? Security?"

Ng scans all of his TV sets. He snaps his fingers and the geisha scurries out of the room. He folds his hands together on his desk and leans forward. He stares at Y.T. "Yes," he says.

Y.T. looks back at him for a bit, waiting for him to continue. After a few seconds his attention drifts back to the monitors.

"I do most of my work under a large contract with Mr. Lee," he blurts.

Y.T. is waiting for the continuation of this sentence: Not "Mr. Lee," but "Mr. Lee's Greater Hong Kong."

Oh, well. If she can drop Uncle Enzo's name, he can drop Mr. Lee's.

"The social structure of any nation-state is ultimately determined by its security arrangements," Ng says, "and Mr. Lee understands this."

Oh, wow, we're going to be profound now. Ng is suddenly talking just like the old white men on the TV pundit powwows, which Y.T.'s mother watches obsessively.

"Instead of hiring a large human security force—which impacts the social environment—you know, lots of minimum-wage earners standing around carrying machine guns—Mr. Lee prefers to use nonhuman systems."

Nonhuman systems. Y.T. is about to ask him, what do you know about the Rat Thing. But it is pointless; he won't say. It would get their relationship off on the wrong foot, Y.T. asking Ng for intel, intel that he would never give her, and that would make this whole scene even weirder than it is now, which Y.T. can't even imagine.

Ng bursts forth with a long string of twangy noises, pops, and glottal stops.

"Fucking bitch," he mumbles.

"Excuse me?"

"Nothing," he says, "a bimbo box cut me off. None of these people understand that with this vehicle, I could crush them like a potbellied pig under an armored personnel carrier."

"A bimbo box—you're driving?"

"Yes. I'm coming to pick you up—remember?"

"Do you mind?"

"No," he sighs, as if he really does.

Y.T. gets up and walks around behind his desk to look.

Each of the little TV monitors is showing a different view out his van: windshield, left window, right window, rearview. Another one has an electronic map showing his position: inbound on the San Bernardino, not far away.

"The van is under voice command," he explains. "I removed the steering-wheel-and-pedal interface because I found verbal commands more convenient. This is why I will sometimes make unfamiliar sounds with my voice—I am controlling the vehicle's systems."

Y.T. signs off from the Metaverse for a while, to clear her head and take a leak. When she takes off the goggles she discovers that she has built up quite an audience of truckers and mechanics, who are standing around the terminal booth in a semicircle listening to her jabber at Ng. When she stands up, attention shifts to her butt, naturally.

Y.T. hits the bathroom, finishes her pie, and wanders out into the ultraviolet glare of the setting sun to wait for Ng.

Recognizing his van is easy enough. It is enormous. It is eight feet high and wider than it is high, which would have made it a wide load in the old days when they had laws. The construction is boxy and angular; it has been welded together out of the type of flat, dimpled steel plate usually used to make manhole lids and stair treads. The tires are huge, like tractor tires with a more subtle tread, and there are six of them: two axles in back and one in front. The engine is so big that, like an evil spaceship in a movie, Y.T. feels its rumbling in her ribs before she can see it; it is kicking out diesel exhaust through a pair of squat vertical red smokestacks that project from the roof, toward the rear. The windshield is a perfectly flat rectangle of glass about three by eight feet, smoked so black that Y.T. can't make out an outline of anything inside. The snout of the van is festooned with every type of high-powered light known to science, like this guy hit a New South Africa franchise on a Saturday night and stole every light off every roll bar, and a grille has been constructed across the front, welded together out of rails torn out of an abandoned railroad somewhere. The grille alone probably weighs more than a small car.

The passenger door swings open. Y.T. walks over and climbs into the front seat. "Hi," she is saying. "You need to take a whiz or anything?"

Ng isn't there.

Or maybe he is.

Where the driver's seat ought to be, there is a sort of neoprene pouch about the size of a garbage can suspended from the ceiling by a web of straps, shock cords, tubes, wires, fiber-optic cables, and hydraulic lines. It is swathed in so much stuff that it is hard to make out its actual outlines.

At the top of this pouch, Y.T. can see a patch of skin with some black hair around it—the top of a balding man's head. Everything else, from the temples downward, is encased in an enormous goggle/mask/headphone/feeding-tube unit, held on-to his head by smart straps that are constantly tightening and loosening themselves to keep the device comfortable and prop-erly positioned.

Below this, on either side, where you'd sort of expect to see arms, huge bundles of wires, fiber optics, and tubes run up out of the floor and are seemingly plugged into Ng's shoulder sockets. There is a similar arrangement where his legs are supposed to be attached, and more stuff going into his groin and hooked up to various locations on his torso. The entire thing is swathed in a one-piece coverall, a pouch, larger than his torso ought to be, that is constantly bulging and throbbing as though alive.

"Thank you, all my needs are taken care of," Ng says.

The door slams shut behind her. Ng makes a yapping sound, and the van pulls out onto the frontage road, headed back toward 405.

"Please excuse my appearance," he says, after a couple of awkward minutes. "My helicopter caught fire during the evacuation of Saigon in 1974—a stray tracer from ground forces."

"Whoa. What a drag."

"I was able to reach an American aircraft carrier off the coast, but you know, the fuel was spraying around quite a bit during the fire."

"Yeah, I can imagine, uh huh."

"I tried prostheses for a while—some of them are very good. But nothing is as good as a motorized wheelchair. And then I got to thinking, why do motorized wheelchairs always have to be tiny pathetic things that strain to go up a little teeny ramp? So I bought this—it is an airport firetruck from Germany—and converted it into my new motorized wheelchair."

"It's very nice."

"America is wonderful because you can get anything on a drive-through basis. Oil change, liquor, banking, car wash, funerals, anything you want—drive through! So this vehicle is much better than a tiny pathetic wheelchair. It is an extension of my body."

"When the geisha rubs your back?"

Ng mumbles something and his pouch begins to throb and undulate around his body. "She is a daemon, of course. As for the massage, my body is suspended in an electrocontractive gel that massages me when I need it. I also have a Swedish girl and an African woman, but those daemons are not as well rendered."

"And the mint julep?"

"Through a feeding tube. Nonalcoholic, ha ha."

"So," Y.T. says at some point, when they are way past LAX,

and she figures it's too late to chicken out, "what's the plan? Do we have a plan?"

"We go to Long Beach. To the Terminal Island Sacrifice Zone. And we buy some drugs," Ng says. "Or you do, actually, since I am indisposed."

"That's my job? To buy some drugs?"

"Buy them, and throw them up in the air."

"In a Sacrifice Zone?"

"Yes. And we'll take care of the rest."

"Who's we, dude?"

"There are several more, uh, entities that will help us."

"What, is the back of the van full of more—people like you?"

"Sort of," Ng says. "You are close to the truth."

"Would these be, like, nonhuman systems?"

"That is a sufficiently all-inclusive term, I think."

Y.T. figures that for a big *yes*.

"You tired? Want me to drive or anything?"

Ng laughs sharply, like distant ack-ack, and the van almost swerves off the road. Y.T. doesn't get the sense that he is laughing at the joke; he is laughing at what a jerk Y.T. is.

30

"Okay, last time we were talking about the clay envelope. But what about this thing? The thing that looks like a tree?" Hiro says, gesturing to one of the artifacts.

"A totem of the goddess Asherah," the Librarian says crisply.

"Now we're getting somewhere," Hiro says. "Lagos said that the Brandy in The Black Sun was a cult prostitute of Asherah. So who is Asherah?"

"She was the consort of El, who is also known as Yahweh," the Librarian says. "She also was known by other names: Elat, her most common epithet. The Greeks knew her as Dione or Rhea. The Canaanites knew her as Tannit or Hawwa, which is the same thing as Eve."

"Eve?"

"The etymology of 'Tannit' proposed by Cross is: feminine of 'tannin,' which would mean 'the one of the serpent.' Furthermore, Asherah carried a second epithet in the Bronze Age, 'dat batni,' also 'the one of the serpent.' The Sumerians knew her as Nintu or Ninhursag. Her symbol is a serpent coiling about a tree or staff: the caduceus."

"Who worshipped Asherah? A lot of people, I gather."

"Everyone who lived between India and Spain, from the second millennium B.C. up into the Christian era. With the exception of the Hebrews, who only worshipped her until the religious reforms of Hezekiah and, later, Josiah."

"I thought the Hebrews were monotheists. How could they worship Asherah?"

"Monolatrists. They did not deny the *existence* of other gods. But they were only supposed to *worship* Yahweh. Asherah was venerated as the consort of Yahweh."

"I don't remember anything about God having a wife in the Bible."

"The Bible didn't exist at that point. Judaism was just a loose collection of Yahwistic cults, each with different shrines and practices. The stories about the Exodus hadn't been formalized into scripture yet. And the later parts of the Bible had not yet happened."

"Who decided to purge Asherah from Judaism?"

"The deuteronomic school—defined, by convention, as the people who wrote the book of Deuteronomy as well as Joshua, Judges, Samuel, and Kings."

"And what kind of people were they?"

"Nationalists. Monarchists. Centralists. The forerunners of the Pharisees. At this time, the Assyrian king Sargon II had recently conquered Samaria—northern Israel—forcing a migration of Hebrews southward into Jerusalem. Jerusalem expanded greatly and the Hebrews began to conquer territory to the west, east, and south. It was a time of intense nationalism and patriotic fervor. The deuteronomic school embodied those attitudes in scripture by rewriting and reorganizing the old tales."

"Rewriting them how?"

"Moses and others believed that the River Jordan was the border of Israel, but the deuteronomists believed that Israel included Transjordan, which justified aggression to the east. There are many other examples: the predeuteronomic law said nothing about a monarch. The Law as laid down by the deuteronomic school reflected a monarchist system. The predeuteronomic law was largely concerned with sacred matters, while the deuteronomic law's main concern is the education of the king and his people—secular matters in other words. The deuteronomists insisted on centralizing the religion in the Temple in Jerusalem, destroying the outlying cult centers. And there is another feature that Lagos found significant."

"And that is?"

"Deuteronomy is the only book of the Pentateuch that refers to a written Torah as comprising the divine will: 'And when he sits on the throne of his kingdom, he shall write for himself in a book a copy of this law, from that which is in charge of the Levitical priests; and it shall be with him, and he shall read in it all the days of his life, that he may learn to fear the LORD his God, by keeping all the words of this law and these statutes, and doing them; that his heart may not be lifted up above his brethren, and that he may not turn aside from the commandment, either to the right hand or to the left; so that he may continue long in his kingdom, he and his children, in Israel.' Deuteronomy 17:18–20."

"So the deuteronomists codified the religion. Made it into an organized, self-propagating entity," Hiro says. "I don't want to say virus. But according to what you just quoted me, the Torah is like a virus. It uses the human brain as a host. The host—the human—makes copies of it. And more humans come to synagogue and read it."

"I cannot process an analogy. But what you say is correct insofar as this: After the deuteronomists had reformed Judaism, instead of making sacrifices, the Jews went to synagogue and read the Book. If not for the deuteronomists, the world's monotheists would still be sacrificing animals and propagating their beliefs through the oral tradition."

"Sharing needles," Hiro says. "When you were going over this stuff with Lagos, did he ever say anything about the Bible being a virus?"

"He said it had certain things in common with a virus, but that it was different. He considered it a benign virus. Like that used for vaccinations. He considered the Asherah virus to be more malignant, capable of being spread through exchange of bodily fluids."

"So the strict, book-based religion of the deuteronomists inoculated the Hebrews against the Asherah virus."

"In combination with strict monogamy and other kosher practices, yes," the Librarian says. "The previous religions, from Sumer up to Deuteronomy, are known as prerational. Judaism was the first of the rational religions. As such, in Lagos's view, it was much less susceptible to viral infection because it was based on fixed, written records. This was the reason for the veneration of the Torah and the exacting care used when making new copies of it—informational hygiene."

"What are we living in nowadays? The postrational era?"

"Juanita made comments to that effect."

"I'll bet she did. She's starting to make more sense to me, Juanita is."

"Oh."

"She never really made much sense before."

"I see."

"I think that if I can just spend enough time with you to figure out what's on Juanita's mind—well, wonderful things could happen."

"I will try to be of assistance."

"Back to work—this is no time for a hard-on. It seems that Asherah was a carrier of a viral infection. The deuteronomists somehow realized this and exterminated her by blocking all the vectors by which she infected new victims."

"With reference to viral infections," the Librarian says, "if I may make a fairly blunt, spontaneous cross-reference—something I am coded to do at opportune moments—you may wish to examine herpes simplex, a virus that takes up residence in the nervous system and never leaves. It is capable of carrying new genes into existing neurons and genetically reengineering them. Modern gene therapists use it for this purpose. Lagos thought that herpes simplex might be a modern, benign descendant of Asherah."

"Not always benign," Hiro says, remembering a friend of his who died of AIDS–related complications; in the last days, he had herpes lesions from his lips all the way down his throat. "It's only benign because we have immunities."

"Yes, sir."

"So did Lagos think that the Asherah virus actually altered the DNA of brain cells?"

"Yes. This was the backbone of his hypothesis that the virus was able to transmute itself from a biologically transmitted string of DNA into a set of behaviors."

"What behaviors? What was Asherah worship like? Did they do sacrifices?"

"No. But there is evidence of cult prostitutes, both male and female."

"Does that mean what I think it does? Religious figures who would hang around the temple and fuck people?"

"More or less."

"Bingo. Great way to spread a virus. Now, I want to jump back to an earlier fork in the conversation."

"As you wish. I can handle nested forkings to a virtually infinite depth."

"You made a connection between Asherah and Eve."

"Eve—whose Biblical name is Hawwa—is clearly the Hebrew interpretation of an older myth. Hawwa is an ophidian mother goddess."

"Ophidian?"

"Associated with serpents. Asherah is also an ophidian mother goddess. And both are associated with trees as well."

"Eve, as I recall, is considered responsible for getting Adam to eat the forbidden fruit, from the tree of *knowledge* of good and evil. Which is to say, it's not just fruit—it's data."

"If you say so, sir."

"I wonder if viruses have always been with us, or not. There's sort of an implicit assumption that they have been around forever. But maybe that's not true. Maybe there was a period of history when they were nonexistent or at least unusual. And at a certain point, when the metavirus showed up, the number of different viruses exploded, and people started getting sick a whole lot. That would explain the fact that all cultures seem to have a myth about Paradise, and the Fall from Paradise."

"Perhaps."

"You told me that the Essenes thought that tapeworms were demons. If they'd known what a virus was, they probably would have thought the same thing. And Lagos told me the other night that, according to the Sumerians, there was no concept of good and evil per se."

"Correct. According to Kramer and Maier, there are good demons and bad demons. 'Good ones bring physical and emotional health. Evil ones bring disorientation and a variety of physical and emotional ills. . . . But these demons can hardly be distinguished from the diseases they personify . . . and many of the diseases sound, to modern ears, as though they must be psychosomatic.' "

"That's what the doctors said about Da5id, that his disease must be psychosomatic."

"I don't know anything about Da5id, except for some rather banal statistics."

"It's as though 'good' and 'evil' were invented by the writer of the Adam and Eve legend to explain why people get sick—why they have physical and mental viruses. So when Eve—or Asherah—got Adam to eat the fruit of the tree of knowledge of good and evil, she was introducing the concept of good and evil into the world—introducing the metavirus, which creates viruses."

"Could be."

"So my next question is: Who wrote the Adam and Eve legend?"

"This is a source of much scholarly argument."

"What did Lagos think? More to the point, what did Juanita think?"

"Nicolas Wyatt's radical interpretation of the Adam and Eve story supposes that it was, in fact, written as a political allegory by the deuteronomists."

"I thought they wrote the later books, not Genesis."

"True. But they were involved in compiling and editing the earlier books as well. For many years, it was assumed that Genesis was written sometime around 900 B.C. or even earlier—long before the advent of the deuteronomists. But more recent analysis of the vocabulary and content suggests that a great deal of edito-

rial work—possibly even authorial work—took place around the
time of the Exile, when the deuteronomists held sway."

"So they may have rewritten an earlier Adam and Eve myth."

"They appear to have had ample opportunity. According to
the interpretation of Hvidberg and, later, Wyatt, Adam in his
garden is a parable for the king in his sanctuary, specifically King
Hosea, who ruled the northern kingdom until it was conquered
by Sargon II in 722 B.C."

"That's the conquest you mentioned earlier—the one that
drove the deuteronomists southward toward Jerusalem."

"Exactly. Now 'Eden,' which can be understood simply as the
Hebrew word for 'delight,' stands for the happy state in which
the king existed prior to the conquest. The expulsion from Eden
to the bitter lands to the east is a parable for the massive depor-
tation of Israelites to Assyria following Sargon II's victory. According to this interpretation, the king was enticed away from the
path of righteousness by the cult of El, with its associated worship of Asherah—who is commonly associated with serpents, and
whose symbol is a tree."

"And his association with Asherah somehow caused him to be
conquered—so when the deuteronomists reached Jerusalem,
they recast the Adam and Eve story as a warning to the leaders
of the southern kingdom."

"Yes."

"And perhaps, because no one was listening to them, perhaps
they invented the concept of good and evil in the process, as a
hook."

"Hook?"

"Industry term. Then what happened? Did Sargon II try to
conquer the southern kingdom also?"

"His successor, Sennacherib, did. King Hezekiah, who ruled
the southern kingdom, prepared for the attack feverishly, making
great improvements in the fortifications of Jerusalem, improving
its supply of drinking water. He was also responsible for a far-
reaching series of religious reforms, which he undertook under
the direction of the deuteronomists."

"How did it work out?"

"The forces of Sennacherib surrounded Jerusalem. 'And that
night the angel of the LORD went forth, and slew a hundred and

eighty-five thousand in the camp of the Assyrians; and when men arose early in the morning, behold, these were all dead bodies. Then Sennacherib king of Assyria departed . . . ' 2 Kings 19:35–36."

"I'll bet he did. So let me get this straight: the deuteronomists, through Hezekiah, impose a policy of informational hygiene on Jerusalem and do some civil-engineering work—you said they worked on the water supply?"

" 'They stopped all the springs and the brook that flowed through the land, saying, "Why should the kings of Assyria come and find much water?" ' 2 Chronicles 32:4. Then the Hebrews carved a tunnel seventeen hundred feet through solid rock to carry that water inside city walls."

"And then as soon as Sennacherib's soldiers came on the scene, they all dropped dead of what can only be understood as an extremely virulent disease, to which the people of Jerusalem were apparently immune. Hmm, interesting—I wonder what got into their water?"

31

Y.T. doesn't get down to Long Beach very much, but when she does, she will do just about anything to avoid the Sacrifice Zone. It's an abandoned shipyard the size of a small town. It sticks out into San Pedro Bay, where the older, nastier Burbclaves of the Basin—unplanned Burbclaves of tiny asbestos-shingled houses patrolled by beetle-browed Kampuchean men with pump shotguns—fade off into the foam-kissed beaches. Most of it's on the appropriately named Terminal Island, and since her plank doesn't run on the water, that means she can only get in or out by one access road.

Like all Sacrifice Zones, this one has a fence around it, with yellow metal signs wired to it every few yards.

SACRIFICE ZONE

WARNING. The National Parks Service has declared this area to be a National Sacrifice Zone. The Sacrifice Zone Program was developed to manage parcels of land whose clean-up cost exceeds their total future economic value.

And like all Sacrifice Zone fences, this one has holes in it and is partially torn down in places. Young men blasted out of their minds on natural and artificial male hormones must have some place to do their idiotic coming-of-age rituals. They come in from Burb-claves all over the area in their four-wheel-drive trucks and tear across the open ground, slicing long curling gashes into the clay cap that was placed on the really bad parts to prevent windblown asbestos from blizzarding down over Disneyland.

Y.T. is oddly satisfied to know that these boys have never even dreamed of an all-terrain vehicle like Ng's motorized wheelchair. It veers off the paved road with no loss in speed—ride gets a little bumpy—and hits the chain-link fence as if it were a fog bank, plowing a hundred-foot section into the ground.

It is a clear night, and so the Sacrifice Zone glitters, an immense carpet of broken glass and shredded asbestos. A hundred feet away, some seagulls are tearing at the belly of a dead German shepherd lying on its back. There is a constant undulation of the ground that makes the shattered glass flash and twinkle; this is caused by vast, sparse migrations of rats. The deep, computer-designed im-prints of suburban boys' fat knobby tires paint giant runes on the clay, like the mystery figures in Peru that Y.T.'s mom learned about at the NeoAquarian Temple. Through the windows, Y.T. can hear occasional bursts of either firecrackers or gunfire.

She can also hear Ng making new, even stranger sounds with his mouth.

There is a built-in speaker system in this van—a stereo, though far be it from Ng to actually listen to any tunes. Y.T. can feel it turning on, can sense a nearly inaudible hiss coming from the speakers.

The van begins to creep forward across the Zone.

The inaudible hiss gathers itself up into a low electronic hum. It's not steady, it wavers up and down, staying pretty low, like Roadkill fooling around with his electric bass. Ng keeps changing the direction of the van, as though he's searching for something, and Y.T. gets the sense that the pitch of the hum is rising.

It's definitely rising, building up in the direction of a squeal.

Ng snarls a command and the volume is reduced. He's driving very slowly now.

"It is possible that you might not have to buy any Snow Crash at all," he mumbles. "We may have found an unprotected stash."

"What is this totally irritating noise?"

"Bioelectronic sensor. Human cell membranes. Grown in vitro, which means in glass—in a test tube. One side is exposed to outside air, the other side is clean. When a foreign substance penetrates the cell membrane to the clean side, it's detected. The more foreign molecules penetrate, the higher the pitch of the sound."

"Like a Geiger counter?"

"Very much like a Geiger counter for cell-penetrating compounds," Ng says.

Like what? Y.T. wants to ask. But she doesn't.

Ng stops the van. He turns on some lights—very dim lights. That's how anal this guy is—he has gone to the trouble to install special dim lights in addition to all the bright ones.

They are looking into a sort of bowl, right at the foot of a major drum heap, that is strewn with litter. Most of the litter is empty beer cans. In the middle is a fire pit. Many tire tracks converge here.

"Ah, this is good," Ng says. "A place where the young men gather to take drugs."

Y.T. rolls her eyes at this display of tubularity. This must be the guy who writes all those antidrug pamphlets they get at school.

Like he's not getting a million gallons of drugs every second through all of those gross tubes.

"I don't see any signs of booby traps," Ng says. "Why don't you go out and see what kind of drug paraphernalia is out there."

She looks at him like, what did you say?

"There's a toxics mask hanging on the back of your seat," he says.

"What's out there, toxic-wise?"

"Discarded asbestos from the snipbuilding industry. Marine antifouling paints that are full of heavy metals. They used PCBs for a lot of things, too."

"Great."

"I sense your reluctance. But if we can get a sample of Snow Crash from this drug-taking site, it will obviate the rest of our mission."

"Well, since you put it that way," Y.T. says, and grabs the mask. It's a big rubber-and-canvas number that covers her whole head and neck. Feels heavy and awkward at first, but whoever designed it had the right idea, all the weight rests in the right places. There's also a pair of heavy gloves that she hauls on. They are way too big. Like the people at the glove factory never dreamed that an actual female could wear gloves.

She trudges out onto the glass-and-asbestos soil of the Zone, hoping that Ng isn't going to slam the door shut and drive away and leave her there.

Actually, she wishes he would. It would be a cool adventure.

Anyway, she goes up to the middle of the "drug-taking site." Is not too surprised to see a little nest of discarded hypodermic needles. And some tiny little empty vials. She picks up a couple of the vials, reads their labels.

"What did you find?" Ng says when she gets back into the van, peels off the mask.

"Needles. Mostly Hyponarxes. But there's also a couple of Ultra Laminars and some Mosquito twenty-fives."

"What does all this mean?"

"Hyponarx you can get at any Buy 'n' Fly, people call them rusty nails, they are cheap and dull. Supposedly the needles of poor black diabetics and junkies. Ultra Laminars and Mosquitos are hip, you get them around fancy Burbclaves, they don't hurt as much when you stick them in, and they have better design. You know, ergonomic plungers, hip color schemes."

"What drug were they injecting?"

"Checkitout," Y.T. says, and holds up one of the vials toward Ng.

Then it occurs to her that he can't exactly turn his head to look.

"Where do I hold it so you can see it?" she says.

Ng sings a little song. A robot arm unfolds itself from the ceiling of the van, crisply yanks the vial from her hand, swings it around, and holds it in front of a video camera set into the dashboard.

The typewritten label stuck onto the vial says, just "Testosterone."

"Ha ha, a false alarm," Ng says. The van suddenly rips forward, starts heading right into the middle of the Sacrifice Zone.

"Want to tell me what's going on?" Y.T. says, "since I have to actually do the work in this outfit?"

"Cell walls," Ng says. "The detector finds any chemical that penetrates cell walls. So we homed in naturally on a source of testosterone. A red herring. How amusing. You see, our biochemists lead sheltered lives, did not anticipate that some people would be so mentally warped as to use hormones like they were some kind of drug. How bizarre."

Y.T. smiles to herself. She really likes the idea of living in a world where someone like Ng can get off calling someone else bizarre. "What are you looking for?"

"Snow Crash," Ng says. "Instead, we found the Ring of Seventeen."

"Snow Crash is the drug that comes in the little tubes," Y.T. says. "I know that. What's the Ring of Seventeen? One of those crazy new rock groups that kids listen to nowadays?"

"Snow Crash penetrates the walls of brain cells and goes to the nucleus where the DNA is stored. So for purposes of this mission, we developed a detector that would enable us to find cell wall–penetrating compounds in the air. But we didn't count on heaps of empty testosterone vials being scattered all over the place. All steroids—artificial hormones—share the same basic structure, a ring of seventeen atoms that acts like a magic key that allows them to pass through cell walls. That's why steroids are such powerful substances when they are unleashed in the human body. They can go deep inside the cell, into the nucleus, and actually change the way the cell functions.

"To summarize: the detector is useless. A stealthy approach will not work. So we go back to the original plan. You buy some Snow Crash and throw it up in the air."

Y.T. doesn't quite understand that last part yet. But she shuts up for a while, because in her opinion, Ng needs to pay more attention to his driving.

Once they get out of that really creepy part, most of the Sacrifice Zone turns out to consist of a wilderness of dry brown weeds and large abandoned hunks of metal. There are big heaps of shit rising up from place to place—coal or slag or coke or smelt or something.

Every time they come around a corner, they encounter a little plantation of vegetables, tended by Asians or South Americans. Y.T. gets the impression that Ng wants to just run them over, but he always changes his mind at the last instant and swerves around them.

Some Spanish-speaking blacks are playing baseball on a broad flat area, using the round lids of fifty-five-gallon drums as bases. They have parked half a dozen old beaters around the edges of the field and turned on their headlights to provide illumination. Nearby is a bar built into a crappy mobile home, marked with a graffiti sign: THE SACRIFICE ZONE. Lines of boxcars are stranded in a yard of rusted-over railway spurs, nopal growing between the ties. One of the boxcars has been turned into a Reverend Wayne's Pearly Gates franchise, and evangelical CentroAmericans are lined up to do their penance and speak in tongues below the neon Elvis. There are no NeoAquarian Temple franchises in the Sacrifice Zone.

"The warehouse area is not as dirty as the first place we went," Ng says reassuringly, "so the fact that you can't use the toxics mask won't be so bad. You may smell some Chill fumes."

Y.T. does a double take at this new phenomenon: Ng using the street name for a controlled substance. "You mean Freon?" she says.

"Yes. The man who is the object of our inquiry is horizontally diversified. That is, he deals in a number of different substances. But he got his start in Freon. He is the biggest Chill wholesaler/retailer on the West Coast."

Finally, Y.T. gets it. Ng's van is air-conditioned. Not with one of those shitty ozone-safe air conditioners, but with the real thing, a heavy metal, high-capacity, bone-chilling Frigidaire blizzard blaster. It must use an incredible amount of Freon.

For all practical purposes, that air conditioner is a part of Ng's body. Y.T.'s driving around with the world's only Freon junkie.

"You buy your supply of Chill from this guy?"

"Until now, yes. But for the future, I have an arrangement with someone else."

Someone else. The Mafia.

_____ They are approaching the waterfront. Dozens of long, skinny, single-story warehouses run parallel down toward the water. They all share the same access road at this end. Smaller roads run between them, down toward where the piers used to be. Abandoned tractor-trailers are scattered around from place to place.

Ng pulls his van off the access road, into a little nook that is partly concealed between an old red-brick power station and a stack of rusted-out shipping containers. He gets it turned around so it's pointed out of here, kind of like he is expecting to leave rapidly.

"There's money in the storage compartment in front of you," Ng says.

Y.T. opens the glove compartment, as anyone else would call it, and finds a thick bundle of worn-out, dirty, trillion-dollar bills. Ed Meeses.

"Jeez, couldn't you get any Gippers? This is kind of bulky."

"This is more the kind of thing that a Kourier would pay with."

"Because we're all pond scum, right?"

"No comment."

"What is this, a quadrillion dollars?"

"One-and-a-half quadrillion. Inflation, you know."

"What do I do?"

"Fourth warehouse on the left," Ng says. "When you get the tube, throw it up in the air."

"Then what?"

"Everything else will be taken care of."

Y.T. has her doubts about that. But if she gets in trouble, well, she can always whip out those dog tags.

While Y.T. climbs down out of the van with her skateboard,

Ng makes new sounds with his mouth. She hears a gliding and clunking noise resonating through the frame of the van, machinery coming to life. Turning back to look, she sees that a steel cocoon on the roof of the van has opened up. There is a miniature helicopter underneath it, all folded up. Its rotor blades spread themselves apart, like a butterfly unfolding. Its name is painted on its side: WHIRLWIND REAPER.

32

It's pretty obvious which warehouse we are looking for here. Fourth one on the left, the road that runs down toward the waterfront is blocked off by several shipping containers—the big steel boxes you see on the backs of eighteen-wheelers. They are arranged in a herringbone pattern, so that in order to get past them you have to slalom back and forth half a dozen times, passing through a narrow mazelike channel between high walls of steel. Guys with guns are perched on top, looking down at Y.T. as she guides her plank through the obstacle course. By the time she makes it out into the clear, she's been heavily checked out.

There is the occasional light-bulb-on-a-wire strung around, and even a couple of strings of Christmas-tree lights. These are switched on, just to make her feel a little more welcome. She can't see anything, just lights making colored halos amid a generalized cloud of dust and fog. In front of her, access to the waterfront is blocked off by another maze of shipping containers. One of them has a graffiti sign: THE UKOD SEZ: TRY SOME COUNTDOWN TODAY!

"What's the UKOD?" she says, just to break the ice a little.

"Undisputed King of the Ozone Destroyers," says a man's voice. He is just in the act of jumping down from the loading dock of the warehouse to her left. Back inside the warehouse, Y.T. can see electric lights and glowing cigarettes. "That's what we call Emilio."

"Oh, right," Y.T. says. "The Freon guy. I'm not here for Chill."

"Well," says the guy, a tall rangy dude in his forties, much too skinny to be forty years old. He yanks the butt of a cigarette from his mouth and throws it away like a dart. "What'll it be, then?"

"What does Snow Crash cost?"

"One point seven five Gippers," the guy says.

"I thought it was one point five," Y.T. says.

The guy shakes his head. "Inflation, you know. Still, it's a bargain. Hell, that plank you're on is probably worth a hundred Gippers."

"You can't even buy these for dollars," Y.T. says, getting her back up. "Look, all I've got is one-and-a-half quadrillion dollars." She pulls the bundle out of her pocket.

The guy laughs, shakes his head, hollers back to his colleagues inside the warehouse. "You guys, we got a chick here who wants to pay in Meeses."

"Better get rid of 'em fast, honey," says a sharper, nastier voice, "or get yourself a wheelbarrow."

It's an even older guy with a bald head, curly hair on the sides, and a paunch. He's standing up on the loading dock.

"If you're not going to take it, just say so," Y.T. says. All of this chatter has nothing to do with business.

"We don't get chicks back here very often," the fat bald old guy says. Y.T. knows that this must be the UKOD himself. "So we'll give you a discount for being spunky. Turn around."

"Fuck you," Y.T. says. She's not going to turn around for this guy.

Everyone within earshot laughs. "Okay, do it," the UKOD says.

The tall skinny guy goes back over to the loading dock and hauls an aluminum briefcase down, sets it on top of a steel drum in the middle of the road so that it's at about waist height. "Pay first," he says.

She hands him the Meeses. He examines the bundle, sneers, throws it back into the warehouse with a sudden backhand motion. All the guys inside laugh some more.

He opens up the briefcase, revealing the little computer keyboard. He shoves his ID card into the slot, types on it for a couple of seconds.

He unsnaps a tube from the top of the briefcase, places it into the socket in the bottom part. The machine draws it inside, does something, spits it back out.

He hands the tube to Y.T. The red numbers on top are counting down from ten.

"When it gets down to one, hold it up to your nose and start inhaling," the guy says.

She's already backing away from him.

"You got a problem, little girl?" he says.

"Not yet," she says. Then she throws the tube up in the air as hard as she can.

The chop of the rotor blades comes out of nowhere. The *Whirlwind Reaper* blurs over their heads; everyone crouches for an instant as surprise buckles their knees. The tube does not come back to earth.

"You fucking bitch," the skinny guy says.

"That was a really cool plan," the UKOD says, "but the part I can't figure out is, why would a nice, smart girl like you participate in a suicide mission?"

The sun comes out. About half a dozen suns, actually, all around them up in the air, so that there are no shadows. The faces of the skinny man and the UKOD look flat and featureless under this blinding illumination. Y.T. is the only person who can see worth a damn because her Knight Visions have compensated for it; the men wince and sag beneath the light.

Y.T. turns to look behind herself. One of the miniature suns is hanging above the maze of shipping containers, casting light into all its crannies, blinding the gunmen who stand guard there. The scene flashes too light and too dark as her goggles' electronics try to make up their mind. But in the midst of this whole visual tangle she gets one image printed indelibly on her retina: the gunmen going down like a treeline in a hurricane, and for just an instant, a line of dark angular things silhouetted above the maze as they crest it like a cybernetic tsunami. Rat Things.

They have evaded the whole maze by leaping over it in long, flat parabolas. Along the way, some of them have slammed right through the bodies of men holding guns, like NFL fullbacks plowing full speed through nerdy sideline photographers. Then, as they land on the road in front of the maze, there is an instant burst of dust with frantic white sparks dancing around at the bottom, and while all this is happening, Y.T. doesn't hear, she feels one of the Rat Things impacting on the body of the tall skinny guy, hears his ribs crackling like a ball of cellophane. Hell is already breaking loose inside the warehouse, but her eyes are trying to follow the action, watching the sparks-and-dust contrails of more Rat Things drawing themselves down the length of the road in an instant and then going airborne to the top of the next barrier.

Three seconds have passed since she threw the tube into the air. She is turning back to look inside the warehouse. But someone's on top of the warehouse, catching her eye for a second. It's another gunman, a sniper, stepping out from behind an air-conditioning unit, just getting used to the light, raising his weapon to his shoulder. Y.T. winces as a red laser beam from his rifle sweeps across her eyes once, twice as he zeroes his sights on her forehead. Behind him she sees the *Whirlwind Reaper,* its rotors making a disk under the brilliant light, a disk that is fore-shortened into a narrow ellipse and then into a steady silver line. Then it flies right past the sniper.

The chopper pulls up into a hard turn, searching for additional prey, and something falls beneath it in a powerless trajectory, she thinks that it has dropped a bomb. But it's the head of the sniper, spinning rapidly, throwing out a fine pink helix under the light. The little chopper's rotor blade must have caught him in the nape of the neck. One part of her is dispassionately watching the head bounce and spin in the dust, and the other part of her is screaming her lungs out.

She hears a crack, the first loud noise so far. She turns to follow the sound, looking in the direction of a water tower that looms above this area, providing a fine vantage point for a sniper.

But then her attention is drawn by the pencil-thin blue-white exhaust of a tiny rocket that lances up into the sky from Ng's van. It doesn't do anything; it just goes up to a certain height and hovers, sitting on its exhaust. She doesn't care, she's kicking her way down the road now on her plank, trying to get something between her and that water tower.

There is a second cracking noise. Before this sound even reaches her ears, the rocket darts horizontally like a minnow, makes one or two minor cuts to correct its course, zeroes in on that sniper's perch, up in the water tower's access ladder. There is a great nasty explosion without any flame or light, like the loud pointless booms that you get sometimes at fireworks shows. For a moment, she can hear the clamor of shrapnel ringing through the ironwork of the water tower.

Just before she kicks her way back into the maze, a dustline whips past her, snapping rocks and fragments of broken glass into her face. It shoots into the maze. She hears it Ping-Pong all the way through, kicking off the steel walls in order to change direction. It's a Rat Thing clearing the way for her.

How sweet!

_____ "Smooth move, Ex-Lax," she says, climbing back into Ng's van. Her throat feels thick and swollen. Maybe it's from screaming, maybe it's the toxic waste, maybe she's getting ready to gag. "Didn't you know about the snipers?" she says. If she can keep talking about the details of the job, maybe she can keep her mind off of what the *Whirlwind Reaper* did.

"I didn't know about the one on the water tower," Ng says. "But as soon as he fired a couple of rounds, we plotted the bullets' trajectories on millimeter-wave and back-traced them." He talks to his van and it pulls out of its hiding place, headed for I-405.

"Seems like kind of an obvious place to look for a sniper."

"He was in an unfortified position, exposed from all sides," Ng says. "He chose to work from a suicidal position. Which is not a typical behavior for drug dealers. Typically, they are more pragmatic. Now, do you have any other criticisms of my performance?"

"Well, did it work?"

"Yes. The tube was inserted into a sealed chamber inside the helicopter before it discharged its contents. It was then flash-frozen in liquid helium before it could chemically self-destruct. We now have a sample of Snow Crash, something that no one else has been able to get. It is the kind of success on which reputations such as mine are constructed."

"How about the Rat Things?"

"How about them?"

"Are they back in the van now? Back there?" Y.T. jerks her head aft.

Ng pauses for a moment. Y.T. reminds herself that he is sitting in his office in Vietnam in 1955 watching all of this on TV.

"Three of them are back," Ng says. "Three are on their way back. And three of them I left behind to carry out additional pacification measures."

"You're leaving them behind?"

"They'll catch up," Ng says. "On a straightaway, they can run at seven hundred miles per hour."

"Is it true they have nuke stuff inside of them?"

"Radiothermal isotopes."

"What happens if one gets busted open? Everyone gets all mutated?"

"If you ever find yourself in the presence of a destructive force powerful enough to decapsulate those isotopes," Ng says, "radiation sickness will be the least of your worries."

"Will they be able to find their way back to us?"

"Didn't you ever watch *Lassie Come Home* when you were a child?" he asks. "Or rather, more of a child than you are now?"

So. She was right. The Rat Things are made from dog parts.

"That's cruel," she says.

"This brand of sentimentalism is very predictable," Ng says.

"To take a dog out of his body—keep him in a hutch all the time."

"When the Rat Thing, as you call it, is in his hutch, do you know what he's doing?"

"Licking his electric nuts?"

"Chasing Frisbees through the surf. Forever. Eating steaks that grow on trees. Lying beside the fire in a hunting lodge. I haven't installed any testicle-licking simulations yet, but now that you have brought it up, I shall consider it."

"What about when he's out of the hutch, running around doing errands for you?"

"Can't you imagine how liberating it is for a pit bullterrier to be capable of running seven hundred miles an hour?"

Y.T. doesn't answer. She is too busy trying to get her mind around this concept.

"Your mistake," Ng says, "is that you think that all mechanically assisted organisms—like me—are pathetic cripples. In fact, we are better than we were before."

"Where do you get the pit bulls from?"

"An incredible number of them are abandoned every day, in cities all over the place."

"You cut up pound puppies?"

"We save abandoned dogs from certain extinction and send them to what amounts to dog heaven."

"My friend Roadkill and I had a pit bull. Fido. We found it in an alley. Some asshole had shot it in the leg. We had a vet fix it up. We kept it in this empty apartment in Roadkill's building for a few months, played with it every day, brought it food. And then one day we came to play with Fido, and he was gone. Someone broke in and took him away. Probably sold him to a research lab."

"Probably," Ng says, "but that's no way to keep a dog."

"It's better than the way he was living before."

There's a break in the conversation as Ng occupies himself with talking to his van, maneuvering onto the Long Beach Freeway, headed back into town.

"Do they remember stuff?" Y.T. says.

"To the extent dogs can remember anything," Ng says. "We don't have any way of erasing memories."

"So maybe Fido is a Rat Thing somewhere, right now."

"I would hope so, for his sake," Ng says.

_____ In a Mr. Lee's Greater Hong Kong franchise in Phoenix, Arizona, Ng Security Industries Semi-Autonomous Guard Unit B-782 comes awake.

The factory that put him together thinks of him as a robot named Number B-782. But he thinks of himself as a pit bullterrier named Fido.

In the old days, Fido was a bad little doggie sometimes. But now, Fido lives in a nice little house in a nice little yard. Now he has become a nice little doggie. He likes to lie in his house and listen to the other nice doggies bark. Fido is part of a big pack.

Tonight there is a lot of barking from a place far away. When he listens to this barking, Fido knows that a whole pack of nice doggies is very excited about something. A lot of very bad men are trying to hurt a nice girl. This has made the doggies very angry and excited. In order to protect the nice girl, they are hurting some of the bad men.

Which is as it should be.

Fido does not come out of his house. When he first heard the barking, he became excited. He likes nice girls, and it makes him especially upset when bad men try to hurt them. Once there was a nice girl who loved him. That was before, when he lived in a scary place and he was always hungry and many people were bad to him. But the nice girl loved him and was good to him. Fido loves the nice girl very much.

But he can tell from the barking of the other doggies that the nice girl is safe now. So he goes back to sleep.

33

" 'Scuse me, pod," Y.T. says, stepping into the Babel/Infocalypse room. "Jeez! This place looks like one of those things full of snow that you shake up."

"Hi, Y.T."

"Got some more intel for you, pod."

"Shoot."

"Snow Crash is a roid. Or else it's similar to a roid. Yeah, that's it. It goes into your cell walls, just like a roid. And then it does something to the nucleus of the cell."

"You were right," Hiro says to the Librarian, "just like herpes."

"This guy I was talking to said that it fucks with your actual DNA. I don't know what half of this shit means, but that's what he said."

"Who's this guy you were talking to?"

"Ng. Of Ng Security Industries. Don't bother talking to him, he won't give you any intel," she says dismissively.

"Why are you hanging out with a guy like Ng?"

"Mob job. The Mafia has a sample of the drug for the first time, thanks to me and my pal Ng. Until now, it always self-destructed before they could get to it. So I guess they're analyzing it or something. Trying to make an antidote, maybe."

"Or trying to reproduce it."

"The Mafia wouldn't do that."

"Don't be a sap," Hiro says. "Of course they would."

Y.T. seems miffed at Hiro.

"Look," he says, "I'm sorry for reminding you of this, but if we still had laws, the Mafia would be a criminal organization."

"But we don't have laws," she says, "so it's just another chain."

"Fine, all I'm saying is, they may not be doing this for the benefit of humanity."

"And why are you in here, holed up with this geeky daemon?" she says, gesturing at the Librarian. "For the benefit of humanity? Or because you're chasing a piece of ass? Whatever her name is."

"Okay, okay, let's not talk about the Mafia anymore," Hiro says. "I have work to do."

"So do I." Y.T. zaps out again, leaving a hole in the Metaverse that is quickly filled in by Hiro's computer.

"I think she may have a crush on me," Hiro explains.

"She seemed quite affectionate," the Librarian says.

"Okay," Hiro says, "back to work. Where did Asherah come from?"

"Originally from Sumerian mythology. Hence, she is also important in Babylonian, Assyrian, Canaanite, Hebrew, and Ugaritic myths, which are all descended from the Sumerian."

"Interesting. So the Sumerian language died out, but the Sumerian myths were somehow passed on in the new languages."

"Correct. Sumerian was used as the language of religion and scholarship by later civilizations, much as Latin was used in Europe during the Middle Ages. No one spoke it as their native language, but educated people could read it. In this way, Sumerian religion was passed on."

"And what did Asherah do in Sumerian myths?"

"The accounts are fragmentary. Few tablets have been discovered, and these are broken and scattered. It is thought that L. Bob Rife has excavated many intact tablets, but he refuses to release them. The surviving Sumerian myths exist in fragments and have a bizarre quality. Lagos compared them to the imaginings of a febrile two-year-old. Entire sections of them simply cannot be translated—the characters are legible and well-known, but when put together they do not say anything that leaves an imprint on the modern mind."

"Like instructions for programming a VCR."

"There is a great deal of monotonous repetition. There is also a fair amount of what Lagos described as 'Rotary Club Boosterism'—scribes extolling the superior virtue of their city over some other city."

"What makes one Sumerian city better than another one? A bigger ziggurat? A better football team?"

"Better *me*."

"What are *me*?"

"Rules or principles that control the operation of society, like a code of laws, but on a more fundamental level."

"I don't get it."

"That is the point. Sumerian myths are not 'readable' or 'enjoyable' in the same sense that Greek and Hebrew myths are. They reflect a fundamentally different consciousness from ours."

"I suppose if our culture was based on Sumer, we would find them more interesting," Hiro says.

"Akkadian myths came after the Sumerian and are clearly based on Sumerian myths to a large extent. It is clear that Akkadian redactors went through the Sumerian myths, edited out the (to us) bizarre and incomprehensible parts, and strung them together into longer works, such as the Epic of Gilgamesh. The Akkadians were Semites—cousins of the Hebrews."

"What do the Akkadians have to say about her?"

"She is a goddess of the erotic and of fertility. She also has a destructive, vindictive side. In one myth, Kirta, a human king, is made grievously ill by Asherah. Only El, king of the gods, can heal him. El gives certain persons the privilege of nursing at Asherah's breasts. El and Asherah often adopt human babies and let them nurse on Asherah—in one text, she is wet nurse to seventy divine sons."

"Spreading that virus," Hiro says. "Mothers with AIDS can spread the disease to their babies by breast-feeding them. But this is the Akkadian version, right?"

"Yes, sir."

"I want to hear some Sumerian stuff, even if it is untranslatable."

"Would you like to hear how Asherah made Enki sick?"

"Sure."

"How this story is translated depends on how it is interpreted. Some see it as a Fall from Paradise story. Some see it as a battle between male and female or water and earth. Some see it as a fertility allegory. This reading is based on the interpretation of Bendt Alster."

"Duly noted."

"To summarize: Enki and Ninhursag—who is Asherah, although in this story she also bears other epithets—live in a place called Dilmun. Dilmun is pure, clean and bright, there is no sickness, people do not grow old, predatory animals do not hunt.

"But there is no water. So Ninhursag pleads with Enki, who is a sort of water-god, to bring water to Dilmun. He does so by masturbating among the reeds of the ditches and letting flow his life-giving semen—the 'water of the heart,' as it is called. At the same time, he pronounces a nam-shub forbidding anyone to enter this area—he does not want anyone to come near his semen."

"Why not?"

"The myth does not say."

"Then," Hiro says, "he must have thought it was valuable, or dangerous, or both."

"Dilmun is now better than it was before. The fields produce abundant crops and so on."

"Excuse me, but how did Sumerian agriculture work? Did they use a lot of irrigation?"

"They were entirely dependent upon it."

"So Enki was responsible, according to this myth, for irrigating the fields with his 'water of the heart.' "

"Enki was the water-god, yes."

"Okay, go on."

"But Ninhursag—Asherah—violates his decree and takes Enki's semen and impregnates herself. After nine days of pregnancy she gives birth, painlessly, to a daughter, Ninmu. Ninmu walks on the riverbank. Enki sees her, becomes inflamed, goes across the river, and has sex with her."

"With his own daughter."

"Yes. She has another daughter nine days later, named Ninkurra, and the pattern is repeated."

"Enki has sex with Ninkurra, too?"

"Yes, and she has a daughter named Uttu. Now, by this time, Ninhursag has apparently recognized a pattern in Enki's behavior, and so she advises Uttu to stay in her house, predicting that Enki will then approach her bearing gifts, and try to seduce her."

"Does he?"

"Enki once again fills the ditches with the 'water of the heart,' which makes things grow. The gardener rejoices and embraces Enki."

"Who's the gardener?"

"Just some character in the story," the Librarian says. "He provides Enki with grapes and other gifts. Enki disguises himself as the gardener and goes to Uttu and seduces her. But this time, Ninhursag manages to obtain a sample of Enki's semen from Uttu's thighs."

"My God. Talk about your mother-in-law from hell."

"Ninhursag spreads the semen on the ground, and it causes eight plants to sprout up."

"Does Enki have sex with the plants, then?"

"No, he eats them—in some sense, he learns their secrets by doing so."

"So here we have our Adam and Eve motif."

"Ninhursag curses Enki, saying 'Until thou art dead, I shall not look upon thee with the "eye of life." ' Then she disappears, and Enki becomes very ill. Eight of his organs become sick, one for each of the plants. Finally, Ninhursag is persuaded to come back. She gives birth to eight deities, one for each part of Enki's body that is sick, and Enki is healed. These deities are the pantheon of Dilmun; i.e., this act breaks the cycle of incest and creates a new race of male and female gods that can reproduce normally."

"I'm beginning to see what Lagos meant about the febrile two-year-old."

"Alster interprets the myth as 'an exposition of a logical problem: Supposing that originally there was nothing but one creator, how could ordinary binary sexual relations come into being?' "

"Ah, there's that word 'binary' again."

"You may remember an unexplored fork earlier in our conversation that would have brought us to this same place by another route. This myth can be compared to the Sumerian creation myth, in which heaven and earth are united to begin with, but the world is not really created until the two are separated. Most Creation myths begin with a 'paradoxical unity of everything, evaluated either as chaos or as Paradise,' and the world as we know it does not really come into being until this is changed. I should point out here that Enki's original name was En-Kur, Lord of Kur. Kur was a primeval ocean—Chaos—that Enki conquered."

"Every hacker can identify with that."

"But Asherah has similar connotations. Her name in Ugaritic, 'atiratu yammi' means 'she who treads on (the) sea (dragon).' "

"Okay, so both Enki and Asherah were figures who had in some sense defeated chaos. And your point is that this defeat of chaos, the separation of the static, unified world into a binary system, is identified with creation."

"Correct."

"What else can you tell me about Enki?"

"He was the *en* of the city of Eridu."

"What's an *en*? Is that like a king?"

"A priest-king of sorts. The *en* was the custodian of the local temple, where the *me*—the rules of the society—were stored on clay tablets."

"Okay. Where's Eridu?"

"Southern Iraq. It has only been excavated within the past few years."

"By Rife's people?"

"Yes. As Kramer has it, Enki is the god of wisdom—but this is a bad translation. His wisdom is not the wisdom of an old man, but rather a knowledge of how to do things, especially occult things. 'He astonishes even the other gods with shocking solutions to apparently impossible problems.' He is a sympathetic god for the most part, who assists humankind."

"Really!"

"Yes. The most important Sumerian myths center on him. As I mentioned, he is associated with water. He fills the rivers, and the extensive Sumerian canal system, with his life-giving semen.

He is said to have created the Tigris in a single epochal act of masturbation. He describes himself as follows: 'I am lord. I am the one whose word endures. I am eternal.' Others describe him: 'a word from you—and heaps and piles stack high with grain.' 'You bring down the stars of heaven, you have computed their number.' He pronounces the name of everything created . . . "

" 'Pronounces the name of everything created?' "

"In many Creation myths, to name a thing is to create it. He is referred to, in various myths, as 'expert who instituted incantations,' 'word-rich,' 'Enki, master of all the right commands,' as Kramer and Maier have it, 'His word can bring order where there had been only chaos and introduce disorder where there had been harmony.' He devotes a great deal of effort to imparting his knowledge to his son, the god Marduk, chief deity of the Babylonians."

"So the Sumerians worshipped Enki, and the Babylonians, who came after the Sumerians, worshipped Marduk, his son."

"Yes, sir. And whenever Marduk got stuck, he would ask his father Enki for help. There is a representation of Marduk here on this stele—the Code of Hammurabi. According to Hammurabi, the Code was given to him personally by Marduk."

Hiro wanders over to the Code of Hammurabi and has a gander. The cuneiform means nothing to him, but the illustration on top is easy enough to understand. Especially the part in the middle:

"Why, exactly, is Marduk handing Hammurabi a one and a zero in this picture?" Hiro asks.

"They were emblems of royal power," the Librarian says. "Their origin is obscure."

"Enki must have been responsible for that one," Hiro says.

"Enki's most important role is as the creator and guardian of the *me* and the *gis-hur,* the 'key words' and 'patterns' that rule the universe."

"Tell me more about the *me.*"

"To quote Kramer and Maier again, '[They believed in] the existence from time primordial of a fundamental, unalterable, comprehensive assortment of powers and duties, norms and standards, rules and regulations, known as *me,* relating to the cosmos and its components, to gods and humans, to cities and countries, and to the varied aspects of civilized life.' "

"Kind of like the Torah."

"Yes, but they have a kind of mystical or magical force. And they often deal with banal subjects—not just religion."

"Examples?"

"In one myth, the goddess Inanna goes to Eridu and tricks Enki into giving her ninety-four *me* and brings them back to her home town of Uruk, where they are greeted with much commotion and rejoicing."

"Inanna is the person that Juanita's obsessed with."

"Yes, sir. She is hailed as a savior because 'she brought the perfect execution of the *me.*' "

"Execution? Like executing a computer program?"

"Yes. Apparently, they are like algorithms for carrying out certain activities essential to the society. Some of them have to do with the workings of priesthood and kingship. Some explain how to carry out religious ceremonies. Some relate to the arts of war and diplomacy. Many of them are about the arts and crafts: music, carpentry, smithing, tanning, building, farming, even such simple tasks as lighting fires."

"The operating system of society."

"I'm sorry?"

"When you first turn on a computer, it is an inert collection of circuits that can't really do anything. To start up the machine, you have to infuse those circuits with a collection of rules that tell it how to function. How to be a computer. It sounds as though these *me* served as the operating system of the society, organizing an inert collection of people into a functioning system."

"As you wish. In any case, Enki was the guardian of the *me.*"

"So he was a good guy, really."

"He was the most beloved of the gods."

"He sounds like kind of a hacker. Which makes his nam-shub very difficult to understand. If he was such a nice guy, why did he do the Babel thing?"

"This is considered to be one of the mysteries of Enki. As you have noticed, his behavior was not always consistent with modern norms."

"I don't buy that. I don't think he actually fucked his sister, daughter, and so on. That story has to be a metaphor for something else. I think it is a metaphor for some kind of recursive informational process. This whole myth stinks of it. To these people, water equals semen. Makes sense, because they probably had no concept of pure water—it was all brown and muddy and full of viruses anyway. But from a modern standpoint, semen is just a carrier of information—both benevolent sperm and malevolent viruses. Enki's water—his semen, his data, his *me*—flow throughout the country of Sumer and cause it to flourish."

"As you may be aware, Sumer existed on the floodplain between two major rivers, the Tigris and the Euphrates. This is where all the clay came from—they took it directly from the riverbeds."

"So Enki even provided them with their medium for conveying information—clay. They wrote on wet clay and then they dried it out—got rid of the water. If water got to it later, the information was destroyed. But if they baked it and drove out all the water, sterilized Enki's semen with heat, then the tablet lasted forever, immutable, like the words of the Torah. Do I sound like a maniac?"

"I don't know," the Librarian says, "but you do sound a little like Lagos."

"I'm thrilled. Next thing you know, I'll turn myself into a gargoyle."

34

Any ped can get into Griffith Park without being noticed. And Y.T. figures that despite the barriers across the road, the Falabala camp isn't too well protected, if you've got off-road capability. For a skate ninja on a brand-new plank in a brand-new pair of Knight Visions (hey, you have to spend money to make money) there will be no problem. Just find a high embankment that ramps down into the canyon, skirt the edge until you see those campfires down below. And then lean down that hill. Trust gravity.

She realizes halfway down that her blue-and-orange coverall, fly as it may be, is going to be a real attention getter in the middle of the night in the Falabala zone, so she reaches up to her collar, feels a hard disk sewn into the fabric, presses it between thumb and finger until it clicks. Her coverall darkens, the colors shimmer through the electropigment like an oil slick, and then it's black.

On her first visit she didn't check this place out all that carefully because she hoped she'd never come back. So the embankment turns out to be taller and steeper than Y.T. remembered. Maybe a little more of a cliff, drop-off, or abyss than she thought. Only thing that makes her think so is that she seems to be doing a lot of free-fall work here. Major plummeting. Big time ballistic styling. That's cool, it's all part of the job, she tells herself. The smartwheels are good for it. The tree trunks are bluish black, standing out not so well against a blackish blue background. The only other thing she can see is the red laser light of the digital speedometer down on the front of her plank, which is not showing any real information. The numbers have vibrated themselves into a cloud of gritty red light as the radar speed sensor tries to lock onto something.

She turns the speedometer off. Running totally black now. Precipitating her way toward the sweet 'crete of the creek bottom like a black angel who has just had the shroud lines of her celestial parachute severed by the Almighty. And when the wheels finally meet the pavement, it just about drives her knees up through her jawbone. She finishes the whole gravitational transaction with not much altitude and a nasty head of dark velocity.

Mental note: Next time just jump off a fucking bridge. That way there's no question of getting an invisible cholla shoved up your nose.

She whips around a corner, heeled over so far she could lick the yellow line, and her Knight Visions reveal all in a blaze of multispectral radiation. On infrared, the Falabala encampment is a turbulating aurora of pink fog punctuated by the white-hot bursts of campfires. All of it rests on dim bluish pavement, which means, in the false-color scheme of things, that it's cold. Behind everything is the jagged horizon line of that funky improvised barrier technology that the Falabalas are so good at. A barrier that has been completely spurned, snubbed, and confounded by Y.T., who dropped out of the sky into the middle of the camp like a Stealth fighter with an inferiority complex.

Once you're into the actual encampment, people don't really notice or care who you are. A couple people see her, watch her slide on by, don't get all hairy about it. They probably get a lot of Kouriers coming through here. A lot of dippy, gullible, Kool-Aid–drinking couriers. And these people aren't hip enough to tell Y.T. apart from that breed. But that's okay, she'll pass for now, as long as they don't check out the detailing on her new plank.

The campfires provide enough plain old regular visible light to show this sorry affair for what it is: a bunch of demented Boy Scouts, a jamboree without merit badges or hygiene. With the IR supered on top of the visible, she can also see vague, spectral red faces out in the shadows where her unassisted eyes would only see darkness. These new Knight Visions cost her a big wad of her Mob drug-running money. Just the kind of thing Mom had in mind when she insisted Y.T. get a part-time job.

Some of the people who were here last time are gone now, and there's a few new ones she doesn't recognize. There's a couple of people actually wearing duct-tape straitjackets. That's a fashion statement reserved for the ones who are totally out of control, rolling and thrashing around on the ground. And there's a few more who are spazzing out, but not as bad, and one or two who are just plain messed up, like plain old derelicts that you might see at the Snooze 'n' Cruise.

"Hey, look!" someone says. "It's our friend the Kourier! Welcome, friend!"

She's got her Liquid Knuckles uncapped, available, and shaken well before use. She's got high-voltage, high-fashion metallic cuffs around her wrists in case someone tries to grab her by same. And a bundy stunner up her sleeve. Only the most tubular throwbacks carry guns. Guns take a long time to work (you have to wait for the victim to bleed to death), but paradoxically they end up killing people pretty often. But nobody hassles you after you've hit them with a bundy stunner. At least that's what the ads say.

So it's not like she exactly feels vulnerable or anything. But still, she'd like to pick her target. So she maintains escape velocity until she's found the woman who seemed friendly—the bald chick in the torn-up Chanel knockoff—and then zeroes in on her.

_____ "Let's get off into the woods, man," Y.T. says, "I want to talk to you about what's going on with what's left of your brain."

The woman smiles, struggles to her feet with the good-natured awkwardness of a retarded person in a good mood. "I like to talk about that," she says. "Because I believe in it."

Y.T. doesn't stop to do a lot of talking, just grabs the woman by the hand, starts leading her uphill, into the scrubby little trees, away from the road. She doesn't see any pink faces lurking up here in the infrared, it ought to be safe. But there are a couple behind her, just ambling along pleasantly, not looking directly at her, like they just decided it was time to go for a stroll in the woods in the middle of the night. One of them is the High Priest.

The woman's probably in her mid-twenties, she's a tall gangly type, nice- but not good-looking, probably was a spunky but low-scoring forward on her high school basketball team. Y.T. sits her down on a rock out in the darkness.

"Do you have any idea where you are?" Y.T. says.

"In the park," the woman says, "with my friends. We're helping to spread the Word."

"How'd you get here?"

"From the _Enterprise_. That's where we go to learn things."

"You mean, like, the Raft? The *Enterprise* Raft? Is that where you guys all came from?"

"I don't know where we came from," the woman says. "Sometimes it's hard to remember stuff. But that's not important."

"Where were you before? You didn't grow up on the Raft, did you?"

"I was a systems programmer for 3verse Systems in Mountain View, California," the woman says, suddenly whipping off a string of perfect, normal-sounding English.

"Then how did you get to be on the Raft?"

"I don't know. My old life stopped. My new life started. Now I'm here." Back to baby talk.

"What's the last thing you remember before your old life stopped?"

"I was working late. My computer was having problems."

"That's it? That's the last normal thing that happened to you?"

"My system crashed," she said. "I saw static. And then I became very sick. I went to the hospital. And there in the hospital, I met a man who explained everything to me. He explained that I had been washed in the blood. That I belonged to the Word now. And suddenly it all made sense. And then I decided to go to the Raft."

"You decided, or someone decided for you?"

"I just wanted to. That's where we go."

"Who else was on the Raft with you?"

"More people like me."

"Like you how?"

"All programmers. Like me. Who had seen the Word."

"Seen it on their computers?"

"Yes. Or sometimes on TV."

"What did you do on the Raft?"

The woman pushes up one sleeve of her raggedy sweatshirt to expose a needle-pocked arm.

"You took drugs?"

"No. We gave blood."

"They sucked your blood out?"

"Yes. Sometimes we would do a little coding. But only some of us."

"How long have you been here?"

"I don't know. They move us here when our veins don't work anymore. We just do things to help spread the Word—drag stuff around, make barricades. But we don't really spend much time working. Most of the time we sing songs, pray, and tell other people about the Word."

"You want to leave? I can get you out of here."

"No," the woman says, "I've never been so happy."

"How can you say that? You were a big-time hacker. Now you're kind of a dip, if I may speak frankly."

"That's okay, it doesn't hurt my feelings. I wasn't really happy when I was a hacker. I never thought about the important things. God. Heaven. The things of the spirit. It's hard to think about those things in America. You just put them aside. But those are really the important things—not programming computers or making money. Now, that's all I think about."

Y.T. has been keeping an eye on the High Priest and his buddy. They keep moving closer, one step at a time. Now they're close enough that Y.T. can smell their dinner. The woman puts her hand on Y.T.'s shoulder pad.

"I want you to stay here with me. Won't you come down and have some refreshments? You must be thirsty."

"Gotta run," Y.T. says, standing up.

"I really have to object to that," the High Priest says, stepping forward. He doesn't say it angrily. Now he's trying to be like Y.T.'s dad. "That's not really the right decision for you."

"What are you, a role model?"

"That's okay. You don't have to agree. But let's go down and sit by the campfire and talk about it."

"Let's just get the fuck away from Y.T. before she goes into a self-defense mode," Y.T. says.

All three Falabalas step back away from her. Very cooperative. The High Priest is holding up his hands, placating her. "I'm sorry if we made you feel threatened," he says.

"You guys just come on a little weird," Y.T. says, flipping her goggles back onto infrared.

In the infrared, she can see that the third Falabala, the one who came up here with the High Priest, is holding a small thing in one hand that is unusually warm.

She nails him with her penlight, spotlighting his upper body in a narrow yellow beam. Most of him is dirty and dun colored and reflects little light. But there is a brilliant glossy red thing, a shaft of ruby.

It's a hypodermic needle. It's full of red fluid. Under infrared, it shows up warm. It's fresh blood.

And she doesn't exactly get it—why these guys would be walking around with a syringe full of fresh blood. But she's seen enough.

The Liquid Knuckles shoots out of the can in a long narrow neon-green stream, and when it nails the needle man in the face, he jerks his head back like he's just been axed across the bridge of the nose and falls back without making a sound. Then she gives the High Priest a shot of it for good measure. The woman just stands there, totally, like, appalled.

_____ Y.T. pumps herself up out of the canyon so fast that when she flies out into traffic, she's going about as fast as it is. As soon as she gets a solid poon on a nocturnal lettuce tanker, she gets on the phone to Mom.

"Mom, listen. No, Mom, never mind the roaring noise. Yes, I am riding my skateboard in traffic. But listen to me for a second, Mom—"

She has to hang up on the old bitch. It's impossible to talk to her. Then she tries to make a voice linkup with Hiro. That takes a couple of minutes to go through.

"Hello! Hello! Hello!" she's shouting. Then she hears the honk of a car horn. Coming out of the telephone.

"Hello?"

"It's Y.T."

"How are you doing?" This guy always seems a little too laid back in his personal dealings. She doesn't really want to talk about how she's doing. She hears another honking horn in the background, behind Hiro's voice.

"Where the hell are you, Hiro?"

"Walking down a street in L.A."

"How can you be goggled in if you're walking down a street?" Then the terrible reality sinks in: "Oh, my God, you didn't turn into a gargoyle, did you?"

"Well," Hiro says. He is hesitant, embarrassed, like it hadn't occurred to him yet that this was what he was doing. "It's not exactly like being a gargoyle. Remember when you gave me shit about spending all my money on computer stuff?"

"Yeah."

"I decided I wasn't spending enough. So I got a beltpack machine. Smallest ever made. I'm walking down the street with this thing strapped to my belly. It's really cool."

"You're a gargoyle."

"Yeah, but it's not like having all this clunky shit strapped all over your body—"

"You're a gargoyle. Listen, I talked to one of these wholesalers."

"Yeah?"

"She says she used to be a hacker. She saw something strange on her computer. Then she got sick for a while and joined this cult and ended up on the Raft."

"The Raft. Do tell."

"On the *Enterprise*. They take their blood, Hiro. Suck it out of their bodies. They infect people by injecting them with the blood of sick hackers. And when their veins get all tracked out like a junkie's, they cut them loose and put them to work on the mainland running the wholesale operation."

"That's good," he says. "That's good stuff."

"She says she saw some static on her computer screen and it made her sick. You know anything about that?"

"Yeah. It's true."

"It's true?"

"Yeah. But you don't have to worry about it. It only affects hackers."

For a minute she can't even speak, she's so pissed. "My mother is a programmer for the Feds. You asshole. Why didn't you warn me?"

Half an hour later, she's there. Doesn't bother to change back into her WASP disguise this time, just bursts into the house in basic, bad black. Drops her plank on the floor on the way in. Grabs one of Mom's curios off the shelf—it's a heavy crystal award—clear plastic, actually—that she got a couple years ago for sucking up to her Fed boss and passing all her polygraph tests—and goes into the den.

Mom's there. As usual. Working on her computer. But she's not looking at the screen right now, she's got some notes on her lap that she's going through.

Just as Mom is looking up at her, Y.T. winds up and throws the crystal award. It goes right over Mom's shoulder, glances off the computer table, flies right through the picture tube. Awesome results. Y.T. always wanted to do that. She pauses to admire her work for a few seconds while Mom just flames off all kinds of weird emotion. What are you doing in that uniform? Didn't I tell you not to ride your skateboard on a real street? You're not supposed to throw things in the house. That's my prized possession. Why did you break the computer? Government property. Just what is going on here, anyway?

Y.T. can tell that this is going to continue for a couple of minutes, so she goes to the kitchen, splashes some water on her face, gets a glass of juice, just letting Mom follow her around and ventilate over her shoulder pads.

Finally Mom winds down, defeated by Y.T.'s strategy of silence.

"I just saved your fucking life, Mom," Y.T. says. "You could at least offer me an Oreo."

"What on earth are you talking about?"

"It's like, if you—people of a certain age—would make some effort to just stay in touch with sort of basic, modern-day events, then your kids wouldn't have to take these drastic measures."

35

Earth materializes, rotating majestically in front of his face. Hiro reaches out and grabs it. He twists it around so he's looking at Oregon. Tells it to get rid of the clouds, and it does, giving him a crystalline view of the mountains and the seashore.

Right out there, a couple of hundred miles off the Oregon coast, is a sort of granulated furuncle growing on the face of the water. Festering is not too strong a word. It's a couple of hundred miles south of Astoria now, moving south. Which explains why Juanita went to Astoria a couple of days ago: she wanted to get close to the Raft. Why is anyone's guess.

Hiro looks up, focuses his gaze on Earth, zooms in for a look. As he gets closer, the imagery he's looking at shifts from the long-range pictures coming in from the geosynchronous satellites to the good stuff being spewed into the CIC computer from a whole fleet of low-flying spy birds. The view he's looking at is a mosaic of images shot no more than a few hours ago.

It's several miles across. Its shape constantly changes, but at the time these pictures were shot, it had kind of a fat kidney shape; that is, it is trying to be a V, pointed southward like a flock of geese, but there's so much noise in the system, it's so amorphous and disorganized, that a kidney is the closest it can come.

At the center is a pair of enormous vessels: the *Enterprise* and an oil tanker, lashed together side by side. These two behemoths are walled in by several other major vessels, an assortment of container ships and other freight carriers. The Core.

Everything else is pretty tiny. There is the occasional hijacked yacht or decommissioned fishing trawler. But most of the boats in the Raft are just that: boats. Small pleasure craft, sampans, junks, dhows, dinghys, life rafts, houseboats, makeshift structures built on air-filled oil drums and slabs of styrofoam. A good fifty percent of it isn't real boat material at all, just a garble of ropes, cables, planks, nets, and other debris tied together on top of whatever kind of flotsam was handy.

And L. Bob Rife is sitting in the middle of it. Hiro doesn't quite know what he's doing, and he doesn't know how Juanita is connected. But it's time to go there and find out.

——————— Scott Lagerquist is standing right on the edge of Mark Norman's 24/7 Motorcycle Mall, waiting, when the man with the swords comes into view, striding down the sidewalk. A pedestrian is a peculiar sight in L.A., considerably more peculiar than a man with swords. But a welcome one. Anyone who drives out to a motorcycle dealership already has a car, by definition, so it's hard to give them a really hard sell. A pedestrian should be cake.

"Scott Wilson Lagerquist!" the guy yells from fifty feet away and closing. "How you doing?"

"Fabulous!" Scott says. A little off guard, maybe. Can't remember this guy's name, which is a problem. Where has he seen this guy before?

"It's great to see you!" Scott says, running forward and pumping the guy's hand. "I haven't seen you since, uh—"

"Is Pinky here today?" the guy says.

"Pinky?"

"Yeah. Mark. Mark Norman. Pinky was his nickname back in college. I guess he probably doesn't like to be called that now that he's running, what, half a dozen dealerships, three McDonaldses, and a Holiday Inn, huh?"

"I didn't know that Mr. Norman was into fast food also."

"Yeah. He's got three franchises down around Long Beach. Owns them through a limited partnership, actually. Is he here today?"

"No, he's on vacation."

"Oh, yeah. In Corsica. The Ajaccio Hyatt. Room 543. That's right, I completely forgot about that."

"Well, were you just stopping by to say hi, or—"

"Nah. I was going to buy a motorcycle."

"Oh. What kind of motorcycle were you looking for?"

"One of the new Yamahas? With the new generation smartwheels?"

Scott grins manfully, trying to put the best face on the awful fact that he is about to reveal. "I know exactly the one you mean.

But I'm sorry to tell you that we don't actually have one in stock today."

"You don't?"

"We don't. It's a brand-new model. Nobody has them."

"You sure? Because you ordered one."

"We did?"

"Yeah. A month ago." Suddenly the guy cranes his neck, looks over Scott's shoulder down the boulevard. "Well, speak of the devil. Here it comes."

A Yamaha semi is pulling into the truck entrance with a new shipment of motorcycles in the back.

"It's on that truck," the guy says. "If you can give me one of your cards, I'll jot down the vehicle identification number on back so you can pull it off the truck for me."

"This was a special order made by Mr. Norman?"

"He claimed he was just ordering it as a display model, you know. But it sort of has my name on it."

"Yes, sir. I understand totally."

——————— Sure enough, the bike comes off the truck, just as the guy described it, right down to color scheme (black) and vehicle ID number. It's a beautiful bike. It draws a crowd just sitting on the parking lot—the other salesmen actually put down their coffee cups and take their feet off their desks to go outside and look at it. It looks like a black land torpedo. Two-wheel drive, natch. The wheels are so advanced they're not even wheels—they look like giant, heavy-duty versions of the smartwheels that high-speed skateboards use, independently telescoping spokes with fat traction pads on the ends. Dangling out over the front, in the nose cone of the motorcycle, is the sensor package that monitors road conditions, decides where to place each spoke as it rolls forward, how much to extend it, and how to rotate the footpad for maximum traction. It's all controlled by a bios—a Built-In Operating System—an onboard computer with a flat-panel screen built into the top of the fuel tank.

They say that this baby will do a hundred and twenty miles per hour on rubble. The bios patches itself into the CIC weather net so that it knows when it's about to run into precip. The aerodynamic cowling is totally flexible, calculates its own most efficient shape for the current speed and wind conditions, changes its curves accordingly, wraps around you like a nympho-maniacal gymnast.

Scott figures this guy is going to waltz off with this thing for dealer invoice, being a friend and confidant of Mr. Norman. And it's not an easy thing for any red-blooded salesman to write out a contract to sell a sexy beast like this one at dealer invoice. He hesitates for a minute. Wonders what's going to happen to him if this is all some kind of mistake.

The guy's watching him intently, seems to sense his nervous-ness, almost as if he can hear Scott's heart beating. So at the last minute he eases up, gets magnanimous—Scott loves these big-spender types—decides to throw in a few hundred Kongbucks over invoice, just so Scott can pull in a meager commission on the deal. A tip, basically.

Then—icing on the cake—the guy goes nuts in the Cycle Shop. Totally berserk. Buys a complete outfit. Everything. Top of the line. A full black coverall that swaddles everything from toes to neck in breathable, bulletproof fabric, with armorgel pads in all the right places and airbags around the neck. Even safety fanatics don't bother with a helmet when they're wearing one of these babies.

So once he's figured out how to attach his swords on the outside of his coverall, he's on his way.

"I gotta say this," Scott says as the guy is sitting on his new bike, getting his swords adjusted, doing something incredi-bly unauthorized to the bios, "you look like one bad mother-fucker."

"Thanks, I guess." He twists the throttle up once and Scott feels, but does not hear, the power of the engine. This baby is so efficient it doesn't waste power by making noise. "Say hi to your brand-new niece," the guy says, and then lets go the clutch. The spokes flex and gather themselves and the bike springs forward out of the lot, seeming to jump off its electric paws. He cuts right across the parking lot of the neighboring NeoAquarian Temple franchise and pulls out onto the road. About half a second later, the guy with the swords is a dot on the horizon. Then he's gone. Northbound.

36

Until a man is twenty-five, he still thinks, every so often, that under the right circumstances he could be the baddest mother-fucker in the world. If I moved to a martial-arts monastery in China and studied real hard for ten years. If my family was wiped out by Colombian drug dealers and I swore myself to revenge. If I got a fatal disease, had one year to live, devoted it to wiping out street crime. If I just dropped out and devoted my life to being bad.

Hiro used to feel that way, too, but then he ran into Raven. In a way, this is liberating. He no longer has to worry about trying to be the baddest motherfucker in the world. The position is taken. The crowning touch, the one thing that really puts true world-class badmotherfuckerdom totally out of reach, of course, is the hydrogen bomb. If it wasn't for the hydrogen bomb, a man could still aspire. Maybe find Raven's Achilles' heel. Sneak up, get a drop, slip a mickey, pull a fast one. But Raven's nuclear umbrella kind of puts the world title out of reach.

Which is okay. Sometimes it's all right just to be a little bad. To know your limitations. Make do with what you've got.

Once he maneuvers his way onto the freeway, aimed up into the mountains, he goggles into his office. Earth is still there, zoomed in tight on the Raft. Hiro contemplates it, superimposed in ghostly hues on his view of the highway, as he rides toward Oregon at a hundred and forty miles per hour.

From a distance, it looks bigger than it really is. Getting closer, he can see that this illusion is caused by an enveloping, self-made slick/cloud of sewage and air pollution, fading out into the ocean and the atmosphere.

It orbits the Pacific clockwise. When they fire up the boilers on the *Enterprise*, it can control its direction a little bit, but real navigation is a practical impossibility with all the other shit lashed onto it. It mostly has to go where the wind and the Coriolis effect take it. A couple of years ago, it was going by the Philip-pines, Vietnam, China, Siberia, picking up Refus. Then it swung up the Aleutian chain, down the Alaska panhandle, and now it's gliding past the small town of Port Sherman, Oregon, near the California border.

As the Raft moves through the Pacific, riding mostly on ocean currents, it occasionally sheds great hunks of itself. Eventually, these fragments wash up in some place like Santa Barbara, still lashed together, carrying a payload of skeletons and gnawed bones.

When it gets to California, it will enter a new phase of its life cycle. It will shed much of its sprawling improvised bulk as a few hundred thousand Refus cut themselves loose and paddle to shore. The only Refus who make it that far are, by definition, the ones who were agile enough to make it out to the Raft in the first place, resourceful enough to survive the agonizingly slow passage through the arctic waters, and tough enough not to get killed by any of the other Refus. Nice guys, all of them. Just the kind of people you'd like to have showing up on your private beach in groups of a few thousand.

Stripped down to a few major ships, a little more maneuverable, the *Enterprise* then will swing across the South Pacific, heading for Indonesia, where it will turn north again and start the next cycle of migration.

Army ants cross mighty rivers by climbing on top of each other and clustering together into a little ball that floats. Many of them fall off and sink, and naturally the ants on the bottom of the ball drown. The ones who are quick and vigorous enough to keep clawing their way to the top survive. A lot of them make it across, and that's why you can't stop army ants by dynamiting the bridges. That's how Refus come across the Pacific, even though they are too poor to book passage on a real ship or buy a sea-worthy boat. A new wave washes up onto the West Coast every five years or so, when the ocean currents bring the *Enterprise* back.

For the last couple of months, owners of beachfront property in California have been hiring security people, putting up spotlights and antipersonnel fences along the tide line, mounting machine guns on their yachts. They have all subscribed to CIC's twenty-four-hour Raft Report, getting the latest news flash, straight from the satellite, on when the latest contingent of twenty-five thousand starving Eurasians has cut itself loose from the *Enterprise* and started dipping its myriad oars into the Pacific, like ant legs.

———————— "Time to do more digging," he tells the Librarian. "But this is going to have to be totally verbal, because I'm headed up I-5 at some incredible speed right now, and I have to watch out for slow-moving bagos and stuff."

"I'll keep that in mind," the voice of the Librarian says into his earphones. "Look out for the jackknifed truck south of Santa Clarita. And there is a large chuckhole in the left lane near the Tulare exit."

"Thanks. Who were these gods anyway? Did Lagos have an opinion on that?"

"Lagos believed that they might have been magicians—that is, normal human beings with special powers—or they might have been aliens."

"Whoa, whoa, hold on. Let's take these one at a time. What did Lagos mean when he talked about 'normal human beings with special powers'?"

"Assume that the nam-shub of Enki really functioned as a virus. Assume that someone named Enki invented it. Then Enki must have had some kind of linguistic power that goes beyond our concept of normal."

"And how would this power work? What's the mechanism?"

"I can only give you forward references drawn by Lagos."

"Okay. Give me some."

"The belief in the magical power of language is not unusual, both in mystical and academic literature. The Kabbalists—Jewish mystics of Spain and Palestine—believed that supernormal insight and power could be derived from properly combining the letters of the Divine Name. For example, Abu Aharon, an early Kabbalist who emigrated from Baghdad to Italy, was said to perform miracles through the power of the Sacred Names."

"What kind of power are we talking about here?"

"Most Kabbalists were theorists who were interested only in pure meditation. But there were so-called 'practical Kabbalists' who tried to apply the power of the Kabbalah in everyday life."

"In other words, sorcerers."

"Yes. These practical kabbalists used a so-called 'archangelic alphabet,' derived from first-century Greek and Aramaic theurgic alphabets, which resembled cuneiform. The Kabbalists referred to this alphabet as 'eye writing,' because the letters were composed of lines and small circles, which resembled eyes."

"Ones and zeroes."

"Some Kabbalists divided up the letters of the alphabet according to where they were produced inside the mouth."

"Okay. So as we would think of it, they were drawing a connection between the printed letter on the page and the neural connections that had to be invoked in order to pronounce it."

"Yes. By analyzing the spelling of various words, they were able to draw what they thought were profound conclusions about their true, inner meaning and significance."

"Okay. If you say so."

"In the academic realm, the literature is naturally not as fanciful. But a great deal of effort has been devoted to explaining Babel. Not the Babel event—which most people consider to be a myth—but the fact that languages tend to diverge. A number of linguistic theories have been developed in an effort to tie all languages together."

"Theories Lagos tried to apply to his virus hypothesis."

"Yes. There are two schools: relativists and universalists. As George Steiner summarizes it, relativists tend to believe that language is not the vehicle of thought but its determining medium. It is the framework of cognition. Our perceptions of everything are organized by the flux of sensations passing over that framework. Hence, the study of the evolution of language is the study of the evolution of the human mind itself."

"Okay, I can see the significance of that. What about the universalists?"

"In contrast with the relativists, who believe that languages need not have anything in common with each other, the universalists believe that if you can analyze languages enough, you can find that all of them have certain traits in common. So they analyze languages, looking for such traits."

"Have they found any?"

"No. There seems to be an exception to every rule."

"Which blows universalism out of the water."

"Not necessarily. They explain this problem by saying that the shared traits are too deeply buried to be analyzable."

"Which is a cop out."

"Their point is that at some level, language has to happen inside the human brain. Since all human brains are more or less the same—"

"The hardware's the same. Not the software."

"You are using some kind of metaphor that I cannot understand."

Hiro whips past a big Airstream that is rocking from side to side in a dangerous wind coming down the valley.

"Well, a French-speaker's brain starts out the same as an English-speaker's brain. As they grow up, they get programmed with different software—they learn different languages."

"Yes. Therefore, according to the universalists, French and English—or any other languages—must share certain traits that have their roots in the 'deep structures' of the human brain. According to Chomskyan theory, the deep structures are innate components of the brain that enable it to carry out certain formal kinds of operations on strings of symbols. Or, as Steiner paraphrases Emmon Bach: These deep structures eventually lead to the actual patterning of the cortex with its immensely ramified yet, at the same time, 'programmed' network of electrochemical and neurophysiological channels."

"But these deep structures are so deep we can't even see them?"

"The universalists place the active nodes of linguistic life—the deep structures—so deep as to defy observation and description. Or to use Steiner's analogy: Try to draw up the creature from the depths of the sea, and it will disintegrate or change form grotesquely."

"There's that serpent again. So which theory did Lagos believe in? The relativist or the universalist?"

"He did not seem to think there was much of a difference. In the end, they are both somewhat mystical. Lagos believed that both schools of thought had essentially arrived at the same place by different lines of reasoning."

"But it seems to me there is a key difference," Hiro says. "The universalists think that we are determined by the prepatterned structure of our brains—the pathways in the cortex. The relativists don't believe that we have any limits."

"Lagos modified the strict Chomskyan theory by supposing that learning a language is like blowing code into PROMs—an analogy that I cannot interpret."

"The analogy is clear. PROMs are Programmable Read-Only Memory chips," Hiro says. "When they come from the factory, they have no content. Once and only once, you can place information into those chips and then freeze it—the information, the software, becomes frozen into the chip—it transmutes into hardware. After you have blown the code into the PROMs, you can read it out, but you can't write to them anymore. So Lagos was trying to say that the newborn human brain has no structure—as the relativists would have it—and that as the child learns a language, the developing brain structures itself accordingly, the language gets 'blown into' the hardware and becomes a permanent part of the brain's deep structure—as the universalists would have it."

"Yes. This was his interpretation."

"Okay. So when he talked about Enki being a real person with magical powers, what he meant was that Enki somehow understood the connection between language and the brain, knew how to manipulate it. The same way that a hacker, knowing the secrets of a computer system, can write code to control it—digital nam-shubs."

"Lagos said that Enki had the ability to ascend into the universe of language and see it before his eyes. Much as humans go into the Metaverse. That gave him power to create nam-shubs. And nam-shubs had the power to alter the functioning of the brain and of the body."

"Why isn't anyone doing this kind of thing nowadays? Why aren't there any nam-shubs in English?"

"Not all languages are the same, as Steiner points out. Some languages are better at metaphor than others. Hebrew, Aramaic, Greek, and Chinese lend themselves to word play and have achieved a lasting grip on reality: 'Palestine had Qiryat Sefer, the "City of the Letter," and Syria had Byblos, the "Town of the Book." By contrast other civilizations seem "speechless" or at

least, as may have been the case in Egypt, not entirely cognizant
of the creative and transformational powers of language.' Lagos
believed that Sumerian was an extraordinarily powerful language—at least it was in Sumer five thousand years ago."

"A language that lent itself to Enki's neurolinguistic hacking."

"Early linguists, as well as the Kabbalists, believed in a fictional
language called the tongue of Eden, the language of Adam. It
enabled all men to understand each other, to communicate without misunderstanding. It was the language of the Logos, the
moment when God created the world by speaking a word. In the
tongue of Eden, naming a thing was the same as creating it. To
quote Steiner again, 'Our speech interposes itself between apprehension and truth like a dusty pane or warped mirror. The
tongue of Eden was like a flawless glass; a light of total understanding streamed through it. Thus Babel was a second Fall.' And
Isaac the Blind, an early Kabbalist, said that, to quote Gershom
Scholem's translation, 'The speech of men is connected with
divine speech and all language whether heavenly or human
derives from one source: the Divine Name.' The practical kabbalists, the sorcerers, bore the title *Ba'al Shem,* meaning 'master of
the divine name.' "

"The machine language of the world," Hiro says.

"Is this another analogy?"

"Computers speak machine language," Hiro says. "It's written
in ones and zeroes—binary code. At the lowest level, all computers are programmed with strings of ones and zeroes. When you
program in machine language, you are controlling the computer
at its brainstem, the root of its existence. It's the tongue of Eden.
But it's very difficult to work in machine language because you
go crazy after a while, working at such a minute level. So a whole
Babel of computer languages has been created for programmers:
FORTRAN, BASIC, COBOL, LISP, Pascal, C, PROLOG,
FORTH. You talk to the computer in one of these languages, and
a piece of software called a compiler converts it into machine
language. But you never can tell exactly what the compiler is
doing. It doesn't always come out the way you want. Like a dusty
pane or warped mirror. A really advanced hacker comes to understand the true inner workings of the machine—he sees through

the language he's working in and glimpses the secret functioning of the binary code—becomes a Ba'al Shem of sorts."

"Lagos believed that the legends about the tongue of Eden were exaggerated versions of true events," the Librarian says. "These legends reflected nostalgia for a time when people spoke Sumerian, a tongue that was superior to anything that came afterward."

"Is Sumerian really that good?"

"Not as far as modern-day linguists can tell," the Librarian says. "As I mentioned, it is largely impossible for us to grasp. Lagos suspected that words worked differently in those days. If one's native tongue influences the physical structure of the developing brain, then it is fair to say that the Sumerians—who spoke a language radically different from anything in existence today—had fundamentally different brains from yours. Lagos believed that for this reason, Sumerian was a language ideally suited to the creation and propagation of viruses. That a virus, once released into Sumer, would spread rapidly and virulently, until it had infected everyone."

"Maybe Enki knew that also," Hiro says. "Maybe the nam-shub of Enki wasn't such a bad thing. Maybe Babel was the best thing that ever happened to us."

37

Y.T.'s mom works in Fedland. She has parked her little car in her own little numbered slot, for which the Feds require her to pay about ten percent of her salary (if she doesn't like it she can take a taxi or walk) and walked up several levels of a blindingly lit reinforced-concrete helix in which most of the spaces—the good spaces closer to the surface—are reserved for people other than her, but empty. She always walks up the center of the ramp, between the rows of parked cars, so that the EBGOC boys won't think she's lurking, loitering, skulking, malingering, or smoking.

Reaching the subterranean entrance of her building, she has taken all metal objects from her pockets and removed what little jewelry she's wearing and dumped them into a dirty plastic bowl and walked through the detector. Flashed her badge. Signed her name and noted down the digital time. Submitted to a frisking from an EBGOC girl. Annoying, but it sure beats a cavity search. They have a right to do a cavity search if they want. She got cavity-searched every day for a month once, right after she had spoken up at a meeting and suggested that her supervisor might be on the wrong track with a major programming project. It was punitive and vicious, she knew it was, but she always wanted to give something back to her country, and whenever you work for the Feds you just accept the fact that there's going to be some politicking. And that as a low-level person you're going to bear the brunt. And later on, you climb the GS ladder, don't have to put up with as much shit. Far be it from her to quarrel with her supervisor. Her supervisor, Marietta, doesn't have an especially stellar GS level, but she does have access. She has connections. Marietta knows people who know people. Marietta has attended cocktail parties that were also attended by some people who, well, your eyes would bug out.

She has passed the frisking with flying collars. Put the metal stuff back into her pockets. Climbed up half a dozen flights of stairs to her floor. The elevators here still work, but some very highly placed people in Fedland have let it be known—nothing official, but they have ways of letting this stuff out—that it is a duty to conserve energy. And the Feds are real serious about duty. Duty, loyalty, responsibility. The collagen that binds us into the United States of America. So the stairwells are filled with sweaty wool and clacking leather. If you took the elevator, no one would actually say anything, but it would be noticed. Noticed and written down and taken into account. People would look at you, glance you up and down, like, what happened, sprain your ankle? Taking the stairs is no problem.

Feds don't smoke. Feds generally don't overeat. The health plan is very specific, contains major incentives, get too heavy or wheezy and, no one says anything about it—which would be rude—but you feel a definite pressure, a sense of not fitting in, as you walk across the sea of desks, eyes glance up to follow you, estimating the mass of your saddlebags, eyes darting back and forth between desks as, by consensus, your co-workers say to themselves, I wonder how much he or she is driving up our health plan premiums?

So Y.T.'s mom has clacked up the stairs in her black pumps and gone into her office, actually a large room with computer workstations placed across it in a grid. Used to be divided up by partitions, but the EBGOC boys didn't like it, said what would happen if there had to be an evacuation? All those partitions would impede the free flow of unhinged panic. So no more partitions. Just workstations and chairs. Not even any desktops. Desktops encourage the use of paper, which is archaic and reflects inadequate team spirit. What is so special about your work that you have to write it down on a piece of paper that only you get to see? That you have to lock it away inside a desk? When you're working for the Feds, everything you do is the property of the United States of America. You do your work on the computer. The computer keeps a copy of everything, so that if you get sick or something, it's all there where your co-workers and supervisors can get access to it. If you want to write little notes or make phone doodles, you're perfectly free to do that at home, in your spare time.

And there's the question of interchangeability. Fed workers, like military people, are intended to be interchangeable parts. What happens if your workstation should break down? You're going to sit there and twiddle your thumbs until it gets fixed? No siree, you're going to move to a spare workstation and get to work on that. And you don't have that flexibility if you've got half a ton of personal stuff cached inside of a desk, strewn around a desktop.

So there is no paper in a Fed office. All the workstations are the same. You come in in the morning, pick one at random, sit down, and get to work. You could try to favor a particular station, try to sit there every day, but it would be noticed. Generally you pick the unoccupied workstation that's closest to the door. That way, whoever came in earliest sits closest, whoever came in latest is way in the back, for the rest of the day it's obvious at a glance who's on the ball in this office and who is—as they whisper to each other in the bathrooms—having problems.

Not that it's any big secret, who comes in first. When you sign on to a workstation in the morning, it's not like the central computer doesn't notice that fact. The central computer notices just about everything. Keeps track of every key you hit on the keyboard, all day long, what time you hit it, down to the microsecond, whether it was the right key or the wrong key, how many mistakes you make and when you make them. You're only required to be at your workstation from eight to five, with a half-hour lunch break and two ten-minute coffee breaks, but if you stuck to that schedule it would definitely be noticed, which is why Y.T.'s mom is sliding into the first unoccupied workstation and signing on to her machine at quarter to seven. Half a dozen other people are already here, signed on to workstations closer to the entrance, but this isn't bad. She can look forward to a reasonably stable career if she can keep up this sort of performance.

The Feds still operate in Flatland. None of this three-dimensional stuff, no goggles, no stereo sound. The computers are all basic flat-screen two-dimensional numbers. Windows appear on the desktop, with little text documents inside. All part of the austerity program. Soon to reap major benefits.

She signs on and checks her mail. No personal mail, just a couple of mass-distributed pronouncements from Marietta.

NEW TP POOL REGULATIONS
I've been asked to distribute the new regulations regarding office pool displays. The enclosed memo is a new subchapter of the EBGOC Procedure Manual, replacing the old subchapter entitled PHYSICAL PLANT/CALIFORNIA/ LOS ANGELES/BUILDINGS/OFFICE AREAS/PHYSI-CAL LAYOUT REGULATIONS/EMPLOYEE INPUT/ GROUP ACTIVITIES.

The old subchapter was a flat prohibition on the use of office space or time for "pool" activities of any kind, whether permanent (e.g., coffee pool) or one-time (e.g., birthday parties).

This prohibition still applies, but a single, one-time exception has now been made for any office that wishes to pursue a joint bathroom-tissue strategy.

By way of introduction, let me just make a few general comments on this subject. The problem of distributing bathroom tissue to workers presents inherent challenges for any

office management system due to the inherent unpredictabil-
ity of usage—not every facility usage transaction necessitates
the use of bathroom tissue, and when it is used, the amount
needed (number of squares) may vary quite widely from person
to person and, for a given person, from one transaction to the
next. This does not even take into account the occasional use
of bathroom tissue for unpredictable/creative purposes such
as applying/removing cosmetics, beverage-spill management,
etc. For this reason, rather than trying to package bathroom
tissue in small one-transaction packets (as is done with pre-
moistened towelettes, for example), which can be wasteful in
some cases and limiting in other cases, it has been traditional
to package this product in bulk distribution units whose size
exceeds the maximum amount of squares that an individual
could conceivably use in a single transaction (barring *force
majeure*). This reduces to a minimum the number of transactions in which the distribution unit is depleted (the roll runs
out) during the transaction, a situation that can lead to emotional stress for the affected employee. However, it does
present the manager with some challenges in that the distribution unit is rather bulky and must be repeatedly used by a
number of different individuals if it is not to be wasted.

Since the implementation of Phase XVII of the Austerity
Program, employees have been allowed to bring their own
bathroom tissue from home. This approach is somewhat bulky
and redundant, as every worker usually brings their own roll.

Some offices have attempted to meet this challenge by
instituting bathroom-tissue pools.

Without overgeneralizing, it may be stated that an inherent
and irreducible feature of any bathroom-tissue pool implemented at the office level, in an environment (i.e., building) in
which comfort stations are distributed on a per-floor basis (i.e.,
in which several offices share a single facility) is that provision
must be made within the confines of the individual office for
temporary stationing of bathroom tissue distribution units
(i.e., rolls). This follows from the fact that if the BTDUs (rolls)
are stationed, while inactive, outside of the purview of the
controlling office (i.e., the office that has collectively purchased the BTDU)—that is, if the BTDUs are stored, for example, in a lobby area or within the facility in which they are

actually utilized, they will be subject to pilferage and "shrink-age" as unauthorized persons consume them, either as part of a conscious effort to pilfer or out of an honest misunderstand-ing, i.e., a belief that the BTDUs are being provided free of charge by the operating agency (in this case the United States Government), or as the result of necessity, as in the case of a beverage spill that is encroaching on sensitive electronic equipment and whose management will thus brook no delay. This fact has led certain offices (which shall go unnamed—you know who you are, guys) to establish makeshift BTDU depots that also serve as pool-contribution collection points. Usually, these depots take the form of a table, near the door closest to the facility, on which the BTDUs are stacked or otherwise deployed, with a bowl or some other receptacle in which par-ticipants may place their contributions, and typically with a sign or other attention-getting device (such as a stuffed animal or cartoon) requesting donations. A quick glance at the current regulations will show that placement of such a display/depot violates the procedure manual. However, in the interests of employee hygiene, morale, and group spirit-building, my higher-ups have agreed to make a one-time exception in the regulations for this purpose.

As with any part of the procedure manual, new or old, it is your responsibility to be thoroughly familiar with this material. Estimated reading time for this document is 15.62 minutes (and don't think we won't check). Please make note of the major points made in this document, as follows:

1) BTDU depot/displays are now allowed, on a trial basis, with the new policy to be reviewed in six months.

2) These must be operated on a voluntary, pool-type basis, as described in the subchapter on employee pools. (Note: This means keeping books and tallying all financial transactions.)

3) BTDUs must be brought in by the employees (not shipped through the mailroom) and are subject to all the usual search-and-seizure regulations.

4) Scented BTDUs are prohibited as they may cause allergic reactions, wheezing, etc. in some persons.

5) Cash pool donations, as with all monetary transactions within the U.S. Government, must use official U.S. cur-rency—no yen or Kongbucks!

Naturally, this will lead to a bulk problem if people try to use the donation bucket as a dumping ground for bundles of old billion- and trillion-dollar bills. The Buildings and Grounds people are worried about waste-disposal problems and the potential fire hazard that may ensue if large piles of billions and trillions begin to mount up. Therefore, a key feature of the new regulation is that the donation bucket must be emptied every day—more often if an excessive build-up situation is seen to develop.

In this vein, the B & G people would also like me to point out that many of you who have excess U.S. currency to get rid of have been trying to kill two birds with one stone by using old billions as bathroom tissue. While creative, this approach has two drawbacks:

1) It clogs the plumbing, and
2) It constitutes defacement of U.S. currency, which is a federal crime.

DON'T DO IT.
Join your office bathroom-tissue pool instead. It's easy, it's hygienic, and it's legal.
Happy pooling!
Marietta.

Y.T.'s mom pulls up the new memo, checks the time, and starts reading it. The estimated reading time is 15.62 minutes. Later, when Marietta does her end-of-day statistical roundup, sitting in her private office at 9:00 P.M., she will see the name of each employee and next to it, the amount of time spent reading this memo, and her reaction, based on the time spent, will go something like this:

Less than 10 min.	Time for an employee conference and possible attitude counseling.
10–14 min.	Keep an eye on this employee; may be developing slipshod attitude.

14–15.61 min.	Employee is an efficient worker, may sometimes miss important details.
Exactly 15.62 min.	Smartass. Needs attitude counseling.
15.63–16 min.	Asswipe. Not to be trusted.
16–18 min.	Employee is a methodical worker, may sometimes get hung up on minor details.
More than 18 min.	Check the security videotape, see just what this employee was up to (e.g., possible unauthorized restroom break).

Y.T.'s mom decides to spend between fourteen and fifteen minutes reading the memo. It's better for younger workers to spend too long, to show that they're careful, not cocky. It's better for older workers to go a little fast, to show good management potential. She's pushing forty. She scans through the memo, hitting the Page Down button at reasonably regular intervals, occasionally paging back up to pretend to reread some earlier section. The computer is going to notice all this. It approves of rereading. It's a small thing, but over a decade or so this stuff really shows up on your work-habits summary.

Having got that out of the way, she dives into work. She is an applications programmer for the Feds. In the old days, she would have written computer programs for a living. Nowadays, she writes fragments of computer programs. These programs are designed by Marietta and Marietta's superiors in massive week-long meetings on the top floor. Once they get the design down, they start breaking up the problem into tinier and tinier segments, assigning them to group managers, who break them down even more and feed little bits of work to the individual programmers. In order to keep the work done by the individual coders from colliding, it all has to be done according to a set of rules and regulations even bigger and more fluid than the Government procedure manual.

So the first thing that Y.T.'s mother does, having read the new subchapter on bathroom tissue pools, is to sign on to a subsystem of the main computer system that handles the particular programming project she's working on. She doesn't know what the project is—that's classified—or what it's called. It's just her project. She shares it with a few hundred other programmers, she's not sure exactly who. And every day when she signs on to it, there's a stack of memos waiting for her, containing new regulations and changes to the rules that they all have to follow when writing code for the project. These regulations make the business with the bathroom tissue seem as simple and elegant as the Ten Commandments.

So she spends until about eleven A.M. reading, rereading, and understanding the new changes in the Project. There are many of these, because this is a Monday morning and Marietta and her higher-ups spent the whole weekend closeted on the top floor, having a catfight about this Project, changing everything.

Then she starts going back over all the code she has previously written for the Project and making a list of all the stuff that will have to be rewritten in order to make it compatible with the new specifications. Basically, she's going to have to rewrite all of her material from the ground up. For the third time in as many months.

But hey, it's a job.

About eleven-thirty, she looks up, startled, to see that half a dozen people are standing around her workstation. There's Marietta. And a proctor. And some male Feds. And Leon the polygraph man.

"I just had mine on Thursday," she says.

"Time for another one," Marietta says. "Come on, let's get this show on the road."

"Hands out where I can see them," the proctor says.

38

Y.T.'s mom stands up, hands to her sides, and starts walking. She walks straight out of the office. None of the other people look up. Not supposed to. Insensitive to co-workers' needs. Makes the testee feel awkward and singled out, when in fact the polygraph is just part of the whole Fed way of life. She can hear the snapping footsteps of the proctor behind her, walking two paces behind, watching, keeping her eyes on those hands so they can't be doing anything, like popping a Valium or something else that might throw off the test.

She stops in front of the bathroom door. The proctor walks in front of her, holds it open, and she walks in, followed by the proctor.

The last stall on the left is oversized, big enough for two people. Y.T.'s mom goes in, followed by the proctor, who closes and locks the door. Y.T.'s mom pulls down her panty hose, pulls up her skirt, squats over a pan, pees. The proctor watches every drop go into the pan, picks it up, empties it into a test tube that is already labeled with her name and today's date.

Then it's back out to the lobby, followed again by the proctor. You're allowed to use the elevators on your way to the polygraph room, so you won't be out of breath and sweaty when you get there.

It used to be just a plain office with a chair and some instruments on a table. Then they got the new, fancy polygraph system. Now it's like going in for some kind of high-tech medical scan. The room is completely rebuilt, no vestige of its original function, the window covered over, everything smooth and beige and smelling like a hospital. There's only one chair, in the middle. Y.T.'s mom goes and sits down in it, puts her arms on the arms of the chair, nestles her fingertips and palms into the little depressions that await. The neoprene fist of the blood-pressure cuff gropes blindly, finds her arm, and seizes it. Meanwhile, the room lights are dimming, the door is closing, she's all alone. The crown of thorns closes over her head, she feels the pricks of the electrodes through her scalp, senses the cool air flowing down over her shoulders from the superconducting quantum-interference devices that serve as radar into her brain. Somewhere on the other side of the wall, she knows, half a dozen personnel techs are sitting in a control room, looking at a big-screen blow-up of her pupils.

Then she feels a burning prick in her forearm and knows she's been injected with something. Which means it's not a normal polygraph exam. Today she's in for something special. The burning spreads throughout her body, her heart thumps, eyes water. She's been shot up with caffeine to make her hyper, make her talkative.

So much for getting any work done today. Sometimes these things go for twelve hours.

"What is your name?" a voice says. It's an unnaturally calm and liquid voice. Computer generated. That way, everything it says to her is impartial, stripped of emotional content, she has no way to pick up any cues as to how the interrogation is going.

The caffeine, and the other things that they inject her with, screw up her sense of time also.

She hates these things, but it happens to everyone from time to time, and when you go to work for the Feds, you sign on the dotted line and give permission for it. In a way, it's a mark of pride and honor. Everyone who works for the Feds has their heart in it. Because if they didn't, it would come out plain as day when it is their turn to sit in this chair.

The questions go on and on. Mostly nonsense questions. "Have you ever been to Scotland? Is white bread more expensive than wheat bread?" This is just to get her settled down, get all systems running smoothly. They throw out all the stuff they get from the first hour of the interrogation, because it's lost in the noise.

She can feel herself relaxing into it. They say that after a few polygraphs, you learn to relax, the whole thing goes quicker. The chair holds her in place, the caffeine keeps her from getting drowsy, the sensory deprivation clears out her mind.

"What is your daughter's nickname?"

"Y.T."

"How do you refer to your daughter?"

"I call her by her nickname. Y.T. She kind of insists on it."

"Does Y.T. have a job?"

"Yes. She works as Kourier. She works for RadiKS."

"How much money does Y.T. make as a Kourier?"

"I don't know. A few bucks here and there."

"How often does she purchase new equipment for her job?"

"I'm not aware. I don't really keep track of that."

"Has Y.T. done anything unusual lately?"

"That depends on what you mean." She knows she's equivocating. "She's always doing things that some people might label as unusual." That doesn't sound too good, sounds like an endorsement of nonconformity. "I guess what I'm saying is, she's always doing unusual things."

"Has Y.T. broken anything in the house recently?"

"Yes." She gives up. The Feds already know this, her house is bugged and tapped, it's a wonder it doesn't short out the electrical grid, all the extra stuff wired into it. "She broke my computer."

"Did she give an explanation for why she broke the computer?"

"Yes. Sort of. I mean, if nonsense counts as an explanation."

"What was her explanation?"

"She was afraid—this is so ridiculous—she was afraid I was going to catch a virus from it."

"Was Y.T. also afraid of catching this virus?"

"No. She said that only programmers could catch it."

Why are they asking her all of these questions? They have all of this stuff on tape.

"Did you believe Y.T.'s explanation of why she broke the computer?"

That's it.

That's what they're after.

They want to know the only thing they can't directly tap—what's going on in her mind. They want to know whether she believes Y.T.'s virus story.

And she knows she's making a mistake just thinking these thoughts. Because those supercooled SQUIDs around her head are picking it up. They can't tell what she's thinking. But they can tell that something's going on in her brain, that she's using parts of her brain right now that she didn't use when they were asking the nonsense questions.

In other words, they can tell that she is analyzing the situation, trying to figure them out. And she wouldn't be doing that unless she wanted to hide something.

"What is it you want to know?" she says. "Why don't you just come out and ask me directly? Let's talk about this face to face. Just sit down together in a room like adults and talk about it."

She feels another sharp prick in her arm, feels numbness and coldness spreading all across her body over an interval of a couple of seconds as the drug mixes with her bloodstream. It's getting harder to follow the conversation.

"What is your name?" the voice says.

39

The Alcan—the Alaska Highway—is the world's longest franchise ghetto, a one-dimensional city two thousand miles long and a hundred feet wide, and growing at the rate of a hundred miles a year, or as quickly as people can drive up to the edge of the wilderness and park their bagos in the next available slot. It is the only way out for people who want to leave America but don't have access to an airplane or a ship.

It's all two-lane, paved but not well paved, and choked with mobile homes, family vans, pickup trucks with camper backs. It starts somewhere in the middle of British Columbia, at the crossroads of Prince George, where a number of tributaries feed in together to make a single northbound highway. South of there, the tributaries split into a delta of feeder roads that crosses the Canadian/American border at a dozen or more places spread out over five hundred miles from the fjords of British Columbia to the vast striped wheatlands of central Montana. Then it ties into the American road system, which serves as the headwaters of the migration. This five-hundred-mile swath of territory is filled with would-be arctic explorers in great wheeled houses, optimistically northbound, and more than a few rejects who have abandoned their bagos in the north country and hitched a ride back down

south. The lumbering bagos and top-heavy four-wheelers form a
moving slalom course for Hiro on his black motorcycle.

All these beefy Caucasians with guns! Get enough of them
together, looking for the America they always believed they'd grow
up in, and they glom together like overcooked rice, form integral,
starchy little units. With their power tools, portable generators,
weapons, four-wheel-drive vehicles, and personal computers, they
are like beavers hyped up on crystal meth, manic engineers without a blueprint, chewing through the wilderness, building things
and abandoning them, altering the flow of mighty rivers and then
moving on because the place ain't what it used to be.

The byproduct of the lifestyle is polluted rivers, greenhouse
effect, spouse abuse, televangelists, and serial killers. But as long
as you have that four-wheel-drive vehicle and can keep driving
north, you can sustain it, keep moving just quickly enough to stay
one step ahead of your own waste stream. In twenty years, ten
million white people will converge on the north pole and park
their bagos there. The low-grade waste heat of their thermody-
namically intense lifestyle will turn the crystalline icescape pli-
able and treacherous. It will melt a hole through the polar icecap,
and all that metal will sink to the bottom, sucking the biomass
down with it.

For a fee, you can drive into a Snooze 'n' Cruise franchise and
umbilical your bago. The magic words are "We Have Pull-
Thrus," which means you can enter the franchise, hook up,
sleep, unhook, and drive out without ever having to shift your
land zeppelin into reverse.

They used to claim it was a campground, tried to design the
franchise with a rustic motif, but the customers kept chopping
up those log-and-plank signs and wooden picnic tables and using
them for cooking fires. Nowadays, the signs are electric polycarbonate bubbles, the corporate identity is all round and polished
and smooth, in the same way that a urinal is, to prevent stuff
from building up in the cracks. Because it's not really camping
when you don't have a house to go back to.

Sixteen hours out of California, Hiro pulls into a Snooze 'n'
Cruise on the eastern slope of the Cascades in northern Oregon.
He's several hundred miles north of where the Raft is, and on the

wrong side of the mountains. But there's a guy here he wants to interview.

There are three parking lots. One out of sight down a pitted dirt road marked with falling-down signs. One a little bit closer, with scary hairys hanging around its edges, silvery disks flashing and popping under the full moon as they aim the bottoms of their beer cans at the sky. And one right in front of the Towne Hall, with gun-toting attendants. You have to pay to park in that lot. Hiro decides to pay. He leaves his bike pointing outward, puts the bios into warm shutdown so he can hot-boot it later if he has to, throws some Kongbucks at an attendant. Then he turns his head back and forth like a hunting dog, sniffing the still air, trying to find the Glade.

There's an area a hundred feet away, under the moonlight, where a few people have been adventurous enough to pitch a tent; usually, these are the ones with the most guns, or the least to lose. Hiro goes in that direction, and pretty soon he can see the spreading canopy over the Glade.

Everyone else calls it the Body Lot. It is, simply, an open patch of ground, formerly grass covered, now covered with successive truckloads of sand that have become mingled with litter, broken glass, and human waste. A canopy is stretched over it to keep out the rain, and big mushroom-shaped hoods stick out of the ground every few feet, exhaling warm air on cold nights. It is pretty cheap to sleep in the Glade. It is an innovation that was created by some of the franchises farther south and has been spreading northward along with its clientele.

About half a dozen of them are scattered around under the warm-air vents, bandaged against the chill in their army blankets. A couple of them have a small fire going, are playing cards by its light. Hiro ignores them, starts wandering around through the remainder.

"Chuck Wrightson," he says. "Mr. President, are you here?"

The second time he says it, a pile of wool off to his left begins to writhe and thrash around. A head comes out of it. Hiro turns toward him, holds up his hands to prove he's unarmed.

"Who is that?" he says. He is abjectly terrified. "Raven?"

"Not Raven," Hiro says. "Don't worry. Are you Chuck Wrightson? Former President of the Temporary Republic of Kenai and Kodiak?"

"Yeah. What do you want? I don't have any money."

"Just to talk. I work for CIC, and my job is to gather intelligence."

"I need a fucking drink," Chuck Wrightson says.

The Towne Hall is a big inflatable building in the middle of the Snooze 'n' Cruise. It is Derelict Las Vegas: convenience store, video arcade, laundromat, bar, liquor store, flea market, whorehouse. It always seems to be ruled by that small percentage of the human population that is capable of partying until five in the morning every single night, and that has no other function.

Most Towne Halls have a few franchises-within-franchises. Hiro sees a Kelley's Tap, which is about the nicest trough you are likely to find at a Snooze 'n' Cruise, and leads Chuck Wrightson into it. Chuck is wearing many layers of clothing that used to be different colors. Now they are the same color as his skin, which is khaki.

All the businesses in a Towne Hall, including this bar, look like something you'd see on a prison ship—everything nailed down, brightly lit up twenty-four hours a day, all of the personnel sealed up behind thick glass barriers that have gone all yellow and murky. Security at this Towne Hall is provided by The Enforcers, so there are a lot of steroid addicts in black armorgel outfits, cruising up and down the arcade in twos and threes, enthusiastically violating people's human rights.

Hiro and Chuck grab the closest thing they can find to a corner table. Hiro buttonholes a waiter and surreptitiously orders a pitcher of Pub Special, mixed half and half with nonalcoholic beer. This way, Chuck ought to remain awake a little longer than he would otherwise.

It doesn't take much to make him open up. He's like one of these old guys from a disgraced presidential administration, forced out by scandal, who devotes the rest of his life to finding people who will listen to him.

"Yeah, I was president of TROKK for two years. And I still consider myself the president of the government in exile."

Hiro tries to keep himself from rolling his eyes. Chuck seems to notice.

"Okay, okay, so that's not much. But TROKK was a thriving country, for a while. There's a lot of people who'd like to see something like that rise again. I mean, the only thing that forced us out—the only way those maniacs were able to seize power—was just totally, you know—" He doesn't seem to have words for it. "How could you have expected something like that?"

"How were you forced out? Was there a civil war?"

"There were some uprisings, early on. And there were remote parts of Kodiak where we never had a firm grip on power. But there was never a civil war per se. See, the Americans liked our government. The Americans had all the weapons, the equipment, the infrastructure. The Orthos were just a bunch of hairy guys running around in the woods."

"Orthos?"

"Russian Orthodox. At first they were a tiny minority. Mostly Indians—you know, Tlingits and Aleuts who'd been converted by the Russians hundreds of years ago. But when things got crazy in Russia, they started to pour across the Dateline in all kinds of different boats."

"And they didn't want a constitutional democracy."

"No. No way."

"What did they want? A tsar?"

"No. Those tsar guys—the traditionalists—stayed in Russia. The Orthos who came to TROKK were total rejects. They had been forced out by the mainline Russian Orthodox church."

"Why?"

"Yeretic. That's how Russians say 'heretic.' The Orthos who came to TROKK were a new sect—all Pentecostals. They were tied in somehow with the Reverend Wayne's Pearly Gates. We had missionaries from Texas coming up all the goddamn time to meet with them. They were always speaking in tongues. The mainline Russian Orthodox church thought it was the work of the devil."

"So how many of these Pentecostal Russian Orthodox people came over to TROKK?"

"Jeez, a hell of a lot of them. At least fifty thousand."

"How many Americans were in TROKK?"

"Close to a hundred thousand."

"Then how exactly did the Orthos manage to take the place over?"

"Well, one morning we woke up and there was an Airstream parked in the middle of Government Square in New Washington, right in the middle of all the bagos where we had set up the government. The Orthos had towed it there during the night, then took the wheels off so it couldn't be moved. We figured it was a protest action. We told them to move it out of there. They refused and issued a proclamation, in Russian. When we got this damn thing translated, it turned out to be an order for us to pack up and leave and turn over power to the Orthos.

"Well, this was ridiculous. So we went up to this Airstream to move it out of there, and Gurov's waiting for us with this nasty grin on his face."

"Gurov?"

"Yeah. One of the Refus who came over the Dateline from the Soviet Union. Former KGB general turned religious fanatic. He was kind of like the Minister of Defense for the government that the Orthos set up. So Gurov opens the side door of the Airstream and lets us get a load of what's inside."

"What was inside?"

"Well, mostly it was a bunch of equipment, you know, a portable generator, electrical wiring, a control panel, and so forth. But in the middle of the trailer, there's this big black cone sitting on the floor. About the shape of an ice cream cone, except it's about five feet long and it's smooth and black. And I asked what the hell is that thing. And Gurov says, that thing is a ten-megaton hydrogen bomb we scavenged from a ballistic missile. A city-buster. Any more questions?"

"So you capitulated."

"Couldn't do much else."

"Do you know how the Orthos came to be in possession of a hydrogen bomb?"

Chuck Wrightson clearly knows. He sucks in his deepest breath of the evening, lets it out, shakes his head, staring off over Hiro's shoulder. He takes a couple of nice long swigs from his glass of beer.

"There was a Soviet nuclear-missile submarine. The commander was named Ovchinnikov. He was religiously faithful, but he wasn't a fanatic like the Orthos. I mean, if he had been a fanatic they wouldn't have given him command of a nuclear-missile submarine, right?"

"Supposedly."

"You had to be psychologically stable. Whatever that means. Anyway, after things fell apart in Russia, he found himself in possession of this very dangerous weapon. He made up his mind that he was going to offload all of the crew and then scuttle it in the Marianas Trench. Bury all those weapons forever.

"But, somehow, he was persuaded to use this submarine to help a bunch of the Orthos escape to Alaska. They, and a lot of other Refus, had started flocking to the Bering coast. And the conditions in some of these Refu camps were pretty desperate. It's not like a lot of food can be grown in that area, you know. These people were dying by the thousands. They just stood on the beaches, starving to death, waiting for a ship to come.

"So Ovchinnikov let himself be persuaded to use his submarine—which is very large and very fast—to evacuate some of these poor Refus to TROKK.

"But, naturally, he was paranoid about the idea of letting a whole bunch of unknown quantities onto his ship. These nuke-sub commanders are real security freaks, for obvious reasons. So they set up a very strict system. All the Refus who were going to get on the ship had to pass through metal detectors, had to be inspected. Then they were under armed guard all the way across to Alaska.

"Well, the Stern Orthos have this guy named Raven—"

"I'm familiar with him."

"Well, Raven got onto that nuclear submarine."

"Oh, my God."

"He got over to the Siberian coast somehow—probably surfed across in his fucking kayak."

"Surfed?"

"That's how the Aleuts get between islands."

"Raven's an Aleut?"

"Yeah. An Aleut whale killer. You know what an Aleut is?"

"Yeah. My Dad knew one in Japan," Hiro says. A bunch of Dad's old prison-camp tales are beginning to stir in Hiro's memory, working their way up out of deep, deep storage.

"The Aleuts just paddle out in their kayaks and catch a wave. They can outrun a steamship, you know."

"Didn't know that."

"Anyway, Raven went to one of these Refu camps and passed himself off as a Siberian tribesman. You can't tell some of those Siberians apart from our Indians. The Orthos apparently had some confederates in these camps who bumped Raven up to the head of the line, so he got to be on the submarine."

"But you said there was a metal detector."

"Didn't help. He uses glass knives. Chips them out of plate glass. It's the sharpest blade in the universe, you know."

"Didn't know that either."

"Yeah. The edge is only a single molecule wide. Doctors use them for eye surgery—they can cut your cornea and not leave a scar. There's Indians who make a living doing that, you know. Chipping out eye scalpels."

"Well, you learn something new every day. That kind of a knife would be sharp enough to go through bulletproof fabric, I guess," Hiro says.

Chuck Wrightson shrugs. "I lost track of the number of people Raven snuffed who were wearing bulletproof fabric."

Hiro says, "I thought he must be carrying some kind of high-tech laser knife or something."

"Think again. Glass knife. He had one on board the submarine. Either smuggled it on board with him, or else found a chunk of glass on the submarine and chipped it out himself."

"And?"

Chuck gets his thousand-yard stare again, takes another slug of beer. "On a sub, you know, there's no place for things to drain to. The survivors claimed that the blood was knee-deep all through the submarine. Raven just killed everyone. Everyone except the Orthos, a skeleton crew, and some other Refus who were able to barricade themselves in little compartments around the ship. The survivors say," Chuck says, taking another swig, "that it was quite a night."

"And he forced them to steer the submarine into the hands of the Orthos."

"To their anchorage off Kodiak," Chuck says. "The Orthos were all ready. They had put together a crew of ex-Navy men, guys who had worked on nuke subs in the past—X-rays, they call them—and they came and took the sub over. As for us, we had no idea that any of this had happened. Until one of the warheads showed up in our goddamn front yard."

Chuck glances up above Hiro's head, noticing someone. Hiro feels a light tap on his shoulder. "Excuse me, sir?" a man is saying. "Pardon me for just a second?"

40

Hiro turns around. It's a big porky white man with wavy, slicked-back red hair and a beard. He's got a baseball cap perched on top of his head, tilted way back to expose the following words, tattooed in block letters across his forehead:

MOOD SWINGS
RACIALLY INSENSITIVE

Hiro is looking up at all of this over the curving horizon of the man's flannel-clad belly.

"What is it?" Hiro says.

"Well, sir, I'm sorry to disturb you in the middle of your conversation with this gentleman here. But me and my friends were just wondering. Are you a lazy shiftless watermelon-eating black-ass nigger, or a sneaky little v.d.-infected gook?"

The man reaches up, pulls the brim of his baseball cap downward. Now Hiro can see the Confederate flag printed on the front, the embroidered words "New South Africa Franchulate #153."

Hiro pushes himself up over the table, spins around, and slides backward on his ass toward Chuck, trying to get the table between him and the New South African. Chuck has conveniently vanished, so Hiro ends up standing with his back comfortably to the wall, looking out over the bar.

At the same time, a dozen or so other men are standing up from their tables, forming up behind the first one in a grinning, sunburned phalanx of Confederate flags and sideburns.

"Let's see," Hiro says, "is that some kind of a trick question?"

There are a lot of Towne Halls in a lot of Snooze 'n' Cruise franchises where you have to check your weapons at the entrance. This is not one of them.

Hiro isn't sure if that is bad or good. Without weapons, the New South Africans would just beat the crap out of him. With weapons, Hiro can fight back, but the stakes are higher. Hiro is bulletproof up to his neck, but that just means the New South Africans will all be going for a head shot. And they pride themselves on marksmanship. It is a fetish with them.

"Isn't there an NSA franchise down the road?" Hiro says.

"Yeah," says the point man, who has a long, spreading body and short stumpy legs. "It's heaven. It really is. Ain't no place on earth like a New South Africa."

"Well, then if you don't mind my asking," Hiro says, "if it's so damn nice, why don't y'all go back to your egg sac and hang out there?"

"There is one problem with New South Africa," the guy says. "Don't mean to sound unpatriotic, but it's true."

"And what is that problem?" Hiro says.

"There's no niggers, gooks, or kikes there to beat the shit out of."

"Ah. That is a problem," Hiro says. "Thank you."

"For what?"

"For announcing your intentions—giving me the right to do this."

Then Hiro cuts his head off.

What else can he do? There are at least twelve of them. They have made a point of blocking the only exit. They have just announced their intentions. And presumably they are all carrying heat. Besides, this kind of thing is going to happen to him about every ten seconds when he's on the Raft.

The New South African has no idea what's coming, but he starts to react as Hiro is swinging the katana at his neck, so he is flying backward when the decapitation occurs. That is good, because about half his blood supply comes lofting out the top of his neck. Twin jets, one from each carotid. Hiro doesn't get a drop on himself.

In the Metaverse, the blade just passes right through, if you

swing it quickly enough. Here in Reality, Hiro's expecting a powerful shock when his blade hits the New South African's neck,
like when you hit a baseball the wrong way, but he hardly feels a
thing. It just goes right through and almost swings around and
buries itself in the wall. He must have gotten lucky and hit a gap
between vertebrae. Hiro's training comes back to him, oddly. He
forgot to squeeze it off, forgot to stop the blade himself, and
that's bad form.

Even though he's expecting it, he's startled for a minute. This
sort of thing doesn't happen with avatars. They just fall down.
For an astonishingly long time, he just stands there and looks at
the guy's body. Meanwhile, the airborne cloud of blood is seeking
its level, dripping from the hung ceiling, spattering down from
shelves behind the bar. A wino sitting there nursing a double shot
of vodka shakes and shivers, staring into his glass at the galactic
swirl of a trillion red cells dying in the ethanol.

Hiro swaps a few long glances with the New South Africans,
like everyone in the bar is trying to come to a consensus as to
what will happen next. Should they laugh? Take a picture? Run
away? Call an ambulance?

He makes his way around toward the exit by running across
people's tables. It is rude, but other patrons scoot back, some of
them are quick enough to snatch their beers out of his way, and
no one gives him any hassles. The sight of the bare katana inspires everyone to a practically Nipponese level of politeness.
There are a couple more New South Africans blocking Hiro's
way out, but not because they want to stop anyone. It's just
where they happen to be standing when they go into shock. Hiro
decides, reflexively, not to kill them.

And Hiro is off into the lurid main avenue of the Towne Hall,
a tunnel of flickering and pulsating loglo through which black
creatures sprint like benighted sperm up the old fallopians, sharp
angular things clenched in their hands. They are The Enforcers.
They make the average MetaCop look like Ranger Rick.

Gargoyle time. Hiro switches everything on: infrared, millimeter-wave radar, ambient-sound processing. The infrared doesn't
do much in these circumstances, but the radar picks out all the
weapons, highlights them in The Enforcers' hands, identifies

them by make, model, and ammunition type. They're all fully automatic.

But The Enforcers and the New South Africans don't need radar to see Hiro's katana with blood and spinal fluid running down the blade.

The music of Vitaly Chernobyl and the Meltdowns is blasting through bad speakers all around him. It is their first single to hit the Billboard charts, entitled "My Heart Is a Smoking Hole in the Ground." The ambient sound processing cuts it to a more reasonable level, evens out the nasty distortion from the speakers so that he can hear his roommate singing more clearly. Which makes it all particularly surreal. It just goes to show that he's out of his element. Doesn't belong here. Lost in the biomass. If there was any justice, he could jump into those speakers and trace up the wires like a digital sylph, follow the grid back to L.A., where he belongs, there on top of the world, where everything comes from, buy Vitaly a drink, crawl into his futon.

He stumbles forward helplessly as something terrible happens to his back..It feels like being massaged with a hundred ballpeen hammers. At the same time, a yellow sputtering light overrides the loglo. A screaming red display flashes up on the goggles informing him that the millimeter-wave radar has noticed a stream of bullets headed in his direction and would you like to know where they came from, sir?

Hiro has just been shot in the back with a burst of machine-gun fire. All of the bullets have slapped into his vest and dropped to the floor, but in doing so they have cracked about half of the ribs on that side of his body and bruised a few internal organs. He turns around, which hurts.

The Enforcer has given up on bullets and whipped out another weapon. It says so right on Hiro's goggles: PACIFIC ENFORCEMENT HARDWARE, INC. MODEL SX-29 RESTRAINT PROJECTION DEVICE (LOOGIE GUN). Which is what he should have used in the first place.

You can't just carry a sword around as an empty threat. You shouldn't draw it, or keep it drawn, unless you intend to kill someone. Hiro runs toward The Enforcer, raising the katana to strike. The Enforcer does the proper thing, namely, gets the hell out of his way. The silver ribbon of the katana shines up above the crowd. It attracts Enforcers and repels everyone else, so as Hiro runs down the center of the Towne Hall, he has no one in front of him and many shiny dark creatures behind him.

He turns off all of the techno-shit in his goggles. All it does is confuse him; he stands there reading statistics about his own death even as it's happening to him. Very post-modern. Time to get immersed in Reality, like all the people around him.

Not even Enforcers will fire their big guns in a crowd, unless it's point-blank range, or they're in a really bad mood. A few loogies shoot past Hiro, already so spread out as to be nothing more than an annoyance, and splat into bystanders, wrapping them in sticky gossamer veils.

Somewhere between the 3-D video-game arcade and the display window full of terminally bored prostitutes, Hiro's eyes clear up and he sees a miracle: the exit of the inflatable dome, where the doors exhale a breeze of synthetic beer breath and atomized body fluids into the cool night air.

Bad things and good things are happening in quick succession. The next bad thing happens when a steel grate falls down to block the doors.

What the hell, it's an inflatable building. Hiro turns on the radar just for a moment and the walls seem to drop away and become invisible; he's seeing through them now, into the forest of steel outside. It doesn't take long to locate the parking lot where he left his bike, supposedly under the protection of some armed attendants.

Hiro fakes toward the whorehouse, then cuts directly toward an exposed section of wall. The fabric of the building is tough, but his katana slices a six-foot rent through it with a single gliding motion, and then he's outside, spat out of the hole on a jet of fetid air.

After that—after Hiro gets onto his motorcycle, and the New South Africans get into their all-terrain pickups, and The Enforcers get into their slick black Enforcer mobiles, and they all go screaming out onto the highway—after that it's just a chase scene.

41

Y.T. has been to some *unusual* places in her career. She has the visas of some three dozen countries laminated onto her chest. And on top of the real countries she has picked up and/or delivered to such charming little vacation spots as the Terminal Island Sacrifice Zone and the encampment in Griffith Park. But the weirdest job of all is this new one: someone wants her to deliver some stuff to the United States of America. Says so right there on the job order.

It's not much of a delivery, just a legal-size envelope.

"You sure you don't just want to mail this?" she asks the guy when she picks it up. It's one of these creepy office parks out in the Burbs. Like a Burbclave for worthless businesses that have offices and phones and stuff but don't actually seem to do anything.

It's a sarcastic question, of course. The mail doesn't work, except in Fedland. All the mailboxes have been unbolted and used to decorate the apartments of nostalgia freaks. But it's also kind of a joke, because the destination is, in fact, a building in the middle of Fedland. So the joke is: If you want to deal with the Feds, why not use their fucked-up mail system? Aren't you afraid that by dealing with anything as incredibly cool as a Kourier you will be tainted in their eyes?

"Well, uh, the mail doesn't come out here, does it?" the guy says.

No point in describing the office. No point in even allowing the office to even register on her eyeballs and take up valuable memory space in her brain. Fluorescent lights and partitions with carpet glued to them. I prefer my carpet on the floor, thank you. A color scheme. Ergonomic shit. Chicks with lipstick. Xerox smell. Everything's pretty new, she figures.

The legal envelope is resting on the guy's desk. Not much point in describing him, either. Traces of a southern or Texan accent. The bottom edge of the envelope is parallel to the edge of the desk, one-quarter inch away from it, perfectly centered between the left and right sides. Like he had a doctor come in here and put it on the desk with tweezers. It is addressed to: ROOM 968A, MAIL STOP MS-1569835, BUILDING LA-6, UNITED STATES OF AMERICA.

"You want a return address on this?" she says.

"That's not necessary."

"If I can't deliver it, there's no way I can get it back to you, because these places all look the same to me."

"It's not important," he says. "When do you think you'll get it there?"

"Two hours max."

"Why so long?"

"Customs, man. The Feds haven't modernized their system like everyone else." Which is why most Kouriers will do anything to avoid delivering to Fedland. But it's a slow day today, Y.T. hasn't been called in to do any secret missions for the Mafia yet, and maybe she can catch Mom on her lunch break.

"And your name is?"

"We don't give out our names."

"I need to know who's delivering this."

"Why? You said it wasn't important."

The guy gets really flustered. "Okay," he says. "Forget it. Just deliver it, please."

Okay, be that way, she mentally says. She mentally says a number of other things, too. The man is an obvious pervert. It's so plain, so open: "And your name is?" Give me a break, man.

Names are unimportant. Everyone knows Kouriers are interchangeable parts. It's just that some happen to be a lot faster and better.

So she skates out of the office. It's all very anonymous. No corporate logos anywhere. So as she's waiting for the elevator, she calls RadiKS, tries to find out who initiated this call.

The answer comes back a few minutes later, as she's riding out of the office park, pooned onto a nice Mercedes: Rife Advanced Research Enterprises. RARE. One of these high-tech outfits. Probably trying to get a government contract. Probably trying to sell sphygmomanometers to the Feds or something like that.

Oh well, she just delivers 'em. She gets the impression that this Mercedes is sandbagging—driving real slow so she'll poon something else—so she poons something else, an outgoing delivery truck. Judging from the way it's riding high on its springs, it must be empty, so it'll probably move along pretty fast.

Ten seconds later, predictably, the Mercedes blasts by in the left lane, so she poons that and rides it nice and hard for a couple of miles.

Getting into Fedland is a drag. Most Fedsters drive tiny, plastic-and-aluminum cars that are hard to poon. But eventually she nails one, a little jellybean with glued-on windows and a three-cylinder engine, and that takes her up to the United States border.

The smaller this country gets, the more paranoid they become. Nowadays, the customs people are just impossible. She has to sign a ten-page document—and they actually make her read it. They say it should take at least half an hour for her just to read the thing.

"But I read it two weeks ago."

"It might have changed," the guard says, "so you have to read it again."

Basically, it just certifies that Y.T. is not a terrorist, Communist (whatever that is), homosexual, national-symbol desecrator, pornography merchant, welfare parasite, racially insensitive, carrier of any infectious disease, or advocate of any ideology tending to impugn traditional family values. Most of it is just definitions of all the words used on the first page.

So Y.T. sits in the little room for half an hour, doing housekeeping work—going over her stuff, changing batteries in all her little devices, cleaning her nails, having her skateboard run its self-maintenance procedures. Then she signs the fucking document and hands it over to the guy. And then she's in Fedland.

It's not hard finding the place. Typical Fed building—a million steps. Like it's built on top of a mountain of steps. Columns. A lot more guys in this one than usual. Chunky guys with slippery hair. Must be some kind of cop building. The guard at the front door is a cop all the way, wants to give her a big hassle about carrying her skateboard into the place. Like they've got a safe place out front to keep skateboards.

The cop guy is completely hard to deal with. But that's okay, so is Y.T.

"Here's the envelope," she says. "You can take it up to the

ninth floor yourself on your coffee break. Too bad you have to take the stairs."

"Look," he says, totally exasperated, "this is EBGOC. This is, like, the headquarters. EBGOC central. You got that? Everything that happens within a mile is being videotaped. People don't spit on the pavement within sight of this building. They don't even say bad words. Nobody's going to steal your skateboard."

"That's even worse. They'll steal it. Then they'll say they didn't steal it, they confiscated it. I know you Feds, you're always confiscating shit."

The guy sighs. Then his eyes go out of focus and he shuts up for a minute. Y.T. can tell he's getting a message over the little earphone that's plugged into his ear, the mark of the true Fed.

"Go on in," he says. "But you gotta sign."

"Naturally," Y.T. says.

The cop hands her the sign-in sheet, which is actually a notebook computer with an electronic pen. She writes "Y.T." on the screen, it's converted to a digital bitmap, automatically time stamped, and sent off to the big computer at Fed Central. She knows she's not going to make it through the metal detector without stripping naked, so she just vaults the cop's table— what's he going to do, shoot her?—and heads on into the building, skateboard under her arm.

"Hey!" he says, weakly.

"What, you got lots of EBGOC agents in here being mugged and raped by female Kouriers?" she says, stomping the elevator button ferociously.

Elevator takes forever. She loses her patience and just climbs the stairs like all the other Feds.

The guy is right, it's definitely Cop Central here on the ninth floor. Every creepy guy in sunglasses and slippery hair you've ever seen, they're all here, all with little fleshtone helices of wire trailing down from their ears. There's even some female Feds. They look even scarier than the guys. The things that a woman can do to her hair to make herself look professional—Jeeezus! Why not just wear a motorcycle helmet? At least then you can take it off.

Except none of the Feds, male or female, is wearing sunglasses. They look naked without them. Might as well be walking around with no pants on. Seeing these Feds without their mirror specs is like blundering into the boys' locker room.

She finds Room 968A easily enough. Most of the floor is just a big pool of desks. All the actual, numbered rooms are around the edges, with frosted glass doors. Each of the creepy guys seems to have a desk of his own, some of them loiter near their desks, the rest of them are doing a lot of hall-jogging and impromptu conferencing at other creepy guys' desks. Their white shirts are painfully clean. Not as many shoulder holsters as she would expect; all the gun-carrying Feds are probably out in what used to be Alabama or Chicago trying to confiscate back bits of United States territory from what is now a Buy 'n' Fly or a toxic-waste dump.

She goes on into Room 968A. It's an office. Four Fed guys are in here, the same as the others except most of them are a tad older, in their forties and fifties.

"Got a delivery for this room," Y.T. says.

"You're Y.T.?" says the head Fed, who's sitting behind the desk.

"You're not supposed to know my name," Y.T. says. "How did you know my name?"

"I recognized you," the head Fed says. "I know your mother."

Y.T. does not believe him. But these Feds have all kinds of ways of finding out stuff.

"Do you have any relatives in Afghanistan?" she says.

The guys all look back and forth at each other, like, did you understand the chick? But it's not a sentence that is intended to be understood. Actually, Y.T. has all kinds of voice recognition ware in her coverall and in her plank. When she says, "Do you have any relatives in Afghanistan?" that's like a code phrase, it tells all of her spook gear to get ready, shake itself down, check itself out, prick up its electronic ears.

"You want this envelope or not?" she says.

"I'll take it," the head Fed says, standing up and holding out one hand.

Y.T. walks into the middle of the room and hands him the envelope. But instead of taking it, he lunges out at the last minute and grabs her forearm.

She sees an open handcuff in his other hand. He brings it out and snaps it down on her wrist so it tightens and locks shut over the cuff of her coverall.

"I'm sorry to do this, Y.T., but I have to place you under arrest," he's saying.

"What the fuck are you doing?" Y.T. is saying. She's holding her free arm back away from the desk so he can't cuff her wrists together, but one of the other Feds grabs her by the free wrist, so now she's stretched out like a tightrope between the two big Feds.

"You guys are dead," she says.

All the guys smile, like they enjoy a chick with some spunk.

"You guys are dead," she says a second time.

This is the key phrase that all of her ware is waiting to hear. When she says it the second time, all the self-defense stuff comes on, which means that among other things, a few thousand volts of radio-frequency electrical power suddenly flood through the outsides of her cuffs.

The head Fed behind the desk blurts out a grunt from way down in his stomach. He flies back away from her, his entire right side jerking spastically, trips over his own chair, and sprawls back into the wall, smacking his head on the marble windowsill. The jerk who's yanking on her other arm stretches out like he's on an invisible rack, accidentally slapping one of the other guys in the face, giving that guy a nice dose of juice to the head. Both of them hit the floor like a sack of rabid cats. There's only one of these guys left, and he's reaching under his jacket for something. She takes one step toward him, swings her arm around, and the end of the loose manacle strokes him in the neck. Just a caress, but it might as well be a two-handed blow from Satan's electric ax handle. That funky juice runs all up and down his spine, and suddenly, he's sprawled across a couple of shitty old wooden chairs and his pistol is rotating on the floor like the spinner in a children's game.

She flexes her wrist in a particular way, and the bundy stunner drops down her sleeve and into her hand. The manacle swinging from the other hand will have a similar effect on that side. She also pulls out the can of Liquid Knuckles, pops the lid, sets the spray nozzle on wide angle.

One of the Fed creeps is nice enough to open the office door for her. He comes into the room with his gun already drawn, backed up by half a dozen other guys who've flocked here from the office pool, and she just lets them have it with the Liquid Knuckles. Whoosh, it's like bug spray. The sound of bodies hitting the floor is like a bass drum roll. She finds that her skateboard has no problem rolling across their prone bodies, and then she's out into the office pool. These guys are converging from all sides, there's an incredible number of them, she just keeps holding that button down, pointed straight ahead, digging at the floor with her foot, building up speed. The Liquid Knuckles acts like a chemical flying wedge, she's skating out of there on a carpet of bodies. Some of the Feds are agile enough to dart in from behind and try to get her that way, but she's ready with the bundy stunner, which turns their nervous systems into coils of hot barbed wire for a few minutes but isn't supposed to have any other effects.

She's made it about three-quarters of the way across the office when the Liquid Knuckles runs out. But it still works for a second or two because people are afraid of it, keep diving out of the way even though there's nothing coming out. Then a couple of them figure it out, make the mistake of trying to grab her by the wrists. She gets one of them with the bundy stunner and the other with the electric manacle. Then *boom* through the door and she's out into the stairwell, leaving four dozen casualties in her wake. Serves them right, they didn't even try to arrest her in a gentlemanly way.

To a man on foot, stairs are a hindrance. But to the smartwheels, they just look like a forty-five-degree angle ramp. It's a little choppy, especially when she's down to about the second floor and is going way too fast, but it's definitely doable.

A lucky thing: One of the first-floor cops is just opening the stairwell door, no doubt alerted by the symphony of alarm bells and buzzers that has begun to merge into a solid wall of hysterical sound. She blows by the guy; he puts one arm out in an attempt to stop her, sort of belts her across the waist in the process, throws her balance off, but this is a very forgiving skateboard, it's smart enough to slow down for her a little bit when her center of mass gets into the wrong place. Pretty soon it's back under her, she's banking radically through the elevator lobby, aiming dead center for the arch of the metal detector, through which the bright outdoor light of freedom is shining.

Her old buddy the cop is up on his feet, and he reacts fast enough to spread-eagle himself across the metal detector. Y.T. acts like she's heading right for him, then kicks the board sideways at the last minute, punches one of the toe switches, coils her legs underneath her, and jumps into the air. She flies right over his little table while the plank is rolling underneath it, and a second later she lands on it, wobbles once, gets her balance back. She's in the lobby, headed for the doors.

It's an old building. Most of the doors are metal. But there's a couple of revolving doors, too, just big sheets of glass.

Early thrashers used to inadvertently skate into walls of glass from time to time, which was a problem. It turned into a bigger problem when the whole Kourier thing got started and thrashers started spending a lot more time trying to go fast through office-type environments where glass walls are considered quite the concept. Which is why on an expensive skateboard, like this one definitely is, you can get, as an extra added safety feature, the RadiKS Narrow Cone Tuned Shock Wave Projector. It works on real short notice, which is good, but you can only use it once (it draws its power from an explosive charge), and then you have to take your plank into the shop to have it replaced.

It's an emergency thing. Strictly a panic button. But that's cool. Y.T. makes sure she's aimed directly at the glass revolving doors, then hits the appropriate toe switch.

It's—my God—like you stretched a tarp across a stadium to turn it into a giant tom-tom and then crashed a 747 into it. She can feel her internal organs move several inches. Her heart trades places with her liver. The bottoms of her feet feel numb and tingly. And she's not even standing in the path of the shock wave.

The safety glass in the revolving doors doesn't just crack and fall to the floor, like she imagined it would. It is blown out of its moorings. It gushes out of the building and down the front steps. She follows, an instant later.

The ridiculous cascade of white marble steps on the front of the building just gives her more ramp time. By the time she reaches the sidewalk, she's easily got enough speed to coast all the way to Mexico.

As she's swinging out across the broad avenue, aiming her crosshairs at the customs post a quarter mile away, which she is going to have to jump over, something tells her to look up.

Because after all, the building she just escaped from is towering above her, many stories full of Fed creeps, and all the alarms are going off. Most of the windows can't be opened, all they can do is look out. But there are people on the roof. Mostly the roof is a forest of antennas. If it's a forest, these guys are the creepy little gnomes who live in the trees. They are ready for action, they have their sunglasses on, they have weapons, they're all looking at her.

But only one guy's taking aim. And the thing he's aiming at her is huge. The barrel is the size of a baseball bat. She can see the muzzle flash poke out of it, wreathed in a sudden doughnut of white smoke. It's not pointed right at her; it's aimed in front of her.

The stun bunny lands on the street, dead ahead, bounces up in the air, and detonates at an altitude of twenty feet.

The next quarter of a second: There's no bright flash to blind her, and so she can actually see the shock wave spreading outward in a perfect sphere, hard and palpable as a ball of ice. Where the sphere contacts the street, it makes a circular wave front, making pebbles bounce, flipping old McDonald's containers that have long been smashed flat, and coaxing fine, flourlike dust out of all the tiny crevices in the pavement, so that it sweeps across the road toward her like a microscopic blizzard. Above it, the shock wave hangs in the air, rushing toward her at the speed of sound, a lens of air that flattens and refracts everything on the other side. She's passing through it.

As Hiro crests the pass on his motorcycle at five in the morning, the town of Port Sherman, Oregon, is suddenly laid out before him: a flash of yellow loglo wrapped into a vast U-shaped valley that was ground out of the rock, a long time ago, by a big tongue of ice in an epochal period of geological cunnilingus. There is just a light dusting of gold around the edges where it fades into the rain forest, thickening and intensifying as it approaches the harbor—a long narrow fjordlike notch cut into the straight coastline of Oregon, a deep cold trench of black water heading straight out to Japan.

Hiro's back on the Rim again. Feels good after that night ride through the sticks. Too many rednecks, too many mounties.

Even from ten miles away and a mile above, it's not a pretty sight. Farther away from the central harbor district, Hiro can make out a few speckles of red, which is a little better than the yellow. He wishes he could see something in green or blue or purple, but there don't seem to be any neighborhoods done up in those gourmet colors.

But then this isn't exactly a gourmet job.

He rides half a mile off the road, sits down on a flat rock in an open space—ambush-proof, more or less—and goggles into the Metaverse.

"Librarian?"

"Yes, sir?"

"Inanna."

"A figure from Sumerian mythology. Later cultures knew her as Ishtar, or Esther."

"Good goddess or bad goddess?"

"Good. A beloved goddess."

"Did she have any dealings with Enki or Asherah?"

"Mostly with Enki. She and Enki were on good and bad terms at different times. Inanna was known as the queen of all the great *me*."

"I thought the *me* belonged to Enki."

"They did. But Inanna went to the Abzu—the watery fortress

in the city of Eridu where Enki stored up the *me*—and got Enki to give her all the *me*. This is how the *me* were released into civilization."

"Watery fortress, huh?"

"Yes, sir."

"How did Enki feel about this?"

"He gave them to her willingly, apparently because he was drunk, and besotted with Inanna's physical charms. When he sobered up, he tried to chase her down and get them back, but she outsmarted him."

"Let's get semiotic," Hiro mumbles. "The Raft is L. Bob Rife's watery fortress. That's where he stores up all of his stuff. All of his *me*. Juanita went to Astoria, which was as close as you could get to the Raft a couple of days ago. I think she's trying to pull an Inanna."

"In another popular Sumerian myth," the Librarian says, "Inanna descends into the nether world."

"Go on," Hiro says.

"She gathers together all of her *me* and enters the land of no return."

"Great."

"She passes through the nether world and reaches the temple that is ruled over by Ereshkigal, goddess of Death. She is traveling under false pretenses, which are easily penetrated by the all-seeing Ereshkigal. But Ereshkigal allows her to enter the temple. As Inanna enters, her robes and jewels and *me* are stripped from her and she is brought, stark naked, before Ereshkigal and the seven judges of the underworld. The judges 'fastened their eyes upon her, the eyes of death; at their word, the word which tortures the spirit, Inanna was turned into a corpse, a piece of rotting meat, and was hung from a hook on the wall.' Kramer."

"Wonderful. Why the hell would she do something like that?"

"As Diane Wolkstein puts it, 'Inanna gave up ... all she had accomplished in life until she was stripped naked, with nothing remaining but her will to be reborn ... because of her journey to the underworld, she took on the powers and mysteries of death and rebirth.' "

"Oh. So I guess there's more to the story?"

"Inanna's messenger waits for three days, and when she fails to return from the nether world, goes to the gods asking for their help. None of the gods is willing to help except for Enki."

"So our buddy, Enki, the hacker god, has to bail her ass out of Hell."

"Enki creates two people and sends them into the netherworld to rescue Inanna. Through their magic, Inanna is brought back to life. She returns from the netherworld, followed by a host of the dead."

"Juanita went to the Raft three days ago," Hiro says. "It's time to get hacking."

_____ Earth is still where he left it, zoomed in to show a magnified view of the Raft. In the light of last night's chat with Chuck Wrightson, it's not hard to find the hunk of raft that was staked out by the Orthos when the *Enterprise* swung by TROKK a few weeks back. There's a couple of big-assed Soviet freighters tied together, a swarm of small boats around them. Most of the Raft is dead brown and organic, but this section is all white fiberglass: pleasure craft looted from the comfortable retirees of TROKK. Thousands of them.

Now the Raft is off Port Sherman, so, Hiro figures, that's where the high priests of Asherah are hanging out. In a few days, they'll be in Eureka, then San Francisco, then L.A.—a floating land link, tying the Orthos' operations on the Raft to the closest available point on the mainland.

He turns away from the Raft, skims across the ocean to Port Sherman to do a bit of reconnoitering there.

Down along the waterfront, there's a nice crescent of cheap motels with yellow logos. Hiro rifles through them, looking for Russian names.

That's easy. There's a Spectrum 2000 right in the middle of the waterfront. As the name implies, each one has a whole range of rooms, from human coin lockers in the lobby all the way to luxury suites on the top. And a whole range of rooms has been rented out by a bunch of people with names ending in -off and -ovski and other dead Slavic giveaways. The foot soldiers sleep in the lobby, laid out straight and narrow in coin lockers next to their AK-47s, and the priests and generals live in nice rooms higher up. Hiro pauses to wonder what a Pentecostal Russian Orthodox priest does with a Magic Fingers.

The suite on the very top is being rented out by a gentleman by the name of Gurov. Mr. KGB himself. Too much of a wimp to hang out on the actual Raft, apparently.

How'd he get from the Raft to Port Sherman? If it involves crossing a couple of hundred miles of North Pacific, it must be a decent-sized vessel.

There are half a dozen marinas in Port Sherman. At the moment, most of them are clogged with small brown boats. It looks like a post-typhoon situation, where a few hundred square miles of ocean have been swept clean of sampans that have piled up against the nearest hard place. Except this is slightly more organized than that.

The Refus are coming ashore already. If they're smart, and aggressive, they probably know that they can walk to California from here.

That explains why the piers are clogged with trashy little boats. But one of them still looks like a private marina. It's got a dozen or so clean white vessels, lined up neatly in their slips, no riffraff. And the resolution of this image is good enough that Hiro can see the pier speckled with little doughnuts: probably rings of sandbags. That'd be the only way to keep your private moorage private when the Raft was hovering offshore.

The numbers, flags, and other identifying goodies are harder to make out. The satellite has a hard time picking that stuff out.

Hiro checks to see whether CIC has a stringer in Port Sherman. They have to, because the Raft is here, and CIC hopes to make a big business out of selling Raft intelligence to all the anxious waterfronters between Skagway and Tierra del Fuego.

Indeed. There are a few people hanging out in this town, uploading the latest Port Sherman intel. And one of them is just a punter with a video camera who goes around shooting pictures of everything.

Hiro reviews this stuff in fast-forward. A lot of it is shot from the stringer's hotel window: hours and hours of coverage of the stream of shitty little brown boats laboring their way up the harbor, tying up to the edge of the mini-Raft that's forming in front of Port Sherman.

But it's semi-organized, in that some apparently self-appointed water cops are buzzing around in a speedboat, aiming guns at people, shouting through a megaphone. And that explains why, no matter how tangled the mess in the harbor becomes, there's always a clear lane down the middle of the fjord, headed out to sea. And the terminus of that clear lane is the nice pier with the big boats.

There are two big vessels there. One is a large fishing boat flying a flag bearing the emblem of the Orthos, which is just a cross and a flame. It is obvious TROKK loot; the name on the stern is KODIAK QUEEN, and the Orthos haven't bothered to change it yet. The other large boat is a small cruise vessel, made to carry rich people comfortably to nice places. It has a green flag and appears to be connected with Mr. Lee's Greater Hong Kong.

Hiro does a little more poking around in the streets of Port Sherman and finds out that there is a pretty good-sized Mr. Lee's Greater Hong Kong franchulate here. In typical Hong Kong style, it is more of a spray of small buildings and rooms all over town. But it's a dense spray. Dense enough that Hong Kong has several full-time employees here, including a proconsul. Hiro pulls up the guy's picture so he'll recognize him: a crusty-looking Chinese-American gent in his fifties. So it's not an automated, unmanned franchulate like you normally see in the Lower 48.

43

When she first woke up, she was still in her RadiKS coverall, mummified in gaffer's tape, lying on the floor of a shitty old Ford van blasting across the middle of nowhere. This did not put her into a very favorable mood. The stun bunny left her with a persistent nosebleed and an eternal throbbing headache, and every time the van hit a chuckhole, her head bounced on the corrugated steel floor.

First she was just pissed. Then she started having brief moments of fear—wanting to go home. After eight hours in the back of the van, there was no doubt in her mind that she wanted to go home. The only thing that kept her from giving up was curiosity. As far as she could tell from this admittedly poor vantage point, this didn't look like a Fed operation.

The van pulled off the highway, onto a frontage road, and into a parking lot. The rear doors of the van opened up, and a couple of women climbed in. Through the open doors, Y.T. could see the Gothic arch logo of a Reverend Wayne's Pearly Gates.

"Oh, you poor baby," one of the women said. The other woman just gasped in horror at her condition. One of them just cradled her head and stroked her hair, letting her sip sweet Kool-Aid from a Dixie cup, while the other tenderly, slowly took the gaffer's tape off.

Her shoes had already been removed when she woke up in the back of the van, and no one offered her another pair. And everything had been removed from her coverall. All the good stuff was gone. But they hadn't gone underneath the coverall. She still had the dog tags. And one other thing, a thing between her legs called a dentata. There's no way they could have found that.

She has always known that the dog tags were probably a fake thing anyway. Uncle Enzo doesn't just go around giving his war souvenirs to fifteen-year-old chicks. But they still might have an effect on someone.

The two women are named Marla and Bonnie. They are with her all the time. Not only with her, but touching her. Lots of hugs, squeezes, hand-holding, and tousled hair. The first time she goes to the bathroom, Bonnie goes with her, opening the stall door and actually standing in there with her. Y.T. thinks that Bonnie is worried that she's going to pass out on the toilet or something. But the next time she has to pee, Marla goes with her. She gets no privacy at all.

The only problem is she can't deny that she likes it, in a way. The ride in the van hurt. It really hurt bad. She never felt so lonely in her life. And now she's barefoot and defenseless in an unfamiliar place and they're giving her what she needs.

After she had a few minutes to freshen up—whatever that means—inside the Reverend Wayne's Pearly Gates, she and Marla and Bonnie climbed into a big stretch van with no windows. The floor was carpeted but there were no seats inside, everyone sat on the floor. The van was jammed when they opened the rear doors. Twenty people were packed into it, all energetic, beaming youths. It looked impossible; Y.T. shrank away from it, backing right into Marla and Bonnie. But a cheerful roar came up from the van people, white teeth flashing in the dimness, and people began to scrunch out a tiny space for them.

She spent most of the next two days packed into the van between Bonnie and Marla, holding hands with them constantly, so she couldn't even pick her nose without permission. They sang happy songs until her brain turned to tapioca. They played wacky games.

A couple of times every hour, someone in the van would start to babble, just like the Falabalas. Just like the Reverend Wayne's Pearly Gates people. The babbling would spread throughout the van like a contagious disease, and soon everyone would be doing it.

Everyone except for Y.T. She couldn't seem to get the hang of it. It just seemed embarrassingly stupid to her. So she just faked it.

Three times a day, they had a chance to eat and eliminate. It always happened in Burbclaves. Y.T. could feel them pulling off the interstate, finding their way down twisty development lanes, courts, ways, and circles. A garage door would rise electrically, the van would pull in, the door would shut behind them. They would go into a suburban house, except stripped of furniture and other family touches, and sit on the floor in empty bedrooms— one for boys, one for girls—and eat cake and cookies. This always happened in a totally empty room in a house, but there was always different decor: in one place, flowery countryish wallpaper and a lingering smell of rancid Glade. In another, bluish wallpaper featuring hockey players, football players, basketball players. In another, just plain white walls with old crayon marks on them. Sitting in these empty rooms, Y.T. would study the old furniture scrapes on the floors, the dents in the sheetrock, and muse over them like an archaeologist, wondering about the long-departed families who had once lived here. But toward the end of the ride, she wasn't paying attention anymore.

In the van, she could hear nothing but singing and chanting, see nothing but the jammed-together faces of her companions. When they stopped for gas, they did it in giant truck stops out in the middle of nowhere, pulling up to the most distant pump island so that no one was near them. And they never stopped driving. They just got relayed from one driver to the next.

Finally, they got to a coast. Y.T. could smell it. They spent a few minutes waiting, engine idling, and then the van bumped over some kind of a threshold, climbed a few ramps, stopped, set its parking brake. The driver got out and left them all alone in the van for the first time. Y.T. felt glad that the trip was over.

Then everything started to rumble, like an engine noise but a lot bigger. She didn't feel any movement until a few minutes later, when she realized that everything was rocking gently. The van was parked on a ship, and the ship was headed out to sea.

——————— It's a real ocean-going ship. An old, shitty, rusty one that probably cost about five bucks at the ship junkyard. But it carries cars, and it goes through the water, and it doesn't sink.

The ship is just like the van, except bigger, with more people. But they eat the same stuff, sing the same songs, and sleep just as rarely as ever. By now, Y.T. finds it perversely comforting. She knows that she's with a lot of other people like her, and that she's safe. She knows the routine. She knows where she belongs.

And so finally they come to the Raft. No one has told Y.T. this is where they're going, but by now it's obvious. She ought to be scared. But they wouldn't be going to the Raft if it was as bad as everyone says.

When it starts coming into view, she half expects them to converge on her with gaffer's tape again. But then she figures out it's not necessary. She hasn't been causing trouble. She's been accepted here, they trust her. It gives her a feeling of pride, in a way.

And she won't cause trouble on the Raft because all she can do is escape from their part of it onto the Raft per se. As such. The real Raft. The Raft of a hundred Hong Kong B-movies and blood-soaked Nipponese comic books. It doesn't take much imagination to think of what happens to lone fifteen-year-old blond American girls on the Raft, and these people know it.

Sometimes, she worries about her mother, then she hardens her heart and thinks maybe the whole thing will be good for her.

Shake her up a little. Which is what she needs. After Dad left, she just folded up into herself like an origami bird thrown into a fire.

There is kind of an outer cloud of small boats surrounding the Raft for a distance of a few miles. Almost all of them are fishing boats. Some of them carry men with guns, but they don't fuck around with this ferry. The ferry swings through this outer zone, making a broad turn, finally zeroing in on a white neighborhood on one flank of the Raft. Literally white. All the boats here are clean and new. There's a couple of big rusty boats with Russian lettering on the side, and the ferry pulls up alongside one of them, ropes are thrown across, then augmented with nets, gangplanks, webs of old discarded tires.

This Raft thing does not look like good skating territory at all.

She wonders if any of the other people on board this ferry are skaters. Doesn't seem likely. Really, they are not her kind of people at all. She has always been a dirty scum dog of the highways, not one of these happy singalong types. Maybe the Raft is just the place for her.

They take her down into one of the Russian ships and give her the grossest job of all time: cutting up fish. She does not want a job, has not asked for one. But that's what she gets. Still, no one really talks to her, no one bothers to explain anything, and that makes her reluctant to ask. She has just run into a massive cultural shock wave, because most of the people on this ship are old and fat and Russian and don't speak English.

For a couple of days, she spends a lot of time sleeping on the job, being prodded awake by the hefty Russian dames who work in this place. She also does some eating. Some of the fish that comes through this place looks pretty rank, but there's a fair amount of salmon. The only way she knows this is from having sushi at the mall—salmon is the orange-red stuff. So she makes some sushi of her own, munches down on some fresh salmon meat, and it's good. It clears her head a little.

Once she gets over the shock of it and settles into a routine, she starts looking around her, watching the other fish-cutting dames, and realizes that this is just like life must be for about 99 percent of the people in the world. You're in this place. There's other people all around you, but they don't understand you and you don't understand them, but people do a lot of pointless babbling anyway. In order to stay alive, you have to spend all day every day doing stupid meaningless work. And the only way to get out of it is to quit, cut loose, take a flyer, and go off into the wicked world, where you will be swallowed up and never heard from again.

She's not especially good at cutting up fish. The big stout Russian chicks—stomping, slab-faced babushkas—keep giving her a hassle. They keep hovering, watching her cut with this look on their face like they can't believe what a dork she is. Then they try to show her how to do it the right way, but still she's not so good at it. It's hard, and her hands are cold and stiff all the time.

After a couple of frustrating days, they give her a new job, farther down the production line: they turn her into a cafeteria dame. Like one of the slop-slingers in the high school lunchroom. She works in the galley of one of the big Russian ships, hauling vats of cooked fish stew out to the buffet line, ladling it out into bowls, shoving it across the counter at an unending line consisting of religious fanatics, religious fanatics, and more religious fanatics. Except this time around, there seem to be a lot more Asians and hardly any Americans at all.

They have a new species here too: people with antennas coming out of their heads. The antennas look like the ones on cop walkie-talkies: short, blunt, black rubber whips. They rise up from behind the ear. The first time she sees one of these people, she figures it must be some kind of new Walkman, and she wants to ask the guy where he got it, what he's listening to. But he's a strange guy, stranger than all of the others, with a permanent thousand-yard stare and a bad case of the mumbles, and he ends up giving her the creeps so bad that she just shoves an extra-large dose of stew in his face and hurries him on down the line.

From time to time, she actually recognizes one of the people who were in her van. But they don't seem to recognize her; they just look right through her. Glassy-eyed. Like they've been brainwashed.

Like Y.T. was brainwashed.

She can't believe it has taken her this long to figure out what they were doing to her. And that just makes her more pissed.

44

In Reality, Port Sherman is a surprisingly tiny little burg, really just a few square blocks. Until the Raft came along, it had a full-time population of a couple of thousand people. Now the population must be pushing fifty thousand. Hiro has to slow down a little bit here because the Refus are all sleeping on the street for the time being, an impediment to traffic.

That's okay, it saves his life. Because shortly after he gets into Port Sherman, the wheels on his motorcycle lock up—the spokes become rigid—and the ride gets very bumpy. A couple of seconds after that, the entire bike goes dead, becomes an inert chunk of metal. Not even the engine works. He looks down into the flat screen on top of the fuel tank, wanting to get a status report, but it's just showing snow. The bios has crashed. Asherah's possessed his bike.

So he abandons it in the middle of the street, starts walking toward the waterfront. Behind him, he can hear the Refus waking up, struggling out of their blankets and sleeping bags, converging over the fallen bike, trying to be the first to claim it.

He can hear a deep thumping in his chest, and for a minute he remembers Raven's motorcycle in L.A., how he felt it first and heard it later. But there are no motorcycles around here. The sound is coming from above. It's a chopper. The kind that flies.

Hiro can smell the seaweed rotting on the beach, he's so close. He comes around a corner and finds himself on the waterfront street, looking straight into the facade of the Spectrum 2000. On the other side is water.

The chopper's coming up the fjord, following it inland from the open sea, headed straight for the Spectrum 2000. It's a small one, an agile number with a lot of glass. Hiro can see the crosses painted all over it where the red stars used to be. It is brilliant and dazzling in the cool blue light of early morning because it's shedding a trail of stars, blue-white magnesium flares tumbling out of it every few seconds, landing in the water below, where they continue to burn, leaving an astral pathway marked out down the length of the harbor. They aren't there to look cool. They are there to confuse heat-seeking missiles.

From where he's standing, he can't see the roof of the hotel, because he's looking straight up at it. But he has the feeling that Gurov must be waiting there, on top of the tallest building in Port Sherman, waiting for a dawn evacuation to carry him away into the porcelain sky, carry him away to the Raft.

Question: Why is he being evacuated? And why are they worried about heat-seeking missiles? Hiro realizes, belatedly, that some heavy shit is going on.

If he still had the bike, he could ride it right up the fire stairs and find out what's happening. But he doesn't have the bike.

A deep thump sounds from the roof of a building on his right. It's an old building, one of the original pioneer structures from a hundred years ago. Hiro's knees buckle, his mouth comes open, shoulders hunch involuntarily, he looks toward the sound. And something catches his eye, something small and dark, darting away from the building and up into the air like a sparrow. But when it's a hundred yards out over the water, the sparrow catches fire, coughs out a great cloud of sticky yellow smoke, turns into a white fireball, and springs forward. It keeps getting faster and faster, tearing down the center of the harbor, until it passes all the way through the little chopper, in through the windshield and out the back. The chopper turns into a cloud of flame shedding dark bits of scrap metal, like a phoenix breaking out of its shell.

Apparently, Hiro's not the only guy in town who hates Gurov. Now Gurov has to come downstairs and get on a boat.

The lobby of the Spectrum 2000 is an armed camp, full of beards with guns. They're still putting their defense together; more soldiers are dragging themselves out of their coin lockers, pulling on their jackets, grabbing their guns. A swarthy guy, probably a Tatar sergeant left over from the Red Army, is running around the lobby in a modified Soviet Marines uniform, screaming at people, shoving them this way and that.

Gurov may be a holy man, but he can't walk on water. He'll have to come out to the waterfront street, make his way two blocks down to the gate that admits him to the secured pier, and get on board the *Kodiak Queen*, which is waiting for him, black smoke starting to cough out of its stacks, lights starting to come on. Just down the pier from the *Kodiak Queen* is the *Kowloon,* which is the big Mr. Lee's Greater Hong Kong boat.

Hiro turns his back on the Spectrum 2000 and starts running up and down the waterfront streets, scanning the logos until he sees the one he wants: Mr. Lee's Greater Hong Kong.

They don't want to let him in. He flashes his passport; the doors open. The guard is Chinese but speaks a bit of English. This is a measure of how weird things are in Port Sherman: they have a guard on the door. Usually, Mr. Lee's Greater Hong Kong is an open country, always looking for new citizens, even if they are the poorest Refus.

"Sorry," the guard says in a reedy, insincere voice, "I did not know—" He points to Hiro's passport.

The franchulate is literally a breath of fresh air. It doesn't have that Third World ambience, doesn't smell like urine at all. Which means it must be the local headquarters, or close to it, because most of Hong Kong's Port Sherman real estate probably consists of nothing more than a gunman hogging a pay phone in a lobby. But this place is spacious, clean, and nice. A few hundred Refus stare at him through the windows, held at bay not by the mere plate glass but by the eloquent promise of the three Rat Thing hutches lined up against one wall. From the looks of it, two of those have just been moved in recently. Pays to beef up your security when the Raft is coming through.

Hiro proceeds to the counter. A man is talking on the phone in Cantonese, which means that he is, in fact, shouting. Hiro recognizes him as the Port Sherman proconsul. He is deeply involved in this little chat, but he has definitely noticed Hiro's swords, is watching him carefully.

"We are very busy," the man says, hanging up.

"Now you are a lot busier," Hiro says. "I would like to charter your boat, the *Kowloon.*"

"It's very expensive," the man says.

"I just threw away a brand-new top-of-the-line motorcycle in the middle of the street because I didn't feel like pushing it half a block to the garage," Hiro says. "I am on an expense account that would blow your mind."

"It's broken."

"I appreciate your politeness in not wanting to come out and just say no," Hiro says, "but I happen to know that it is, in fact, not broken, and so I must consider your refusal equivalent to a no."

"It's not available," the man says. "Someone else is using it."

"It has not yet left the pier," Hiro says, "so you can cancel that engagement, using one of the excuses you have just given me, and then I will pay you more money."

"We cannot do this," the man says.

"Then I will go out into the street and inform the Refus that the *Kowloon* is leaving for L.A. in exactly one hour, and that they have enough room to take twenty Refus along with them, first come, first served," Hiro says.

"No," the man says.

"I will tell them to contact you personally."

"Where do you want to go on the *Kowloon*?" the man says.

"The Raft."

"Oh, well, why didn't you say so," the man says. "That's where our other passenger is going."

"You've got someone else who wants to go to the Raft?"

"That's what I said. Your passport, please."

Hiro hands it over. The man shoves it into a slot. Hiro's name, personal data, and mug shots are digitally transferred into the franchulate's bios, and with a little bit of key-pounding, the man persuades it to spit out a laminated photo ID card.

"You get onto the pier with this," he says. "It's good for six hours. You make your own deal with the other passenger. After that, I never want to see you again."

"What if I need more consular services?"

"I can always go out and tell people," the man says, "that a nigger with swords is out raping Chinese refugees."

"Hmm. This isn't exactly the best service I've ever had at a Mr. Lee's Greater Hong Kong."

"This is not a normal situation," the man says. "Look out the window, asshole."

Not much has apparently changed down at the waterfront. The Orthos have organized their defense in the lobby of the Spectrum 2000: furniture has been overturned, barricades set up. Inside the hotel itself, Hiro presumes furious activity is going on.

It's still not clear whom the Orthos are defending themselves against. Making his way through the waterfront area, Hiro doesn't see much: just more Chinese Refus in baggy clothes. It's just that some of them look a lot more alert than others. They have a whole different affect. Most of the Chinese have their eyes on the mud in front of their feet, and their minds on something else. But some of them are just strolling up and down the street, looking all around, alertly, and most of these people happen to be young men wearing bulky jackets. And haircuts that are from a whole other stylistic universe than what the others are sporting. There is evidence of styling gel.

The entrance to the rich people's pier is sandbagged, barbwired, and guarded. Hiro approaches slowly, his hands in plain sight, and shows his pass to the head guard, who is the only white person Hiro has seen in Port Sherman.

And that gets him onto the pier. Just like that. Like the Hong Kong franchulate, it's empty, quiet, and doesn't stink. It bobs up and down gently on the tide, in a way that Hiro finds relaxing. It's really just a train of rafts, plank platforms built over floating hunks of styrofoam, and if it weren't guarded it would probably end up getting dragged out and lashed onto the Raft.

Unlike a normal marina, it's not quiet and isolated. Usually, people moor their boats, lock them up, and leave. Here, at least one person is hanging out on each boat, drinking coffee, keeping their weapons in plain sight, watching Hiro very intently as he strolls up the pier. Every few seconds, the pier thunders with footsteps, and one or two Russians run past Hiro, making for the *Kodiak Queen*. They are all young men, all sailor/soldier types, and they're diving onto the *Kodiak Queen* as if it's the last boat out of Hell, being shouted at by officers, running to their stations, frantically attending to their sailor chores.

Things are a lot calmer on the *Kowloon*. It's guarded too, but most of the people appear to be waiters and stewards, wearing snappy uniforms with brass buttons and white gloves. Uniforms that are intended to be used indoors, in pleasant, climate-controlled dining rooms. A few crew members are visible from place to place, their black hair slicked back, clad in dark windbreakers to protect them from the cold and spray. Hiro can only see one man on the *Kowloon* who appears to be a passenger: a tall slender Caucasian in a dark suit, strolling around chatting into a portable telephone. Probably some Industry jerk who wants to go out for a day cruise, look at the Refus on the Raft while he's sitting in a dining room having a gourmet dinner.

Hiro's about halfway down the pier when all hell breaks loose on shore, in front of the Spectrum 2000. It starts with a long series of heavy machine-gun bursts that don't appear to do much damage, but do clear the street pretty fast. Ninety-nine percent of the Refus just evaporate. The others, the young men Hiro noticed, pull interesting high-tech weapons out of their jackets and disappear into doorways and buildings. Hiro picks up the pace a little, starts walking backward down the pier, trying to get some of the larger vessels in between him and the action so he doesn't get hit by a stray burst.

A fresh breeze comes off the water and down the pier. Passing by the *Kowloon*, it picks up the smell of bacon frying and coffee brewing, and Hiro can't help but meditate on the fact that his last meal was half of a cheap beer in a Kelley's Tap in a Snooze 'n' Cruise.

The scene in front of the Spectrum 2000 has devolved into a generalized roar of unbelievably loud white noise as all the people inside and outside of the hotel fire their weapons back and forth across the street.

Something touches his shoulder. Hiro turns to brush it away, sees that he's looking down at a short Chinese waitress who has come down the pier from the *Kowloon*. Having gotten his attention, she puts her hands back where they were originally, to wit, plastered over her ears.

"You Hiro Protagonist?" she mouths, basically inaudible over the ridiculous noise of the firefight.

Hiro nods. She nods back, steps away from him, jerks her head toward the *Kowloon*. With her hands plastered over her ears this way, it looks like some kind of a folk-dance move.

Hiro follows her down the pier. Maybe they're going to let him charter the *Kowloon* after all. She ushers him onto the aluminum gangplank.

As he's walking across it, he looks up to one of the higher decks, where a couple of the crew members are hanging out in their dark windbreakers. One of them is leaning against a railing, watching the firefight through binoculars. Another one, an older one, approaches him, leans over to examine his back, slaps him a couple of times between the shoulder blades.

The guy drops his binoculars to see who's pounding him on the back. His eyes are not Chinese. The older guy says something to him, gestures at his throat. He's not Chinese, either.

The binocular guy nods, reaches up with one hand and presses a lapel switch. The next time he turns around, a word is written across his back in neon green electropigment: MAFIA.

The older guy turns away; his windbreaker says the same thing.

Hiro turns around in the middle of the gangplank. There are twenty crew members in plain sight all around him. Suddenly, their black windbreakers all say, MAFIA. Suddenly, they are all armed.

45

"I was planning to get in touch with Mr. Lee's Greater Hong Kong and file a complaint about their proconsul here in Port Sherman," Hiro jokes. "He was very uncooperative this morning when I insisted on renting this boat out from under you."

Hiro is sitting in the first-class dining room of the *Kowloon*. On the other side of the white linen tablecloth is the man Hiro had previously pegged as the Industry creep on vacation. He's impeccably dressed in a black suit, and he has a glass eye. He has not bothered to introduce himself, as though he's expecting Hiro to know who he is already.

The man does not seem amused by Hiro's story. He seems, rather, nonplussed. "So?"

"Don't see any reason to file a complaint now," Hiro says.

"Why not?"

"Well, because now I understand his reluctance not to displace you guys."

"How come? You got money, don't you?"

"Yeah, but—"

"Oh!" the man with the glass eye says, and allows himself sort of a forced smile. "Because we're the Mafia, you're saying."

"Yeah," Hiro says, feeling his face get hot. Nothing like making a total dickhead out of yourself. Nothing in the world like it, nosireebob.

Outside, the gun battle is just a dim roar. This dining room is insulated from noise, water, wind, and hot flying lead by a double layer of remarkably thick glass, and the space between the panes is full of something cool and gelatinous. The roar does not seem as steady as it used to be.

"Fucking machine guns," the man says. "I hate 'em. Maybe one out of a thousand rounds actually hits something worth hitting. And they kill my ears. You want some coffee or something?"

"That'd be great."

"We got a big buffet coming up soon. Bacon, eggs, fresh fruit you wouldn't believe."

The guy that Hiro saw earlier, up on the deck, pounding Binocular Man on the back, sticks his head into the room.

"Excuse me, boss, but we're moving into, like, the third phase of our plan. Just thought you'd wanna know."

"Thank you, Livio. Let me know when the Ivans make it to the pier." The guy sips his coffee, notices Hiro looking confused. "See, we got a plan, and the plan is divided up into different phases."

"Yeah, I got that."

"The first phase was immobilization. Taking out their chopper. Then we had Phase Two, which was making them think we were trying to kill them in the hotel. I think that this phase succeeded wonderfully."

"Me, too."

"Thank you. Another important part of this phase was getting your ass in here, which is also done."

"I'm part of this plan?"

The man with the glass eye smiles crisply. "If you were not part of this plan, you would be dead."

"So you knew I was coming to Port Sherman?"

"You know that chick Y.T.? The one you have been using to spy on us?"

"Yeah." No point in denying it.

"Well, we have been using her to spy on you."

"Why? Why the hell do you care about me?"

"That would be a tangent from our main conversation, which is about all the phases of the plan."

"Okay. We just finished Phase Two."

"Now, in Phase Three, which is ongoing, we allow them to think that they are making an incredible, heroic escape, running down the street toward the pier."

"Phase Four!" shouts Livio, the lieutenant.

"*Scusi,*" the man with the glass eye says, scooting his chair back, folding his napkin back onto the table. He gets up and walks out of the dining room. Hiro follows him above deck.

A couple of dozen Russians are all trying to force their way through the gate onto the pier. Only a few of them can get through at once, and so they end up strung out over a couple of hundred feet, all running toward the safety of the *Kodiak Queen.*

But a dozen or so manage to stay together in a clump: a group of soldiers, forming a human shield around a smaller cluster of men in the center.

"Bigwigs," the man with the glass eye says, shaking his head philosophically.

They all run crablike down the pier, bent down as far as they can go, firing the occasional covering burst of machine-gun fire back into Port Sherman.

The man with the glass eye is squinting against a cool, sudden breeze. He turns to Hiro with a hint of a grin. "Check this out," he says, and presses a button on a little black box in his hand.

The explosion is like a single drumbeat, coming from everywhere at once. Hiro can feel it coming up out of the water, shaking his feet. There's no big flame or cloud of smoke, but there is a sort of twin geyser effect that shoots out from underneath the *Kodiak Queen,* sending jets of white, steamy water upward like unfolding wings. The wings collapse in a sudden downpour, and then the *Kodiak Queen* seems shockingly low in the water. Low and getting lower.

All the men who are running down the pier suddenly stop in their tracks.

"Now," Binocular Man mumbles into his lapel.

There are some smaller explosions down on the pier. The entire pier buckles and writhes like a snake in the water. One segment in particular, the segment with the bigwigs on it, is rocking and seesawing violently, smoke rising from both ends. It has been blown loose from the rest of the pier.

All of its occupants fall down in the same direction as it jerks sideways and begins to move, yanked out of its place. Hiro can see the tow cable rising up out of the water as it is stretched tight, running a couple of hundred feet to a small open boat with a big motor on it, which is now pulling out of the harbor.

There's still a dozen bodyguards on the segment. One of them sizes up the situation, aims his AK-47 across the water at the boat that's towing them, and loses his brains. There's a sniper on the top deck of the *Kowloon*.

All the other bodyguards throw their guns into the water.

"Time for Phase Five," the man with the glass eye says. "A big fucking breakfast."

By the time he and Hiro have sat back down in the dining room, the *Kowloon* has pulled away from the pier and is headed down the fjord, following a course parallel to the smaller boat that is towing the segment. As they eat, they can look out the window, across a few hundred yards of open water, and see the segment keeping pace with them. All the bigwigs and the bodyguards are on their asses now, keeping their centers of gravity low as the segment bucks nastily.

"When we get farther away from land, the waves get bigger," the man with the glass eye says. "I hate that shit. All I want is to hang on to the breakfast long enough to tamp it down with some lunch."

"Amen," says Livio, heaping some scrambled eggs onto his plate.

"Are you going to pick those guys up?" Hiro says. "Or just let them stay out there for a while?"

"Fuck 'em. Let 'em freeze their asses off. Then when we bring them onto this boat, they'll be ready for it. Won't put up too much of a fight. Hey, maybe they'll even talk to us."

Everyone seems pretty hungry. For a while, they just dig into breakfast. After a while, the man with the glass eye breaks the ice by announcing how great the food is, and everyone agrees. Hiro figures it's okay to talk now.

"I was wondering why you guys were interested in me." Hiro

figures that this is always a good thing to know in the case of the Mafia.

"We're all in the same happy gang," the man with the glass eye says.

"Which gang is that?"

"Lagos's gang."

"Huh?"

"Well, it's not really his gang. But he's the guy who put it together. The nucleus around which it formed."

"How and why and what are you talking about?"

"Okay." He shoves his plate away from him, folds up his napkin, puts it on the table. "Lagos had all these ideas. Ideas about all kinds of stuff."

"So I noticed."

"He had stacks all over the place, on all different topics. Stacks where he would pull together knowledge from all over the fucking map and tie it all together. He had these things stashed here and there around the Metaverse, waiting for the information to become useful."

"More than one of them?" Hiro says.

"Supposedly. Well, a few years ago, Lagos approached L. Bob Rife."

"He did?"

"Yeah. See, Rife has a million programmers working for him. He was paranoid that they were stealing his data."

"I know that he was bugging their houses and so on."

"The reason you know that is because you found it in Lagos's stack. And the reason Lagos bothered to look it up is because he was doing market research. Looking for someone who might pay him hard cash for the stuff he dug up in the Babel/Infocalypse stack."

"He thought," Hiro says, "that L. Bob Rife might have a use for some viruses."

"Right. See, I don't understand all this shit. But I guess he found an old virus or something that was aimed at the elite thinkers."

"The technological priesthood," Hiro says. "The infocrats. It wiped out the whole infocracy of Sumer."

"Whatever."

"That's crazy," Hiro says. "That's like if you find out your employees are stealing ballpoint pens, you take them out and kill them. He wouldn't be able to use it without destroying all his programmers' minds."

"In its original form," the man with the glass eye says. "But the whole point is, Lagos wanted to do research on it."

"Informational warfare research."

"Bingo. He wanted to isolate this thing and modify it so it could be used to control the programmers without blowing their brains sky high."

"And did it work?"

"Who knows? Rife stole Lagos's idea. Just took it and ran with it. And after that, Lagos had no idea what Rife did with it. But a couple of years later, he started getting worried about a lot of stuff he was seeing."

"Like the explosive growth in Reverend Wayne's Pearly Gates."

"And these Russkies who speak in tongues. And the fact that Rife was digging up this old city—"

"Eridu."

"Yeah. And the radio astronomy thing. Lagos had a lot of stuff he was worried about. So he began to approach people. He approached us. He approached that girl you used to go out with—"

"Juanita."

"Yeah. Nice girl. And he approached Mr. Lee. So you might say that a few different people have been working on this little project."

46

"Where'd they go?" Hiro says.

Everyone's already looking for the float, as though they all noticed at once that it was missing. Finally they see it, a quarter mile behind them, dead in the water. The bigwigs and the bodyguards are standing up now, all looking in the same direction. The speedboat is circling around to retrieve it.

"They must have figured out a way to detach the tow cable," Hiro says.

"Not likely," the man with the glass eye says. "It was attached to the bottom, under the water. And it's a steel cable, so there's no way they could cut it."

Hiro sees another small craft bobbing on the water, about halfway between the Russians and the speedboat that was towing them. It's not obvious, because it's tiny, close to the water, done up in dull natural colors. It's a one-man kayak. Carrying a long-haired man.

"Shit," Livio says. "Where the hell did he come from?"

The kayaker looks behind himself for a few moments, reading the waves, then suddenly turns back around and begins to paddle hard, accelerating, glancing back every few strokes. A big wave is coming, and just as it swells up underneath the kayak, he's matching its speed. The kayak stays on top of the wave and shoots forward like a missile, riding the swell, suddenly going twice as fast as anything else on the water.

Digging at the wave with one end of his paddle, the kayaker makes a few crude changes in his direction. Then he parks the paddle athwart the kayak, reaches down inside, and hauls out a small dark object, a tube about four feet long, which he hoists up to one shoulder.

He and the speedboat shoot past each other going in opposite directions, separated by a gap of only about twenty feet. Then the speedboat blows up.

The *Kowloon* has overshot the site of all this action by a few thousand yards. It's pulling around into as tight a turn as a vessel of this size can handle, trying to throw a one-eighty so it can go back and deal with the Russians and, somewhat more problematically, with Raven.

Raven is paddling back toward his buddies.

"He's such an asshole," Livio says. "What's he going to do, tow them out to the Raft behind his fucking kayak?"

"This gives me the creeps," the man with the glass eye says. "Make sure we got some guys up there with Stingers. They must have a chopper coming or something."

"No other ships on the radar," says one of the other soldiers, coming in from the bridge. "Just us and them. And no choppers either."

"You know Raven carries a nuke, right?" Hiro says.

"So I heard. But that kayak's not big enough. It's tiny. I can't believe you'd go out to sea in something like that."

A mountain is growing out of the sea. A bubble of black water that keeps rising and broadening. Well behind the bobbing raft, a black tower has appeared, jutting vertically out of the water, a pair of wings sprouting from its top. The tower keeps getting taller, the wings getting higher out of the water, as before and aft, the mountain rises and shapes itself. Red stars and a few numbers. But no one has to read the numbers to know it's a submarine. A nuclear-missile submarine.

Then it stops. So close to the Russians on their little raft that Gurov and friends can practically jump onto it. Raven paddles toward them, cutting through the waves like a glass knife.

"Fuck me," the man with the glass eye says. He is utterly astounded. "Fuck me, fuck me, fuck me. Uncle Enzo's gonna be pissed."

"You couldn't of known," Livio says. "Should we shoot at 'em?"

Before the man with the glass eye can make a policy decision, the deck gun on the top of the nukesub opens up. The first shell misses them by just a few yards.

"Okay, we got a rapidly evolving situation. Hiro, you come with me."

The crew of the *Kowloon* has already sized up the situation and placed their bets on the nuclear submarine. They are running up and down the rails, dropping large fiberglass capsules into the water. The capsules break open to reveal bright orange folds, which blossom into life rafts.

Once the deck gunners on the nukesub figure out how to hit the *Kowloon*, the situation begins to evolve even more rapidly. The *Kowloon* can't decide whether to sink, burn, or simply disintegrate, so it does all three at once. By that time, most of the people who were on it have made their way onto a life raft. They all bob on the water, zip themselves into orange survival suits, and watch the nukesub.

Raven is the last person to go belowdecks on the submarine. He spends a minute or two removing some gear from his kayak: a few items in bags, and one eight-foot spear with a translucent, leaf-shaped head. Before he disappears into the hatch, he turns toward the wreckage of the *Kowloon* and holds the harpoon up over his head, a gesture of triumph and a promise all at once. Then he's gone. A couple of minutes later, the submarine is gone, too.

"That guy gives me the creeps," the man with the glass eye says.

47

Once it starts coming clear to her, again, that these people are all twisted freaks, she starts to notice other things about them. For example, the whole time, no one ever looks her in the eye. Especially the men. No sex at all in these guys, they've got it pushed so far down inside of them. She can understand why they don't look at the fat babushkas. But she's a fifteen-year-old American chick, and she is used to getting the occasional look. Not here.

Until she looks up from her big vat of fish one day and finds that she is looking into some guy's chest. And when she follows his chest upward to his neck, and his neck all the way up to his face, she sees dark eyes staring right back at her, right over the top of the counter.

He's got something written on his forehead: POOR IMPULSE CONTROL. Which is kind of scary. Sexy, too. It gives him a certain measure of romance that none of these other people have. She was expecting the Raft to be dark and dangerous, and instead it's just like working where her mother works. This guy is the first person she's seen around this place who really looks like he belongs on the Raft.

And he's got the look down, too. Incredibly rank style. Although he has a long wispy mustache that doesn't do much for his face. Doesn't bring out his features well at all.

"Do you take the nasty stuff? One fish head or two?" she says, dangling the ladle picturesquely. She always talks trash to people because none of them can understand what she's saying.

"I'll take whatever you're offering," the guy says. In English. Sort of a crisp accent.

"I'm not offering anything," she says, "but if you want to stand there and browse, that's cool."

He stands there and browses for a while. Long enough that people farther back in line stand up on tiptoe to see what the problem is. But when they see that the problem is this particular individual, they get down off their toes real fast, hunch down, sort of blend in to the mass of fishy-smelling wool.

"What's for dessert today?" the guy asks. "Got anything sweet for me?"

"We don't believe in dessert," Y.T. says. "It's a fucking sin, remember?"

"Depends on your cultural orientation."

"Oh, yeah? What culture are you oriented to?"

"I am an Aleut."

"Oh. I've never heard of that."

"That's because we've been fucked over," the big scary Aleut says, "worse than any other people in history."

"Sorry to hear that," Y.T. says. "So, uh, do you want me to serve up some fish, or are you gonna stay hungry?"

The big Aleut stares at her for a while. Then he jerks his head sideways and says, "Come on. Let's get the fuck out of here."

"What, and skip out on this cool job?"

He grins ridiculously. "I can find you a better job."

"In this job, do I get to leave my clothes on?"

"Come on. We're going now," he says, those eyes burning into her. She tries to ignore a sudden warm tense feeling down between her legs.

She starts following him down the cafeteria line, heading for a gap where she can exit into the dining area. The head babushka bitch comes stomping out from in back, hollers at her in some incomprehensible language.

Y.T. turns to look back. She feels a pair of big hands sliding up her sides, coming up into her armpits, and she pulls her arms to her sides, trying to stop it. But it's no good, the hands come all the way up and keep lifting, keep rising into the air, bringing her with them. The big guy hoists her right up over the counter like she's a three-year-old and sets her down next to him.

Y.T. turns back around to see the head babushka bitch, but

she is frozen in a mixture of surprise, fear, and sexual outrage. But in the end, fear wins out, she averts her eyes, turns away, and goes to replace Y.T. at vat position number nine.

"Thanks for the lift," Y.T. says, her voice wowing and fluttering ridiculously. "Uh, didn't you want to eat something?"

"I was thinking of going out anyway," he says.

"Going out? Where do you go out on the Raft?"

"Come on, I'll show you."

――――――――― He leads her down passageways and up steep steel stairways and out onto the deck. It's getting close to twilight, the control tower of the *Enterprise* looms hard and black against a deep gray sky that's getting dark and gloomy so fast that it seems darker, now, than it will at midnight. But for now, none of the lights are on and that's all there is, black steel and slate sky.

She follows him down the deck of the ship to the stern. From here it's a thirty-foot drop to the water, they are looking out across the prosperous, clean white neighborhood of the Russian people, separated from the squalid dark tangle of the Raft per se by a wide canal patrolled by gun-toting blackrobes. There's no stairway or rope ladder here, but there is a thick rope hanging from the railing. The big Aleut guy hauls up a chunk of rope and drapes it under one arm and over one leg in a quick motion. Then he throws one arm around Y.T.'s waist, gathering her in the crook of his arm, leans back, and falls off the ship.

She absolutely refuses to scream. She feels the rope stop his body, feels his arm squeeze her so tight she chokes for a moment, and then she's hanging there, hanging in the crook of his arm.

She's got her arms down to her side, defiant. But just for the hell of it, she leans into him, wraps her arms around his neck, puts her head on his shoulder, and hangs on tight. He rappels them down the rope, and soon they are standing on the sanitized, prosperous Russian version of the Raft.

"What's your name anyway?" she says.

"Dmitri Ravinoff," he says. "Better known as Raven."

Oh, shit.

_____ The connections between boats are tangled and unpredictable. To get from point A to point B, you have to wander all over the place. But Raven knows where he's going. Occasionally, he reaches out, grabs her hand, but he doesn't yank her around even though she's going a lot slower than he is. Every so often, he looks back at her with a grin, like, I could hurt you, but I won't.

They come to a place where the Russian neighborhood is joined to the rest of the Raft by a wide plank bridge guarded by Uzi dudes. Raven ignores them, takes Y.T.'s hand again, and walks right across the bridge with her. Y.T. hardly has time to think through the implications of this before it hits her, she looks around, sees all these gaunt Asians, staring back at her like she's a five-course meal, and realizes: I'm on the Raft. Actually on the Raft.

"These are Hong Kong Vietnamese," Raven says. "Started out in Vietnam, came to Hong Kong as boat people after the war there—so they've been living on sampans for a couple of generations now. Don't be scared, this isn't dangerous for you."

"I don't think I can find my way back here," Y.T. says.

"Relax," he says. "I've never lost a girlfriend."

"Have you ever _had_ a girlfriend?"

Raven throws back his head and laughs. "A lot, in the old days. Not as many in the past few years."

"Oh, yeah? The old days? Is that when you got your tattoo?"

"Yeah. I'm an alcoholic. Used to get in a lot of trouble. Been sober for eight years."

"Then how come everyone's scared of you?"

Raven turns to her, smiles broadly, shrugs. "Oh, because I'm an incredibly ruthless, efficient, cold-blooded killer, you know."

Y.T. laughs. So does Raven.

"What's your job?" Y.T. asks.

"I'm a harpooneer," he says.

"Like in _Moby Dick_?" Y.T. likes this idea. She read that book in school. Most of the people in her class, even the power tools, thought that the book was totally entrenched. But she liked all the stuff about harpooning.

"Nah. Compared to me, those Moby Dicksters were faggots."

"What kind of stuff do you harpoon?"

"You name it."

From there on out, she just looks at him. Or at inanimate objects. Because otherwise she wouldn't see anything except thousands of dark eyes staring back at her. In that way, it's a big change from being a slop-slinger for the repressed.

Part of it is just because she's so different. But part of it is that there's no privacy on the Raft, you make your way around by hopping from one boat to the next. But each boat is home to about three dozen people, so it's like you are constantly walking through people's living rooms. And bathrooms. And bedrooms. Naturally, they look.

They tromp across a makeshift platform built on oil drums. A couple of Vietnamese dudes are there arguing or haggling over something, looks like a slab of fish. The one who's turned toward them sees them coming. His eyes flicker across Y.T. without pausing, fix on Raven, and go wide. He steps back. The guy he's talking to, who has his back to them, turns around and literally jumps into the air, letting out a suppressed grunt. Both of them back well out of Raven's path.

And then she figures out something important: These people aren't looking at her. They're not even giving her a second glance. They're all looking at Raven. And it's not just a case of celebrity watching or something like that. All of these Raft dudes, these tough scary homeboys of the sea, are scared shitless of this guy.

And she's on a date with him.

And it's just started.

Suddenly, walking through another Vietnamese living room, Y.T. has a flashback to the most excruciating conversation she ever had, which was a year ago when her mother tried to give her advice on what to do if a boy got fresh with her. Yeah, Mom, right. I'll keep that in mind. Yeah, I'll be sure to remember that. Y.T. knew that advice was worthless, and this goes to show she was right.

48

There are four men in the life raft: Hiro Protagonist, self-employed stringer for the Central Intelligence Corporation, whose practice used to be limited to so-called "dry" operations, meaning that he sat around and soaked up information and then later spat it back into the Library, the CIC database, without ever actually doing anything. Now his practice has become formidably wet. Hiro is armed with two swords and a nine-millimeter semi-automatic pistol, known colloquially as a nine, with two ammunition clips, each carrying eleven rounds.

Vic, unspecified last name. If there was still such a thing as income tax, then every year when Vic filled out his 1040 form he would put down, as his occupation, "sniper." In classic sniper style, Vic is reticent, unobtrusive. He is armed with a long, large-caliber rifle with a bulky mechanism mounted on its top, where a telescopic sight might be found if Vic were not at the leading edge of his profession. The exact nature of this device is not obvious, but Hiro presumes that it is an exquisitely precise sensor package with fine crosshairs superimposed on the middle. Vic may safely be presumed to be carrying additional small concealed weapons.

Eliot Chung. Eliot used to be the skipper of a boat called the *Kowloon*. At the moment, he is between jobs. Eliot grew up in Watts, and when he speaks English, he sounds like a black guy. Genetically speaking, he is entirely Chinese. He is fluent in both black and white English as well as Cantonese, Taxilinga, and some Vietnamese, Spanish, and Mandarin. Eliot is armed with a .44 Magnum revolver, which he carried on board the *Kowloon* "just for the halibut," i.e., he used it to execute halibut before passengers hauled them on board. Halibut grow very large and can thrash so violently that they can easily kill the people who hook them; hence it is prudent to fire a number of shells through their heads before taking them on board. This is the only reason Eliot carries a weapon; the other defensive needs of the *Kowloon* were seen to by crew members who were specialists in that kind of thing.

"Fisheye." This is the man with the glass eye. He will only identify himself by his nickname. He is armed with a large, fat black suitcase.

The suitcase is massively constructed, with built-in wheels, and weighs somewhere between three hundred pounds and a metric ton, as Hiro discovers when he tries to move it. Its weight turns the normally flat bottom of the life raft into a puckered cone. The suitcase has a noteworthy attachment: a flexible three-inch-thick cable or hose or something, a couple of meters long, that emerges from one corner, runs up the sloping floor of the life raft, over the edge, and trails in the water. At the end of this mysterious tentacle is a hunk of metal about the size of a waste-basket, but so finely sculpted into so many narrow fins and vanes that it appears to have a surface area the size of Delaware. Hiro only saw this thing out of the water for a few chaotic moments, when it was being transferred into the life raft. At that time it was glowing red hot. Since then, it has lurked below the surface, light gray, impossible to see clearly because the water around it is forever churning in a full, rolling boil. Fist-sized bubbles of steam coalesce amid its fractal tracery of hot vanes and pummel the surface of the ocean, ceaselessly, all day and all night. The pow-erless life raft, sloshing around the North Pacific, emits a vast, spreading plume of steam like that of an Iron Horse chugging full blast over the Continental Divide. Neither Hiro nor Eliot ever mentions, or even notices, the by-now-obvious fact that Fisheye is traveling with a small, self-contained nuclear power source—al-most certainly radiothermal isotopes like the ones that power the Rat Thing. As long as Fisheye refuses to notice this fact, it would be rude for them to bring it up.

All of the participants are clad in bright orange padded suits that cover their entire bodies. They are the North Pacific version of life vests. They are bulky and awkward, but Eliot Chung likes to say that in northern waters, the only thing a life vest does is make your corpse float.

The lifeboat is an inflatable raft about ten feet long that does not come equipped with a motor. It has a tentlike, waterproof canopy that they can zip up all the way around, turning it into a sealed capsule so that the water stays out even in the most violent weather.

For a couple of days, a powerful chill wind coming down out off the mountains drives them out of Oregon, out toward the open water. Eliot explains, cheerfully, that this lifeboat was invented back in the old days, when they had navies and coast guards that would come and rescue stranded travelers. All you had to do was float and be orange. Fisheye has a walkie-talkie, but it is a short-range device. And Hiro's computer is capable of jacking into the net, but in this regard it functions much like a cellular telephone. It doesn't work out in the middle of nowhere.

When the weather is extremely rainy, they sit under the canopy. When it's less rainy, they sit above it. They all have ways of passing the time.

Hiro dicks around with his computer, naturally. Being stranded on a life raft in the Pacific is a perfect venue for a hacker.

Vic reads and rereads a soaked paperback novel that he had in the pocket of his MAFIA windbreaker when the *Kowloon* got blown out from under them. These days of waiting are much easier for him. As a professional sniper, he knows how to kill time.

Eliot looks at things with his binoculars, even though there is very little to look at. He spends a lot of time messing around with the raft, fretting about it in the way that boat captains do. And he does a lot of fishing. They have plenty of stored food on the raft, but the occasional fresh halibut and salmon are nice to eat.

Fisheye has taken what appears to be an instruction manual from the heavy black suitcase. It is a miniature three-ring binder with pages of laser-printed text. The binder is just a cheap unmarked one bought from a stationery store. In these respects, it is perfectly familiar to Hiro: it bears the earmarks of a high-tech product that is still under development. All technical devices require documentation of a sort, but this stuff can only be written by the techies who are doing the actual product development, and they absolutely hate it, always put the dox question off to the very last minute. Then they type up some material on a word processor, run it off on the laser printer, send the departmental secretary out for a cheap binder, and that's that.

But this only occupies Fisheye for a little while. He spends the rest of the time just staring off at the horizon, as though he's expecting Sicily to heave into view. It doesn't. He is despondent over the failure of his mission, and spends a lot of time mumbling under his breath, trying to find a way to salvage it.

"If you don't mind my asking," Hiro says, "what was your mission anyway?"

Fisheye thinks this one over for a while. "Well it depends on how you look at it. Nominally, my objective is to get a fifteen-year-old girl back from these assholes. So my tactic was to take a bunch of their bigwigs hostage, then arrange a trade."

"Who's this fifteen-year-old girl?"

Fisheye shrugs. "You know her. It's Y.T."

"Is that really your whole objective?"

"The important thing is, Hiro, that you have to understand the Mafia way. And the Mafia way is that we pursue larger goals under the guise of personal relationships. So, for example, when you were a pizza guy you didn't deliver pizzas fast because you made more money that way, or because it was some kind of a fucking policy. You did it because you were carrying out a personal covenant between Uncle Enzo and every customer. This is how we avoid the trap of self-perpetuating ideology. Ideology is a virus. So getting this chick back is more than just getting a chick back. It's the concrete manifestation of an abstract policy goal. And we like concrete—right, Vic?"

Vic allows himself a judicious sneer and a deep grinding laugh.

"What's the abstract policy goal in this case?" Hiro says.

"Not my department," Fisheye says. "But I think Uncle Enzo is real pissed at L. Bob Rife."

_____ Hiro is messing around in Flatland. He is doing this partly to conserve the computer's batteries; rendering a three-dimensional office takes a lot of processors working full-time, while a simple two-dimensional desktop display requires minimal power.

But his real reason for being in Flatland is that Hiro Protagonist, last of the freelance hackers, is hacking. And when hackers are hacking, they don't mess around with the superficial world of Metaverses and avatars. They descend below this surface layer and into the netherworld of code and tangled nam-shubs that supports it, where everything that you see in the Metaverse, no matter how lifelike and beautiful and three-dimensional, reduces to a simple text file: a series of letters on an electronic page. It is a throwback to the days when people programmed computers through primitive teletypes and IBM punch cards.

Since then, pretty and user-friendly programming tools have been developed. It's possible to program a computer now by sitting at your desk in the Metaverse and manually connecting little preprogrammed units, like Tinkertoys. But a real hacker would never use such techniques, any more than a master auto mechanic would try to fix a car by sliding in behind the steering wheel and watching the idiot lights on the dashboard.

Hiro does not know what he is doing, what he is preparing for. That's okay, though. Most of programming is a matter of laying groundwork, building structures of words that seem to have no particular connection to the task at hand.

He knows one thing: The Metaverse has now become a place where you can get killed. Or at least have your brain reamed out to the point where you might as well be dead. This is a radical change in the nature of the place. Guns have come to Paradise.

It serves them right, he realizes now. They made the place too vulnerable. They figured that the worst thing that could happen was that a virus might get transferred into your computer and force you to ungoggle and reboot your system. Maybe destroy a little data if you were stupid enough not to install any medicine. Therefore, the Metaverse is wide open and undefended, like airports in the days before bombs and metal detectors, like elementary schools in the days before maniacs with assault rifles. Anyone can go in and do anything that they want to. There are no cops. You can't defend yourself, you can't chase the bad people. It's going to take a lot of work to change that—a fundamental rebuilding of the whole Metaverse, carried out on a planetwide, corporate level.

In the meantime, there may be a role for individuals who know their way around the place. A few hacks can make a lot of difference in this situation. A freelance hacker could get a lot of shit done, years before the giant software factories bestir themselves to deal with the problem.

_____ The virus that ate through Da5id's brain was a string of binary information, shone into his face in the form of a bitmap—a series of white and black pixels, where white represents zero and black represents one. They put the bitmap onto scrolls and gave the scrolls to avatars who went around the Metaverse looking for victims.

The Clint who tried to infect Hiro in The Black Sun got away, but he left his scroll behind—he didn't reckon on having his arms lopped off—and Hiro dumped it into the tunnel system below the floor, the place where the Graveyard Daemons live. Later, Hiro had a Daemon take the scroll back to his workshop. And anything that is in Hiro's house is, by definition, stored inside his own computer. He doesn't have to jack into the global network in order to access it.

It's not easy working with a piece of data that can kill you. But that's okay. In Reality, people work with dangerous substances all the time—radioactive isotopes and toxic chemicals. You just have to have the right tools: remote manipulator arms, gloves, goggles, leaded glass. And in Flatland, when you need a tool, you just sit down and write it. So Hiro starts by writing a few simple programs that enable him to manipulate the contents of the scroll without ever seeing it.

The scroll, like any other visible thing in the Metaverse, is a piece of software. It contains some code that describes what it looks like, so that your computer will know how to draw it, and some routines that govern the way it rolls and unrolls. And it contains, somewhere inside of itself, a resource, a hunk of data, the digital version of the Snow Crash virus.

Once the virus has been extracted and isolated, it is easy enough for Hiro to write a new program called SnowScan. SnowScan is a piece of medicine. That is, it is code that protects Hiro's system—both his hardware and, as Lagos would put it, his bioware—from the digital Snow Crash virus. Once Hiro has installed it in his system, it will constantly scan the information coming in from outside, looking for data that matches the contents of the scroll. If it notices such information, it will block it.

There's other work to do in Flatland. Hiro's good with avatars, so he writes himself an invisible avatar—just because, in the new and more dangerous Metaverse, it might come in handy. This is easy to do poorly and surprisingly tricky to do well. Almost anyone can write an avatar that doesn't look like anything, but it will lead to a lot of problems when it is used. Some Metaverse real estate—including The Black Sun—wants to know how big your avatar is so that it can figure out whether you are colliding with another avatar or some obstacle. If you give it an answer of zero—you make your avatar infinitely small—you will either crash that piece of real estate or else make it think that something is very wrong. You will be invisible, but everywhere you go in the Metaverse you will leave a swath of destruction and confusion a mile wide. In other places, invisible avatars are illegal. If your avatar is transparent and reflects no light whatsoever—the easiest kind to write—it will be recognized instantly as an illegal avatar and alarms will go off. It has to be written in such a way that other people can't see it, but the real estate software doesn't realize that it's invisible.

There are about a hundred little tricks like this that Hiro wouldn't know about if he hadn't been programming avatars for people like Vitaly Chernobyl for the last couple of years. To write a really good invisible avatar from scratch would take a long time, but he puts one together in several hours by recycling bits and pieces of old projects left behind in his computer. Which is how hackers usually do it.

While he's doing that, he comes across a rather old folder with some transportation software in it. This is left over from the very old days of the Metaverse, before the Monorail existed, when the only way to get around was to walk or to write a piece of ware that simulated a vehicle.

In the early days, when the Metaverse was a featureless black ball, this was a trivial job. Later on, when the Street went up and people started building real estate, it became more complicated. On the Street, you can pass through other people's avatars. But you can't pass through walls. You can't enter private property. And you can't pass through other vehicles, or through permanent Street fixtures such as the Ports and the stanchions that support the monorail line. If you try to collide with any of these things, you don't die or get kicked out of the Metaverse; you just come to a complete stop, like a cartoon character running spang into a concrete wall.

In other words, once the Metaverse began to fill up with obstacles that you could run into, the job of traveling across it at high speed suddenly became more interesting. Maneuverability became an issue. Size became an issue. Hiro and Da5id and the rest of them began to switch away from the enormous, bizarre vehicles they had favored at first—Victorian houses on tank treads, rolling ocean liners, mile-wide crystalline spheres, flaming chariots drawn by dragons—in favor of small maneuverable vehicles. Motorcycles, basically.

A Metaverse vehicle can be as fast and nimble as a quark. There's no physics to worry about, no constraints on acceleration, no air resistance. Tires never squeal and brakes never lock up. The one thing that can't be helped is the reaction time of the user. So when they were racing their latest motorcycle software, holding wild rallies through Downtown at Mach 1, they didn't worry about engine capacity. They worried about the user interface, the controls that enabled the rider to transfer his reactions into the machine, to steer, accelerate, or brake as quickly as he could think. Because when you're in a pack of bike racers going through a crowded area at that speed, and you run into something and suddenly slow down to a speed of exactly zero, you can forget about catching up. One mistake and you've lost.

Hiro had a pretty good motorcycle. He probably could have had the best one on the Street, simply because his reflexes are unearthly. But he was more preoccupied with sword fighting than motorcycle riding.

He opens up the most recent version of his motorcycle software, gets familiar with the controls again. He ascends from Flatland into the three-dimensional Metaverse and practices riding his bike around his yard for a while. Beyond the boundaries of his yard is nothing but blackness, because he's not jacked into the net. It is a lost, desolate sensation, kind of like floating on a life raft in the Pacific Ocean.

49

Sometimes they see boats in the distance. A couple of these even swing close by to check them out, but none of them seems to be in that rescuing mood. There are few altruists in the vicinity of the Raft, and it must be evident that they don't have much to steal.

From time to time, they see an old deep-water fishing boat, fifty to a hundred feet long, with half a dozen or so small fast boats clustered around it.

When Eliot informs them that these are pirate vessels, Vic and Fisheye prick up their ears. Vic unwraps his rifle from the collection of Hefty bags that he uses to protect it from the salt spray, and detaches the bulky sight so that they can use it as a spyglass. Hiro can't see any reason to pull the sight off the rifle in order to do this, other than the fact that if you don't, it looks like you're drawing a bead on whatever you're looking at.

Whenever a pirate vessel comes into view, they all take turns looking at it through the sight, playing with all the different sensor modes: visible, infrared, and so on. Eliot has spent enough time knocking around the Rim that he has become familiar with the colors of the different pirate groups, so by examining them through the sight he can tell who they are: Clint Eastwood and his band parallel them for a few minutes one day, checking them out, and the Magnificent Seven send out one of their small boats to zoom by them and look for potential booty. Hiro's almost hoping they get taken prisoner by the Seven, because they have the nicest-looking pirate ship: a former luxury yacht with Exocet launch tubes kludged to the foredeck. But this reconnaissance leads nowhere. The pirates, unschooled in thermodynamics, do not grasp the implications of the eternal plume of steam coming from beneath the life raft.

One morning, a big old trawler materializes very close to them, congealing out of nothing as the fog lifts. Hiro has been hearing its engines for a while, but didn't realize how close it was.

"Who are they?" Fisheye says, choking on a cup of the freeze-dried coffee he despises so much. He's wrapped up in a space blanket and partly snuggled underneath the boat's waterproof canopy, just his face and hands visible.

Eliot scopes them out with the sight. He is not a real demonstrative guy, but it's clear that he is not very happy with what he sees. "That is Bruce Lee," he says.

"How is that significant?" Fisheye says.

"Well, check out the colors," Eliot says.

The ship is close enough that everyone can see the flag pretty clearly. It's a red banner with a silver fist in the middle, a pair of nunchuks crossed beneath it, the initials B and L on either side.

"What about 'em?" Fisheye says.

"Well, the guy who calls himself Bruce Lee, who's like the leader? He got a vest with those colors on the back."

"So?"

"So, it's not just embroidered or painted, it's actually done in scalps. Patchwork, like."

"Say what?" Hiro says.

"There's a rumor, just a rumor, man, that he went through the Refu ships looking for people with red or silver hair so he could collect the scalps he needed."

Hiro is still absorbing that when Fisheye makes an unexpected decision. "I want to talk to this Bruce Lee character," he says. "He interests me."

"Why the hell do you want to talk to this fucking psycho?" Eliot says.

"Yeah," Hiro says. "Didn't you see that series on *Eye Spy*? He's a maniac."

Fisheye throws up his hands as if to say the answer is, like Catholic theology, beyond mortal comprehension. "This is my decision," he says.

"Who the fuck are you?" Eliot says.

"President of the fucking boat," Fisheye says. "I hereby nominate myself. Is there a second?"

"Yup," Vic says, the first time he has spoken in forty-eight hours.

"All in favor say aye," Fisheye says.

"Aye," Vic says, bursting into florid eloquence.

"I win," Fisheye says. "So how do we get these Bruce Lee guys to come over here and talk to us?"

"Why should they want to?" Eliot says. "We got nothing they want except for poontang."

"Are you saying these guys are homos?" Fisheye says, his face shriveling up.

"Shit, man," Eliot says, "you didn't even blink when I told you about the scalps."

"I knew I didn't like any of this boat shit," Fisheye says.

"If this makes any difference to you, they're not gay in the sense that we usually think of it," Eliot explains. "They're het, but they're pirates. They'll go after anything that's warm and concave."

Fisheye makes a snap decision. "Okay, you two guys, Hiro and Eliot, you're Chinese. Take off your clothes."

"What?"

"Do it. I'm the president, remember? You want Vic to do it for you?"

Eliot and Hiro can't help looking over at Vic, who is just sitting there like a lump. There is something about his extremely blasé attitude that inspires fear.

"Do it or I'll fucking kill you," Fisheye says, finally driving the point home.

Eliot and Hiro, bobbing awkwardly on the unsteady floor of the raft, peel off their survival suits and step out of them. Then they pull off the rest of their clothes, exposing smooth bare skin to the air for the first time in a few days.

The trawler comes right alongside of them, no more than twenty feet away, and cuts its engines. They are nicely equipped: half a dozen Zodiacs with new outboards, an Exocet-type missile, two radars, and a fifty-caliber machine gun at each end of the boat, currently unmanned. A couple of speedboats are being towed behind the trawler like dinghys and each of these also has a heavy machine gun. And there is also a thirty-six-foot motor yacht, following them under its own power.

There are a couple of dozen guys in Bruce Lee's pirate band, and they are now lined up along the trawler's railing, grinning, whistling, howling like wolves, and waving unrolled trojans in the air.

"Don't worry, man, I'm not going to let 'em fuck you," Fisheye says, grinning.

"What you gonna do," Eliot says, "hand them a papal encyclical?"

"I'm sure they'll listen to reason," Fisheye says.

"These guys aren't scared of the Mafia, if that's what you have in mind," Eliot says.

"That's just because they don't know us very well."

Finally, the leader comes out, Bruce Lee himself, a fortyish guy in a Kevlar vest, an ammo vest stretched over that, a diagonal bandolier, samurai sword—Hiro would love to take him on—nunchuks, and his colors, the patchwork of human scalps.

He flashes them a nice grin, has a look at Hiro and Eliot, gives them a highly suggestive, thrusting thumbs-up gesture, and then struts up and down the length of the boat one time, swapping high fives with his merry men. Every so often, he picks out one of the pirates at random and gestures at the man's trojan. The pirate puts his condom to his lips and inflates it into a slippery ribbed balloon. Then Bruce Lee inspects it, making sure there are no leaks. Obviously, the man runs a tight ship.

Hiro can't help staring at the scalps on Bruce Lee's back. The pirates note his interest and mug for him, pointing to the scalps, nodding, looking back at him with wide, mocking eyes. The colors look much too uniform—no change in the red from one to the next. Hiro concludes that Bruce Lee, contrary to his reputation, must have just gone out and gotten scalps of any old color, bleached them, and dyed them. What a wimp.

Finally, Bruce Lee works his way back to midship and flashes them another big grin. He has a great, dazzling grin and he knows it; maybe it's those one-karat diamonds Krazy Glued to his front teeth.

"Jammin' boat," he says. "Maybe you, me swap, huh? Hahaha."

Everyone on the life raft, except for Vic, just smiles a brittle smile.

"Where you goin'? Key West? Hahaha."

Bruce Lee examines Hiro and Eliot for a while, rotates his index finger to indicate that they should spin around and display their business ends. They do.

"*Quanto?*" Bruce Lee says, and all the pirates get uproarious, most of all Bruce Lee. Hiro can feel his anal sphincter contracting to the size of a pore.

"He's asking how much we cost," Eliot says. "It's a joke, see, because they know they can come over and have our asses for free."

"Oh, hilarious!" Fisheye says. While Hiro and Eliot literally freeze their asses, he's still snuggled up under the canopy, that bastard.

"Poonmissile, like?" Bruce Lee says, pointing to one of the antiship missiles on the deck. "Bugs? Motorolas?"

"Poonmissile is a Harpoon antiship missile, real expensive," Eliot says. "A bug is a microchip. Motorola would be one brand, like Ford or Chevy. Bruce Lee deals in a lot of electronics—you know, typical Asian pirate dude."

"He'd give us a Harpoon missile for you guys?" Fisheye says.

"No! He's being sarcastic, shithead!" Eliot says.

"Tell him we want a boat with an outboard motor," Fisheye says.

"Want one zode, one kicker, fillerup," Eliot says.

Suddenly Bruce Lee gets real serious and actually considers it. "Scope clause, chomsayen? Gauge and gag."

"He'll consider it if they can come and check out the merchandise first," Eliot says. "They want to check out how tight we are, and whether we are capable of suppressing our gag reflex. These are all terms from the Raft brothel industry."

"Ombwas scope like twelves to me, hahaha."

"Us homeboys look like we have twelve-gauge assholes," Eliot says, "i.e., that we are all stretched out and worthless."

Fisheye speaks up on his own. "No, no, four-tens, totally!" The entire deck of the pirate ship titters with excitement.

"No way," Bruce Lee says.

"These ombwas," Fisheye says, "still got cherries up in there!"

The whole deck erupts in rude, screaming laughter. One of the pirates scrambles up to balance on the railing, gyrates one fist in the air, and hollers: "ba ka na zu ma lay ga no ma la aria ma na po no a ab zu ... " By that point all the other pirates have stopped laughing, gotten serious looks on their faces, and joined in, bellowing their own private streams of babble, rattling the air with a profound hoarse ululation.

Hiro's feet go out from under him as the raft moves suddenly; he can see Eliot falling down next to him.

He looks up at Bruce Lee's ship and flinches involuntarily as he sees what looks like a dark wave cresting over the rail, washing over the row of standing pirates, starting at the stern of the trawler and working its way forward. But this is just some kind of optical illusion. It is not really a wave at all. Suddenly, they are fifty feet away from the trawler, not twenty feet. As the laughter on the railing dies away, Hiro hears a new sound: a low whirring noise from the direction of Fisheye, and from the atmosphere around them, a tearing, hissing noise, like the sound just before a thunderbolt strikes, like the sound of sheets being ripped in half.

Looking back at Bruce Lee's trawler, he sees that the dark wavelike phenomenon was a wave of blood, as though someone hosed down the deck with a giant severed aorta. But it didn't come from outside. It erupted from the pirates' bodies, one at a time, moving from the stern to the bow. The deck of Bruce Lee's ship is now utterly quiet and motionless except for blood and gelatinized internal organs sliding down the rusted steel and plopping softly into the water.

Fisheye is up on his knees now and has torn away the canopy and space blanket that have covered him until this point. In one hand he is holding a long device a couple of inches in diameter, which is the source of the whirring noise. It is a circular bundle of parallel tubes about pencil-sized and a couple of feet long, like a miniaturized Gatling gun. It whirs around so quickly that the individual tubes are difficult to make out; when it is operating, it is in fact ghostly and transparent because of this rapid motion, a glittering, translucent cloud jutting out of Fisheye's arm. The device is attached to a wrist-thick bundle of black tubes and cables that snake down into the large suitcase, which lies open on the bottom of the raft. The suitcase has a built-in color monitor screen with graphics giving information about the status of this weapons system: how much ammo is left, the status of various subsystems. Hiro just gets a quick glimpse at it before all of the ammunition on board Bruce Lee's ship begins to explode.

"See, I told you they'd listen to Reason," Fisheye says, shutting down the whirling gun.

Now Hiro sees a nameplate tacked onto the control panel.

> REASON
> version 1.0B7
> Gatling-type 3-mm hypervelocity railgun system
> Ng Security Industries, Inc.
> PRERELEASE VERSION—NOT FOR FIELD USE
> DO NOT TEST IN A POPULATED AREA
> — ULTIMA RATIO REGUM —

"Fucking recoil pushed us halfway to China," Fisheye says appreciatively.

"Did you do that? What just happened?" Eliot says.

"I did it. With Reason. See, it fires these teeny little metal splinters. They go real fast—more energy than a rifle bullet. Depleted uranium."

The spinning barrels have now slowed almost to a stop. It looks like there are about two dozen of them.

"I thought you hated machine guns," Hiro says.

"I hate this fucking raft even more. Let's go get ourselves something that goes, you know. Something with a motor on it."

Because of the fires and small explosions going off on Bruce Lee's pirate ship, it takes them a minute to realize that several people are still alive there, still shooting at them. When Fisheye becomes aware of this, he pulls the trigger again, the barrels whirl themselves up into a transparent cylinder, and the tearing, hissing noise begins again. As he waves the gun back and forth, hosing the target down with a hypersonic shower of depleted uranium, Bruce Lee's entire ship seems to sparkle and glitter, as though Tinkerbell was flying back and forth from stem to stern, sprinkling nuclear fairy dust over it.

Bruce Lee's smaller yacht makes the mistake of coming around to see what's going on. Fisheye turns toward it for a moment and its high, protruding bridge slides off into the water.

Major structural elements of the trawler are losing their integrity. Enormous popping and wrenching noises are coming from inside as big pieces of Swiss-cheesed metal give way, and the superstructure is slowly collapsing down into the hull like a botched soufflé. When Fisheye notes this, he ceases fire.

"Cut it out, boss," Vic says.

"I'm melting!" Fisheye crows.

"We could have used that trawler, asshole," Eliot says, vindictively yanking his pants back on.

"I didn't mean to blow it all up. I guess the little bullets just go through everything."

"Sharp thinking, Fisheye," Hiro says.

"Well, I'm sorry I took a little action to save our asses. Come on, let's go get one of them little boats before they all burn."

_____ They paddle in the direction of the decapitated yacht. By the time they reach it, Bruce Lee's trawler is just a listing, empty steel hull with flames and smoke pouring out of it, spiced by the occasional explosion.

The remaining portion of the yacht has many, many tiny little holes in it, and glitters with exploded fragments of fiberglass: a million tiny little glass fibers about a millimeter long. The skipper and a crew member, or rather the stew that they turned into when the bridge was hit by Reason, slid off into the water along with the rest of the debris, leaving behind no evidence of their having been there except for a pair of long parallel streaks trailing off into the water. But there is a Filipino boy down in the galley, the galley so low, unhurt and only dimly aware of what happened.

A number of electrical cables have been sawn in half. Eliot digs up a toolbox from belowdecks and spends the next twelve hours patching things together to the point where the engine can be started and the yacht can be steered. Hiro, who has a rudimentary knowledge of electrical stuff, acts as gofer and limp-dicked adviser.

"Did you hear the way the pirates were talking, before Fisheye opened up on them?" Hiro asks Eliot while they are working.

"You mean in pidgin?"

"No. At the very end. The babbling."

"Yeah. That's a Raft thing."

"It is?"

"Yeah. One guy will start in and the rest will follow. I think it's just a fad."

"But it's common on the Raft?"

"Yeah. They all speak different languages, you know, all those different ethnic groups. It's like the fucking Tower of Babel. I think when they make that sound—when they babble at each other—they're just imitating what all the other groups sound like."

The Filipino kid starts making them some food. Vic and Fisheye sit down in the main cabin belowdecks, eating, going through Chinese magazines, looking at pictures of Asian chicks, and occasionally looking at nautical charts. When Eliot gets the electrical system back up and running, Hiro plugs his personal computer in, to recharge its batteries.

By the time the yacht is up and running again, it's dark. To the southwest, a fluctuating column of light is playing back and forth against the low overhanging cloud layer.

"Is that the Raft over there?" Fisheye says, pointing to the light, as all hands converge on Eliot's makeshift control center.

"It is," Eliot says. "They light it up at night so that the fishing boats can find their way back to it."

"How far away do you think it is?" Fisheye says.

Eliot shrugs. "Twenty miles."

"And how far to land?"

"I have no idea. Bruce Lee's skipper probably knew, but he's been pureed along with everyone else."

"You're right," Fisheye says. "I should have set it on 'whip' or 'chop.'"

"The Raft usually stays at least a hundred miles offshore," Hiro says, "to reduce the danger of snags."

"How we doing on gas?"

"I dipped the tank," Eliot says, "and it looks like we're not doing so well, to tell you the truth."

"What does that mean, not doing so well?"

"It's not always easy to read the level when you're out to sea," Eliot says. "And I don't know how efficient these engines are. But if we're really eighty or a hundred miles offshore, we might not make it."

"So we go to the Raft," Fisheye says. "We go to the Raft and persuade someone it's in his best interests to give us some fuel. Then, back to the mainland."

No one really believes it's going to happen this way, least of all Fisheye. "And," he continues, "while we're there—on the Raft—after we get the fuel and before we go home—some other stuff might happen, too, you know. Life's unpredictable."

"If you have something in mind, why don't you just spit it out?" Hiro says.

"Okay. Policy decision. The hostage tactic failed. So we go for an extraction."

"Extraction of what?"

"Of Y.T."

"I go along with that," Hiro says, "but I have another person I want to extract also, as long as we're extracting."

"Who?"

"Juanita. Come on, you said yourself she was a nice girl."

"If she's on the Raft, maybe she's not so nice," Fisheye says.

"I want to extract her anyway. We're all in this together, right? We're all part of Lagos's gang."

"Bruce Lee has some people there," Eliot says.

"Correction. Had."

"But what I'm saying is, they're going to be pissed."

"You think they're going to be pissed. I think they're going to be scared shitless," Fisheye says. "Now drive the boat, Eliot. Come on, I'm sick of all this fucking water."

50

Raven ushers Y.T. onto a flat-assed boat with a canopy on top. It is some kind of a riverboat that has been turned into a Vietnamese/American/Thai/Chinese business establishment, kind of a bar/restaurant/whorehouse/gambling den. It has a few big rooms, where lots of people are letting it all hang out, and a lot of little tiny steel-walled rooms down below where God knows what kind of activity is taking place.

The main room is packed with lowlife revelry. The smoke ties her bronchial passages into granny knots. The place is equipped with a shattering Third World sound system: pure distortion echoing off painted steel walls at three hundred decibels. A television set bolted onto one wall is showing foreign cartoons, done up in a two-color scheme of faded magenta and lime green, in which a ghoulish wolf, kind of like Wile E. Coyote with rabies, gets repeatedly executed in ways more violent than even Warner Bros. could think up. It's a snuff cartoon. The soundtrack is either turned off completely or else overwhelmed by the screeching melody coming out of the speakers. A bunch of erotic dancers are performing at one end of the room.

It's impossibly crowded, they'll never get a place to sit. But shortly after Raven comes into the room, half a dozen guys in the corner suddenly stand bolt upright and scatter from a table, snatching up their cigarettes and drinks almost as an afterthought. Raven pushes Y.T. through the room ahead of him, like she's a figurehead on his kayak, and everywhere they go, people are shoved out of her way by Raven's almost palpable personal force field.

Raven bends down and looks under the table, picks a chair up off the floor and looks at the underside—you can never be too careful about those chair bombs—sets it down, pushed all the way back into the corner where two steel walls meet, and sits down. He gestures for Y.T. to do the same, and she does, her back to the action. From here, she can see Raven's face, illuminated mostly by occasional stabs of light filtering through the crowd from the mirrored ball over the erotic dancers, and by the generalized green-and-magenta haze coming out of the TV set, spiked by the occasional flash when the cartoon wolf makes the mistake of swallowing another hydrogen bomb, or has the misfortune to get hosed down again with a flamethrower.

A waiter's there immediately. Raven commences hollering across the table at her. She can't hear him, but maybe he's asking her what she wants.

"A cheeseburger!" she screams back at him.

Raven laughs, shakes his head. "You see any cows around here?"

"Anything but fish!" she screams.

Raven talks to the waiter for a while in some variant of Taxilinga.

"I ordered you some squid," he hollers. "That's a mollusk."

Great. Raven, the last of the true gentlemen.

There is a shouted conversation lasting the better part of an hour. Raven does most of the shouting. Y.T. just listens, smiles, and nods. Hopefully, he's not saying something like "I enjoy really violent, abusive sex acts."

She doesn't think he's talking about that at all. He's talking politics. She hears a fragmented history of the Aleuts, a burst here and a burst here, when Raven isn't poking squid into his mouth and the music isn't too loud:

"Russians fucked us over ... smallpox had a ninety-percent mortality rate ... worked as slaves in their sealing industry ... Seward's folly ... Fucking Nipponese took away my father in forty-two, put him in a POW camp for the duration ...

"Then the Americans fucking nuked us. Can you believe that shit?" Raven says. There's a lull in the music; suddenly she can hear complete sentences. "The Nipponese say they're the only people who were ever nuked. But every nuclear power has one aboriginal group whose territory they nuked to test their weapons. In America, they nuked the Aleutians. Amchitka. My father," Raven says, grinning proudly, "was nuked twice: once at Nagasaki, when he was blinded, and then again in 1972, when the Americans nuked our homeland."

Great, Y.T. thinks. She's got a new boyfriend and he's a mutant. Explains one or two things.

"I was born a few months later," Raven continues, by way of totally hammering that point home.

"How did you get hooked up with these Orthos?"

"I got away from our traditions and ended up living in Soldotna, working on oil rigs," Raven says, like Y.T. is supposed to just know where Soldotna is. "That was when I did my drinking and got this," he says, pointing to his tattoo. "That's also when I learned how to make love to a woman—which is the only thing I do better than harpooning."

Y.T. can't help but think that fucking and harpooning are closely related activities in Raven's mind. But as crude as the man is, she can't get around the fact that he's making her uncomfortably horny.

"I used to work fishing boats too, to make a little extra money.

We would come back from a forty-eight-hour halibut opening—this was back in the old days when they had fishing regulations—and we'd put on our survival suits, stick beers into the pockets, and jump into the water and just float around drinking all night long. And one time we were doing this and I drank until I passed out. And when I woke up, it was the next day, or maybe a couple of days later, I don't know. And I was floating in my survival suit out in the middle of the Cook Inlet, all alone. The other guys on my fishing boat had forgotten about me."

Conveniently enough, Y.T. thinks.

"Anyway, I floated for a couple of days. Got real thirsty. Ended up washing ashore on Kodiak Island. By this time, I was real sick with the DTs and everything else. But I washed up near a Russian Orthodox church and they found me, took me in, and straightened me out. And that was when I saw that the Western, American lifestyle had come this close to killing me."

Here comes the sermon.

"And I saw that we can only live through faith, living a simple lifestyle. No booze. No television. None of that stuff."

"So what are we doing in this place?"

He shrugs. "This is an example of the bad places I used to hang out. But if you're going to get decent food on the Raft, you have to come to a place like this."

A waiter approaches the table. His eyes are big, his movements tentative. He's not coming to take an order; he's coming to deliver bad news.

"Sir, you are wanted on the radio. I'm sorry."

"Who is it?" Raven says.

The waiter just looks around him like he can't even speak the name in public. "It's very important," he says.

Raven heaves a big sigh, grabs one last piece of fish and pokes it into his mouth. He stands up, and before Y.T. can react, gives her a kiss on the cheek. "Honey, I got a job to do, or something. Just wait right here for me, okay?"

"Here?"

"Nobody will fuck with you," Raven says, as much for the benefit of the waiter as for Y.T.

51

The Raft looks uncannily cheerful from a few miles away. A dozen searchlights, and at least that many lasers, are mounted on the towering superstructure of the *Enterprise,* waving back and forth against the clouds like a Hollywood premiere. Closer up, it doesn't look so bright and crisp. The vast matted tangle of small boats radiates a murky cloud of yellow light that spoils the contrast.

A couple of patches of the Raft are burning. Not a nice cheery bonfire type of thing, but a high burbling flame with black smoke sliding out of it, like you get from a large quantity of gasoline.

"Gang warfare, maybe," Eliot theorizes.

"Energy source," Hiro guesses.

"Entertainment," Fisheye says. "They don't have cable on the fucking Raft."

Before they really plunge into Hell, Eliot takes the lid off the fuel tank and slides the dipstick into there, checking the fuel supply. He doesn't say anything, but he doesn't look especially happy.

"Turn off all the lights," Eliot says when it seems they are still miles away. "Remember that we have already been sighted by several hundred or even several thousand people who are armed and hungry."

Vic is already going around the boat shutting off lights via the simple expedient of a ball peen hammer. Fisheye just stands there and listens intently to Eliot, suddenly respectful. Eliot continues. "Take off all the bright orange clothing, even if it means we get cold. From now on, we lay down on the decks, expose ourselves as little as possible, and we don't talk to each other unless necessary. Vic, you stay midships with your rifle and wait for someone to hit us with a spotlight. Anyone hits us with a spotlight from any direction, you shoot it out. That includes flashlights from small boats. Hiro, your job is gunwale patrol. You just keep going around the edges of this yacht, anywhere that a swimmer could climb up over the edge and slip on board, and when that happens, cut his arms off. Also, be on the lookout for any kind of grappling-hook type stuff. Fisheye, if any other floating object comes within a hundred feet of us, sink it.

"If you see Raft people with antennas coming out of their heads, try to kill them first, because they can talk to each other."

"Antennas coming out of their heads?" Hiro says.

"Yeah. Raft gargoyle types," Eliot says.

"Who are they?"

"How the fuck should I know? I've just seen 'em a few times, from a distance. Anyway, I'm going to take us straight in toward the center, and once we get close enough, I'll turn to starboard and swing around the Raft counterclockwise, looking for someone who might be willing to sell us fuel. If worse comes to worst and we end up on the Raft itself, we stick together and we hire ourselves a guide, because if we try to move across the Raft without the help of someone who knows the web, we'll get into a bad situation."

"Like what kind of a bad situation?" Fisheye asks.

"Like hanging on a rotted-out slime-covered cargo net between two ships rocking different ways, with nothing underneath us except ice water full of plague rats, toxic waste, and killer whales. Any questions?"

"Yeah," Fisheye says. "Can I go home now?"

Good. If Fisheye is scared, so's Hiro.

"Remember what happened to the pirate named Bruce Lee," Eliot says. "He was well-armed and powerful. He pulled up alongside a life raft full of Refus one day, looking for some poontang, and he was dead before he knew it. Now there are a lot of people who want to do that to us."

"Don't they have some kind of cops or something?" Vic says. "I heard they did."

In other words, Vic has killed a lot of time going to Raft movies in Times Square.

"The people up on the *Enterprise* operate in kind of a wrath-of-God mode," Eliot says. "They have big guns mounted around the edge of the flight deck—big Gatling guns like Reason except with larger bullets. They were originally put there to shoot down Exocet missiles. They strike with the force of a meteorite. If people act up out on the Raft, they will make the problem go away. But a little murder or riot isn't enough to get their attention. If it's a rocket duel between rival pirate organizations, that's different."

Suddenly, they've been nailed with a spotlight so big and powerful they can't look anywhere near it.

Then it's dark again, and a gunshot from Vic's rifle is searing and reverberating across the water.

"Nice shooting, Vic," Fisheye says.

"It's, like, one of them drug dealer boats," Vic says, looking through his magic sight. "Five guys on it. Headed our way." He fires another round. "Correction. Four guys on it." Boom. "Correction, they're not headed our way anymore." Boom. A fireball erupts from the ocean two hundred feet away. "Correction. No boat."

Fisheye laughs and actually slaps his thigh. "You recording all of this, Hiro?"

"No," Hiro says. "Wouldn't come out."

"Oh." Fisheye seems taken aback, like this changes everything.

"That's the first wave," Eliot says. "Rich pirates looking for easy pickings. But they've got a lot to lose, so they scare easy."

"Another big yacht-type boat is out there," Vic says, "but they're turning away now."

Above the deep chortling noise of their yacht's big diesel, they can hear the high whine of outboard motors.

"Second wave," Eliot says. "Pirate wannabes. These guys will come in a lot faster, so stay sharp."

"This thing has millimeter wave on it," Fisheye says. Hiro looks at him; his face is illuminated from below by the glow of Reason's built-in screen. "I can see these guys like it's fucking daylight."

Vic fires several rounds, pops the clip out of his rifle, shoves in a new one.

A zodiac zips past, skittering across the wavetops, strafing them with weak flashlight beams. Fisheye fires a couple of short bursts from Reason, blasting clouds of warm steam into the cold night air, but misses them.

"Save your ammo," Eliot says. "Even with Uzis, they can't hit us until they slow down a little bit. And even with radar, you can't hit them."

A second zodiac whips past them on the other side, closer than the last one. Vic and Fisheye both hold their fire. They hear it orbiting them, swinging back around the way it came.

"Those two boats are getting together out there," Vic says. "They got two more of them. A total of four. They're talking."

"We've been reconned," Eliot says, "and they're planning their tactics. The next time is for real."

A second later, two fantastically loud blasts sound from the rear of the yacht, where Eliot is, accompanied by brief flashes of light. Hiro turns around to see a body collapsing to the deck. It's not Eliot. Eliot is crouching there holding his oversized halibut shooter.

Hiro runs back, looks at the dead swimmer in the dim light scattering off the clouds. He's naked except for a thick coating of black grease and a belt with a gun and a knife in it. He's still holding on to the rope that he used to pull himself onboard. The rope is attached to a grappling hook that has caught in the jagged, broken fiberglass on one side of the yacht.

"Third wave is coming a little early," Eliot says, his voice high and shaky. He's trying so hard to sound cool that it has the opposite effect. "Hiro, this gun's got three rounds left in it, and I'm saving the last one for you if any more of these motherfuckers get on board."

"Sorry," Hiro says. He draws the short wakizashi. He would feel better if he could carry his nine in the other hand, but he needs one hand free to steady himself and keep from falling overboard. He makes a quick circuit of the yacht, looking for more grappling hooks, and actually finds one on the other side, hooked into one of the railing stanchions, a taut rope trailing out behind it into the sea.

Correction: It's a taut cable. His sword won't cut it. And the tension on the rope is such that he can't get it unhooked from the stanchion.

As he's squatting there playing with the grappling hook, a greasy hand rises up out of the water and grabs his wrist. Another hand gropes for Hiro's other hand and grabs the sword instead. Hiro yanks the weapon free, feeling it do damage, and shoves the wakizashi point first into the place between those two hands just as someone is sinking his teeth into Hiro's crotch. But Hiro's crotch is protected—the motorcycle outfit has a hard plastic cup—and so this human shark just gets a mouthful of bulletproof fabric. Then his grip loosens, and he falls into the sea. Hiro releases the grappling hook and drops it in with him.

Vic fires three rounds in quick succession, and a fireball illuminates one whole side of the ship. For a moment, they can see everything around them for a distance of a hundred yards, and the effect is like turning on your kitchen lights in the middle of the night and finding your countertops aswarm with rats. At least a dozen small boats are around them.

"They got Molotov cocktails," Vic says.

The people in the boats can see them, too. Tracers fly around them from several directions. Hiro can see muzzle flashes in at least three places. Fisheye opens up once, twice with Reason, just firing short bursts of a few dozen rounds each, and produces one fireball, this one farther away from the yacht.

It's been at least five seconds since Hiro moved, so he checks this area for grappling hooks again and resumes his circuit around the edge of the yacht. This time it's clear. The two greaseballs must have been working together.

A Molotov cocktail arcs through the sky and impacts on the starboard side of the yacht, where it's not going to do much damage. Inside would be a lot worse. Fisheye uses Reason to hose down the area from which the Molotov was thrown, but now that the side of the boat is all lit up from the flames, they draw more small-arms fire. In that light, Hiro can see trickles of blood running down from the area where Vic ensconced himself.

On the port side, he sees something long and narrow and low in the water, with the torso of a man rising out of it. The man has long hair that falls down around his shoulders, and he's holding an eight-foot pole in one hand. Just as Hiro sees him, he's throwing it.

The harpoon darts across twenty feet of open water. The million chipped facets of its glass head refract the light and make it look like a meteor. It takes Fisheye in the back, slices easily through the bulletproof fabric he's wearing under his suit, and comes all the way out the other side of his body. The impact lifts Fisheye into the air and throws him off the boat; he lands face-first in the water, already dead.

Mental note: Raven's weapons do not show up on radar.

Hiro looks back in the direction of Raven, but he's already gone. A couple more greaseballs, side by side, vault over the railing about ten feet forward of Hiro, but for a moment they're dazzled by the flames. Hiro pulls out his nine, aims it their way, and keeps pulling the trigger until both of them have fallen back into the water. He's not sure how many rounds are left in the gun now.

There's a coughing, hissing noise, and the flame light gets dim and finally goes out. Eliot nailed it with a fire extinguisher.

The yacht jerks out from under Hiro's feet, and he hits the deck with his face and shoulder. Getting up, he realizes that either they've just rammed, or been rammed by, something big. There is a thudding noise, feet running on the deck. Hiro hears some of these feet near him, drops his wakizashi, pulls his katana, whirls at the same time, snapping the long blade into someone's midsection. Meanwhile they're dragging a long knife down his back, but it doesn't penetrate the fabric, just hurts a little. His katana comes free easily, which is dumb luck, because he forgot to squeeze off the blow, could have gotten it wedged in there. He turns again, instinctively parries a knife thrust from another greaseball, raises the katana and snaps it down into his brainpan. This time he does it right, kills him without sticking the blade. There are greaseballs on two sides of him now. Hiro chooses a direction, swings it sideways, decapitates one of them. Then he turns around. Another greaseball is staggering toward him across the pitching deck with a spiked club, but unlike Hiro he's not keeping his balance. Hiro shuffles up to meet him, keeping his center of gravity over his feet, and impales him on the katana.

Another greaseball is watching all of this in astonishment from up near the bow. Hiro shoots him, and he collapses to the deck. Two more greaseballs jump off the boat voluntarily.

The yacht is tangled up in a spider's web of shitty old ropes and cargo nets that were stretched out across the surface of the water as a snare for poor suckers like them. The yacht's engine is still straining, but the prop isn't moving; something got wrapped around the shaft.

There's no sign of Raven now. Maybe it was just a one-time contract hit on Fisheye. Maybe he didn't want to get tangled up in the spiderweb. Maybe he figured that, once Reason was taken out, the greaseballs would take care of the rest.

Eliot's no longer at the controls. He's no longer even on the yacht. Hiro calls out his name, but there's no response. Not even thrashing in the water. The last thing he did was lean over the edge with the fire extinguisher, putting out the Molotov flame; when they were jerked to a halt he must have tumbled overboard.

They're a lot closer to the *Enterprise* than he had ever thought. They covered a lot of water during the fight, got closer in than they should have. In fact, Hiro's surrounded on all sides by the Raft at this point. Meager, flickering illumination is provided by the burning remains of the Molotov cocktail–carrying Zodiacs, which have become tangled in the net around them.

Hiro does not think it would be wise to take the yacht back out toward open water. It's a little too competitive there. He goes up forward. The suitcase that serves as Reason's power supply and ammo dump is open on the deck next to him, its color monitor screen reading: *Sorry, a fatal system error occurred. Please reboot and try again.*

Then, as Hiro's looking at it, it fritzes out completely and dies of a snow crash.

Vic got hit by one of the machine-gun bursts and is also dead. Around them, half a dozen other boats ride on the waves, caught in the spiderweb, nice-looking yachts all of them. But they are all empty hulks, stripped of their engines and everything else. Just like duck decoys in front of a hunter's blind. A hand-painted sign rides on a buoy nearby, reading FUEL in English and other languages.

Farther out to sea, a number of the ships that were chasing them earlier are lingering, steering well clear of the spiderweb. They know they can't come in here; this is the exclusive domain of the black grease swimmers, the spiders in the web, almost all of whom are now dead.

If he goes onto the Raft itself, it can't be any worse. Can it?

The yacht has its own little dinghy, the smallest size of inflatable zodiac, with a small outboard motor. Hiro gets it into the water.

"I go with you," a voice says.

Hiro whirls, hauling out his gun, and finds himself aiming it into the face of the Filipino cabin boy. The boy blinks, looks a little surprised, but not especially scared. He has been hanging out with pirates, after all. For that matter, all the dead guys on the yacht don't seem to faze him either.

"I be your guide," the boy says. "ba la zin ka nu pa ra ta . . . "

52

Y.T. waits so long that she thinks the sun must have come up by now, but she knows it can't really be more than a couple of hours. In a way, it doesn't even matter. Nothing ever changes: the music plays, the cartoon videotape rewinds itself and starts up again, men come in and drink and try not to get caught staring at her. She might as well be shackled to the table anyway; there's no way she could ever find her way back home from here. So she waits.

Suddenly, Raven's standing in front of her. He's wearing different clothes, wet slippery clothing made out of animal skins or something. His face is red and wet from being outside.

"You get your job all done?"

"Sort of," Raven says. "I did enough."

"What do you mean, enough?"

"I mean I don't like being called out of a date to do bullshit work," Raven says. "So I got things in order out there and my attitude is, let his gnomes worry about the details."

"Well, I've been having a great time here."

"Sorry, baby. Let's get out of here," he says, speaking with the intense, strained tones of a man with an erection.

"Let's go to the Core," he says, once they get into the cool air above deck.

"What's there?"

"Everything," he says. "The people who run this whole place. Most of these people"—he waves his hand out over the Raft—"can't go there. I can. Want to see it?"

"Sure, why not," she says, hating herself for sounding like such a sap. But what else is she going to say?

He starts leading her down a long moonlit series of gangplanks, in toward the big ships in the middle of the Raft. You could almost skate here, but you'd have to be really good.

"Why are you different from the other people?" Y.T. says. She kind of blurts it out without doing a whole lot of thinking first. But it seems like a good question.

He laughs. "I'm an Aleut. I'm different in a lot of ways—"

"No. I mean your brain works in a different way," Y.T. says. "You're not wacked out. You know what I mean? You haven't mentioned the Word all night."

"We have a thing we do in kayaks. It's like surfing," Raven says.

"Really? I surf, too—in traffic," Y.T. says.

"We don't do this for fun," Raven says. "It's part of how we live. We get from island to island by surfing on waves."

"Same here," Y.T. says, "except we go from one franchulate to the next by surfing on cars."

"See, the world is full of things more powerful than us. But if you know how to catch a ride, you can go places," Raven says.

"Right. I'm totally hip to what you're saying."

"That's what I'm doing with the Orthos. I agree with some of their religion. But not all of it. But their movement has a lot of power. They have a lot of people and money and ships."

"And you're surfing on it."

"Yeah."

"That's cool, I can relate. What are you trying to do? I mean, what's your real goal?"

They're crossing a big broad platform. Suddenly he's right behind her, his arms are around her body, and he draws her back into him. Her toes are just barely touching the ground. She can feel his cool nose against her temple and his hot breath coming into one ear. It sends a tingle straight down to her toes.

"Short-term goal or long-term goal?" Raven whispers.

"Um—long term."

"I used to have this plan—I was going to nuke America."

"Oh. Well, that'd be kind of harsh," she says.

"Maybe. Depends on what kind of a mood I'm in. Other than that, no long-term goals." Every time he whispers something, another breath tickles her ear.

"How about medium-term then?"

"In a few hours, the Raft comes apart," Raven says. "We're headed for California. Looking for a decent place to live. Some people might try to stop us. It's my job to help the people make it safe and sound up onto the shore. So you might say I'm going to war."

"Oh, that's a shame," she mumbles.

"So it's hard to think of anything besides the here and now."

"Yeah, I know."

"I rented a nice room to spend my last night in," Raven says. "It's got clean sheets."

Not for long, she thinks.

_____ She had thought that his lips would be cold and stiff, like a fish. But she's shocked at how warm they are. Every part of his body feels hot, like that's his only way of keeping warm up in the Arctic.

About thirty seconds into the kiss, he bends down, wraps his great thigh-sized forearms around her waist, cinches her up into the air, lifting her feet up off the deck.

She was afraid he would take her to some horrible place, but it turns out he rented a whole shipping container, stacked way up high on one of the containerships in the Core. The place is like a luxury hotel for big Core wheels.

She's trying to decide what to do with her legs, which are now dangling uselessly. She's not quite ready to wrap them around him, not this early in the date. Then she feels them spreading apart—way, way apart—Raven's thighs must be bigger around than his waist. He has lifted one leg up into her crotch and put the foot up on a chair so she's straddling his thigh, and with his arms he's holding her body up against him, squeezing and relaxing, squeezing and relaxing, so that she's helplessly rocking back and forth, all her weight on her crotch. Some huge muscle, the upmost part of his quadricep, angles up where it attaches to the bone in his pelvis, and as he rocks her in closer and tighter she ends up straddling that, shoved against it so tight that she can feel the seams in the crotch of her coverall, feel the coins in the key pocket of Raven's black jeans. When he slides his hands downward, still pressing her inward, and squeezes her butt in both hands, so big it must be like squeezing an apricot, fingers so long they wrap around and push up into her crack and she rocks forward to get away from it but there's nowhere to go except into his body, her face breaking away from the kiss and sliding against the perspiration of his broad, smooth, whiskerless neck. She can't help letting out a yelp that turns into a moan, and then she knows he's got her. Because she never makes noises during sex, but this time she can't help it.

And once she's decided that, she's impatient to get on with it. She can move her arms, she can move her legs, but the middle part of her body is pinned in place, it's not going to move until Raven moves it. And he's not going to move it until she makes him want to. So she goes to work on his ear. That usually does it.

He tries to get away from her. Raven, trying to run away from something. She likes that idea. She has arms that are as strong as a man's, strong from hanging on to that poon on the freeway, so she wraps them around his head like a vise and presses her forehead against the side of his head and starts orbiting the tip of her tongue around the little folded-over rim of his outer ear.

He stands paralyzed for a couple of minutes, breathing shallowly, while she works her way inward, and when she finally shoves her tongue into his ear canal, he bucks and grunts like he's just been harpooned, lifts her up off his leg, kicks the chair across the room so hard it cracks against the steel wall of the shipping container. She feels herself falling backward toward the futon, thinks for a moment she's about to get crushed beneath him, but he catches all the weight on his elbows, except for his lower body, which slams into hers all at once, sending another electric shot of pleasure up her back and down her legs. Her thighs and calves have turned solid and tight, like they've been pumped full of juice, she can't relax them. He leans up on one elbow, separating their bodies for a moment, plants his mouth on hers to maintain the contact, fills her mouth with his tongue, holds her there with it while he one-hands the fastener at the collar of her coverall and yanks the zipper all the way down to the crotch. It's open now, exposing a broad V of skin converging from her shoulders. He rolls back onto her, grabs the top of the coverall with both hands and pulls it down behind her, forcing her arms down and to her sides, stuffing the mass of fabric and pads down underneath the small of her back so she stays arched up toward him. Then he's in between her tight thighs, all those skating muscles strained to the limit, and his hands come back inside to squeeze her butt again, this time his hot skin against hers, it's like sitting on a warm buttered griddle, makes the whole body feel warmer.

There's something she's supposed to remember at this point. Something she has to take care of. Something important. One of those dreary duties that always seems so logical when you think about it in the abstract and, at moments like this, seems so utterly beside the point that it never even occurs to you.

It must be something to do with birth control. Or something like that. But Y.T. is helpless with passion, so she has an excuse. So she squirms and kicks her knees until the coverall and her panties have slid down to her ankles.

Raven gets completely naked in about three seconds. He pulls his shirt off over his head and throws it somewhere, bucks out of his pants and kicks them off onto the floor. His skin is as smooth as hers, like the skin of a mammal that swims through the sea, but he feels hot, not cold and fishy. She doesn't see his cock, but she doesn't want to, what's the point, right?

She does something she's never done before: comes as soon as he goes into her. It's like a bolt of lightning shoots out from the middle, down the backs of her tensed legs, up her spine, into her nipples, she sucks in air until her whole ribcage is poking out through the skin and then screams it all out. She just rips one. Raven's probably deaf now. Which is his fucking problem.

She goes limp. So does he. He must have come at the same time. Which is okay. It's early, and poor Raven was horny as a goat from being out to sea. Later on, she'll expect more endurance.

Right now, she's content to lie underneath him and suck the warmth out of his body. She's been cold for days. Her feet are still cold, hanging out in the air, but that just makes the rest of her feel much better.

Raven seems content, too. Uncharacteristically so. Talk about bliss. Most guys would already be flipping through channels on the TV. Not Raven. He's content to lie here all night, breathing softly into her neck. As a matter of fact, he's gone to sleep right on top of her. Like something a woman would do.

She dozes, too. Lies there for a minute or two, all these thoughts going through her head.

This is a pretty nice place. Like a mid-priced business hotel in the Valley. She never figured anything like this existed on the Raft. But there's rich people and poor people here, too, just like anywhere else.

When they came to a certain place on the walkway, not far from the first of the big Core ships, there was an armed guard blocking the way. He let Raven go on through, and Raven took Y.T. with him, leading her by the hand, and the guard gave her a look but he didn't say anything, he was keeping most of his attention on Raven.

After that, the walkway got a lot nicer. It was broad, like the boardwalk at the beach, and not quite so crowded with old Chinese ladies carrying gigantic bundles on their backs. And it didn't smell like shit quite so much.

When they got to the first Core ship, there was a stairway that took them from sea level up to its deck. From there, they took a gangplank across to the innards of another ship, and Raven led her through the place like he'd been through it a million times, and eventually they crossed another gangplank into this containership. And it was just like a fucking hotel in there: bellhops with white gloves carrying luggage for guys in suits, a registration desk, everything. It was still a ship—everything's made out of steel that has been painted white a million times over—but nothing like what she expected. There's even a little helipad where the suits can come and go. There's a chopper parked next to it with a logo she's seen before: Rife Advanced Research Enterprises. RARE. The people who gave her the envelope to deliver to EBGOC headquarters. All of this is fitting together now: the Feds and L. Bob Rife and the Reverend Wayne's Pearly Gates and the Raft are all part of the same deal.

"Who the hell are all these people?" she asked Raven when she first saw it. But he just shushed her.

She asked him again later, as they were wandering around looking for their room, and he told her: These guys all work for

L. Bob Rife. Programmers and engineers and communications people. Rife's an important man. Got a monopoly to run.

"Rife's here?" she asked him. Putting on an act, of course; she had it figured out by that point.

"Ssh," he said.

It's a nice piece of intel. Hiro should like it, if she can just get it to him. And even that's going to be easy. She never thought there'd be Metaverse terminals here on the Raft, but on this ship there's a whole row of them, so that visiting suits can call back to civilization. All she has to do is get to one without waking up Raven. Which could be tricky. It's too bad she couldn't drug him with something, like in the Raft movies.

That's when the realization comes. It swims up out of her subconscious in the same way that a nightmare does. Or when you leave the house and remember half an hour later that you left a teakettle going on the stove. It's a cold clammy reality that she can't do a damn thing about.

She has finally remembered what that nagging thing was that bothered her for a moment, right before the actual moment of fucking.

It was not birth control. It was not a hygiene thing.

It was her dentata. The last line of personal self-defense. Along with Uncle Enzo's dog tags, the one piece of stuff that the Orthos didn't take. They didn't take it because they don't believe in cavity searches.

Which means that at the moment Raven entered her, a very small hypodermic needle slipped imperceptibly into the engorged frontal vein of his penis, automatically shooting a cocktail of powerful narcotics and depressants into his bloodstream.

Raven's been harpooned in the place where he least expected it. Now he's going to sleep for at least four hours.

And then, boy, is he ever going to be pissed.

53

Hiro remembers Eliot's warning: Don't go onto the Raft itself without a local guide. This kid must be a Refu that Bruce Lee recruited from some Filipino neighborhood on the Raft.

The kid's name is Transubstanciacion. Tranny for short. He climbs into the zodiac before Hiro tells him to.

"Wait a sec," Hiro says. "We have to do some packing first."

Hiro risks turning on a small flashlight, uses it to rummage around the yacht, picking up valuable stuff: a few bottles of (presumably) drinkable water, some food, extra ammunition for his nine. He takes one of the grappling hooks, too, coiling its rope neatly. Seems like the kind of thing that might be useful on the Raft.

He has one other chore to take care of, not something he's looking forward to.

Hiro has lived in a lot of places where mice and even rats were a problem. He used to get rid of them using traps. But then he had a run of bad luck with the things. He would hear a trap snap shut in the middle of the night, and then instead of silence he would hear pitiable squeaking and thrashing, whacking noises as the stricken rodent tried to drag itself back to safety with a trap snapped over some part of its anatomy, usually its head. When you have gotten up at three in the morning to find a live mouse on your kitchen counter leaving a contrail of brain tissue across the formica, it is hard to get back to sleep, and so he prefers to set out poison now.

Somewhat in the same vein, a severely wounded man—the last man Hiro shot—is thrashing around on the deck of the yacht, up near the bow, babbling.

More than anything he has ever wanted to do, Hiro wants to get into the zodiac and get away from this person. He knows that in order to go up and help him, or put him out of his misery, he's going to have to shine the flashlight on him, and when he does that he's going to see something he'll never be able to forget.

But he has to do it. He swallows a couple of times because he's already gagging and follows his flashlight beam up to the bow.

It's much worse than he had expected.

This man apparently took a bullet somewhere around the bridge of his nose, aimed upward. Everything above that point has been pretty much blown off. Hiro's looking into a cross-section of his lower brain.

Something is sticking up out of his head. Hiro figures it must be fragments of skull or something. But it's too smooth and regular for that.

Now that he's gotten over his initial nausea, he's finding this easier to look at. It helps to know that the guy is out of his misery. More than half of his brain is gone. He's still talking—his voice sounds whistly and gaseous, like a pipe organ gone bad, because of the changes in his skull—but it's just a brainstem function, just a twitch in the vocal cords.

The thing sticking up out of his head is a whip antenna about a foot long. It is encased in black rubber, like the antennas on cop walkie-talkies, and it is strapped onto his head, above the left ear. This is one of the antenna-heads that Eliot warned them about.

Hiro grabs the antenna and pulls. He might as well take the headset with him—it must have something to do with the way L. Bob Rife controls the Raft.

It doesn't come off. When Hiro pulls, what's left of the guy's head twists around, but the antenna doesn't come loose. And that's how Hiro figures out that this isn't a headset at all. The antenna has been permanently grafted onto the base of the man's skull.

Hiro switches his goggles into millimeter-wave radar and stares into the man's ruined head.

The antenna is attached to the skull by means of short screws that go into the bone, but do not pierce all the way through. The base of the antenna contains a few microchips, whose purpose Hiro cannot divine by looking at them. But nowadays you can put a supercomputer on a single chip, so anytime you see more than one chip together in one place, you're looking at significant ware.

A single hair-thin wire emerges from the base of the antenna and penetrates the skull. It passes straight through to the brainstem and then branches and rebranches into a network of invisibly tiny wires embedded in the brain tissue. Coiled around the base of the tree.

Which explains why this guy continues to pump out a steady stream of Raft babble even when his brain is missing: It looks like L. Bob Rife has figured out a way to make electrical contact with the part of the brain where Asherah lives. These words aren't originating here. It's a pentecostal radio broadcast coming through on his antenna.

Reason is still up top, its monitor screen radiating blue static toward heaven. Hiro finds the hard power switch and turns it off. Computers this powerful are supposed to shut themselves down, after you've asked them to. Turning one off with the hard switch is like lulling someone to sleep by severing their spinal column. But when the system has snow-crashed, it loses even the ability to turn itself off, and primitive methods are required. Hiro packs the Gatling gun assembly back into the case and latches it shut.

Maybe it's not as heavy as he thought, or maybe he's on adrenaline overdrive. Then he realizes why it seems so much lighter: most of its weight was ammunition, and Fisheye used up quite a bit. He half-carries, half-drags it back to the stern, making sure the heat exchanger stays in the water, and somersaults it into the zodiac.

Hiro climbs in after it, joining Tranny, and starts attending to the motor.

"No motor," Tranny says. "It snag bad."

Right. The spiderweb would get wrapped around the propeller. Tranny shows Hiro how to snap the zodiac's oars into the oarlocks.

Hiro rows for a while and finds himself in a long clear zone that zigzags its way through the Raft, like a lead of clear water between ice floes in the Arctic.

"Motor okay," Tranny says.

He drops the motor into the water. Tranny pumps up the fuel line and starts it up. It starts on the first pull; Bruce Lee ran a tight ship.

As Hiro begins to motor down the open space, he is afraid that it is just a little cove in the ghetto. But this is just a trick of the lights. He rounds a corner and finds it stretching out for some distance. It is a sort of beltway that runs all the way around the Raft. Small streets and even smaller alleys lead from this beltway into the various ghettos. Through the scope, Hiro can see that their entrances are guarded. Anyone's free to cruise around the beltway, but people are more protective of their neighborhoods.

The worst thing that can happen on the Raft is for your neighborhood to get cut loose. That's why the Raft is such a tangled mess. Each neighborhood is afraid that the neighboring 'hoods are going to gang up on them, cut them loose, leave them to starve in the middle of the Pacific. So they are constantly finding new ways to tie themselves into each other, running cables over, under, and around their neighbors, tying into more far-flung 'hoods, or preferably into one of the Core ships.

The neighborhood guards are armed, needless to say. Looks like the weapon of choice is a small Chinese knockoff of the AK-47. Its metal frame jumps out pretty clearly on radar. The Chinese government must have stamped out an unimaginable number of these things, back in the days when they spent a lot of time thinking about the possibility of fighting a land war with the Soviets.

Most of them just look like indolent Third World militia the world over. But at the entrance to one neighborhood, Hiro sees that the guard in charge has a whip antenna sticking straight up in the air, sprouting from his head.

A few minutes later, they get to a point where the beltway is intersected by a broad street that runs straight into the middle of the Raft, where the big ships are—the Core. The closest one is a Nipponese containership—a low, flat-decked number with a high bridge, stacked with steel shipping containers. It's webbed over with rope ladders and makeshift stairways that enable people to climb up into this container or that. Many of the containers have lights burning in them.

"Apartment building," Tranny jokes, noting Hiro's interest. Then he shakes his head and rolls his eyes and rubs his thumb against his fingertips. Apparently, this is quite the swell neighborhood.

The nice part of the cruise comes to an end when they notice several fast skiffs emerging from a dark and smoky neighborhood.

"Vietnam gang," Tranny says. He puts his hand on Hiro's and

gently but firmly removes it from the outboard motor's throttle. Hiro checks them out on radar. A couple of these guys have the little AK-47s, but most of them are armed with knives and pistols, obviously looking forward to some close-up, face-to-face contact. These guys in the boats are, of course, the peons. More important-looking gents stand along the edge of the neighborhood, smoking and watching. A couple of them are wireheads.

Tranny revs it up, turns into a sparse neighborhood of loosely connected Arabian dhows, and maneuvers through the darkness for a while, occasionally putting his hand on Hiro's head and gently pressing it down so he doesn't catch a rope with his neck.

When they emerge from the fleet of dhows, the Vietnamese gang is no longer in evidence. If this happened in daylight, the gangsters could track them by following Reason's steam. Tranny steers them across a medium-sized street and into a cluster of fishing boats. In the middle of this area an old trawler sits, being cut up for scrap, cutting torches illuminating the black surface of the water all around. But most of the work is being done with hammers and cold chisels, which radiate appalling noise across the flat echoing water.

"Home," Tranny says, smiling, and points to a couple of houseboats lashed together. Lights are still burning here, a couple of guys are out on the deck smoking fat, makeshift cigars, through the windows they can see a couple of women working in the kitchen.

As they approach, the guys on the deck sit up, take notice, draw revolvers out of their waistbands. But then Tranny speaks up in a happy stream of Tagalog. And everything changes.

Tranny gets the full Prodigal Son welcome: crying, hysterical fat ladies, a swarm of little kids piling out of their hammocks, sucking their thumbs and jumping up and down. Older men beaming, showing great gaps and black splotches in their smiles, watching and nodding and diving in to give him the occasional hug.

And on the edge of the mob, way back in the darkness, is another wirehead.

"You come in, too," says one of the women, a lady in her forties named Eunice.

"That's okay," Hiro says. "I won't intrude."

This statement is translated and moves like a wave through the some eight hundred and ninety-six Filipinos who have now converged on the area. It is greeted with the utmost shock. Intrude? Unthinkable! Nonsense! How dare you so insult us?

One of the gap-toothed guys, a miniature old man and probable World War II veteran, jumps onto the rocking zodiac, sticks to the floor like a gecko, wraps his arm around Hiro's shoulders, and pokes a spliff into his mouth.

He looks like a solid guy. Hiro leans into him. "Compadre, who is the guy with the antenna? A friend of yours?"

"Nah," the guy whispers, "he's an asshole." Then he puts his index finger dramatically to his lips and shushes.

54

It's all in the eyes. Along with picking handcuffs, vaulting Jersey barriers, and fending off perverts, it is one of the quintessential Kourier skills: walking around in a place where you don't belong without attracting suspicion. And you do it by not looking at anyone. Keep those eyes straight ahead no matter what, don't open them too wide, don't look tense. That, and the fact that she just came in here with a guy that everyone is scared of, gets her back through the containership to the reception area.

"I need to use a Street terminal," she says to the reception guy. "Can you charge it to my room?"

"Yes, ma'am," the reception guy says. He doesn't have to ask which room she's in. He's all smiles, all respect. Not the kind of thing you get very often when you're a Kourier.

She could really get to like this relationship with Raven, if it weren't for the fact that he's a homicidal mutant.

55

Hiro ducks out of Tranny's celebratory dinner rather early, drags Reason off the zodiac and onto the front porch of the houseboat, opens it up, and jacks his personal computer into its bios.

Reason reboots with no problems. That's to be expected. It's also to be expected that later, probably when he most needs Reason to work, it will crash again, the way it did for Fisheye. He could keep turning it off and on every time it does this, but this is awkward in the heat of battle, and not the type of solution that hackers admire. It would be much more sensible just to debug it.

Which he could do by hand, if he had time. But there may be a better way of going about it. It's possible that, by now, Ng Security Industries has fixed the bug—come out with a new version of the software. If so, he should be able to get a copy of it on the Street.

Hiro materializes in his office. The Librarian pokes his head out of the next room, just in case Hiro has any questions for him.

"What does *ultima ratio regum* mean?"

" 'The Last Argument of Kings,' " the Librarian says. "King Louis XIV had it stamped onto the barrels of all of the cannons that were forged during his reign."

Hiro stands up and walks out into his garden. His motorcycle is waiting for him on the gravel path that leads to the gate. Looking up over the fence, Hiro can see the lights of Downtown rising in the distance again. His computer has succeeded in jacking into L. Bob Rife's global network; he has access to the Street. This is as Hiro had expected. Rife must have a whole suite of satellite uplinks there on the *Enterprise*, patched into a cellular network covering the Raft. Otherwise, he wouldn't be able to reach the Metaverse from his very own watery fortress, which would never do for a man like Rife.

Hiro climbs on his bike, eases it through the neighborhood and onto the Street, and then gooses it up to a few hundred miles an hour, slaloming between the stanchions of the monorail, practicing. He runs into a few of them and stops, but that's to be expected.

Ng Security Industries has a whole floor of a mile-high neon skyscraper near Port One, right in the middle of Downtown. Like everything else in the Metaverse, it's open twenty-four hours, because it's always business hours somewhere in the world. Hiro leaves his bike on the Street, takes the elevator up to the 397th floor, and comes face to face with a receptionist daemon. For a moment, he can't peg her racial background; then he realizes that this daemon is half-black, half-Asian—just like him. If a white man had stepped off the elevator, she probably would have been a blonde. A Nipponese businessman would have come face to face with a perky Nipponese office girl.

"Yes, sir," she says. "Is this in regard to sales or customer service?"

"Customer service."

"Whom are you with?"

"You name it, I'm with them."

"I'm sorry?" Like human receptionists, the daemon is especially bad at handling irony.

"At the moment, I think I'm working for the Central Intelligence Corporation, the Mafia, and Mr. Lee's Greater Hong Kong."

"I see," says the receptionist, making a note. Also like a human receptionist, it is not possible to impress her. "And what product is this in regards to?"

"Reason."

"Sir! Welcome to Ng Security Industries," says another voice.

It is another daemon, an attractive black/Asian woman in highly professional dress, who has materialized from the depths of the office suite.

She ushers Hiro down a long, nicely paneled hallway, down another long paneled hallway, and then down a long paneled hallway. Every few steps, he passes by a reception area where avatars from all over the world sit in chairs, passing the time. But Hiro doesn't have to wait. She ushers him straight into a nice big paneled office where an Asian man sits behind a desk littered with models of helicopters. It is Mr. Ng himself. He stands up; they swap bows; the usher lady checks out.

"You working with Fisheye?" Ng says, lighting up a cig. The smoke swirls in the air ostentatiously. It takes as much computing power realistically to model the smoke coming out of Ng's mouth as it does to model the weather system of the entire planet.

"He's dead," Hiro says. "Reason crashed at a critical juncture, and he ate a harpoon."

Ng doesn't react. Instead, he just sits there motionless for a few seconds, absorbing this data, as if his customers get harpooned all the time. He's probably got a mental database of everyone who has ever used one of his toys and what happened to them.

"I told him it was a beta version," Ng says. "And he should have known not to use it for infighting. A two-dollar switchblade would have served him better."

"Agreed. But he was quite taken with it."

Ng blows out more smoke, thinking. "As we learned in Vietnam, high-powered weapons are so sensorily overwhelming that they are similar to psychoactive drugs. Like LSD, which can convince people they can fly—causing them to jump out of windows—weapons can make people overconfident. Skewing their tactical judgment. As in the case of Fisheye."

"I'll be sure and remember that," Hiro says.

"What kind of combat environment do you want to use Reason in?" Ng says.

"I need to take over an aircraft carrier tomorrow morning."

"The *Enterprise?*"

"Yes."

"You know," Ng says, apparently in a conversational mood, "there's a guy who actually took over a nuclear-missile submarine armed with nothing more than a piece of glass—"

"Yeah, that's the guy who killed Fisheye. I might have to tangle with him, too."

Ng laughs. "What is your ultimate objective? As you know, we are all in this together, so you may share your thoughts with me."

"I'd prefer a little more discretion in this case ... "

"Too late for that, Hiro," says another voice. Hiro turns around; it is Uncle Enzo, being ushered through the door by the receptionist—a striking Italian woman. Just a few paces behind him is a small Asian businessman and an Asian receptionist.

"I took the liberty of calling them in when you arrived," Ng says, "so that we could have a powwow."

"Pleasure," Uncle Enzo says, bowing slightly to Hiro.

Hiro bows back. "I'm really sorry about the car, sir."

"It's forgotten," Uncle Enzo says.

The small Asian man has now come into the room. Hiro finally recognizes him. It is the photo that is on the wall of every Mr. Lee's Greater Hong Kong in the world.

Introductions and bows all around. Suddenly, a number of extra chairs have materialized in the office, so everyone pulls one up. Ng comes out from behind his desk, and they sit in a circle.

"Let us cut to the chase, since I assume that your situation, Hiro, may be more precarious than ours," Uncle Enzo says.

"You got that right, sir."

"We would all like to know what the hell is going on," Mr. Lee says. His English is almost devoid of a Chinese accent; clearly his cute, daffy public image is just a front.

"How much of this have you guys figured out so far?"

"Bits and pieces," Uncle Enzo says. "How much have you figured out?"

"Almost all of it," Hiro says. "Once I talk to Juanita, I'll have the rest."

"In that case, you are in possession of some very valuable intel," Uncle Enzo says. He reaches into his pocket and pulls out a hypercard and hands it toward Hiro. It says

TWENTY-FIVE
MILLION
HONG KONG
DOLLARS

Hiro reaches out and takes the card.

Somewhere on earth, two computers swap bursts of electronic noise and the money gets transferred from the Mafia's account to Hiro's.

"You'll take care of the split with Y.T.," Uncle Enzo says.

Hiro nods. You bet I will.

56

"I'm here on the Raft looking for a piece of software—a piece of medicine to be specific—that was written five thousand years ago by a Sumerian personage named Enki, a neurolinguistic hacker."

"What does that mean?" Mr. Lee says.

"It means a person who was capable of programming other people's minds with verbal streams of data, known as nam-shubs."

Ng is totally expressionless. He takes another drag on his cigarette, spouts the smoke up above his head in a geyser, watches it spread out against the ceiling. "What is the mechanism?"

"We've got two kinds of language in our heads. The kind we're using now is acquired. It patterns our brains as we're learning it. But there's also a tongue that's based in the deep structures of the brain, that everyone shares. These structures consist of basic neural circuits that have to exist in order to allow our brains to acquire higher languages."

"Linguistic infrastructure," Uncle Enzo says.

"Yeah. I guess 'deep structure' and 'infrastructure' mean the same thing. Anyway, we can access those parts of the brain under the right conditions. Glossolalia—speaking in tongues—is the output side of it, where the deep linguistic structures hook into our tongues and speak, bypassing all the higher, acquired languages. Everyone's known that for some time."

"You're saying there's an input side, too?" Ng says.

"Exactly. It works in reverse. Under the right conditions, your ears—or eyes—can tie into the deep structures, bypassing the higher language functions. Which is to say, someone who knows the right words can speak words, or show you visual symbols, that go past all your defenses and sink right into your brainstem. Like a cracker who breaks into a computer system, bypasses all the security precautions, and plugs himself into the core, enabling him to exert absolute control over the machine."

"In that situation, the people who own the computer are helpless," Ng says.

"Right. Because they access the machine at a higher level, which has now been overridden. In the same sense, once a neurolinguistic hacker plugs into the deep structures of our brain, we can't get him out—because we can't even control our own brain at such a basic level."

"What does this have to do with a clay tablet on the *Enterprise?*" Mr. Lee says.

"Bear with me. This language—the mother tongue—is a vestige of an earlier phase of human social development. Primitive societies were controlled by verbal rules called *me*. The *me* were like little programs for humans. They were a necessary part of the transition from caveman society to an organized, agricultural society. For example, there was a program for plowing a furrow in the ground and planting grain. There was a program for baking bread and another one for making a house. There were also *me* for higher-level functions such as war, diplomacy, and religious ritual. All the skills required to operate a self-sustaining culture were contained in these *me*, which were written down on tablets or passed around in an oral tradition. In any case, the repository for the *me* was the local temple, which was a database of *me*, controlled by a priest/king called an *en*. When someone needed bread, they would go to the *en* or one of his underlings and download the bread-making *me* from the temple. Then they would carry out the instructions—run the program—and when they were finished, they'd have a loaf of bread.

"A central database was necessary, among other reasons, because some of the *me* had to be properly timed. If people carried out the plowing-and-planting *me* at the wrong time of year, the harvest would fail and everyone would starve. The only way to make sure that the *me* were properly timed was to build astronomical observatories to watch the skies for the changes of season. So the Sumerians built towers 'with their tops with the heavens'—topped with astronomical diagrams. The *en* would watch the skies and dispense the agricultural *me* at the proper times of year to keep the economy running."

"I think you have a chicken-and-egg problem," Uncle Enzo says. "How did such a society first come to be organized?"

"There is an informational entity known as the metavirus, which causes information systems to infect themselves with customized viruses. This may be just a basic principle of nature, like Darwinian selection, or it may be an actual piece of information that floats around the universe on comets and radio waves—I'm not sure. In any case, what it comes down to is this: Any information system of sufficient complexity will inevitably become infected with viruses—viruses generated from within itself.

"At some point in the distant past, the metavirus infected the human race and has been with us ever since. The first thing it did was to spawn a whole Pandora's box of DNA viruses—smallpox, influenza, and so on. Health and longevity became a thing of the past. A distant memory of this event is preserved in legends of the Fall from Paradise, in which mankind was ejected from a life of ease into a world infested with disease and pain.

"That plague eventually reached some kind of a plateau. We still see new DNA viruses from time to time, but it seems that our bodies have developed a resistance to DNA viruses in general."

"Perhaps," Ng says, "there are only so many viruses that will work in the human DNA, and the metavirus has created all of them."

"Could be. Anyway, Sumerian culture—the society based on *me*—was another manifestation of the metavirus. Except that in this case, it was in a linguistic form rather than DNA."

"Excuse me," Mr. Lee says. "You are saying that civilization started out as an infection?"

"Civilization in its primitive form, yes. Each *me* was a sort of virus, kicked out by the metavirus principle. Take the example of the bread-baking *me*. Once that *me* got into society, it was a self-sustaining piece of information. It's a simple question of natural selection: people who know how to bake bread will live better and be more apt to reproduce than people who don't know how. Naturally, they will spread the *me*, acting as hosts for this self-replicating piece of information. That makes it a virus. Sumerian culture—with its temples full of *me*—was just a collection of successful viruses that had accumulated over the millennia. It was a franchise operation, except it had ziggurats instead of golden arches, and clay tablets instead of three-ring binders.

"The Sumerian word for 'mind,' or 'wisdom,' is identical to the word for 'ear.' That's all those people were: ears with bodies attached. Passive receivers of information. But Enki was different. Enki was an *en* who just happened to be especially good at his job. He had the unusual ability to write new *me*—he was a hacker. He was, actually, the first modern man, a fully conscious human being, just like us.

"At some point, Enki realized that Sumer was stuck in a rut. People were carrying out the same old *me* all the time, not coming up with new ones, not thinking for themselves. I suspect that he was lonely, being one of the few—perhaps the only—conscious human being in the world. He realized that in order for the human race to advance, they had to be delivered from the grip of this viral civilization.

"So he created the nam-shub of Enki, a countervirus that spread along the same routes as the *me* and the metavirus. It went into the deep structures of the brain and reprogrammed them. Henceforth, no one could understand the Sumerian language, or any other deep structure–based language. Cut off from our common deep structures, we began to develop new languages that had nothing in common with each other. The *me* no longer worked and it was not possible to write new *me*. Further transmission of the metavirus was blocked."

"Why didn't everyone starve from lack of bread, having lost the bread-making *me?*" Uncle Enzo says.

"Some probably did. Everyone else had to use their higher brains and figure it out. So you might say that the nam-shub of Enki was the beginnings of human consciousness—when we first had to think for ourselves. It was the beginning of rational religion, too, the first time that people began to think about abstract issues like God and Good and Evil. That's where the name Babel comes from. Literally it means 'Gate of God.' It was the gate that allowed God to reach the human race. Babel is a gateway in our minds, a gateway that was opened by the nam-shub of Enki that broke us free from the metavirus and gave us the ability to think—moved us from a materialistic world to a dualistic world—a binary world—with both a physical and a spiritual component.

"There was probably chaos and upheaval. Enki, or his son Marduk, tried to reimpose order on society by supplanting the old system of *me* with a code of laws—The Code of Hammurabi.

It was partially successful. Asherah worship continued in many places, though. It was an incredibly tenacious cult, a throwback to Sumer, that spread itself both verbally and through the exchange of bodily fluids—they had cult prostitutes, and they also adopted orphans and spread the virus to them via breast milk."

"Wait a minute," Ng says. "Now you are talking about a biological virus again."

"Exactly. That's the whole point of Asherah. It's both. As an example, look at herpes simplex. Herpes heads straight for the nervous system when it enters the body. Some strains stay in the peripheral nervous system, but other strains head like a bullet for the *central* nervous system and take up permanent residence in the cells of the brain—coiling around the brainstem like a serpent around a tree. The Asherah virus, which may be related to herpes, or they may be one and the same, passes through the cell walls and goes to the nucleus and messes with the cell's DNA in the same way that steroids do. But Asherah is a lot more complicated than a steroid."

"And when it alters that DNA, what is the result?"

"No one has studied it, except maybe for L. Bob Rife. I think it definitely brings the mother tongue closer to the surface, makes people more apt to speak in tongues and more susceptible to *me*. I would guess that it also tends to encourage irrational behavior, maybe lowers the victim's defenses to viral ideas, makes them sexually promiscuous, perhaps all of the above."

"Does every viral idea have a biological virus counterpart?" Uncle Enzo says.

"No. Only Asherah does, as far as I know. That is why, of all the *me* and all the gods and religious practices that predominated in Sumer, only Asherah is still going strong today. A viral idea can be stamped out—as happened with Nazism, bell bottoms, and Bart Simpson T-shirts—but Asherah, because it has a biological aspect, can remain latent in the human body. After Babel, Asherah was still resident in the human brain, being passed on from mother to child and from lover to lover.

"We are all susceptible to the pull of viral ideas. Like mass hysteria. Or a tune that gets into your head that you keep on humming all day until you spread it to someone else. Jokes. Urban legends. Crackpot religions. Marxism. No matter how smart we get, there is always this deep irrational part that makes us potential hosts for self-replicating information. But being physically infected with a virulent strain of the Asherah virus makes you a whole lot more susceptible. The only thing that keeps these things from taking over the world is the Babel factor—the walls of mutual incomprehension that compartmentalize the human race and stop the spread of viruses.

"Babel led to an explosion in the number of languages. That was part of Enki's plan. Monocultures, like a field of corn, are susceptible to infections, but genetically diverse cultures, like a prairie, are extremely robust. After a few thousand years, one new language developed—Hebrew—that possessed exceptional flexibility and power. The deuteronomists, a group of radical monotheists in the sixth and seventh centuries B.C., were the first to take advantage of it. They lived in a time of extreme nationalism and xenophobia, which made it easier for them to reject foreign ideas like Asherah worship. They formalized their old stories into the Torah and implanted within it a law that insured its propagation throughout history—a law that said, in effect, 'make an exact copy of me and read it every day.' And they encouraged a sort of informational hygiene, a belief in copying things strictly and taking great care with information, which as they understood, is potentially dangerous. They made data a controlled substance.

"They may have gone beyond that. There is evidence of carefully planned biological warfare against the army of Sennacherib when he tried to conquer Jerusalem. So the deuteronomists may have had an *en* of their very own. Or maybe they just understood viruses well enough that they knew how to take advantage of naturally occurring strains. The skills cultivated by these people were passed down in secret from one generation to the next and manifested themselves two thousand years later, in Europe, among the kabbalistic sorcerers, ba'al shems, masters of the divine name.

"In any case, this was the birth of rational religion. All of the subsequent monotheistic religions—known by Muslims, appropriately, as religions of the Book—incorporated those ideas to some extent. For example, the Koran states over and over again that it is a transcript, an exact copy, of a book in Heaven. Naturally, anyone who believes that will not dare to alter the text in any way! Ideas such as these were so effective in preventing the spread of Asherah that, eventually, every square inch of the territory where the viral cult had once thrived—from India to Spain—was under the sway of Islam, Christianity, or Judaism.

"But because of its latency—coiled about the brainstem of those it infects, passed from one generation to the next—it always finds ways to resurface. In the case of Judaism, it came in the form of the Pharisees, who imposed a rigid legalistic theocracy on the Hebrews. With its rigid adherence to laws stored in a temple, administered by priestly types vested with civil authority, it resembled the old Sumerian system, and was just as stifling.

"The ministry of Jesus Christ was an effort to break Judaism out of this condition—sort of an echo of what Enki did. Christ's gospel is a new nam-shub, an attempt to take religion out of the temple, out of the hands of the priesthood, and bring the Kingdom of God to everyone. That is the message explicitly spelled out by his sermons, and it is the message symbolically embodied in the empty tomb. After the crucifixion, the apostles went to his tomb hoping to find his body and instead found nothing. The message was clear enough: We are not to idolize Jesus, because his ideas stand alone, his church is no longer centralized in one person but dispersed among all the people.

"People who were used to the rigid theocracy of the Pharisees couldn't handle the idea of a popular, nonhierarchical church. They wanted popes and bishops and priests. And so the myth of the Resurrection was added onto the gospels. The message was changed to a form of idolatry. In this new version of the gospels, Jesus came back to earth and organized a church, which later became the Church of the Eastern and Western Roman Empire—another rigid, brutal, and irrational theocracy.

"At the same time, the Pentecostal church was being founded. The early Christians spoke in tongues. The Bible says, 'And all were amazed and perplexed, saying to one another, "What does this mean?" ' Well, I think I may be able to answer that question. It was a viral outbreak. Asherah had been present, lurking in the population, ever since the triumph of the deuteronomists. The informational hygiene measures practiced by the Jews kept it suppressed. But in the early days of Christianity, there must have been a lot of chaos, a lot of radicals and free thinkers running around, flouting tradition. Throwbacks to the days of prerational religion. Throwbacks to Sumer. And sure enough, they all started talking to each other in the tongue of Eden.

"The mainline Christian church refused to accept glossolalia. They frowned on it for a few centuries and officially purged it at the Council of Constantinople in 381. The glossolalic cult remained on the fringes of the Christian world. The Church was willing to accept a little bit of xenoglossia if it helped convert heathens, as in the case of St. Louis Bertrand who converted thousands of Indians in the sixteenth century, spreading glossolalia across the continent faster than smallpox. But as soon as they were converted, those Indians were supposed to shut up and speak Latin like everyone else.

"The Reformation opened the door a little wider. But Pentecostalism didn't really take off until the year 1900, when a small group of Bible-college students in Kansas began to speak in tongues. They spread the practice to Texas. There it became known as the revival movement. It spread like wildfire, all across the United States, and then the world, reaching China and India in 1906. The twentieth century's mass media, high literacy rates, and high-speed transportation all served as superb vectors for the infection. In a packed revival hall or a Third World refugee encampment, glossolalia spread from one person to the next as fast as panic. By the eighties, the number of Pentecostals worldwide numbered in the tens of millions.

"And then came television, and the Reverend Wayne, backed up by the vast media power of L. Bob Rife. The behavior that the Reverend Wayne promulgates through his television shows, pamphlets, and franchises can be traced in an unbroken line back to the Pentecostal cults of early Christianity, and from there back to pagan glossolalia cults. The cult of Asherah lives. The Reverend Wayne's Pearly Gates is the cult of Asherah."

57

"Lagos figured all of this out. He was originally a researcher at the Library of Congress, later became part of CIC when it absorbed the Library. He made a living by discovering interesting things in the Library, facts no one else had bothered to dig up. He would organize these facts and sell them to people. Once he figured out all of this Enki/Asherah stuff, he went looking for someone who would pay for it and settled on L. Bob Rife, Lord of Bandwidth, owner of the fiber-optics monopoly, who at that time employed more programmers than anyone else on earth.

"Lagos, typically for a nonbusinessman, had a fatal flaw: he thought too small. He figured that with a little venture capital, this neurolinguistic hacking could be developed as a new technology that would enable Rife to maintain possession of information that had passed into the brains of his programmers. Which, moral considerations aside, wasn't a bad idea.

"Rife likes to think big. He immediately saw that this idea could be much more powerful. He took Lagos's idea and told Lagos himself to buzz off. Then he started dumping a lot of money into Pentecostal churches. He took a small church in Bayview, Texas, and built it up into a university. He took a small-time preacher, the Reverend Wayne Bedford, and made him more important than the Pope. He constructed a string of self-supporting religious franchises all over the world, and used his university, and its Metaverse campus, to crank out tens of thousands of missionaries, who fanned out all over the Third World and began converting people by the hundreds of thousands, just like St. Louis Bertrand. L. Bob Rife's glossolalia cult is the most successful religion since the creation of Islam. They do a lot of talking about Jesus, but like many self-described Christian churches, it has nothing to do with Christianity except that they use his name. It's a postrational religion.

"He also wanted to spread the biological virus as a promoter or enhancer of the cult, but he couldn't really get away with doing that through the use of cult prostitution because it is flagrantly anti-Christian. But one of the major functions of his Third World missionaries was to go out into the hinterlands and vaccinate people—and there was more than just vaccine in those needles.

"Here in the First World, everyone has already been vaccinated, and we don't let religious fanatics come up and poke needles into us. But we do take a lot of drugs. So for us, he devised a means for extracting the virus from human blood serum and packaged it as a drug known as Snow Crash.

"In the meantime, he got the Raft going as a way of transporting hundreds of thousands of his cultists from the wretched parts of Asia into the United States. The media image of the Raft is that it is a place of utter chaos, where thousands of different languages are spoken and there is no central authority. But it's not like that at all. It's highly organized and tightly controlled. These people are all talking to each other in tongues. L. Bob Rife has taken xenoglossia and perfected it, turned it into a science.

"He can control these people by grafting radio receivers into their skulls, broadcasting instructions—me—directly into their brainstems. If one person in a hundred has a receiver, he can act as the local en and distribute the me of L. Bob Rife to all the others. They will act out L. Bob Rife's instructions as though they have been programmed to. And right now, he has about a million of these people poised off the California coast.

"He also has a digital metavirus, in binary code, that can infect computers, or hackers, via the optic nerve."

"How did he translate it into binary form?" Ng says.

"I don't think he did. I think he found it in space. Rife owns the biggest radio astronomy network in the world. He doesn't do real astronomy with it—he just listens for signals from other planets. It stood to reason that sooner or later, one of his dishes would pick up the metavirus."

"How does that stand to reason?"

"The metavirus is everywhere. Anywhere life exists, the metavirus is there, too, propagating through it. Originally, it was spread around on comets. That's probably how life first came to the Earth, and that's probably how the metavirus came here also. But comets are slow, whereas radio waves are fast. In binary form, a virus can bounce around the universe at the speed of light. It infects a civilized planet, gets into its computers, reproduces, and inevitably gets broadcast on television or radio or whatever. Those transmissions don't stop at the edge of the atmosphere—they radiate out into space, forever. And if they hit a planet with another civilized culture, where people are listening to the stars the way Rife was doing, then that planet gets infected, too. I think that was Rife's plan, and I think it worked. Except that Rife was smart—he caught it in a controlled manner. He put it in a bottle. An informational warfare agent for him to use at his discretion. When it is placed into a computer, it snow-crashes the computer by causing it to infect itself with new viruses. But it is much more devastating when it goes into the mind of a hacker, a person who has an understanding of binary code built into the deep structures of his brain. The binary metavirus will destroy the mind of a hacker."

"So Rife can control two kinds of people," Ng says. "He can control Pentecostals by using *me* written in the mother tongue. And he can control hackers in a much more violent fashion by damaging their brains with binary viruses."

"Exactly."

"What do you think Rife wants?" Ng says.

"He wants to be Ozymandias, King of Kings. Look, it's simple: Once he converts you to his religion, he can control you with *me*. And he can convert millions of people to his religion because it spreads like a fucking virus—people have no resistance to it because no one is used to thinking about religion, people aren't rational enough to argue about this kind of thing. Basically, anyone who reads the *National Enquirer* or watches pro wrestling on TV is easy to convert. And with Snow Crash as a promoter, it's even easier to get converts.

"Rife's key realization was that there's no difference between modern culture and Sumerian. We have a huge workforce that is illiterate or aliterate and relies on TV—which is sort of an oral tradition. And we have a small, extremely literate power elite—the people who go into the Metaverse, basically—who understand that information is power, and who control society because they have this semimystical ability to speak magic computer languages.

"That makes us a big stumbling block to Rife's plan. People like L. Bob Rife can't do anything without us hackers. And even if he could convert us, he wouldn't be able to use us, because what we do is creative in nature and can't be duplicated by people running *me*. But he can threaten us with the blunt instrument of Snow Crash. That, I think, is what happened to Da5id. It may have been an experiment, just to see if Snow Crash worked on a real hacker, and it may have been a warning shot intended to demonstrate Rife's power to the hacker community. The message: If Asherah gets broadcast into the technological priesthood—"

"Napalm on wildflowers," Ng says.

"As far as I know, there's no way to stop the binary virus. But there's an antidote to Rife's bogus religion. The nam-shub of Enki still exists. He gave a copy to his son Marduk, who passed it on to Hammurabi. Now, Marduk may or may not have been a real person. The point is that Enki went out of his way to *leave the impression* that he had passed on his nam-shub in some form. In other words, he was planting a message that later generations of hackers were supposed to decode, if Asherah should rise again.

"I am fairly certain that the information we need is contained within a clay envelope that was excavated from the ancient Sumerian city of Eridu in southern Iraq ten years ago. Eridu was the seat of Enki; in other words, Enki was the local *en* of Eridu, and the temple of Eridu contained his *me*, including the nam-shub that we are looking for."

"Who excavated this clay envelope?"

"The Eridu dig was sponsored entirely by a religious university in Bayview, Texas."

"L. Bob Rife's?"

"You got it. He created an archaeology department whose sole function was to dig up the city of Eridu, locate the temple where Enki stored all of his *me*, and take it all home. L. Bob Rife wanted to reverse-engineer the skills that Enki possessed; by analyzing Enki's *me*, he wanted to create his very own neurolinguistic hackers, who could write new *me* that would become the ground rules, the program, for the new society that Rife wants to create."

"But among these *me* is a copy of the nam-shub of Enki," Ng says, "which is dangerous to Rife's plan."

"Right. He wanted that tablet, too—not to analyze but to keep to himself, so no one could use it against him."

"If you can obtain a copy of this nam-shub," Ng says, "what effect would it have?"

"If we could transmit the nam-shub of Enki to all of the *en* on the Raft, they would relay it to all of the Raft people. It would jam their mother-tongue neurons and prevent Rife from programming them with new *me*," Hiro says. "But we really need to get this done before the Raft breaks up—before the Refus all come ashore. Rife talks to his *en* through a central transmitter on the *Enterprise*, which I take to be a fairly short-range, line-of-sight type of thing. Pretty soon he'll use this system to distribute a big *me* that will cause all the Refus to come ashore as a unified army with coordinated marching orders. In other words, the Raft will break up, and after that it won't be possible to reach all of these people anymore with a single transmission. So we have to do it as soon as possible."

"Mr. Rife will be most unhappy," Ng predicts. "He will try to retaliate by unleashing Snow Crash against the technological priesthood."

"I know that," Hiro says, "but I can only worry about one thing at a time. I could use a little help here."

"Easier said than done," Ng says. "To reach the Core, one must fly over the Raft or drive a small boat through its midst. Rife has a million people there with rifles and missile launchers. Even high-tech weapons systems cannot defeat organized small-arms fire on a massive scale."

"Get some choppers out to this vicinity, then," Hiro says. "Something. Anything. If I can get my hands on the nam-shub of Enki and infect everyone on the Raft with it, then you can approach safely."

"We'll see what we can come up with," Uncle Enzo says.

"Fine," Hiro says. "Now, what about Reason?"

Ng mumbles something and a card appears in his hand. "Here's a new version of the system software," he says. "It should be a little less buggy."

"A little less?"

"No piece of software is ever bug free," Ng says.

Uncle Enzo says, "I guess there's a little bit of Asherah in all of us."

58

Hiro finds his own way out and takes the elevator all the way back down to the Street. When he exits the neon skyscraper, a black-and-white girl is sitting on his motorcycle, messing with the controls.

"Where are you?" she says.

"I'm on the Raft, too. Hey, we just made twenty-five million dollars."

He is sure that just this one time, Y.T. is going to be impressed by something that he says. But she's not.

"That'll buy me a really happening funeral when they mail me home in a piece of Tupperware," she says.

"Why would that happen?"

"I'm in trouble," she admits—for the first time in her life. "I think my boyfriend is going to kill me."

"Who's your boyfriend?"

"Raven."

If avatars could turn pale and woozy and have to sit down on the sidewalk, Hiro's would. "Now I know why he has POOR IMPULSE CONTROL tattooed across his forehead."

"This is great. I was hoping to get a little cooperation or at least maybe some advice," she says.

"If you think he's going to kill you, you're wrong, because if you were right, you'd be dead," Hiro says.

"Depends on your assumptions," she says. She goes on to tell him a highly entertaining story about a dentata.

"I'm going to try to help you," Hiro says, "but I'm not necessarily the safest guy on the Raft to hang out with, either."

"Did you hook up with your girlfriend yet?"

"No. But I have high hopes for that. Assuming I can stay alive."

"High hopes for what?"

"Our relationship."

"Why?" she asks. "What's changed between then and now?"

This is one of these utterly simple and obvious questions that is irritating because Hiro's not sure of the answer. "Well, I think I figured out what she was doing—why she came here."

"So?"

Another simple and obvious question. "So, I feel like I understand her now."

"You *do?*"

"Yeah, well, sort of."

"And is that supposed to be a *good* thing?"

"Well, sure."

"Hiro, you are such a geek. She's a woman, you're a dude. You're not *supposed* to understand her. That's *not* what she's after."

"Well, what is she after, do you suppose—keeping in mind that you've never actually met the woman, and that *you're* going out with Raven?"

"She doesn't want you to understand *her.* She knows *that's* impossible. She just wants you to understand *yourself.* Everything else is negotiable."

"You figure?"

"Yeah. Definitely."

"What makes you think I don't understand myself?"

"It's just obvious. You're a really smart hacker and the greatest sword fighter in the world—and you're delivering pizzas and promoting concerts that you don't make any money off of. How do you expect her to—"

The rest is drowned out by sound breaking in through his earphones, coming in from Reality: a screeching, tearing noise riding in high and sharp above the rumbling noise of heavy impact. Then there is just the screaming of terrified neighborhood children, the cries of men in Tagalog, and the groaning and popping sound of a steel fishing trawler collapsing under the pressure of the sea.

"What was that?" Y.T. says.

"Meteorite," Hiro says.

"Huh?"

"Stay tuned," Hiro says, "I think I just got into a Gatling gun duel."

"Are you going to sign off?"

"Just shut up for a second."

This neighborhood is U-shaped, built around a sort of cove in the Raft where half a dozen rusty old fishing boats are tied up. A floating pier, pieced together from mismatched pontoons, runs around the edge.

The empty trawler, the one they've been cutting up for scrap, has been hit by a burst from the big gun on the deck of the *Enterprise*. It looks as though a big wave picked it up and tried to wrap it around a pillar: one whole side is collapsed in, the bow and the stern are actually bent toward each other. Its back is broken. Its empty holds are ingurgitating a vast, continuous rush of murky brown seawater, sucking in that variegated sewage like a drowning man sucks air. It's heading for the bottom fast.

Hiro shoves Reason back into the zodiac, jumps in, and starts the motor. He doesn't have time to untie the boat from the pontoon, so he snaps through the line with his wakizashi and takes off.

The pontoons are already sagging inward and down, pulled together by the ruined ship's mooring lines. The trawler is falling off the surface of the water, trying to pull in the entire neighborhood like a black hole.

A couple of Filipino men are already out with short knives, hacking at the stuff that webs the neighborhood together, trying to cut loose the parts that can't be salvaged. Hiro buzzes over to a pontoon that is already knee-deep under the water, finds the ropes that connect it to the next pontoon, which is even more deeply submerged, and probes them with his katana. The remaining ropes pop like rifle shots, and then the pontoon breaks loose, shooting up to the surface so fast that it almost capsizes the zodiac.

A whole section of the pontoon pier, along the side of the trawler, can't be salvaged. Men with fishing knives and women with kitchen cleavers are down on their knees, the water already rising up under their chins, cutting their neighborhood free. It breaks loose one rope at a time, haphazardly, tossing the Filipinos up into the air. A boy with a machete cuts the one remaining line, which pops up and lashes him across the face. Finally, the raft is free and flexible once again, bobbing and waving back toward equilibrium, and where the trawler was, there's nothing but a bubbling whirlpool that occasionally vomits up a loose piece of floating debris.

Some others have already clambered up onto the fishing boat that was tied up next to the trawler. It has suffered some damage, too: several men cluster around and lean over the rail to examine a couple of large impact craters on the side. Each hole is surrounded by a shiny dinner plate–sized patch that has been blown free of all paint and rust. In the middle is a hole the size of a golf ball.

Hiro decides it's time to leave.

But before he does, he reaches into his coverall, pulls out a money clip, and counts out a few thousand Kongbucks. He puts them on the deck and weighs them down under the corner of a red steel gasoline tank. Then he hits the road.

He has no trouble finding the canal that leads to the next neighborhood. His paranoia level is way up, and so he glances back and forth as he pilots his way out of there, looking up all the little alleys. In one of those niches, he sees a wirehead, mumbling something.

The next neighborhood is Malaysian. Several dozen of them are gathered near the bridge, attracted by the noise. As Hiro is entering their neighborhood, he sees men running down the undulating pontoon bridge that serves as the main street, carrying guns and knives. The local constabulary. More men of the same description emerge from the byways and skiffs and sampans, joining them.

A tremendous whacking and splintering and tearing noise sounds right beside him, as though a lumber truck has just crashed into a brick wall. Water splashes his body, and an exhalation of steam passes over his face. Then it's quiet again. He turns around, slowly and reluctantly. The nearest pontoon isn't there anymore, just a bloody, turbulent soup of splinters and chaff.

He turns around and looks behind him. The wirehead he saw a few seconds ago is out in the open now, standing all by himself at the edge of a raft. Everyone else has cleared out of there. He can see the bastard's lips moving. Hiro whips the boat around and returns to him, drawing his wakizashi with his free hand, and cuts him down on the spot.

But there will be more. Hiro knows they're all out looking for him now. The gunners up there on the *Enterprise* don't care how many of these Refus they have to kill in order to nail Hiro.

From the Malaysian neighborhood, he passes into a Chinese neighborhood. This one's a lot more built up, it contains a number of steel ships and barges. It extends off into the distance, away from the Core, for as far as Hiro can see from his worthless sea-level vantage point.

He's being watched by a man high up in the superstructure of one of those Chinese ships, another wirehead. Hiro can see the guy's jaw flapping as he sends updates to Raft Central.

The big Gatling gun on the deck of the *Enterprise* opens up again and fires another meteorite of depleted uranium slugs into the side of an unoccupied barge about twenty feet from Hiro. The entire side of the barge chases itself inward, like the steel has become liquid and is running down a drain, and the metal turns bright as shock waves simply turn that thick layer of rust into an aerosol, blast it free from the steel borne on a wave of sound so powerful that it hurts Hiro down inside his chest and makes him feel sick.

The gun is radar controlled. It's very accurate when it's shooting at a piece of metal. It's a lot less accurate when it's trying to hit flesh and blood.

"Hiro? What the fuck's going on?" Y.T. is shouting into his earphones.

"Can't talk. Get me to my office," Hiro says. "Pull me onto the back of the motorcycle and then drive it there."

"I don't know how to drive a motorcycle," she says.

"It's only got one control. Twist the throttle and it goes."

And then he points his boat out toward the open water and drills it. Dimly superimposed on Reality, he can see the black-and-white figure of Y.T. sitting in front of him on the motorcycle; she reaches out for the throttle and both of them jerk forward and slam into the wall of a skyscraper at Mach 1.

He turns off his view of the Metaverse entirely, making the goggles totally transparent. Then he switches his system into full gargoyle mode: enhanced visible light with false-color infrared, plus millimeter-wave radar.

His view of the world goes into grainy black and white, much brighter than it was before. Here and there, certain objects glow fuzzily in pink or red. This comes from the infrared, and it means that these things are warm or hot; people are pink, engines and fires are red.

The millimeter-wave radar stuff is superimposed much more cleanly and crisply in neon green. Anything made of metal shows up. Hiro is now navigating down a grainy, charcoal-gray avenue of water lined with grainy, light gray pontoon bridges tied up to crisp neon-green barges and ships that glow reddishly from place to place, wherever they are generating heat. It's not pretty. In fact, it's so ugly that it probably explains why gargoyles are, in general, so socially retarded. But it's a lot more useful than the charcoal-on-ebony view he had before.

And it saves his life. As he's buzzing down a curving, narrow canal, a narrow green parabola appears hanging across the water in front of him, suddenly rising out of the water and snapping into a perfectly straight line at neck level. It's a piece of piano wire. Hiro ducks under it, waves to the young Chinese men who set the booby trap, and keeps going.

The radar picks out three fuzzy pink individuals holding Chinese AK-47s standing by the side of the channel. Hiro cuts into a side channel and avoids them. But it's a narrower channel, and he's not sure where it goes.

"Y.T.," he says, "where the hell are we?"

"Driving down the street toward your house. We overshot it about six times."

Up ahead, the channel dead-ends. Hiro does a one-eighty. With the big heat exchanger dragging behind it, the boat is not nearly as maneuverable or as fast as Hiro wants it to be. He passes back underneath the booby-trap wire and starts exploring another narrow channel that he passed earlier.

"Okay, we're home. You're sitting at your desk," Y.T. says.

"Okay," Hiro says, "this is going to be tricky."

He coasts down to a dead stop in the middle of the channel, makes a scan for militia men and wireheads, and finds none. There is a five-foot-tall Chinese woman in the boat next to him holding a square cleaver, chopping something. Hiro figures it's a risk he can handle, so he turns off Reality and returns to the Metaverse.

He's sitting at his desk. Y.T. is standing next to him, arms crossed, radiating Attitude.

"Librarian?"

"Yes, sir," the Librarian says, padding in.

"I need blueprints of the aircraft carrier *Enterprise*. Fast. If you can get me something in 3-D, that'd be great."

"Yes, sir," the Librarian says.

Hiro reaches out and grabs Earth.

"YOU ARE HERE," he says.

Earth spins around until he's staring straight down at the Raft. Then it plunges toward him at a terrifying rate. It takes all of three seconds for him to get there.

If he were in some normal, stable part of the world like lower Manhattan, this would actually work in 3-D. Instead, he's got to put up with two-dimensional satellite imagery. He is looking at a red dot superimposed on a black-and-white photograph of the Raft. The red dot is in the middle of a narrow black channel of water: YOU ARE HERE.

It's still an incredible maze. But it's a lot easier to solve a maze when you're looking down on it. Within about sixty seconds, he's out in the open Pacific. It's a foggy gray dawn. The plume of steam coming out of Reason's heat exchanger just thickens it a little.

"Where the hell are you?" Y.T. says.

"Leaving the Raft."

"Gee, thanks for all your help."

"I'll be back in a minute. I just need a second to get myself organized."

"There's a lot of scary guys around here," Y.T. says. "They're watching me."

"It's okay," Hiro says. "I'm sure they'll listen to Reason."

59

He flips open the big suitcase. The screen is still on, showing him a flat desktop display with a menu bar at the top. He uses a trackball to pull down a menu:

HELP
Getting ready
Firing Reason
Tactical tips
Maintenance
Resupply
Troubleshooting
Miscellaneous

Under the "Getting ready" heading is more information than he could possibly want on that subject, including half an hour of badly overexposed video starring a stocky, scar-faced Asian guy whose face seems paralyzed into a permanent look of disdain. He puts on his clothes. He limbers up with special stretching exercises. He opens up Reason. He checks the barrels for damage or dirt. Hiro fast-forwards through all of this.

Finally the stocky Asian man puts on the gun.

Fisheye wasn't really using Reason the right way; it comes with its own mount that straps to your body so that you can soak up the recoil with your pelvis, taking the force right in your body's center of gravity. The mount has shock absorbers and miniature hydraulic goodies to compensate for the weight and the recoil. If you put all this stuff on the right way, the gun's a lot easier to use accurately. And if you're goggled into a computer, it'll superimpose a handy cross hairs over whatever the gun's aimed at.

"Your information, sir," the Librarian says.

"Are you smart enough to tie that information into YOU ARE HERE?" Hiro says.

"I'll see what I can do, sir. The formats appear to be reconcilable. Sir?"

"Yes?"

"These blueprints are several years old. Since they were made, the *Enterprise* has been purchased by a private owner—"

"Who may have made some changes. Gotcha."

Hiro's back in Reality.

He finds an open boulevard of water that leads inward to the Core. It has a sort of pedestrian catwalk running along one side of it, pieced together haphazardly, a seemingly endless procession of gangplanks, pontoons, logs, abandoned skiffs, aluminum canoes, oil drums. Anywhere else in the world, it would be an obstacle course; here in the Fifth World, it's a superhighway.

Hiro takes the boat straight down the middle, not very fast. If he runs into something, the boat might flip. Reason will sink. And Hiro's strapped onto Reason.

Flipping into gargoyle mode, he can clearly make out a sparse picket line of hemispherical domes running along the edge of the *Enterprise*'s flight deck. The radar gear thoughtfully identifies these, onscreen, as the radar antennas of Phalanx antimissile guns. Underneath each dome, a multibarreled gun protrudes.

He slows to a near stop and waves the barrel of Reason back and forth for a while until a cross hairs whips across his field of vision. That's the aiming point. He gets it settled down in the middle, right on one of those Phalanx guns, and jerks the trigger for half a second.

The big dome turns into a fountain of jagged, flaky debris. Underneath it, the gun barrels are still visible, speckled with a few red marks; Hiro lowers the cross hairs a tad and fires another fifty-round burst that cuts the gun loose from its mount. Then its ammunition belt starts to burst sporadically, and Hiro has to look away.

He looks at the next Phalanx gun and finds himself staring straight down its barrels. That's so scary he jerks the trigger involuntarily and fires a long burst that appears to do nothing at all. Then his view is obscured by something close up; the recoil has pushed him back behind a decrepit yacht tied up along the side of the channel.

He knows what's going to happen next—the steam makes him easy to find—so he whips out of there. A second later, the yacht gets simply forced under the water by a burst from the big gun.

Hiro runs for a few seconds, finds a pontoon where he can steady himself, and opens up again with a long burst; when he's finished, the edge of the *Enterprise* has a jagged semicircular bite taken out of it where the Phalanx gun used to be.

He takes to the main channel again and follows it inward until it terminates beneath one of the Core ships, a containership converted into a high-rise apartment complex. A cargo net serves as a ramp from one to the other. It probably serves as a drawbridge also, when undesirables try to clamber up out of the ghetto. Hiro is about as undesirable as anyone can be on the Raft, but they leave the cargo net there for him.

That's quite all right. He's staying on the little boat for now. He buzzes down the side of the containership, makes a U-turn around its prow.

The next vessel is a big oil tanker, mostly empty and riding high in the water. Looking up the sheer steel canyon separating the two ships, he sees no handy cargo nets stretched between them. They don't want thieves or terrorists to come up onto the tanker and drill for oil.

The next ship is the *Enterprise*.

The two giant vessels, the tanker and the aircraft carrier, ride parallel, anywhere from ten to fifty feet apart, joined by a number of gigantic cables and held apart by huge airbags, like they squished a few blimps between them to keep them from rubbing. The heavy cables aren't just lashed from one ship to another; they've done something clever with weights and pulleys, he suspects, to allow for some slack when rough seas pull the ships opposite ways.

Hiro rides his own little airbag in between them. This gray steel tunnel is quiet and isolated compared to the Raft; except for him, no one has any reason to be here. For a minute, he just wants to sit there and relax.

Which is not too likely, when you think about it. "YOU ARE HERE," he says.

His view of the *Enterprise*'s hull—a gently curved expanse of gray steel—turns into a three-dimensional wire frame drawing, showing him all the guts of the ship on the other side.

Down here along the waterline, the *Enterprise* has a belt of thick antitorpedo armor. It's not too promising. Farther up, the armor is thinner, and there's good stuff on the other side of it, actual rooms instead of fuel tanks or ammunition holds.

Hiro chooses a room marked WARDROOM and opens fire.

The hull of the *Enterprise* is surprisingly tough. Reason doesn't just blow a crater straight through; it takes a few moments for the burst to penetrate. And then all it does is make a hole about six inches across. The recoil pushes Hiro back against the rusted hull of the oil tanker.

He can't take the gun with him anyway. He holds the trigger down and just tries to keep it aimed in a consistent direction until all the ammunition is gone. Then he unstraps it from his body and dumps the whole thing overboard. It'll go to the bottom and mark its position with a column of steam; later, Mr. Lee's Greater Hong Kong can dispatch one of its environmental direct-action posses to pick it up. Then they can haul Hiro before the Tribunal of Environmental Crimes, if they want to. Right now he doesn't care.

It takes half a dozen tries to secure the grappling hook in the jagged hole, twenty feet above the waterline.

As he's wriggling through the hole, his coverall makes popping and hissing noises as the hot, sharp metal melts and tears through the synthetic material. He ends up leaving scraps of it behind, welded to the hull. He's got a few first- and second-degree burns on the parts of his skin that are now exposed, but they don't really hurt yet. That's how wound up he is. Later, they'll hurt. The soles of his shoes melt and sizzle as he treads on glowing hunks of shrapnel. The room is rather smoky, but aircraft carriers are nothing if not fire conscious, and not too much in this place is flammable. Hiro just walks through the smoke to the door, which has been carved into a steel doily by Reason. He kicks it out of its frame and enters a place that, in the blueprints, is simply marked PASSAGEWAY. Then, because this seems as good a time as any, he draws his katana.

60

When her partner is off doing something in Reality, his avatar goes kind of slack. The body sits there like an inflatable love doll, and the face continues to go through all kinds of stretching exercises. She does not know what he's doing, but it looks like it must be exciting, because most of the time he's either extremely surprised or scared shitless.

Shortly after he gets done talking to the Librarian dude about the aircraft carrier, she begins to hear deep rumbling noises—Reality noises—from outside. Sounds like a cross between a machine gun and a buzz saw. Whenever she hears that noise, Hiro's face gets this astonished look like: I'm about to die.

Someone is tapping her on the shoulder. Some suit who has an early morning appointment in the Metaverse, figures that whatever this Kourier is doing can't be all that important. She ignores it for a minute.

Then Hiro's office goes out of focus, jumps up in the air like it is painted on a window shade, and she's looking into the face of a guy. An Asian guy. A creep. A wirehead. One of the scary antenna dudes.

"Okay," she says, "what do you want?"

He grabs her by the arm and hauls her out of the booth. There's another one with him, and he grabs her other arm. They all start walking out of there.

"Let go my fucking arm," she says. "I'll go with you. It's okay."

It's not the first time she's been thrown out of a building full of suits. This time it's a little different, though. This time, the bouncers are a couple of life-sized plastic action figures from Toys R Us.

And it's not just that these guys probably don't speak English. They just don't act normal. She actually manages to twist one of her arms loose and the guy doesn't smack her or anything, just turns rigidly toward her and paws at her mechanically until he's got her by the arm again. No change in his face. His eyes stare like busted headlights. His mouth is open enough to let him breathe through it, but the lips never move, never change expression.

They are in a complex of ship cabins and sliced-open containers that acts as the lobby of the hotel. The wireheads drag her out the door, over the blunt cross hairs of the helipad. Just in time, too, because a chopper happens to be coming in for a landing. The safety procedures in this place suck; they could have got their heads chopped off. It is the slick corporate chopper with the RARE logo that she saw earlier.

The wireheads try to drag her over a gangplank thingy that leads them across open water to the next ship. She manages to get turned around backward, grabs the railings with both hands, hooks her ankles into the stanchions, and hangs on. One of them grabs her around the waist from behind and tries to yank her body loose while the other one stands in front of her and pries her fingers loose, one at a time.

Several guys are piling out of the RARE chopper. They are wearing coveralls with gear stuck into the pockets, and she sees at least one stethoscope. They haul big fiberglass cases out of the chopper, with red crosses painted on their sides, and run into the containership. Y.T. knows that this is not being done for the benefit of some fat businessman who stroked a lobe over his stewed prunes. They are going in there to reanimate her boyfriend. Raven pumped full of speed: just what the world needs right now.

They drag her across the deck of the next ship. From there they take a stairway thingy up to the next ship after that, which is very big. She thinks it's an oil tanker. She can look across its broad deck, through a tangle of pipes, rust seeping through white paint, and see the *Enterprise* on the other side. That's where they're going.

There's no direct connection. A crane on the deck of the *Enterprise* has swung itself over to dangle a small wire cage over the tanker, just a few feet off the deck; it bobs up and down and glides back and forth over a fairly large area as the two ships rock in different ways and it swings like a pendulum at the end of its cable. It has a door on one side, which is hanging open.

They sort of toss her into it head first, keeping her arms pinned to her sides so she can't push it away from her, and then they spend a few seconds folding her legs in behind her. It's obvious by now that talking doesn't work, so she just fights silently. She manages to give one of them a good stomp to the bridge of the nose, and both feels and hears the bone break, but the man doesn't react in any way, other than snapping his head back on impact. She's so busy watching him, waiting to see when he's going to figure out that his nose is broken and that she's responsible for it, that she stops kicking and flailing long enough to get all shoved into the cage. Then the door snaps shut.

An experienced raccoon could get the latch open. This cage isn't made to hold people. But by the time she gets her body worked around to the point where she can reach it, she's twenty feet above the deck, looking down on a lead of black water between the tanker and the *Enterprise*. Down below, she can see an abandoned zodiac caroming back and forth between the steel walls.

Not everything is exactly right on the *Enterprise*. Something is burning somewhere. People are firing guns. She's not entirely sure she wants to be there. As long as she is high up in the air, she reconnoiters the ship and confirms that there is no way off, no handy gangplanks or stairway thingies.

She is being lowered toward the *Enterprise*. The cage is careening back and forth, skimming just over the deck on its cable, and when it finally touches the deck, it skids for a few feet before coming to a halt. She pops the latch and climbs out of there. Now what?

There's a bullseye painted on the deck, a few helicopters parked around the edges and lashed down. And there is one helicopter, a mammoth twin-engine jet number, kind of a flying bathtub festooned with guns and missiles, sitting right in the middle of the bullseye, all of its lights on, engine whining, rotors spinning desultorily. A small cluster of men is standing next to it.

Y.T. walks toward it. She hates this. She knows this is exactly what she's supposed to do. But there really is no other choice. She wishes, profoundly, that she had her plank with her. The deck of this aircraft carrier is some of the best skating territory she has ever seen. She has seen, in movies, that carriers have big steam catapults for throwing airplanes into the sky. Think of what it would be like to ride a steam catapult on your plank!

As she is walking toward the helicopter, one of the men standing by it detaches himself from the group and walks toward her.

He's big, with a body like a fifty-five-gallon drum, and a mustache that turns up at the corners. And as he comes toward her he is laughing in a satisfied way, which pisses her off.

"Well, don't you look like a forlorn lil thang!" he says. "Shit, honey, you look like a drowned rat that got dried out again."

"Thanks," she says. "You look like chiseled Spam."

"Very funny," he says.

"Then how come you're not laughing? Afraid it's true?"

"Look," he says, "I don't have time for this fucking adolescent banter. I grew up and got old 'pecifically to get away from this."

"It's not that you don't have time," she says. "It's that you're not very good at it."

"You know who I am?" he asks.

"Yeah, I know. You know who I am?"

"Y.T. A fifteen-year-old Kourier."

"And personal buddy of Uncle Enzo," she says, whipping off the string of dog tags and tossing them. He holds out one hand, startled, and the chain whips around his fingers. He holds them up and reads them.

"Well, well," he says, "this is quite a little memento." He throws them back at her. "I know you're buddies with Uncle Enzo. Otherwise I just woulda dunked you instead a bringing you here to my spread. And I frankly don't give a shit," he says, "because by the time this day is through, either Uncle Enzo will be out of a job, or else I'll be, as you said, chiseled Spam. But I figure that the Big Wop will be a lot less likely to throw a Stinger through the turbine of my chopper there if he knows his little chiquita is on board."

"It's not like that," Y.T. says. "It's not a relationship where fucking is part of it." But she is chagrined to learn that the dog tags, after all this time, did not have any magical effect on the bad guys.

Rife turns around and starts walking back to the chopper. After a few steps, he turns back and looks at her, just standing there, trying not to cry. "You coming?" he says.

She looks at the chopper. A ticket off the Raft.

"Can I leave a note for Raven?"

"Far as Raven is concerned, I think you already made your

point—haw haw haw. Come on, girl, we're wasting jet fuel over there—that ain't good for the goddamn environment."

She follows him to the chopper, climbs on board. It's warm and light inside here, with nice seats. Like coming in off a hard February day of thrashing the grittier highways and settling into a padded easy chair.

"Had the interior redone," Rife says. "This is a big old Sov gunship and it wasn't made for comfort. But that's the price you pay for all that armor plating."

There's two other guys in here. One is about fifty, sort of gaunt, big pores, wire-rimmed bifocals, carrying a laptop. A techie. The other is a bulky African-American with a gun. "Y.T.," says the always polite L. Bob Rife, "meet Frank Frost, my tech director, and Tony Michaels, my security chief."

"Ma'am," says Tony.

"Howdy," says Frank.

"Suck my toes," says Y.T.

"Don't step on that, please," Frank says.

Y.T. looks down. Climbing into the empty seat nearest the door, she has stepped on a package resting on the floor. It's about the dimensions of a phone book, but irregular, very heavy, swaddled in bubble pack and clear plastic. She can see glimpses of what's inside. Light reddish brown in color. Covered with chicken scratches. Hard as a rock.

"What's that?" Y.T. says. "Homemade bread from Mom?"

"It's an ancient artifact," Frank says, all pissed off. Rife chuckles, pleased and relieved that Y.T. is now insulting someone else.

Another man duck-walks across the flight deck, in mortal fear of the whirling rotor blades, and climbs in. He's about sixty, with a dirigible of white hair that was not ruffled in any way by the downdraft.

"Hello, everyone," he says cheerfully. "I don't think I've met all of you. Just got here this morning and now I'm on my way back again!"

"Who are you?" Tony says.

The new guy looks crestfallen. "Greg Ritchie," he says.

Then, when no one seems to react, he jogs their memory. "President of the United States."

"Oh! Sorry. Nice to meet you, Mr. President," Tony says, extending his hand. "Tony Michaels."

"Frank Frost," Frank says, extending his hand and looking bored.

"Don't mind me," Y.T. says, when Ritchie looks her way. "I'm a hostage."

"Torque this baby," Rife says to the pilot. "Let's go to L.A. We got a Mission to Control."

The pilot has an angular face that, after her experiences on the Raft, Y.T. recognizes as typically Russian. He starts dicking with his controls. The engines whine louder and the thwacking of the chopper blades picks up. Y.T. feels, but does not hear, a couple of small explosions. Everyone else feels it, too, but only Tony reacts; he crouches down on the floor of the chopper, pulls a gun out from under his jacket, and opens the door on his side. Meanwhile, the engines sigh back down in pitch and the rotor coasts back down to an idle.

Y.T. can see him out the window. It's Hiro. He's all covered with smoke and blood, and he's holding a pistol in one hand. He's just fired a couple of shots in the air, to get their attention, and now he backs behind one of the parked choppers, taking cover.

"You're a dead man," Rife shouts. "You're stuck on the Raft, asshole. I got a million Myrmidons here. You gonna kill 'em all?"

"Swords don't run out of ammo," Hiro shouts.

"Well, what do you want?"

"I want the tablet. You give me the tablet, then you can take off and let your million wireheads kill me. You don't give me the tablet, I'm gonna empty this clip into the windshield of your chopper."

"It's bulletproof! Haw!" Rife says.

"No it isn't," Hiro says, "as the rebels in Afghanistan found out."

"He is right," the pilot says.

"Fucking Soviet piece of shit! They put all that steel in its belly and then made the windshield out of *glass*?"

"Give me the tablet," Hiro says, "or I'm taking it."

"No you ain't," Rife says, "cause I got Tinkerbell here."

At the last minute, Y.T. tries to duck down and hide, so he

won't see her. She's ashamed. But Hiro locks eyes with her for just a moment, and she can see the defeat come into his face.

She makes a dive for the door and gets halfway out, under the downblast of the rotors. Tony grabs her coverall's collar and hauls her back inside. He shoves her down on her belly and puts one knee in the small of her back to hold her there. Meanwhile, the engine is powering up again, and out the open door she can see the steel horizon of the carrier's deck drop from view.

After all this time, she fucked up the plan. She owes Hiro a refund.

Or maybe not.

She puts the heel of one hand against the edge of the clay tablet and shoves as hard as she can. It slides across the floor, teeters on the threshold, and spins out of the chopper.

Another delivery made, another satisfied customer.

61

For a minute or so, the chopper hovers twenty feet overhead. All the people inside are staring down at the tablet, which has burst out of its wrappings in the middle of the bullseye. The plastic has torn apart around the corners and fragments—large fragments—of the tablet have sprayed out for a few feet in either direction.

Hiro stares at it, too, still safe behind the cover of a parked chopper. He stares at it so hard that he forgets to stare at anything else. Then a couple of wireheads land on his back, smashing his face into the flank of the chopper. He slides down and lands on his belly. His gun arm is still free, but a couple more wireheads sit on that. A couple on his legs, too. He can't move at all. He can't see anything but the broken tablet, twenty feet away on the flight deck. The sound and wind of Rife's chopper diminish into a distant puttering noise that takes a long time to go away completely.

He feels a tingling behind his ear, anticipating the scalpel and the drill.

These wireheads are operating under remote control from
somewhere else. Ng seemed to think that they had an organized
Raft defense system. Maybe there's a hacker-in-charge, an *en*,
sitting in the *Enterprise*'s control tower, moving these guys
around like an air traffic controller.

In any case, they are not very big on spontaneity. They sit on
him for a few minutes before they decide what to do next. Then,
many hands reach down and clasp him around the wrists and
ankles, elbows and knees. They haul him across the flight deck
like pallbearers, face up. Hiro looks up into the control tower and
sees a couple of faces looking down at him. One of them—the
en—is talking into a microphone.

Eventually, they come to a big flat elevator that sinks down
into the guts of the ship, out of view of the control tower. It
comes to rest on one of the lower decks, apparently a hangar deck
where they used to maintain airplanes.

Hiro hears a woman's voice, speaking words gently but clearly:
"me lu lu mu al nu um me en ki me en me lu lu mu me al nu um
me al nu ume me me mu lu e al nu um me dug ga mu me mu lu
e al nu um me . . . "

It's three feet straight down to the deck, and he covers the
distance in free fall, slamming down on his back, bumping his
head. All his limbs bounce loosely on the metal. Around him he
sees and hears the wireheads collapsing like wet towels falling off
a rack.

He cannot move any part of his body. He has a little control
over his eyes. A face comes into view, and he has trouble resolv-
ing it, can't quite focus, but he recognizes something in her
posture, the way she tosses her hair back over her shoulder when
it falls down. It's Juanita. Juanita with an antenna rising out of
the base of her skull.

She kneels down beside him, bends down, cups one hand
around his ear, and whispers. The hot air tickles his ear, he tries
to move away from it but can't. She's whispering another long
string of syllables. Then she straightens up and gooses him in the
side. He jerks away from her.

"Get up, lazybones," she says.

He gets up. He's fine now. But all the wireheads lay around
him, perfectly motionless.

"Just a little nam-shub I whipped up," she says. "They'll be fine."

"Hi," he says.

"Hi. It's good to see you, Hiro. I'm going to give you a hug now—watch out for the antenna."

She does. He hugs her back. The antenna is upside his nose, but that's okay.

"Once we get this thing taken off, all the hair and stuff should grow back," she whispers. Finally, she lets him go. "That hug was really more for me than for you. It's been a lonely time here. Lonely and scary."

This is typically paradoxical behavior for Juanita—getting touchy-feely at a time like this.

"Don't get me wrong," Hiro says, "but aren't you one of the bad guys now?"

"Oh, you mean this?"

"Yeah. Don't you work for them?"

"If so, I'm not doing a very good job." She laughs, gesturing at the ring of motionless wireheads. "No. This doesn't work on me. It sort of did, for a while, but there are ways to fight it."

"Why? Why doesn't it work on you?"

"I've spent the last several years hanging around with Jesuits," she says. "Look. Your brain has an immune system, just like your body. The more you use it—the more viruses you get exposed to—the better your immune system becomes. And I've got a hell of an immune system. Remember, I was an atheist for a while, and then I came back to religion the hard way."

"Why didn't they screw you up the way they did Da5id?"

"I came here voluntarily."

"Like Inanna."

"Yes."

"Why would anyone come here voluntarily?"

"Hiro, don't you realize? This is it. This is the nerve center of a religion that is at once brand new and very ancient. Being here is like following Jesus or Mohammed around, getting to observe the birth of a new faith."

"But it's terrible. Rife is the Antichrist."

"Of course he is. But it's still interesting. And Rife has got something else going for him: Eridu."

"The city of Enki."

"Exactly. He's got every tablet Enki ever wrote. For a person who's interested in religion and hacking, this is the only place in the world to be. If those tablets were in Arabia, I'd put on a chador and burn my driver's license and go there. But the tablets are here, and so I let them wire me up instead."

"So all this time, your goal was to study Enki's tablets."

"To get the *me*, just like Inanna. What else?"

"And have you been studying them?"

"Oh, yes."

"And?"

She points to the fallen wireheads. "And I can do it now. I'm a ba'al shem. I can hack the brainstem."

"Okay, look. I'm happy for you, Juanita. But at the time being, we have a little problem. We are surrounded by a million people who want to kill us. Can you paralyze all of them?"

"Yes," she says, "but then they'd die."

"You know what we have to do, don't you, Juanita?"

"Release the nam-shub of Enki," she says. "Do the Babel thing."

"Let's go get it," Hiro says.

"First things first," Juanita says. "The control tower."

"Okay, you get ready to grab the tablet, and I'll take out the control tower."

"How are you going to do that? By cutting people up with swords?"

"Yeah. That's the only thing they're good for."

"Let's do it the other way around," Juanita says. She gets up and walks off across the hangar deck.

             The nam-shub of Enki is a tablet wrapped up in a clay envelope covered with the cuneiform equivalent of a warning sticker. The entire assembly has shattered into dozens of pieces. Most of them have stayed wrapped up inside the plastic, but some have gone spinning across the flight deck. Hiro gathers them up from the helipad and returns them to the center.

By the time he's got the plastic wrapper cut away, Juanita is waving to him from the windows on top of the control tower.

He takes all the pieces that look to be part of the envelope and puts them into a separate pile. Then he assembles the remains of the tablet itself into a coherent group. It's not obvious, yet, how to piece them together, and he doesn't have time for jigsaw puzzles. So he goggles into his office, uses the computer to take an electronic snapshot of the fragments, and calls the Librarian.

"Yes, sir?"

"This hypercard contains a picture of a shattered clay tablet. Do you know of some software that would be good at piecing it back together?"

"One moment, sir," the Librarian says. Then a hypercard appears in his hand. He gives it to Hiro. It contains a picture of an assembled tablet. "That's how it looks, sir."

"Can you read Sumerian?"

"Yes, sir."

"Can you read this tablet out loud?"

"Yes, sir."

"Get ready to do it. And hold on a second."

Hiro walks over to the base of the control tower. There's a door there that gives him access to a stairwell. He climbs up to the control room, a strange mixture of Iron Age and high-tech. Juanita's waiting there, surrounded by peacefully slumbering wireheads. She taps a microphone that is projecting from a communications panel at the end of a flexible gooseneck—the same mike that the *en* was speaking into.

"Live to the Raft," she says. "Go for it."

Hiro puts his computer into speakerphone mode and stands up next to the microphone. "Librarian, read it back," he says. And a string of syllables pours out of the speaker.

In the middle of it, Hiro glances up at Juanita. She's standing in the far corner of the room with her fingers stuck in her ears.

Down at the base of the stairs, a wirehead begins to talk. Deep down inside the *Enterprise,* there's more talking going on. And none of it makes any sense. It's just a lot of babbling.

There's an external catwalk on the control tower. Hiro goes out there and listens to the Raft. From all around them comes a dim roar, not of waves or wind, but of a million unchained human voices speaking in a confusion of tongues.

Juanita comes out to listen, too. Hiro sees a trickle of red under her ear.

"You're bleeding," he says.

"I know. A little bit of primitive surgery," she says. Her voice is strained and uncomfortable. "I've been carrying around a scalpel blade for cases like this."

"What did you do?"

"Slid it up under the base of the antenna and cut the wire that goes into my skull," she says.

"When did you do that?"

"While you were down on the flight deck."

"Why?"

"Why do you think?" she says. "So I wouldn't be exposed to the nam-shub of Enki. I'm a neurolinguistic hacker now, Hiro. I went through hell to obtain this knowledge. It's a part of me. Don't expect me to submit to a lobotomy."

"If we get out of this, will you be my girl?"

"Naturally," she says. "Now let's get out of it."

62

"I was just doing my job, man," she says. "This Enki dude wanted to get a message to Hiro, and I delivered it."

"Shut up," Rife says. He doesn't say it like he's pissed. He just wants her to be quiet. Because what she did doesn't make any difference now that all those wireheads have piled on top of Hiro.

Y.T. looks out the window. They are buzzing across the Pacific, keeping pretty low down so that the water skims quickly beneath them. She doesn't know how fast they're going, but it looks to be pretty damn fast. She always thought the ocean was supposed to be blue, but in fact it's the most boring gray color she's ever seen. And there's miles and miles of it.

After a few minutes, another chopper catches up with them and begins flying alongside, pretty close, in formation. It's the RARE chopper, the one full of medics.

Through its cabin window, she can see Raven sitting in one of the seats. At first she thinks he's still unconscious because he's kind of hunched over, not moving.

Then he lifts his head and she sees that he's goggled in to the Metaverse. He reaches up with one hand and pulls the goggles up onto his forehead for a moment, squints out the window, and sees her watching him. Their eyes meet and her heart starts flopping around weakly, like a bunny in a Ziploc bag. He grins and waves.

Y.T. sits back in her seat and pulls the shade down over the window.

63

From Hiro's front yard to L. Bob Rife's black cube at Port 127 is halfway around the Metaverse, a distance of 32,768 kilometers. The only hard part, really, is getting out of Downtown. He can ride his bike straight through the avatars as usual, but the Street is also cluttered with vehicles, animercials, commercial displays, public plazas, and other bits of solid-looking software that get in his way.

Not to mention a few distractions. Off to his right, about a kilometer away from The Black Sun, is a deep hole in the hyper-Manhattan skyline. It is an open plaza about a mile wide, a park of sorts where avatars can gather for concerts and conventions and festivals. Most of it is occupied by a deep-dish amphitheater that is capable of seating close to a million avatars at once. Down at the bottom is a huge circular stage.

Normally, the stage is occupied by major rock groups. Tonight, it is occupied by the grandest and most brilliant computer hallucinations that the human mind can invent. A three-dimensional marquee hangs above it, announcing tonight's event: a benefit graphics concert staged on behalf of Da5id Meier, who is still hospitalized with an inexplicable disease. The amphitheater is half filled with hackers.

Once he gets out of Downtown, Hiro twists his throttle up to the max and covers the remaining thirty-two thousand and some kilometers in the space of about ten minutes. Over his head, the express trains are whooshing down the track at a metaphorical speed of ten thousand miles per hour; he passes them like they're standing still. This only works because he's riding in an absolutely

straight line. He's got a routine coded into his motorcycle software that makes it follow the monorail track automatically so that
he doesn't even have to worry about steering it.

Meanwhile, Juanita's standing next to him in Reality. She's got
another pair of goggles; she can see all the same things that Hiro
sees.

"Rife's got a mobile uplink on his corporate chopper, just like
the one on commercial airliners, so he can patch into the Metaverse when he's in the air. As long as he's airborne, that's his only
link to the Metaverse. We may be able to hack our way into that
one link and block it or something. ... "

"That low-level communications stuff is too full of medicine
for us to mess with it in this decade," Hiro says, braking his
motorcycle to a stop. "Holy shit. It's just like Y.T. described it."

He's in front of Port 127. Rife's black cube is there, just as Y.T.
described it. There's no door.

Hiro starts walking away from the Street, toward the cube. It
reflects no light at all, so he can't tell whether it's ten feet or ten
miles away from him until the security daemons begin to materialize. There are half a dozen of them, all big sturdy avatars in blue
coveralls, sort of quasi-military looking, but without rank. They
don't need rank because they're all running the same program.
They materialize around him in a neat semicircle with a radius of
about ten feet, blocking Hiro's way to the cube.

Hiro mumbles a word under his breath and vanishes—he slips
into his invisible avatar. It would be very interesting to hang
around and see how these security daemons deal with it, but right
now he has to get moving before they get a chance to adjust.

They don't, at least not very well. Hiro runs between two of
the security daemons and heads for the wall of the cube. He
finally gets there, slamming into it, coming to a dead stop. The
security daemons have all turned around and are chasing him.
They can figure out where he is—the computer tells them that
much—but they can't do much to him. Like the bouncer daemons in The Black Sun, which Hiro helped write, they shove
people around by applying basic rules of avatar physics. When
Hiro is invisible, there is very little for them to shove. But if they
are well written, they may have more subtle ways of messing him

up, so he's not wasting any time. He pokes his katana through the side of the cube and follows it through the wall and out the other side.

This is a hack. It is really based on a very old hack, a loophole that he found years ago when he was trying to graft the sword-fighting rules onto the existing Metaverse software. His blade doesn't have the power to cut a hole in the wall—this would mean permanently changing the shape of someone else's build-ing—but it does have the power to penetrate things. Avatars do not have that power. That is the whole purpose of a wall in the Metaverse; it is a structure that does not allow avatars to pene-trate it. But like anything else in the Metaverse, this rule is noth-ing but a protocol, a convention that different computers agree to follow. In theory, it cannot be ignored. But in practice, it depends upon the ability of different computers to swap informa-tion very precisely, at high speed, and at just the right times. And when you are connected to the system over a satellite uplink, as Hiro is, out here on the Raft, there is a delay as the signals bounce up to the satellite and back down. That delay can be taken advan-tage of, if you move quickly and don't look back. Hiro passes right through the wall on the tail end of his all-penetrating katana.

Rifeland is a vast, brightly lit space occupied by elementary shapes done up in primary colors. It is like being inside an educa-tional toy designed to teach solid geometry to three-year-olds: cubes, spheres, tetrahedrons, polyhedrons, connected with a web of cylinders and lines and helices. But in this case, it has gone way, way out of control, as if every Tinkertoy set and Lego block ever made had been slapped together according to some long-forgotten scheme.

Hiro's been around the Metaverse long enough to know that despite the bright cheery appearance of this thing, it is, in fact, as simple and utilitarian as an Army camp. This is a model of a system. A big complicated system. The shapes probably repre-sent computers, or central nodes in Rife's worldwide network, or Pearly Gates franchises, or any other kind of local and regional offices that Rife has going around the world. By clambering over this structure and going into those bright shapes, Hiro could probably uncover some of the code that makes Rife's network operate. He could, perhaps, try to hack it up, as Juanita suggested.

But there is no point in messing with something he doesn't understand. He might waste hours fooling around with some piece of code only to find out that it was the software to control the automatic toilet flushers at Rife Bible College. So Hiro keeps moving, keeps looking up at the tangle of shapes, trying to find a pattern. He knows, now, that he has found his way into the boiler room of the entire Metaverse. But he has no idea what he's looking for.

This system, he realizes, really consists of several separate networks all tangled together in the same space. There's an extremely complicated tangle of fine red lines, millions of them, running back and forth between thousands of small red balls. Just as a wild guess, Hiro figures that this may represent Rife's fiberoptics network, with its innumerable local offices and nodes spread all over the world. There are a number of less complicated networks in other colors, which might represent coaxial lines, such as they used to use for cable television, or even voice phone lines.

And there is a crude, heavily built, blocky network all done up in blue. It consists of a small number—fewer than a dozen—of big blue cubes. They are connected to each other, but to nothing else, by massive blue tubes; the tubes are transparent, and inside of them, Hiro can see bundles of smaller connections in various colors. It has taken Hiro a while to see all of this, because the blue cubes are nearly obscured; they are all surrounded by little red balls and other small nodes, like trees being overwhelmed with kudzu. It appears to be an older, preexisting network of some kind, with its own internal channels, mostly primitive ones like voice phone. Rife has patched into it, heavily, with his own, higher-tech systems.

Hiro maneuvers until he can get a closer look at one of the blue cubes, peering through the clutter of lines that has grown around it. The blue cube has a big white star on each of its six faces.

"It's the Government of the United States," Juanita says.

"Where hackers go to die," Hiro says. The largest, and yet the least efficient, producer of computer software in the world.

Hiro and Y.T. have eaten a lot of junk food together in different joints all over L.A.—doughnuts, burritos, pizza, sushi, you name it—and all Y.T. ever talks about is her mother and the terrible job that she has with the Feds. The regimentation. The lie-detector tests. The fact that for all the work she does, she really has no idea what it is that the government is really working on.

It's always been a mystery to Hiro, too, but then, that's how the government is. It was invented to do stuff that private enterprise doesn't bother with, which means that there's probably no reason for it; you never know what they're doing or why. Hackers have traditionally looked upon the government's coding sweatshops with horror and just tried to forget that all of that shit ever existed.

But they have thousands of programmers. The programmers work twelve hours a day out of some twisted sense of personal loyalty. Their software-engineering techniques, while cruel and ugly, are very sophisticated. They must have been up to something.

"Juanita?"

"Yeah?"

"Don't ask me why I think this. But I think that the government has been undertaking a big software development project for L. Bob Rife."

"Makes sense," she says. "He has such a love-hate relationship with his programmers—he needs them, but he won't trust them. The government's the only organization he would trust to write something important. I wonder what it is?"

"Hold on," Hiro says. "Hold on."

He is now a stone's throw away from a big blue cube sitting at ground level. All the other blue cubes sort of feed into it. There is a motorcycle parked next to the cube, rendered in color, but just one notch above black and white: big jaggedy pixels and a limited color palette. It has a sidecar. Raven's standing next to it.

He is carrying something in his arms. It is another simple geometric construction, a long smooth blue ellipsoid a couple of feet in length. From the way he's moving, Hiro thinks that Raven has just removed it from the blue cube; he carries it over to the motorcycle and nestles it into the sidecar.

"The Big One," Hiro says.

"It's exactly what we were afraid of," Juanita says. "Rife's revenge."

"Headed for the amphitheater. Where all the hackers are gathered in one place. Rife's going to infect all of them at once. He's going to burn their minds."

64

Raven's already on the motorcycle. If Hiro chases him on foot, he might catch him before he reaches the Street.

But he might not. In that case, Raven would be on his way to Downtown at tens of thousands of miles per hour while Hiro was still trying to get back to his own motorcycle. At those speeds, once Hiro has lost sight of Raven, he's lost him forever.

Raven starts his bike, begins maneuvering carefully through the tangle, headed for the exit. Hiro takes off as fast as his invisible legs can carry him, headed straight for the wall.

He punches through a couple of seconds later, runs back to the Street. His tiny little invisible avatar can't operate the motorcycle, so he returns to his normal look, hops on his bike, and gets it turned around. Looking back, he sees Raven riding out toward the Street, the logic bomb glowing a soft blue, like heavy water in a reactor. He doesn't even see Hiro yet.

Now's his chance. He draws his katana, aims his bike at Raven, pumps it up to sixty or so miles an hour. No point in coming in too fast; the only way to kill Raven's avatar is to take its head off. Running it over with the motorcycle won't have any effect.

A security daemon is running toward Raven, waving his arms. Raven looks up, sees Hiro bearing down on him, and bursts forward. The sword cuts air behind Raven's head.

It's too late. Raven must be gone now—but turning himself around, Hiro can see him in the middle of the Street. He slammed into one of the stanchions that holds up the monorail track—a perennial irritation to high-speed motorcyclists.

"Shit!" both of them say simultaneously.

Raven gets turned toward Downtown and twists his throttle just as Hiro is pulling in behind him on the Street, doing the same. Within a couple of seconds, they're both headed for Downtown at something like fifty thousand miles an hour. Hiro's half a mile behind Raven but can see him clearly: the streetlights have merged into a smooth twin streak of yellow, and Raven blazes in the middle, a storm of cheap color and big pixels.

"If I can take his head off, they're finished," Hiro says.

"Gotcha," Juanita says. "Because if you kill Raven, he gets kicked out of the system. And he can't sign back on until the Graveyard Daemons dispose of his avatar."

"And I control the Graveyard Daemons. So all I have to do is kill the bastard once."

"Once they get their choppers back to land, they'll have better access to the net—they can have someone else go into the Metaverse and take over for him," Juanita warns.

"Wrong. Because Uncle Enzo and Mr. Lee are waiting for them on land. They have to do it during the next hour, or never."

65

Y.T. suddenly wakes up. She hadn't realized that she was asleep. Something about the thwop of the rotor blades must have lulled her. She must be tired as shit, is what it really is.

"What the *fuck* is going on with my com net?" L. Bob Rife is squalling.

"No one answers," the Russian pilot says. "Not Raft, not L.A., not Khyooston."

"Get me LAX on the phone, then," Rife says. "I want to take the jet to Houston. We'll get our butts over to the campus and find out what's going on."

The pilot messes around on his control panel. "Problem," he says.

"*What?*"

The pilot just shakes his head forlornly. "Someone is messing with the skyphone. We're being jammed."

"I might be able to get a line," the President says. Rife just gives him a look like, *right, asshole.*

"Anybody got a fucking quarter?" Rife hollers. Frank and

Tony are startled for a minute. "We're gonna have to touch down at the first pay phone we see and make a goddamn phone call." He laughs. "Can you believe that? Me, using a *telephone?*"

A second later, Y.T. looks out the window and is blown away to see actual land down there, and a two-lane highway winding its way down a warm sandy coastline. It's California.

The chopper slows, cuts in closer to land, begins following the highway. Most of it is free of plastic and neon lights, but before long they home in on a short bit of franchise ghetto, built on both sides of the road in a place where it has cut away from the beach some distance.

The chopper sets down in the parking lot of a Buy 'n' Fly. Fortunately, the lot's mostly empty, they don't cut any heads off. A couple of youths are playing video games inside, and they barely look up at the astonishing sight of the chopper. She's glad; Y.T. is totally embarrassed to be seen with this dull assortment of old farts. The chopper just sits there, idling, while L. Bob Rife jumps out and runs over to the pay phone bolted to the front wall.

These guys were stupid enough to put her in the seat right next to the fire extinguisher. No reason not to take advantage of that fact. She jerks it out of its bracket, pulling out the safety pin in virtually the same motion, and squeezes the trigger, aiming it right into Tony's face.

Nothing happens.

"Fuck!" she shouts, and throws it at him, or rather pushes it toward him. He's just leaning forward, grabbing at her wrist, and the impact of the extinguisher hitting his face is enough to put a major dent in his 'tude. Gives her enough time to swing her legs out of the chopper.

Everything's getting fucked up. One of her pockets is zipped open, and as she's half-falling, half-rolling out of the chopper, the fire-extinguisher bracket catches in that pocket and holds her. By the time she's gotten free of that, Tony's back, now on his hands and knees, reaching out for her arm.

That she manages to avoid. She's running out freely into the parking lot. At the back, she's hemmed in by the Buy 'n' Fly, along the sides by the tall border fence that separates this place from a NeoAquarian Temple on one side and a Mr. Lee's Greater

Hong Kong franchulate on the other. The only way to escape is out onto the road—on the other side of the chopper. But the pilot and Frank and Tony have already jumped out and are blocking her exit out onto the road.

NeoAquarian Temple isn't going to help her. If she begs and pleads, they might just include her in their mantras next week. But Mr. Lee's Greater Hong Kong is another story. She runs to the fence and starts trying to climb it. Eight feet of chain link with razor ribbon on top. But her clothing should stop the razor ribbon. Mostly.

She gets about halfway up. Then, pudgy but strong arms are around her waist. She's out of luck. L. Bob Rife lifts her right off the fence, both arms and both legs kicking the air uselessly. He backs up a couple of steps and starts carrying her back toward the chopper.

She looks back at the Hong Kong franchise. It was a close thing.

Someone's in the parking lot. A Kourier, cruising in off the highway, just kind of chilling out and taking it real easy.

"Hey!" she screams. She reaches up and punches the lapel switch on her coverall, turning it bright blue and orange. "Hey! I'm a Kourier! My name's Y.T.! These maniac scum guys kidnapped me!"

"Wow," the Kourier says. "What a drag." Then he asks her something. But she can't hear it because the helicopter is whirling up its blades.

"They're taking me to LAX!" she screams at the top of her lungs. Then Rife slams her into the chopper face first. The chopper lifts off, tracked precisely by an audience of antennas on the roof of Mr. Lee's Greater Hong Kong.

In the parking lot, the Kourier watches the chopper taking off. It's really cool to watch, and it has a lot of bumping guns on it.

But those dudes inside of the chopper were harshing that chick *major.*

The Kourier pulls his personal phone out of its holster, jacks into RadiKS Central Command, and punches a big red button. He calls a Code.

_____ Twenty-five hundred Kouriers are massed on the reinforced-concrete banks of the L.A. River. Down in the bottom trench of the river, Vitaly Chernobyl and the Meltdowns are just hitting the really good part of their next major hit single, "Control Rod Jam." A number of the Kouriers are taking advantage of this sound track to style up and down the banks of the river; only Vitaly, live, can get their adrenaline pumping hard enough to enable them to skate a sharp bank at eighty miles per hour plus without doing a wilson into the crete.

And then the dark mass of Meltdown fans turns into a gyrating, orange-red galaxy as twenty-five hundred new stars appear. It's a mind-blowing sight, and at first they think it's a new visual effect put together by Vitaly and his imageers. It is like a mass flicking of Bics, except brighter and more organized; each Kourier looks down on his or her belt to see that a red light is flashing on their personal telephone. Looks like some poor skater called in a Code.

_____ In a Mr. Lee's Greater Hong Kong franchise on the outskirts of Phoenix, Rat Thing number B-782 comes awake.

Fido is waking up because the dogs are barking tonight.

There is always barking. Much of the barking is very far away. Fido knows that faraway barks are not as important as close barks, and so he often sleeps through these.

But sometimes a faraway bark will carry a special sound that makes Fido excited, and he can't help waking up.

He is hearing one of those barks right now. It comes from far away but it is urgent. Some nice doggie somewhere is very upset. He is so upset that his barking has spread to all the other doggies in the pack.

Fido listens to the bark. He gets excited, too. Some bad strangers have just been very close to a nice doggie's yard. They were in a flying thing. They had lots of guns.

Fido doesn't like guns very much. A stranger with a gun shot him once and made him hurt. Then the nice girl came and helped him.

These are extremely bad strangers. Any nice doggie in his right mind would want to hurt them and make them go away. As Fido listens to the bark, he sees what they look like and hears the way they sound. If any of these very bad strangers ever come into his yard, he will be extremely upset.

Then Fido notices that the bad strangers are chasing someone. He can tell they are hurting her by the way her voice sounds and the way she moves.

The bad strangers are hurting the nice girl who loves him!

Fido gets more angry than he has ever been, even more angry than when a bad man shot him long ago.

His job is to keep bad strangers out of his yard. He does not do anything else.

But it's even more important to protect the nice girl who loves him. That is more important than anything. And nothing can stop him. Not even the fence.

The fence is very tall. But he can remember a long time ago when he used to jump over things that were taller than his head.

Fido comes out of his doggie house, curls his long legs beneath him, and jumps over the fence around his yard before he has remembered that he is not capable of jumping over it. This contradiction is lost on him, though; as a dog, introspection is not one of his strong points.

The bark is spreading to another place far away. All the nice doggies who live in this faraway place are being warned to look out for the very bad strangers and the girl who loves Fido, because they are going to that place. Fido sees the place in his mind. It is big and wide and flat and open, like a nice field for chasing Frisbees. It has lots of big flying things. Around the edges are a couple of yards where nice doggies live.

Fido can hear those nice doggies barking in reply. He knows where they are. Far away. But you can get there by streets. Fido knows a whole lot of different streets. He just runs down streets, and he knows where he is and where he's going.

At first, the only trace that B-782 leaves of his passage is a dancing trail of sparks down the center of the franchise ghetto. But once he makes his way out onto a long straight piece of highway, he begins to leave further evidence: a spume of shattered blue safety glass spraying outward in parallel vanes from all four lanes of traffic as the windows and the windshields of the cars blow out of their frames, spraying into the air like rooster tails behind a speedboat.

As part of Mr. Lee's good neighbor policy, all Rat Things are programmed never to break the sound barrier in a populated area. But Fido's in too much of a hurry to worry about the good neighbor policy. Jack the sound barrier. Bring the noise.

66

"Raven," Hiro says, "let me tell you a story before I kill you."

"I'll listen," Raven says. "It's a long ride."

All vehicles in the Metaverse have voice phones on them. Hiro simply called home to the Librarian and had him look up Raven's number. They are riding in lockstep across the black surface of the imaginary planet now, though Hiro is gaining on Raven, meter by meter.

"My dad was in the Army in World War Two. Lied about his age to get in. They put him in the Pacific doing scut work. Anyway, he got captured by the Nipponese."

"So?"

"So they took him back to Nippon. Put him in a prison camp. There were a lot of Americans there, plus some Brits and some Chinese. And a couple of guys that they couldn't place. They looked like Indians. Spoke a little English. But they spoke Russian even better."

"They were Aleuts," Raven says. "American citizens. But no one had ever heard of them. Most people don't know that the Japanese conquered American territory during the war—several islands at the end of the Aleutian chain. Inhabited. By my people. They took the two most important Aleuts and put them in prison camps in Japan. One of them was the mayor of Attu—the most important civil authority. The other was even more important, to us. He was the chief harpooneer of the Aleut nation."

Hiro says, "The mayor got sick and died. He didn't have any immunities. But the harpooneer was one tough son of a bitch. He got sick a few times, but he survived. Went out to work in the fields along with the rest of the prisoners, growing food for the war effort. Worked in the kitchen, preparing slop for the prisoners and the guards. He kept to himself a lot. Everyone avoided him because he smelled terrible. His bed stank up the barracks."

"He was cooking up aconite whale poison from mushrooms and other substances that he found in the fields and secreted in his clothing," Raven says.

"Besides," Hiro continues, "they were pissed at him because he broke out a windowpane in the barracks once, and it let cold air in for the rest of the winter. Anyway, one day, after lunch, all of the guards became terribly sick."

"Whale poison in the fish stew," Raven says.

"The prisoners were already out working in the fields, and when the guards began to get sick, they began to march them all back in toward the barracks, because they couldn't keep watch over them when they were doubled over with stomach cramps. And this late in the war, it wasn't easy to bring in reinforcements. My father was last in the line of prisoners. And this Aleut guy was right in front of him."

Raven says, "As the prisoners were crossing an irrigation ditch, the Aleut dove into the water and disappeared."

"My father didn't know what to do," Hiro says, "until he heard a grunt from the guard who was bringing up the rear. He turned around and saw that this guard had a bamboo spear stuck all the way through his body. Just came out of nowhere. And he still couldn't see the Aleut. Then another guard went down with his throat slit, and there was the Aleut, winding up and throwing another spear that brought down yet another guard."

"He had been making harpoons and hiding them under the water in the irrigation ditches," Raven says.

"Then my father realized," Hiro continues, "that he was doomed. Because no matter what he said to the guards, they would consider him to have been a part of an escape attempt, and they would bring a sword and lop his head off. So, figuring that he might as well bring down a few of the enemy before they got to him, he took the gun from the first guard who had been hit, jumped down into the cover of the irrigation ditch, and shot another couple of guards who were coming over to investigate."

Raven says, "The Aleut ran for the border fence, which was a flimsy bamboo thing. There was supposedly a minefield there, but he ran straight across it with no trouble. Either he was lucky or else the mines—if there were any—were few and far between."

"They didn't bother to have strict perimeter security," Hiro says, "because Japan is an island—so even if someone escaped, where could they run to?"

"An Aleut could do it, though," Raven says. "He could go to the nearest coastline and build himself a kayak. He could take to the open water and make his way up the coastline of Japan, then surf from one island to the next, all the way back to the Aleutians."

"Right," Hiro says, "which is the only part of the story that I never understood—until I saw you on the open water, outrunning a speedboat in your kayak. Then I put it all together. Your father wasn't crazy. He had a perfectly good plan."

"Yes. But your father didn't understand it."

"My father ran in your father's footsteps across the minefield. They were free—in Nippon. Your father started heading downhill, toward the ocean. My father wanted to head uphill, into the mountains, figuring that they could maybe live in an isolated place until the war was over."

"It was a stupid idea," Raven says. "Japan is heavily populated. There is no place where they could have gone unnoticed."

"My father didn't even know what a kayak was."

"Ignorance is no excuse," Raven says.

"Their arguing—the same argument we're having now—was their downfall. The Nipponese caught up with them on a road just outside of Nagasaki. They didn't even have handcuffs, so they tied their hands behind their backs with bootlaces and made them kneel on the road, facing each other. Then the lieutenant took his sword out of its sheath. It was an ancient sword; the lieutenant was from a proud family of samurai, and the only reason he was on this home-front detail was that he had nearly had one leg blown off earlier in the war. He raised the sword up above my father's head."

"It made a high ringing sound in the air," Raven says, "that hurt my father's ears."

"But it never came down."

"My father saw your father's skeleton kneeling in front of him. That was the last thing he ever saw."

"My father was facing away from Nagasaki," Hiro says. "He was temporarily blinded by the light; he fell forward and pressed his face into the ground to get the terrible light out of his eyes. Then everything was back to normal again."

"Except my father was blind," Raven says. "He could only listen to your father fighting the lieutenant."

"It was a half-blind, one-legged samurai with a katana versus a big strong healthy man with his arms tied behind his back," Hiro says. "A pretty interesting fight. A pretty fair one. My father won. And that was the end of the war. The occupation troops got there a couple of weeks later. My father went home and kicked around for a while and finally had a kid during the seventies. So did yours."

Raven says, "Amchitka, 1972. My father got nuked twice by you bastards."

"I understand the depth of your feelings," Hiro says. "But don't you think you've had enough revenge?"

"There's no such thing as enough," Raven says.

Hiro guns his motorcycle forward and closes on Raven, swinging his katana. But Raven reaches back—watching him in the rearview mirror—and blocks the blow; he's carrying a big long knife in one hand. Then Raven cuts his speed down to almost nothing and dives in between a couple of the stanchions. Hiro overshoots him, slows down too much, and gets a glimpse of Raven screaming past him on the other side of the monorail; by the time he's accelerated and cut through another gap, Raven has already slalomed over to the other side.

And so it goes. They run down the length of the Street in an interlacing zigzag pattern, cutting back and forth under the monorail. The game is a simple one. All Raven has to do is make Hiro run into a stanchion. Hiro will come to a stop for a moment. By that time Raven will be gone, out of visual range, and Hiro will have no way to track him.

It's an easier game for Raven than for Hiro. But Hiro's better at this kind of thing than Raven is. That makes it a pretty even match. They slalom down the monorail track at speeds from sixty to sixty thousand miles per hour; all around them, low-slung commerical developments and high-tech labs and amusement parks sprawl off into the darkness. Downtown is before them, as high and bright as the aurora borealis rising from the black water of the Bering Sea.

67

The first poon smacks into the belly of the chopper as they are coming in low over the Valley. Y.T. feels it rather than hears it; she knows that sweet impact so well that she can sense it like one of those supersensitive seismo-thingies that detects earthquakes on the other side of the planet. Then half a dozen other poons strike in quick succession, and she has to force herself not to lean over and look out the window. Of course. The chopper's belly is a solid wall of Soviet steel. It'll hold poons like glue. If they just keep flying low enough to poon—which they have to, to keep the chopper under the Mafia's radar.

She can hear the radio crackling up front. "Take it up, Sasha, you're picking up some parasites."

She looks out the window. The other chopper, the little aluminum corporate number, is flying alongside them, a little bit higher in the air, and all the people inside of it are peering out the windows, watching the pavement underneath them. Except for Raven. Raven is still goggled into the Metaverse.

Shit. The pilot's pulling the chopper to a higher altitude.

"Okay, Sasha. You lost 'em," the radio says. "But you still got a couple of them poon things hanging off your belly, so make sure you don't snag 'em on anything. The cables are stronger than steel."

That's all Y.T. needs. She opens the door and jumps out of the chopper.

At least that's how it looks to the people inside. Actually she grabs a handhold on her way down and ends up dangling from the swinging, open door, looking inward toward the belly of the chopper. A couple of poons are stuck to it; thirty feet below, she can see the handles dangling on the ends of their lines, fluttering in the airstream. Looking into the open door she can't hear Rife but she can see him, sitting there next to the pilot, motioning: Down, take it down!

Which is what she figured. This hostage thing works two ways. She's no good to Rife unless he's got her, and she's in one piece.

The chopper starts losing altitude again, heading back down toward the twin stripe of loglo that marks out the avenue beneath them. Y.T. gets swinging back and forth on the door a little, finally swings in far enough that she can hook one of the poon cables with her foot.

This next bit is going to hurt like hell. But the tough fabric of the coverall should prevent her from losing too much skin. And the sight of Tony lunging at her, trying to grab her sleeve, reinforces her own natural tendency not to think about it too hard. She lets go of the chopper's door with one of her hands, grabs the poon cable, winds it around the outside of her glove a couple of times, then lets go with the other hand.

She was right. It does hurt like hell. As she swings down under the belly of the chopper, out of Tony's grasp, something pops inside her hand—probably one of those dinky little bones. But she gets the poon cable wrapped around her body the same way Raven did when he rappeled off the ship with her, and manages a controlled, burning slide down to the end.

Down to the handle, that is. She hooks it onto her belt so she can't fall and then thrashes around for what seems like a whole minute until she's not tangled up in the cable anymore, just dangling by the waist, twisting around and around between the chopper and the street, out of control. Then she gets the handle in both hands and unhooks it from her belt so she's hanging by the arms again, which was the whole point of the exercise. As she rotates, she sees the other chopper above her and off to the side, glimpses the faces watching her, knows that all of this is being relayed, over the radio, to Rife.

Sure enough. The chopper cuts to about half its former speed, loses some altitude.

She clicks another control and reels out the line all the way to the end, dropping twenty feet in one thrill-packed moment. Now she's flying along, ten or fifteen feet above the highway, doing maybe forty-five miles an hour. The logo signs shoot past her on

either side like meteors. Other than a swarm of Kouriers, traffic
is light.

The RARE chopper comes thwacking in, dangerously close,
and she looks up at it, just for an instant, and sees Raven looking
at her through the window. He's pulled his goggles up on his
forehead, just for a second. He's got a certain look on his face,
and she realizes that he's not pissed at her at all. He loves her.

She lets go of the handle and goes into free fall.

At the same time, she jerks the manual release on her cervical
collar and goes into full Michelin Man mode as tiny gas car-
tridges detonate in several strategic locations around her bod.
The biggest one goes off like an M-80 at the nape of her neck,
unfurling the coverall's collar into a cylindrical gasbag that
shoots straight up and encases her entire head. Other airbags go
off around her torso and her pelvis, paying lots of attention to
that spinal column. Her joints are already protected by the armorgel.

Which is not to say that it doesn't hurt when she lands. She
can't see anything because of the airbag around her head, of
course. But she feels herself bouncing at least ten times. She
skids for a quarter of a mile and apparently caroms off several cars
along the way; she can hear their tires squealing. Finally, she goes
butt first through someone's windshield and ends up sprawled
across their front seat; they veer into a Jersey barrier. The airbag
deflates as soon as everything stops moving, and she claws it away
from her face.

Her ears are ringing or something. She can't hear anything.
Maybe she busted her eardrums when the airbags went off.

But there's also the question of the big chopper, which has a
talent for making noise. She drags herself out onto the hood of
the car, feeling little hunks of safety glass beneath her carving
parallel scratches into the paint job.

Rife's big Soviet chopper is right there, hovering about twenty
feet above the avenue, and by the time she sees it, it has already
accumulated a dozen more poons. Her eyes follow the cables
down to street level, and she sees Kouriers straining at the lines;
this time, they're not letting go.

Rife gets suspicious, and the chopper gains altitude, lifting the
Kouriers off their planks. But a passing double-bottom semi

sheds a small army of Kouriers—there must be a hundred of them pooned onto the poor thing—and within a few seconds, all their MagnaPoons are airborne and at least half of them stick to the armor plating on the first try. The chopper lurches downward until all of the Kouriers are on the ground again. Twenty more Kouriers come flying in and nail it; those that can't, grab onto someone else's handle and add their weight. The chopper tries several times to rise, but it may as well be tethered to the asphalt by this point.

It starts to come down. The Kouriers fan out away from it so that the chopper comes down in the middle of a radial burst of poon cables.

Tony, the security guy, climbs down out of the open door, moving slowly, high-stepping his way through the web of cables but somehow retaining his balance and his dignity. He walks away from the chopper until he is out from under the rotor blades, then pulls an Uzi out from under his windbreaker and fires a short air burst.

"Get the fuck away from our chopper!" he is shouting.

The Kouriers, by and large, do. They're not stupid. And Y.T. is now walking around safe on the pavement, the mission is accomplished, the Code is finished, there's no reason to hassle these chopper dudes anymore. They detach their poons from the belly of the chopper and reel in the cables.

Tony looks around and sees Y.T. She's walking directly toward the chopper. Her sprained body moves awkwardly.

"Get back in the chopper, you lucky bitch!" he says.

Y.T. picks up a loose poon handle that no one has bothered to reel in yet. She hits the button that turns off the electromagnet and its head drops off the chopper's armor. She reels it in until about four feet of slack is there between the reel and the head.

"There was this dude named Ahab that I read about," she says, whirling the poon around her head. "He got his poon cable all wrapped up around the thing he was trying to poon. It was a big mistake."

She lets the poon fly. It passes up through the plane of the rotor blades, near the center, and she can see the unbreakable cable start to wind itself around the delicate parts of the rotor's axle, like a garrote around a ballerina's neck. Through the chopper's windshield she can see Sasha reacting, flipping switches frantically, pulling levers, his mouth making a long string of Russian curses. The poon's handle gets snapped out of her hand, and she sees it get whipped into the center like it's a black hole.

"I guess he just didn't know when to let go, like some people," she says. Then she turns around and walks away from the chopper. Behind her, she can hear large pieces of metal going the wrong way, running into one another at high speed.

Rife has figured it out a long time ago. He's already running down the middle of the highway with a submachine gun in one hand, looking for a car to commandeer. Above, the RARE chopper hovers and watches; Rife looks up to it and motions forward with one hand, shouting, "Go to LAX! Go to LAX!"

The chopper makes one last orbit over the scene, watching as Sasha puts the ruined gunship into cold shutdown, watching furious Kouriers overwhelming and disarming Tony and Frank and the President, watching as Rife stands in the middle of the left lane and forces a CosaNostra Pizza car to a stop, forces the driver out. But Raven isn't watching any of these things. He's looking out the window at Y.T. And as the chopper finally tilts forward and accelerates into the night, he grins at her and gives her the thumbs up. Y.T. bites her lower lip and flips him the bird. With that, the relationship is over, hopefully for all time.

Y.T. borrows a plank from an awed skater and pushes herself across the street to the nearest Buy 'n' Fly and starts trying to call Mom for a ride home.

Hiro loses Raven a few miles outside of Downtown, but it doesn't matter by this point; he goes straight to the plaza and then starts to orbit the rim of the amphitheater at high speed, a one-man picket fence. Raven makes his approach within a few seconds. Hiro breaks out of his orbit and heads straight for him, and they come together like a couple of medieval jousters. Hiro loses his left arm and Raven drops a leg. The limbs topple to the ground. Hiro drops his katana and uses his remaining arm to draw his

one-handed sword—a better match for Raven's long knife anyway. He cuts Raven off just as he's about to plummet over the lip
of the amphitheater and forces him aside; Raven's momentum
takes him half a mile away in half a second. Hiro chases him down
by following a series of educated guesses—he knows this territory
like Raven knows the currents of the Aleutians—and then they
are blasting through the narrow streets of the Metaverse's financial district, waving long knives at each other, slicing and dicing
hundreds of pinstriped avatars who happen to get in their way.

But they never seem to hit each other. The speeds are just too
great, the targets too small. Hiro's been lucky so far—he has got
Raven caught up in the thrill of competition, made him spoil for
a fight. But Raven doesn't need this. He can get back to the
amphitheater pretty easily without bothering to kill Hiro first.

And finally, he realizes it. He sheaths his knife and dives into
an alley between skyscrapers. Hiro follows him, but by the time
he's gotten into that same alley, Raven's gone.

_____ Hiro goes over the lip of the amphitheater doing
a couple of hundred miles per hour and soars out into space, in
free fall, above the heads of a quarter of a million wildly cheering
hackers.

They all know Hiro. He's the guy with the swords. He's a
friend of Da5id's. And as his own personal contribution to the
benefit, he's apparently decided to stage a sword fight with some
kind of hulking, scary-looking daemon on a motorcycle. Don't
touch that dial, it's going to be a hell of a show.

He lands on the stage and bounces to a halt next to his motorcycle. The bike still works, but it's worthless down here. Raven is
ten meters away, grinning at him.

"Bombs away," Raven says. He pulls the glowing blue lozenge
out of his sidecar with one hand and drops it on the center of the
amphitheater. It breaks open like the shell of an egg and light
shines out of it. The light begins to grow and take shape.

The crowd goes wild.

Hiro runs toward the egg. Raven cuts him off. Raven can't
move around on his feet now, because he's lost a leg. But he can
still control the bike. He's got his long knife out now, and the two

blades come together above the egg, which has become the vortex of a blinding, deafening tornado of light and sound. Colored shapes, foreshortened by their immense speed, shoot from the center of it and take positions above their heads, building a three-dimensional picture.

The hackers are going nuts. Hiro knows that the Hacker Quadrant in The Black Sun is, at this moment, emptying itself out. They are all cramming through the exit and running down the Street toward the plaza, coming to see Hiro's fantastic show of light, sound, swords, and sorcery.

Raven tries to shove Hiro back. It would work in Reality because Raven has such overpowering strength. But avatars are equally strong, unless you hack them up in just the right way. So Raven gives a mighty push and then pulls his knife back so that he can take a cut at Hiro's neck when Hiro flies away from him; but Hiro doesn't fly away. He waits for the opening and then takes Raven's sword hand off. Then, just in case, he takes Raven's other hand off. The crowd screams in delight.

"How do I stop this thing?" Hiro says.

"Beats me. I just deliver 'em," Raven says.

"Do you have any concept of what you just did?"

"Yeah. Realized my lifelong ambition," Raven says, a huge relaxed grin spreading across his face. "I nuked America."

Hiro cuts his head off. The crowd of doomed hackers rises to its feet and shrieks.

Then they go silent as Hiro abruptly disappears. He has switched over to his small, invisible avatar. He is hovering in the air now above the shattered remains of the egg; gravity takes him right down into the center of it. As he falls, he is muttering to himself: "SnowScan." It's the piece of software he wrote while he was killing time on the liferaft. The one that searches for Snow Crash.

_____ With Hiro Protagonist seemingly gone from the stage, the hackers turn their attention toward the giant construction rising up out of the egg. All that nonsense with the sword fight must have been just a wacky introductory piece—Hiro's typically offbeat way of getting their attention. This light and sound show is the main attraction. The amphitheater is now filling up rapidly as thousands of hackers pour in from all over the place: running down the Street from The Black Sun, streaming out of the big office towers where the major software corporations are headquartered, goggling into the Metaverse from all points in Reality as word of the extravaganza spreads down the fiber-optic grapevine at the speed of light.

The light show is designed as if late comers were anticipated. It builds to false climax after false climax, like an expensive fireworks show, and each one is better. It is so vast and complicated that no one sees more than 10 percent of it; you could spend a year watching it over and over again and keep seeing new things.

It is a mile-high structure of moving two- and three-dimensional images, interlocked in space and time. It's got everything in it. Leni Riefenstahl films. The sculptures of Michelangelo and the fictional inventions of Da Vinci made real. World War II dogfights zooming in and out of the middle, veering out over the crowd, shooting and burning and exploding. Scenes from a thousand classic films, flowing and merging together into a single vast complicated story.

But in time, it begins to simplify itself and narrow into a single bright column of light. By this point, it is the music that is carrying the show: a pounding bass beat and a deep, threatening ostinato that tells everyone to keep watching, the best is yet to come. And everyone does watch. Religiously.

The column of light begins to flow up and down and resolve itself into a human form. Actually, it is four human forms, female nudes standing shoulder to shoulder, facing outward, like caryatids. Each of them is carrying something long and slender in her hands: a pair of tubes.

A third of a million hackers stare at the women, towering above the stage, as they raise their arms above their heads and unroll the four scrolls, turning each one of them into a flat television screen the size of a football field. From the seats in the amphitheater, the screens virtually blot out the sky; they are all that anyone can see.

The screens are blank at first, but finally the same image snaps into existence on all four of them at once. It is an image consisting of words; it says

---

IF THIS WERE A VIRUS
YOU WOULD BE DEAD NOW
FORTUNATELY IT'S NOT
THE METAVERSE IS A DANGEROUS PLACE;
HOW'S YOUR SECURITY?
CALL HIRO PROTAGONIST SECURITY ASSOCIATES
FOR A FREE INITIAL CONSULTATION.

"This is exactly the kind of high-tech nonsense that never, ever worked when we tried it in Vietnam," Uncle Enzo says.

"Your point is well taken. But technology has come a long way since then," says Ky, the surveillance man from Ng Security Industries. Ky is talking to Uncle Enzo over a radio headset; his van, full of electronic gear, is lurking a quarter of a mile away in the shadows next to a LAX cargo warehouse. "I am monitoring the entire airport, and all its approaches, with a three-dimensional Metaverse display. For example, I know that your dog tags, which you customarily wear around your neck, are missing. I know that you are carrying one Kongbuck and eighty-five Kongpence in change in your left pocket. I know that you have a straight razor in your other pocket. Looks like a nice one, too."

"Never underestimate the importance of good grooming," Uncle Enzo says.

"But I do not understand why you are carrying a skateboard."

"It's a replacement for the one Y.T. lost in front of EBGOC," Uncle Enzo says. "It's a long story."

"Sir, we have a report from one of our franchulates," says a young lieutenant in a Mafia windbreaker, jogging across the apron with a black walkie-talkie in one hand. He is not really a lieutenant; the Mafia is not very keen on the use of military ranks. But for some reason, Uncle Enzo thinks of him as the lieutenant. "The second chopper set down in a strip-mall parking lot about ten miles from here and met the pizza car and picked up Rife, then took off again. They are on their way in now."

"Send someone out to pick up the abandoned pizza car. And give the driver a day off," Uncle Enzo says.

The lieutenant looks somewhat taken aback that Uncle Enzo is concerning himself with such a tiny detail. It is as if the don were going up and down highways picking up litter or something. But he nods respectfully, having just learned something: details matter. He turns away and begins talking into his radio.

Uncle Enzo has serious doubts about this fellow. He is a blazer person, adept at running the small-time bureaucracy of a Nova Sicilia franchulate, but lacking in the kind of flexibility that, for example, Y.T. has. A classic case of what is wrong with the Mafia today. The only reason the lieutenant is even here is because the situation has been changing so rapidly, and, of course, because of all the fine men they lost on the *Kowloon*.

Ky comes in over the radio again. "Y.T. has just contacted her mother and asked for a ride," he says. "Would you like to hear their conversation?"

"Not unless it has tactical significance," Uncle Enzo says briskly. This is one more thing to check off his list; he has been worried about Y.T.'s relationship with her mother and was meaning to speak with her about it.

Rife's jet sits on the tarmac, engines idling, waiting to taxi out onto the runway. In the cockpit are a pilot and copilot. Until half an hour ago, they were loyal employees of L. Bob Rife. Then they sat and watched out the windshield as the dozen Rife security drones who were stationed around the hangar variously got their heads blown off, their throats slit, or else just plain dropped their weapons and fell to their knees and surrendered. Now the pilot and copilot have taken lifelong oaths of loyalty to Uncle Enzo's organization. Uncle Enzo could have just dragged them out and replaced them with his own pilots, but this way is better. If Rife should, somehow, actually make it onto the plane, he will recognize his own pilots and think that everything is fine. And the fact that the pilots are alone there in the cockpit without any direct Mafia supervision will merely emphasize the great trust that Uncle Enzo has placed in them and the oath that they have taken. It will actually enhance their sense of duty. It will amplify Uncle Enzo's displeasure if they should break their oaths. Uncle Enzo has no doubt about the pilots at all.

He is less happy with the arrangements here, which were made rather hastily. The problem is, as usual, the unpredictable Y.T. He was not expecting her to jump out of a moving helicopter and get free from L. Bob Rife. He was, in other words, expecting a hostage negotiation somewhat later on, after Rife had flown Y.T. back to his headquarters in Houston.

But the hostage situation no longer obtains, and so Uncle Enzo feels it is important to stop Rife now, before he gets back to his home turf in Houston. He has called for a major realignment of Mafia forces, and right now, dozens of helicopters and tactical units are hastily replotting their courses and trying to converge on LAX as quickly as they can. But in the meantime, Enzo is here with a small number of his own personal bodyguards, and this technical surveillance man from Ng's organization.

They have shut down the airport. This was easy to do: they just pulled Lincoln Town Cars onto all the runways, for starters, and then went into the control tower and announced that in a few minutes they would be going to war. Now, LAX is probably quieter than it has been at any point since it was built. Uncle Enzo can actually hear the faint crashing of surf on the beach, half a mile away. It is almost pleasant here. Weenie-roasting weather.

Uncle Enzo is cooperating with Mr. Lee, which means working with Ng, and Ng, while highly competent, has a technological bias that Uncle Enzo distrusts. He would prefer a single good soldier in polished shoes, armed with a nine, to a hundred of Ng's gizmos and portable radar units.

When they came out here, he was expecting a broad open space in which to confront Rife. Instead, the environment is cluttered. Several dozen corporate jets and helicopters are parked on the apron. Nearby is an assortment of private hangars, each with its own fenced-in parking area containing a number of cars and utility vehicles. And they are rather close to the tank farm where the airport's supply of jet fuel is stored. That means lots of pipes and pumping stations and hydraulic folderol sprouting out of the ground. Tactically, the area has more in common with a jungle than with a desert. The apron and runway themselves are, of course, more desertlike, although they have drainage ditches where any number of men could be concealed. So a better analogy would be beach warfare in Vietnam: a broad open area that abruptly turns into jungle. Not Uncle Enzo's favorite place.

"The chopper is approaching the perimeter of the airport," Ky says.

Uncle Enzo turns to his lieutenant. "Everyone in place?"

"Yes, sir."

"How do you know that?"

"They all checked in a few minutes ago."

"That means absolutely nothing. And how about the pizza car?"

"Well, I thought I would do that later, sir—"

"You need to be capable of doing more than one thing at a time."

The lieutenant turns away, shamed and awed. "Ky," Uncle Enzo says, "anything interesting happening on our perimeter?"

"Nothing at all," Ng says.

"Anything uninteresting?"

"A few maintenance workers, as normal."

"How do you know they are maintenance workers and not Rife soldiers in costume? Did you check their IDs?"

"Soldiers carry guns. Or at least knives. Radar shows that these men do not. Q.E.D."

"Still trying to get all our men to check in," the lieutenant says. "Having a little radio trouble, I guess."

Uncle Enzo puts one arm around the lieutenant's shoulders. "Let me tell you a story, son. From the first moment I saw you, I thought you seemed familiar. Finally I realized that you remind me of someone I used to know: a lieutenant who was my commanding officer, for a while, in Vietnam."

The lieutenant is thrilled. "Really?"

"Yes. He was young, bright, ambitious, well educated. And well meaning. But he had certain deficiencies. He had a stubborn inability to grasp the fundamentals of our situation over there. A sort of mental block, if you will, that caused those of us who were serving under him to experience the most intense kind of frustration. It was touch and go for a while, son, I don't mind telling you that."

"How did it work out, Uncle Enzo?"

"It worked out fine. You see, one day, I took it upon myself to shoot him in the back of the head."

The lieutenant's eyes get very big, and his face seems paralyzed. Uncle Enzo has no sympathy for him at all: if he screws this up, people could die.

Some new piece of radio babble comes in over the lieutenant's headset. "Oh, Uncle Enzo?" he says, very quietly and reluctantly.

"Yes?"

"You were asking about that pizza car?"

"Yes?"

"It's not there."

"Not there?"

"Apparently, when they set down to pick up Rife, a man got out of the chopper and climbed into the pizza car and drove it away."

"Where did he drive it to?"

"We don't know, sir, we only had one spotter in the area, and he was tracking Rife."

"Take off your headset," Uncle Enzo says. "And turn off that walkie-talkie. You need your ears."

"My ears?"

Uncle Enzo drops into a crouch and walks briskly across the pavement until he is between a couple of small jets. He sets the skateboard down quietly. Then he unties his shoelaces and pulls his shoes off. He takes his socks off, too, and stuffs them into the shoes. He takes the straight razor out of his pocket, flips it open, and slits both of his trouser legs from the hem up to his groin, then bunches the material up and cuts it off. Otherwise the fabric will slide over his hairy legs when he walks and make noise.

"My God!" the lieutenant says, a couple of planes over. "Al is down! My God, he's dead!"

70

Uncle Enzo leaves his jacket on, for now, because it's dark, and because it's lined with satin so that it is relatively quiet. Then he climbs up onto the wing of one of the planes so that his legs cannot be seen by someone crouching on the ground. He hunkers down on the end of the wing, opens his mouth so that he can hear better, and listens.

The only thing he can hear at first is an uneven spattering noise that wasn't there before, like water falling out of a half-open faucet onto bare pavement. The sound seems to be coming from a nearby airplane. Uncle Enzo is afraid that it may be jet fuel leaking onto the ground, as part of a scheme to blow up this whole section of the airport and take out all opposition at a stroke. He drops silently to the ground, makes his way carefully around a couple of adjacent planes, stopping every few feet to listen, and finally sees it: one of his soldiers has been pinned to the aluminum fuselage of a Learjet by means of a long wooden pole. Blood runs out of the wound, down his pant legs, drips from his shoes, and spatters onto the tarmac.

From behind him, Uncle Enzo hears a brief scream that suddenly turns into a sharp gaseous exhalation. He has heard it before. It is a man having a sharp knife drawn across his throat. It is undoubtedly the lieutenant.

He has a few seconds to move freely now. He doesn't even know what he's up against, and he needs to know that. So he runs in the direction the scream came from, moving quickly from cover of one jet to the next, staying down in a crouch.

He sees a pair of legs moving on the opposite side of a jet's fuselage. Uncle Enzo is near the tip of the jet's wing. He puts both hands on it, shoves down with all his weight, and then lets it go.

It works: the jet rocks toward him on its suspension. The assassin thinks that Uncle Enzo has just jumped up onto the wingtip, so he climbs up onto the opposite wing and waits with his back to the fuselage, waiting to ambush Enzo when he climbs over the top.

But Enzo is still on the ground. He runs in toward the fuselage on silent, bare feet, ducks beneath it, and comes up from underneath with his straight razor in one hand. The assassin—Raven—is right where Enzo expected him.

But Raven is already getting suspicious; he stands up to look over the top of the fuselage, and that puts his throat out of reach. Enzo's looking at his legs instead.

It's better to be conservative and take what you can get than take a big gamble and blow it, so Enzo reaches in, even as Raven is looking down at him, and severs Raven's left Achilles tendon.

As he's turning away to protect himself, something hits him very hard in the chest. Uncle Enzo looks down and is astonished to see a transparent object protruding from the right side of his rib cage. Then he looks up to see Raven's face three inches from his.

Uncle Enzo steps back away from the wing. Raven was hoping to fall on top of him but instead tumbles to the ground. Enzo steps back in, reaching forward with his razor, but Raven, sitting on the tarmac, has already drawn a second knife. He lunges for the inside of Uncle Enzo's thigh and does some damage; Enzo sidesteps away from the blade, throwing off his attack, and ends up making a short but deep cut on the top of Raven's shoulder. Raven knocks his arm aside before Enzo can go for the throat again.

Uncle Enzo's hurt and Raven's hurt. But Raven can't outrun him anymore; it's time to take stock of things a little bit. Enzo runs away, though when he moves, terrible pains run up and down the right side of his body. Something thuds into his back, too; he feels a sharp pain above one kidney, but only for a moment. He turns around to see a bloody piece of glass shattering on the pavement. Raven must have thrown it into his back. But without Raven's arm strength behind it, it didn't have enough momentum to penetrate all the way through the bulletproof fabric, and it fell out.

Glass knives. No wonder Ky didn't see him on millimeter wave.

By the time he gets behind the cover of another plane, his sense of hearing is being overwhelmed by the approach of a chopper.

It is Rife's chopper, settling down on the tarmac a few dozen meters away from the jet. The thunder of the rotor blades and the blast of the wind seem to penetrate into Uncle Enzo's brain. He closes his eyes against the wind and utterly loses his balance, has no idea where he is until he slams full-length into the pavement. The pavement beneath him is slippery and warm, and Uncle Enzo realizes that he is losing a great deal of blood.

Staring across the tarmac, he sees Raven making his way toward the aircraft, limping horrendously, one leg virtually useless. Finally, he gives up on it and just hops on his good leg.

Rife has climbed down out of the chopper. Raven and Rife are talking, Raven gesticulating back in Enzo's direction. Then Rife nods his approval, and Raven turns around, his teeth bright and white. He's not grimacing so much as he is smiling in anticipation. He begins to hop toward Uncle Enzo, pulling another glass knife out of his jacket. The bastard is carrying a million of those things.

He's coming after Enzo, and Enzo can't even stand up without passing out.

He looks around and sees nothing but a skateboard and a pair of expensive shoes and socks about twenty feet away. He can't stand up, but he can do the GI crawl, and so he begins to pull himself forward on his elbows even as Raven is hopping toward him one-legged.

They meet in an open lane between two adjacent jets. Enzo is on his belly, slumped over the skateboard. Raven is standing, supporting himself with one hand on the wing of the jet, the glass knife glittering in his other hand. Enzo is now seeing the world in dim black and white, like a cheap Metaverse terminal; this is how his buddies used to describe it in Vietnam right before they succumbed to blood loss.

"Hope you've done your last rites," Raven says, "because there ain't no time to call a priest."

"There is no need for one," Uncle Enzo says, and punches the button on the skateboard labeled "RadiKS Narrow Cone Tuned Shock Wave Projector."

The concussion nearly blows his head off. Uncle Enzo, if he survives, will never hear well again. But it does wake him up a little bit. He lifts his head off the board to see Raven standing there stunned, empty-handed, a thousand tiny splinters of broken glass raining down out of his jacket.

Uncle Enzo rolls over on his back and waves his straight razor in the air. "I prefer steel myself," he says. "Would you like a shave?"

71

Rife sees it all and understands it clearly enough. He would love to see how it all comes out, but he's a very busy man; he would like to get out of here before the rest of the Mafia and Ng and Mr. Lee and all those other assholes come after him with their heat-seeking missiles. And there's no time to wait for the gimpy Raven to hop all the way back. He gives a thumbs up to the pilot and begins climbing the steps into his private jet.

It's daytime. A wall of billowing orange flame grows up silently from the tank farm a mile away, like a time-lapse chrysanthemum. It is so vast and complicated in its blooming, uncontrolled growth that Rife stops halfway up the stairs to watch.

A powerful disturbance is moving through the flame, leaving a linear trail in the light, like a cosmic ray fired through a cloud chamber. By the force of its passage, it leaves behind a shock wave that is clearly visible in the flame, a bright spreading cone that is a hundred times larger than the dark source at its apex: a black bulletlike thing supported on four legs that are churning too fast to be visible. It is so small and so fast that L. Bob Rife would not be able to see it, if it were not headed directly for him.

It is picking its way over a broad tangle of open-air plumbing, the pipes that carry the fuel to the jets, jumping over some obstacles, digging its metallic claws into others, tearing them open with the explosive thrust of its legs, igniting their contents with the sparks that fly whenever its feet touch the pavement. It gathers its four legs under it, leaps a hundred feet to the top of a buried tank, uses that as a launch pad for another long, arcing leap over the chain link fence that separates the fuel installation from the airport proper, and then it settles into a long, steady, powerful lope, accelerating across the perfect geometric plane of the runway, chased by a long tongue of flame that extends lazily from the middle of the conflagration, whorling inward upon itself as it traces the currents in the Rat Thing's aftershock.

Something tells L. Bob Rife to get away from the jet, which is loaded with fuel. He turns and half jumps, half falls off the stairs, moving clumsily because he's looking at the Rat Thing, not at the ground.

The Rat Thing, just a tiny dark thing close to the ground, visible only by virtue of its shadow against the flames, and by the chain of white sparks where its claws dig into the pavement, makes a tiny correction in its course.

It's not headed for the jet; it's headed for him. Rife changes his mind and runs up the stairway, taking the steps three at a time. The stairway flexes and recoils under his weight, reminding him of the jet's fragility.

The pilot has seen it coming, doesn't wait to retract the stairway before he releases the brakes and sends the jet taxiing down the runway, swinging the nose away from the Rat Thing. He punches the throttles, nearly throwing the jet onto one wing as it whips around in a tight curve, and redlines the engines as soon as he sees the center line of the runway. Now they can only see forward and sideways. They can't see what is chasing them.

Y.T. is the only person who can see it happen. Having easily penetrated airport security with her Kourier pass, she is coasting onto the apron near the cargo terminal. From here, she has an excellent view across half a mile of open runway, and she sees it all happen: the plane roars down the runway, hauling its door closed as it goes, shooting pale blue flames out its engine nozzles, trying to build up speed for takeoff, and Fido chases it down like a dog going after a fat mailman, makes one final tremendous leap into the air and, turning himself into a Sidewinder missile, flies nose-first into the tailpipe of its left engine.

The jet explodes about ten feet off the ground, catching Fido and L. Bob Rife and his virus all together in its fine, sterilizing flame.

How sweet!

She stays for a while and watches the aftermath: Mafia choppers coming in, doctors jumping out with doc boxes and blood bags and stretchers. Mafia soldiers scurrying between the private jets, apparently looking for someone. A pizza delivery car takes off from one of the parking areas, tires squealing, and a Mafia car peels out after it in hot pursuit.

But after a while it gets boring, and so she skates back to the main terminal, under her own power mostly, though she manages to poon a fuel tanker for a while.

Mom's waiting for her in her stupid little jellybean car, by the United baggage claim, just like they arranged on the phone. Y.T. opens the door, throws her plank into the back seat, and climbs in.

"Home?" Mom says.

"Yeah, home seems about right."

ACKNOWLEDGMENTS

This book germinated in a collaboration between me and the artist Tony Sheeder, the original goal of which was to publish a computer-generated graphic novel. In general, I handled the words and he handled the pictures; but even though this work consists almost entirely of words, certain aspects of it stem from my discussions with Tony.

This novel was very difficult to write, and I received a great deal of good advice from my agents Liz Darhansoff, Chuck Verrill, and Denise Stewart, who read early drafts. Other people subjected to the early drafts were Tony Sheeder; Dr. Steve Horst of Wesleyan University, who made extensive and very lucid comments on everything having to do with brains and computers (and who suddenly came down with a virus about one hour after reading it); and my brother-in-law, Steve Wiggins, currently at the University of Edinburgh, who got me started on Asherah to begin with and also fed me useful papers and citations as I thrashed around pitifully in the Library of Congress.

Marco Kaltofen, as usual, functioned in the same quick, encyclopedic way as the Librarian when I had questions about certain whys and wheres of the toxic-waste business. Richard Green, my agent in L.A., gave me some help with the geography of that town.

Bruck Pollock read the galleys attentively, but with blistering speed, and made several useful suggestions. He was the first and certainly not the last to point out that BIOS actually stands for "Basic Input/Output System," not "Built-In Operating System" as I have it here (and as it *ought* to be); but I feel that I am entitled to trample all other considerations into the dirt in my pursuit of a satisfying pun, so this part of the book is unchanged.

The idea of a "virtual reality" such as the Metaverse is by now widespread in the computer-graphics community and is being implemented in a number of different ways. The particular vision of the Metaverse as expressed in this novel originated from idle discussion between me and Jaime (Captain Bandwidth) Taaffe—which does not imply that blame for any of the unrealistic or tawdry aspects of the Metaverse should be placed on anyone but me. The words "avatar" (in the sense used here) and "Metaverse" are my inventions, which I came up with when I decided that existing words (such as "virtual reality") were simply too awkward to use.

In thinking about how the Metaverse might be constructed, I was influenced by the Apple *Human Interface Guidelines,* which is a book that explains the philosophy behind the Macintosh. Again, this point is made only to acknowledge the beneficial influence of the people who compiled said document, not to link these poor innocents with its results.

In a nice twist, which I include only because it is pleasingly self-referential, I became intimately familiar with the inner workings of the Macintosh during the early phases of the doomed and maniacal graphic-novel project when it became clear that the only way to make the Mac do the things we needed was to write a lot of custom image-processing software. I have probably spent more hours coding during the production of this work than I did actually writing it, even though it eventually turned away from the original graphic concept, rendering most of that work useless from a practical viewpoint.

Finally, it should be pointed out that when I wrote the Babel material, I was standing on the shoulders of many, many historians and archaeologists who actually did the research; most of the words spoken by the Librarian originated with these people and I have tried to make the Librarian give credit where due, verbally footnoting his comments like a good scholar, which I am not.

After the first publication of Snow Crash, I learned that the term 'avatar' has actually been in use for a number of years as part of a virtual reality system called Habitat, developed by F. Randall Farmer and Chip Morningstar. The system runs on Commodore 64 computers, and though it has all but died out in the U.S., is still popular in Japan. In addition to avatars, Habitat includes many of the basic features of the Metaverse as described in this book.

NEAL STEPHENSON

THE DIAMOND AGE

The future is small. The future is nano . . .

And who could be smaller or more insignificant than poor Little Nell – an orphan girl alone and adrift in a world of Confucian Law, Neo-Victorian values and warring nano-technology?

Well, not quite alone. Because Nell has a friend, of sorts. A guide, a teacher, an armed and unarmed combat instructor, a book and a computer: the Young Lady's Illustrated Primer is all these and much much more. It is illicit, magical, dangerous.

And it isn't Nell's. It was stolen. And now some very powerful people want to get their hands on this highly desirable object. Nell is about to discover that the world can feel very small indeed . . .

'The Quentin Tarantino of postcyberpunk science fiction. Stephenson has upped the form's ante with rambunctious glee' *Village Voice*

'A new era in science fiction. People will walk around slack-jawed for days and reemerge with a radically redefined sense of reality' Bruce Sterling

'Establishes Stephenson as a powerful voice for the cyber age. At once whimsical, satirical, and cautionary' *USA Today*

'A brilliant, tricky, twenty-first-century version of Pygmalion' *Guardian*

'A wealth of hip, social and technological riffs, stories-within-stories and not a few good jokes. Invest' *Time Out*

He just wanted a decent book to read ...

Not too much to ask, is it? It was in 1935 when Allen Lane, Managing Director of Bodley Head Publishers, stood on a platform at Exeter railway station looking for something good to read on his journey back to London. His choice was limited to popular magazines and poor-quality paperbacks – the same choice faced every day by the vast majority of readers, few of whom could afford hardbacks. Lane's disappointment and subsequent anger at the range of books generally available led him to found a company – and change the world.

'We believed in the existence in this country of a vast reading public for intelligent books at a low price, and staked everything on it'
Sir Allen Lane, 1902–1970, founder of Penguin Books

The quality paperback had arrived – and not just in bookshops. Lane was adamant that his Penguins should appear in chain stores and tobacconists, and should cost no more than a packet of cigarettes.

Reading habits (and cigarette prices) have changed since 1935, but Penguin still believes in publishing the best books for everybody to enjoy. We still believe that good design costs no more than bad design, and we still believe that quality books published passionately and responsibly make the world a better place.

So wherever you see the little bird – whether it's on a piece of prize-winning literary fiction or a celebrity autobiography, political tour de force or historical masterpiece, a serial-killer thriller, reference book, world classic or a piece of pure escapism – you can bet that it represents the very best that the genre has to offer.

Whatever you like to read – trust Penguin.